5

WIND
WITHOUT
RAIN

Into this lusty, vivid story Mr. Krause has put the soil and the seasons, and the spirit of the people who worked to wrest a hard livelihood from the fields of Minnesota.

It was land that dominated Johan Vildvogel's life, and it was Johan Vildvogel who dominated the lives of his wife and four sons. To all of them this domination was complete, but to Franz it was particularly cruel for it was he who was sensitive to the beauty and harmony of a nature that to the others seemed only hard.

The drama of the Vildvogels is told with a suspense and beauty that mark it as a truly unusual novel — one that is mature and masterly both in conception and execution.

WIND WITHOUT RAIN

By HERBERT KRAUSE

*"Beams smooth and brown
with the wear of hay."*
—JOHN CLIFFORD DANIELSON

THE BOBBS-MERRILL COMPANY

INDIANAPOLIS   *Publishers*   NEW YORK

PRINTED AND BOUND BY
BRAUNWORTH & CO., INC.
BUILDERS OF BOOKS
BRIDGEPORT, CONN.

To
MY FATHER
*who spun yarns for me
while he pumped the fire*
and
MY MOTHER
*who taught me courage
and patience with my
ABC's*

Wind in the east
Rain heaps the harvest feast;
Wind in the south
The tongue goes dry in the mouth.

Part One

THIS SAPLING
OUT OF SEED

1

FATHER felt the rasp of our unquietness better than most. Much better, I think, remembering how, when we were little, he stood as he usually did the day after each Christmas, tall and dark beside the first page of the new year, a curved finger hooked over the calendar.

"*Na, na;* run out again; one on the heels of another. Nothing different," resentment edging his words. "Stuck; stuck fast, that's what I am. A hill farmer, and out there, all the north country—." I remember once how he turned then and looked at Mother and Franz, not at the rest of us, as if they had scattered the years and were alone to blame. I try to bring back what he said but hear only the echoes of words, tantalizing in their unguessable nearness. Something about a load on the bones and the sheep's foolishness of women.

I can look back now, quietly from this white interlude of peace, and see as one from a far hill how all our days were spent. Wasted in a sort of hen-fight to snatch from life a moldy rind of happiness, avoiding when we could the nettle-patches of hurt. But there were hours, like that night back there in Franz's tenth autumn, when four walls and the rock foundations underneath seemed to have no more permanence than honeycomb ice in spring. When uphill acres and the oaks in the pasture alone seemed to promise strength, and quiet rained down with the shadows.

Father had an eighty, more than half in timber standing on the root, the rest under plow except a few patches blanket-sized and tough with sod for grass, and the hay bottoms along the rice lake. Land so young the brown shells of roots forked up with the share and stumps lifted gray butts in the wheat; heavy with clay, most of it, like the high field south, burning to rock under July suns. Clearings on lower ground were better and the ten-acre piece by the meadow wallowed in thick wet loam.

The trees marched in from the ridges off south, miles of them, with here a cleared space and there a slash on the bark to show where a farm's end might be. Far back where second growth leaved in fainter green than older wood, loops of wire lost in the kinnikinnicks told of work begun by men, fox-hearted and with eyes elsewhere than on home-building, and of post and rail fence soon left and forgotten. But near us the timber was thick and solid and the windfalls of no account. Only the creek and the willows bordering it stopped the elms and basswood from climbing over the hog-fence and taking root in our barnyards. So Franz imagined it once. We laughed his face red that day, and Walter said, "Where you get your crazy ideas in your head, don't ask me." Fritzie barked up sharply, "Quit owling about so much, you'd get more weeds pulled in the potatoes, mabbe."

I wondered in a half-hearted way about the woods marching, those forests beyond the Maises' and the Prinzings' west and north and the great slopes of red oak to the east . . . the puny cleanings lost in maple and ash . . . the brush in spring creeping out into winter rye, and oaks the size of milk buckets across, standing in the corn rows—woods hanging their dark cliffs to the four quarters of our world. They stopped the eye and even in summer, long before the sun flamed down in the notch between two shoulders, they spilled thick shadows across the fields and crowded them into our house. Night crept out of the woods like a black cat and with it came murk-bred forms and noises . . . sometimes wolves howling on a rabbit's trail and often the crazy whimper of a loon. I remember that Franz didn't mind, small as he was then, but Mother's face was a white blur moving in a dusk-filled room. Since Father grumbled about burning up the evening with oil when the long days gave light enough for early bed, the lamp on the bracket stayed cold. The high field would still be catching the light and only the low places slipping from the eye, when she'd call us and Franz would whisper, "She's scared—alone there."

"Well," we'd put it up to him, "you go stay." If we headed for the creek in a wild race, she'd cry out, "Not far, *Kinder*. Stay close by." As if the four of us added up to something she could put a hand on; something more than a huddle of shadows in a corner. The days Father was away she used to lock the door early, shoving down the bar with a kind of frightened haste and breathing quickly when whatever belonged to the woods and the night was shut out. Then she'd hold Franz in her arms and sometimes cry, and Walter and Fritzie would sneak off to the lean-to.

Hours after we'd be warm in bed, she'd wait, listening for the rattle of stones in the road, and run to put up the bar before Father came, so that he wouldn't know. Half-asleep in the loft, I'd hear her swift steps and the silence before he walked in. Those hours must have creaked in their slow passing, heavy as weights. I think Mother was glad when he found out at last—glad not so much that the hurt of waiting was ended, for it never was or would be, but glad with a kind of soured joy that the dread of what he might do was dragged into reality.

I remember that night as one who is jerked from sleep to awful wakefulness . . . Mother almost screaming she was afraid of the dark and the loneliness and wanted a lamp, and Father shouting her down with words about knowing what kind of a woman she was, locking her man out, and she could have a lamp and lakes of oil if she wanted to put him into the poor-house.

She had beggar's little to be thankful for, less than most, and I wonder now that she could smile at all, knowing within her how the fear rankled—fear of winter and the wolf tracks under the window; loneliness that began with the squeak of the door closing, on her wedding night, and grew with the days

Father put in, grubbing or brushing or lending a knife and a hand, butchering time, at one neighbor's or another.

Few came to tell her the time of the day, and fresh faces to wonder at were scarce, except at church. The Blubers lived nearest, two ridges on, but Father was bearish when they shuffled over, prowling to find out something and sour-faced when they didn't. Even when the Maises came and a neighbor's door was near, talk and recipes weren't exchanged very fast, for Father hated the goose gabble of Mrs. Mais's tongue and said so.

But I remember her smile when Franz wrote in the Bible; tremulous, as if her lips were asking for song and received only sorrow. She met us at the door when we tramped back from the closing school day, Franz seven then, Walter kicking his heels and impatient with hunger. "Come, *Kinder;* I'll get the Book," she called. "Lunch afterward." Father was in Mary's Hill that afternoon, we knew, as we nibbled at the batch of cookies she'd made. She opened the large book to the certificate page, her name and Father's—Johan Vildvogel—at the top, and helped Franz write his under "Children," next to our names; crabbed fists, all of them written when each of us had finished his first year at school and showing how Mother labored with us over slate and pencil. Walter's was there, thick and heavy with ink, the "Vildvogel" pressed in so hard a stain spread across the face of Moses on the other side; Fritzie's scrawly "Friederich" thin-lined as if he'd used a needle, his "d's" looking like dogs sitting upright and scratching themselves; Jepthah's—mine— plain as a fence post; and Franz's, airy as to the "F" but the last "l" gone in a black rill of ink; for Mother, hearing a noise out in the yard, suddenly dragged his hand away and shut the book with haste, and shoved it on the shelf. Then we saw that it was only Mrs. Bauer, wanting a recipe for eggless cake and talk about Mary's Hill and the time they were girls there. But Mother was almost wordless over the cookies, her eye on the stain the pen had made on Franz's fingers—he'd gripped the steel in such a scared way.

[14]

It runs in the mind like a thought half-muddled through that there was this fear when Father was away balanced up with the fear that sidled over when he was at home—of never being sure how he'd take a word of hers or a batch of bread; of never knowing when he'd be standing not far and watching her, his eyes saying as little as his lips. But even then, I think she feared most what his hands might do to Franz.

2

We had more time than enough to forget whatever shadows made us uneasy, bent over most of the day, with a hoe or a cow's teats or the wood of a pail caught in our hands. Aching sometimes. We'd be out pulling weeds in young corn with the sun hardly topping the trees, and I remember once we shivered under the stars, husking corn late, when we'd sneaked off to watch the shiners in the creek and Father coming home caught us. We husked every bundle in the pile that night before he'd let us in to bed. Fritzie began to milk the black heifer when he was seven but Franz hated it from the first, and would look at the brown streams of wet and smelly dirt caking between his fingers as if no soap that ever came out of Mother's sooty kettle could wash them off. Walter'd growl, "Look at him . . . the little Bull Calf. Cow dirt spoil your daisy hands?" Fritzie would snicker shortly, "Lady Fingers, how do you smell today?" "Ain't half through yet, Franz," I'd remind him. "Tonight you feed the calves, too." He'd pick up a stool as if it were a rock he'd like to throw, and we'd laugh, going back under the cows.

But when Father drove to town with the mares or was out in the back fields, we'd sneak along the dark paths on the ridges; at first not so far that we couldn't see our place in a break among trees—the knob of hill where our house stood with trees back of it and an oak prying at the eaves; the barn, and the hoghouse of posts and boards covered with straw;

the hencoop snug in a clay bank. Once Fritzie said, "House needs a new roof." Walter growled, "Old shack, that's what it is; wind'll take it along someday." But Franz wouldn't have it so. "It's home," he said, "and Mother's there and supper. Even if it ain't as nice as the Prinzings'.''

When we came up in years, though, we kicked over the traces and went farther. The blood up close under our skins, we wriggled like cats through hazel and Indian buckskin to watch a partridge begin his slow and muffled thuds on a drumming log, or tiptoed on a squirrel in a tree-fork, stretched belly-length to the sun. All four together, sometimes. Walter went first, a scowl for whoever cracked a stick, Fritzie next, second oldest and therefore important; and Franz trailed after me, getting the bushes slapped in his teeth. He liked to tease woodchucks and poke them out of the rail piles. They climbed trees as if they hated it, clumsily, as men do. Franz let go a stone too well-aimed once and shouted as the furry animal crashed down. But when blood squirted out of its nose and dribbled on his foot, he stood as if ax-struck. Fritzie broke off a dry club but Franz howled and wouldn't look. We saw to it that he stayed home the next two times for that.

How often in this white room, twisting and hot with pain, I have thought about coolness and wet swamp grass, and wood ducks brooding in knots of branches low over water; a partridge exploding from the bushes one evening, and the chicks scattering—the hours walking together that would have knitted us closer but for the weevil that ate and ate under the laughter and low whispers. If Father comes home . . . if Father finds out . . . if Father catches us.

We used to pull hop vines in the lower woods—tangles of stiff green yarn—and on them thread the dark balls of fruit lying under the whisky cherry. The tree stood in the pasture, the length of the cowyard from the barn—an old tree, pitted by the hammers of flicker and redhead, with a girth six hands around, and dangling more cherries than all the birds in a township could eat. It was shady-cool there, in the middle of plum and hazel. The whisky fruit bled wine stains on our fingers. Fritzie made a lasso of his string and mine spliced together, and tried to snare us. He flung a twirling loop one afternoon, a good throw, and poor Franz came near being strangled with a rope of cherries.

A part of that day is clear to me because of the horse Father sold and the look on Franz's face. Frightened and mixed with tears. It bothered me then, I didn't guess why, seeing it for the first time and not knowing it for the beginning of hate. We had the rope on Franz's wrists, ready for "Prisoner's Back," when Fritzie stopped us.

"Look," he called out. "Old Man Ochstock. He's got a halter for the roan."

"He can't." Franz dropped the cord, thinking of the horse in the back pasture—a devil in red hide. "He's mean, the roan; he kicks and bites—and Old Ochstock is good—" Words stuck in his throat.

Walter balled a fist. "Can't, hey, Bull Calf? Old Ochstock bought him with silver; if he's that foolish—"

"He's not." Franz came up close. "He gave me a hatful of apples last year. All Father wants is money and—"

"The Bank wants it," said Fritzie; "little we've got."

"It's wrong." Franz stood his ground but Walter growled fiercely, "Shut your face," and slapped him. Franz stood there, not looking at Walter, seeing the crook-backed old man with the halter. I noticed for the first time how the birthmark lay red on Franz's cheek—and wondered if it would bleed if I'd hit it along the edge; a fool notion, I decided afterward.

Wherever we dug up "Prisoner's Back" gets away from me; probably in Fritzie's shifty brain. We tied one of us to the tree, face against the bark; rolled his shirt up under his ears, and laid whips of strung cherries across his back. Every lash spattered the white skin with red—streaks of it, and the prisoner howled like a kicked dog, the louder and more doglike, the

[17]

better. But it hurt, this make-believe, the cherry stones rattling against our ribs like pebbles; sometimes we went home with blue lumps under the shoulder blades. Mother always said we smelled like the bag she crushed wild cherries in, at jelly-making time. But Father mumbled about wasting the day, if he opened his mouth at all, and usually put a chore in our hands.

For all that the screak of the gate might send us scattering like a catch of rabbits, we romped stolen hours in the pale green light shaken from the branches of the whisky cherry, Franz counting the white petals of the bloodroot. Violets flowered there, thin blue clouds of them, and the ribbed leaves of wild onion. A circle of quiet, with the cowyard and sour milk cans and the stink of the pigpen fenced off by hazel and plum. It was a woods place, until that spring when Father cut the tree and the brush and piled manure around the stump. He hauled thick stuff from the horse stalls and the heap where the strawstack rotted; piled it up. Purposely, I guess, although he muttered the tree was dry and bird-pricked anyway, and the fruit wormy. Which didn't say much about the manure, though we had to haul and pile it there winters afterward, and all the rains in Christendom will never wash the place clean of stink. But the next summer Franz found a yellow lady's-slipper swaying on the edge of manure. What wind blew the seed there is now gone under heaven. I put my hand out but Franz said, "Don't pick it, Jeppy."

"Why?" I wanted to know. "The shoe will sail dandy on the creek. We'll put a bug in and see how he goes." He had a funny look on his face, queer as if he saw more than gold bars and yellow satin on the toe of the slipper.

"Jeppy, it's growing in manure," he said; "in manure."

"Well, why not? Good and rich for it." I pulled it, roots and all. He didn't say anything but I could see he had his mind elsewhere, when we sailed the lady's-slipper boat that afternoon.

Change crept like a blind beggar over our farm, slowly and with no more hurry than rust. The fields broadened, true.

Father'd say, "Next fall we'll add the south clearing," and
we'd mark the increase. One year we dragged a fence an odd
hundred feet farther over, all the length of the ten-acre patch.
But when the moldboard turned new breaking and old plowing
into acres of even furrows, there was little to crow about—not
enough for the sweat of grubbing and hauling stumps and ripping up the hide of new land. Even Father grumbled we weren't
getting anywhere fast. Not by half. We left too much of ache
in our footsteps, coming and going, and the last strip added
seemed small and unimportant finally. The house wanted
paper, and the barn glass instead of rags for windows, but
there never seemed to be money for nails or putty to stop a
crack ("Use clay," ordered Father), and the fences got down
and lost in the burning bushes. We learned to expect corn meal
and potatoes twice a day and rye brew when the coffee failed.
We took it, though, as we took measles or the heifer's dropping a dead calf—something that couldn't be shouldered aside
any more than the hog-back knolls or a thunderbolt. But there
was that which we knew—common as rock. I can't remember the time when there wasn't a slant of hill back of the barn,
or a blue gulf beyond the tamaracks where Long Lake fretted
in the cattails edging Diemer's swamp. Nor a spring when
Father didn't stomp across our cleared patches to the high field,
gray with rocks and steeping to a dubious angle. He'd come
back, yellow to his shoe-tops with clay, and mumble something about throwing seed to the groundhog on acres like
those.

"Corn'll wash and wheat burn. What is a man to plant?"
He'd jerk about irritably, as if shoving off the blame, as if he'd
done better than his best, and it wasn't his fault. I remember
the tiredness of Mother's eyes, the violet-blue in them fading
to no color at all. And one spring he shouted so that we heard
him in the lower pigpen, "Get me the grub hoe, kids." Clods
flew like dark birds in the east clearing that day, as if in exasperation he wanted to chop a ridge of trees back to root in an

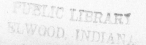

hour and bare new acres in a day. Fields bulged out carefully. The plow rolled up black loam where lately oaks and elm clung stubbornly to sod and rock, and the high field went into pastures. But not so many years ago, the sun two hours high could almost stretch a shadow clean across the largest of our fields.

3

So far back that the thread of my remembering becomes unraveled and confused, Father remains one who came out of the night and shouted and stopped my throat with crying. We were held tight in Mother's arms, Franz and I, so my memory goes, and Father was yelling about being hexed into it and not wanting her, and Mother not saying a word but trembling when he raged on, "I wanted to go my way; now I'm stuck with you—you and four kids. And this one—" He jerked Franz out of her arms; roughly, as if blind with a mist fogging his eyes. Franz tipped forward and fell against the bench, tearing his cheek where the birthmark lay reddish blue, and the blood came. I can hear Franz whimpering now and Father's thick anger. "This is yours—not mine; yours—yours." The rest is gone, smeared over with forgetfulness.

But the hammer-mark of awful fear remains; even in this white room and the safety of walls and bottles on the table, hills away from the farm, I have a strange feeling that it had no beginning, this gnawing, but came with the first breath. What will Father say? . . . what will Father do? . . . nagged us like an itch. I can hardly believe that any of us really knew him, or said more words than the day and the work required. The four of us might shut out the world of Mother and the water kettle on the stove, pretending an overturned chair in a corner was a den and we wolves inside, and growl our throats hog-dry and hoarse; but with Father's voice or step we clenched up tight and the room became hush-quiet.

A bullheaded man, Johan Vildvogel, leathered and tough as

an ox. Oh, I've heard it enough from the neighbors, times enough, and worse, too. And the congregation said "Amen," except when they needed the stout lever of his strength. They came, then. I've watched him at the Maises', at threshing time. He'd be slanted forward a little under two bags, one on each shoulder propped against his head, and running up nine steps to the loft bins—running because they were shorthanded and needed hurry. What breath failed him he caught again between the bin and the load. But Franz wanted to know, after a while of woolgathering, "Do you s'pose he could laugh—out loud, I mean, like Mr. Mais?" I hadn't even words to stick in my throat, only blankness.

He came to Mary's Hill with a timber sweep one spring—out of nowhere up north. A logger, he said. The townsmen crinkled up their eyes and let it go at that. Here for supper, gone for breakfast—loggers were like that. They went like the last shim-ice on the ponds, if you locked up your girls at nine o'clock. He stayed, though, Vildvogel, keeping whatever dark secret his past knew behind a prickly hedge of curtness. Hiding something, they said, wetting their lips to whisper. But Pastor Sunnenbaum brought him before the congregation and went good for him, and the deacons pried into every jot and tittle of what he knew about the Lord's Supper and baptism; even nosed around to uncover a manure pile or two in his life; hopefully, I guess, like dogs sniffing in places where bones are hid. But they didn't find more than a smell to egg them on. He was from over east, he said; had come up on a farm and knew more about pitching hay than swinging an ax in half a circle. But the woods had money under the bark, and he came. He had his bellyful of sawdust now, though, and hankered to settle him somewhere, and this looked like a good place to set, with clearings in the hills, and when there weren't, miles of timber on the root where a man could slash out an acre and step on nobody's toes. The deacons said him aye. From that day the Pastor and he were friends. But the members peeped over their knuckles, hoping, and Father knew they did, but not how to strike back. I'd like to forget the gritty thought that he spent most of his life being afraid of what people said.

Some things in those muddled years back beyond Franz's tenth autumn have about them a firm clarity not yet worn thin with forgetting. There were summers with storms when the sky, torn with lightning, cracked and broke like a dropped plate and fell in a roar of hail and rain, and thunder jolted the rafters. Franz used to sit white-faced and voiceless, wanting to shut out sight and hearing in Mother's apron but staying to watch the trees swish violently around as if shaken by the limbs, and the ridges dim away in streamers that pitched from the sky. Father'd say, "Up and off the step, Franz, and close the door." Franz when he came moved woodenly. And there were harvest days, when we gathered wheat heads, each with a basket, picking in the space between the bull-wheel tracks, bent over to scratch earth. I remember how the stubbles punched the skin bloody under the toes; how Fritzie crouched down, pinching out the thistle stings, and Father bellowed over the field he'd streak hot leather across our butts if we didn't pick up our heels. "Old devil," Walter'd snarl; "someday when I'm man-sized—" He crushed a head so hard that the kernels snapped out of his hand.

There was the autumn when the morning-glories tangled along the side of the house, green curtains of them, with trumpets the color of violets and deeper. They came out clear on days cloudy and promising wet, and Franz used to think they were horns to catch whatever blue came down with the rain. But Fritzie teetered with laughing and Walter growled about loon-headed notions.

Franz herded the cows in the meadows each fall; began when he was six. He let the hours dribble on while he pried into the crooks and crannies of ravine and rocky dry wash, or climbed the oaks where the kingbirds had nested, one eye open for the cows. They got away sometimes, obstinate as oxen, headed for the cornfield or the haystacks, and tearing out fork-fuls with their curved horns. Franz ran his legs off, then, the breath rattling in his throat like a pump rod with the leathers worn, shouting them back. And three summers, before Father fenced in the south woods, he drove the cattle early each day to the Diemer hills and the swamps, where neither post nor wire barred a cow's way. Franz'd lug home anything that stirred his fancy with its strangeness—moccasin flowers by the handful; a snakeskin, still vivid with the print of scales; until Fritzie, stumbling among the junk he brought up into the loft, howled, "Near knocked out an eye—old bee's nest hanging around. Get that truck out of here, Dough-pan." He'd come home head down, sometimes; his tongue hanging out as far as the heifers', Walter said one evening; trudging, hot and tired to his toes, and drink with the cows at the pasture spring.

Mother'd shake her head over him. "Thin legs like yours—not meant for these hills," she'd say and wipe his dusty face. "Sweat in the eyes—bad as an ant flying in them. Rest, now, and to bed—with the sparrows." She'd go for wood then, and split kindling; or carry a bucket to the calves; more than a few times milked the black heifer, pushing Franz off with a shoo of her hands. "Run, now, and ease your bones. Down by the creek, or somewhere." But I saw her stumble, pushing the cart piled heaping with dry cobs, and her mouth crinkle with pain. Long after we were in the loft, furrows under in sleep, she'd splash dishes in the pan and swish out the dirtied buckets. Fritzie said sharply, "Ain't nobody helping *us,* chore-time." Meaning himself. He was spiteful, when anybody else got the better share, and in no hurry to mind that she broke her back, taking on work, for him as for the rest of us. Father'd grumble, with a jerk toward Franz, "Let him busy himself. The Devil sits in idle hands."

But on a late-September day when the hazels were rusting to the tan of old iron and the nuts stuck ends out like brown thumbs from the greenish husks, the Prinzing kids came by, tin pails swinging, to gather a fall crop on the south ridges, and wanted Franz along. Father said, "No; Franz picks potatoes today." Mother wrinkled her apron; uneasy. "Johan, *bitte*—let him go; not often he gets to be with others; we five, picking—"

"*Na,* Minna; jaw rattling with talk again. You can help with the manure tomorrow, if you got time to gabble." Mother put her fingers to her lips to hide their trembling, so that the Prinzings, faces puckered like old apples with scared curiosity and ready to clank off, wouldn't see.

But on Saturdays when Father went to Mary's Hill—and other times when he was away—she'd slip over to the hills, with lunch for Franz, and tend the cows while he hopped from one cow-hummock to another; often stirring up a flutter of wings and finding a song sparrow still haunting the summer nest of hair wound under the side of a hummock; or he'd lie at Mother's feet, body to earth, listening to her soft voice, and waiting for the deer to come with the long shadows and browse with the cattle.

Fritzie ruffled with ire those days. "Guess Father'd like to know. I've a mind to tell—" Walter caught him by the looseness of his pants once and set him on the manure pile. "Shut that hole in your face; or I'll ram it full of cow-flop." Fritzie mumbled, his tail lowered, "You gonna stand for it—him getting the best of it and—" Walter shrugged, uncertain. "Take it out on the Bull Calf; all you please." He slammed a fork against the wall. "But let *her* alone." Fritzie rolled his lip but said nothing.

We dragged out half the days of one February with Anders Jaahcobs and the squeal of the accordion. That was the year the Griebers came, and Father was over there part of the time, helping them widen a clearing. Anders wallowed through a broken section of drifts after dark, slow and with patience in each step, like the oxen Old Man Prinzing drove. But he came, poofing and scattering snow, to sit near the stove and steam before he unbuttoned the accordion. A heavy man, thick and clumsy, with a belly that threatened to haul down his suspenders. His spoonlike fingers dug at the keys, tweedling out a waltz with leaky sighs, and, after much coaxing, perhaps a hiccoughy polka. Walter beat time with his heels, dolefully, a couple of winks behind, but seven-year-old Franz whirled until his head buzzed and he had to put out his hands to walk straight. He always begged for *Liebeslied* but Anders was stingy about playing it, and did so only when Mother asked and promised him a glass of pieplant wine, and then as if he didn't want to— a sad little melody from the old country that brought Franz to a standstill beside Mother and sometimes on her knee. Her lips trembled more than once, I know, the tune reminding her maybe of dreams she whispered to herself under who knows what night of stars—fancies spun as bright and as fragile as new frost on the pane; broken now, shattered, as tinsel between finger and thumb. The rest of us sat dead-still in our shoes.

But Father shoved back his chair with heavy scrapings in the middle of the piece one night and stood near the door, growling that such a push-and-pull rag—*ja* all right for women; but a man—*na, na*. Hinting, we knew, as we watched him. The accordion sobbed gustily and was still. Anders hooked a plug of black twist from his pocket and bit off a crablike chew. After that time, he went elsewhere, and music at our house dwindled for a while to Walter's sloppy whistling. The hand organ came a year later, with hymns and German songs enough; quadrilles and marches when we were alone. And Franz leaning his ear over the *Barcarolle*, winter or April time.

There were springs in thaw when we spaded caves in the five-foot drifts back of the hill and watched the snow darken with water. Fields began to break through the crusts, the plowed acres first, blackening in a night and holding at noon pints of water caught in hollow places where the clods jutted up. Snow on the unfurrowed patches became stubble-pocked and gray. Before we left off and forgot February cold, April sent the creek roaring in the willows, and earth slipped away underfoot.

It was in such a spring that the Griebers slopped through the mud one Sunday to visit us for the first time. I spent the shank end of the day before, dragging up wood and wondering about them. How they'd like our rye coffee and barley *Kuchen;* whether they had chairs around the table like the Maises, or a bench shoved against the wall to sit on as we had. Anything new swung our ears and eyes open like cupboard doors to take in what we saw and heard. A fresh calf, or a baby, or teeth knocked loose in a fight, left us in an upset of feeling, as if the event belonged in part to us, and we had a say in it. I remember how frog-eyed we stood when Walter brought home a black-oak stick, crooked and twisted like a snake caught in a wriggle and hardened to wood. And there was the unbelievable length of a timber wolf, snarling even in death, that Mr. Mais shot behind a rock pile and carried home. Afterward we spent hours in chasing the marvel through the heavy thickets of our wonder, saying what we said before six times over and yet finding repetition good to the ear and the tongue; contriving much out of little, stretched thin to make it last.

Mother fussed over her pots and loaves, thinking of the Griebers too, I guess, and hunted in the dugout by candlelight time and again to see whether she had overlooked a jar of plums or Juneberries she could dish up for them instead of sour pie-plant sauce. "Bitter as vinegar," she said with a wry face, slapping the sugar bag to beat out a few grains. But no amount could sweeten it, even if she had the sugar. The corn sirup she heated and poured in added stickiness but little else. She was worried and flustered; shamed, too, when the cups didn't go around and she had to set up a tin mug for one of us.

She put on a dress we'd never seen before, I remember; the color of light apple butter, with tucks and ruffles and large puffs at the shoulders; faded a little but gay with bright buttons. "It's been up in the chest years," she whispered; "too much fuss and feathers for church. He'd scold me for a hussy, the Pastor would." I could see Father didn't like it but held his peace. He carried the oak bench in and put it against the wall back of the table. The one room of our house had an air of waiting, as Mother had; she was tremulous, more than any of us except Franz. I remember how her eyes turned bluer when they came, and Mrs. Grieber kissed her. We stood awkwardly near the door, knees half-bent, wondering what we ought to do or say, glad without knowing why. Even Father nearly grinned when Mr. Grieber without a smile unwrapped a small jug of blackberry cordial.

He was a dried-up man no wider than a board and about as thin, though tougher than bull leather. No one I ever met had less to say, except Father—few words to spare and those were short. I think it was for this that Father liked him and went to his house often. They sat by the half-hour Sundays, letting the grandpa clock speak out loud for them. (Fritzie heehawed afterward when I told him. " 'Tain't Old Grieber, no; it's the blackberry cordial Father likes. Don't you see how it oils his tongue?") But I like to think of that day, years back in there, and the supper we had. A strange meal, with Mrs. Grieber gibble-gabbling like a turkey hen and Mother venturing a word once in a while, shyly; unused to company. Mr. Grieber said little over his noodles and sowbelly, and Father less, though they gave and took words man-fashion about plows that wanted cutting bars . . . the heifer that wouldn't calve . . . the trouble they had with spring rye. We took easier breaths, somehow, as if whatever dark goblins lurking in the shadows behind our thought were beaten off with laughter and talk and the neighborly face of heartiness. Not all, though; some crept back when Franz, his mouth crooked with barley crusts, cried out suddenly, "Stay here, Uncle Grieber—can't you—all night? You can have my bed." Father looked at him so that he turned to his potato mush with a red and scared face.

That spring sticks in my mind because of the man and the yellow-haired girl. The fields were sloos of mud; a wagon drawn across them left tracks so deep and wide not even the plow

could erase the scars. Roads bounced off into side tracks to
avoid the drifts, and on the level were broken and pitchy with
sled-wallows. They came to the Griebers', asking the way to
Too Far Lake; the Griebers didn't know, being new then, and
sent them to us. We were ditching the pond by the barn, ankle-
deep in brown ooze, when they drove up. Franz was making a
noise about wet feet but hushed when he saw the girl; took a
step ahead and stopped. Fritzie ran inside to call Father. We
leaned on our spades, Walter and I, staring like pumpkin faces;
scared and uneasy for no earthly reason except that they were
strangers and their ways unknown to us. The man was gentle-
fisted, we saw by the way he handled his team, with no more
fire in his pale blue eyes than in a lamb's; soft-spoken, too.
The little girl looked up at him before she observed us frankly
with dark eyes. She is clear in my mind—a faint leaf-curl of a
smile on her lips; about Franz's age, maybe, seven or eight;
with a bowl-like gray cap from under which yellow curls got
away and crawled over her collar. I felt how dirty and manure-
soaked my pants were because she looked at them. But Franz
stared and stared at her with a puzzled wonder, as though she
weren't real. I remember this, for when Father came and had
gruffly marked the way in a patch of snow, Franz suddenly
moved like one walking in sleep and climbed into the sled,
shyly yet purposefully, afraid, yet not to be stopped either.
Before a mouth could say "Don't," he gently pulled off her
cap and let the yellow curls tumble and make her dark coat
darker because of the golden light. She watched him like a
fawn ready to spring at the flick of danger, quietly but unafraid, even when he gathered a fistful of curls. He put a
finger on them as if they were hummingbirds and no more
tangible to nerve-ends than the pale ghost candles in the marsh.
Softly, with tenderness. Then Father had a boot on the runner,
shouting "Franz," and pulled him down with a yank. He fell,
the water spurting from the puddle. The little girl hid behind
the man, watching sorrowfully.

"You—you—get to the house." Father was dark with anger. Franz got up slowly, half of him wet to the neck. He was not sorry, though; you could see that. I felt shame in a hot sweat go over me. That anyone in our family should behave so— bold and clumsy, and as if he didn't know better. Before strangers, too. Without looking back, he went. Father mumbled about kids' notions and the man laughed. They drove off, Father with them, to point out the snags in the short cut. Nobody knew till later that Franz turned at the door and streaked across to a hill in the field, where he could see the road. He watched the girl until the basswood clumps hid her, before he came home. We caught him sneaking back and gave him our thought, a good square piece of it.

"A couple of licks across your hinder, that's what you'll get," promised Fritzie; "you wait." Franz hadn't a word for himself. Months later he spoke of her one day when we were helping Walter drive posts. He brought her out of his mind in the sudden way he had. He'd look for her around Too Far Lake and ask—well, he didn't know what. But there would be a trail blazed, he knew, for him to find her. He'd have us know that much.

Thereafter, we prodded him with his own words; dug them from the pockets of our memory, when we thought he was uppish and needed setting down. "Getting kinda lonesome, over there, ain't she, your Yellow Head? Waiting so long." Walter pulled at the words, slowly, watching him dig at his nails. "I tell you what, Dough-pan." Fritzie couldn't hide the cunning in his face. "You can have the buggy Saturday night. We'll get it washed and shiny. And put a ribbon in the mare's tail." Not for years did we let him forget. But a light burned in a hidden part of him, I think, at the thought of golden curls.

I don't believe that any of us cared; or wanted to know his fancies, even when he spoke out. We put them aside as something he didn't come by natural as being a boy, but notions that she-kids have, like playing house with dolls and bits of broken saucers, as Tinkla Bauer did. Not worth a man's thought. Franz felt this in those years not far from his tenth birthday and after, without being able to do much but spill tears. He got clawing mad when we hooted at the way he split kindling.

"You do it like a girl," said Fritzie and stuck a finger into his mouth; "a little teasy easy girl. Here, take a hold of the handle like this."

"Get away from that ax," Franz howled. "I can do it," and tried to swing.

Fritzie grabbed the handle. "Can't sit here all night. Take the wood so, and hit straight. Chop hard." But Franz balked. "You can do it yourself now. You spoiled it for me," and left, looking as if he hated us. When he didn't run off bawling, he'd stand watching us with the eyes of a tormented cat. Ready to spit, the mark on his cheek a smear of crimson.

He let off steam, though, a winter's afternoon, when we least expected it. We were loading straw in the field, Fritzie and I pitching up the rack and Franz waist-deep in the loose stuff, tromping the edge to keep the load solid and the chaff from falling away. He coughed when a forkful struck him, filling his mouth. Fritzie suddenly jammed his fork down. "Enough to make a cow laugh, the way you work." He climbed on the load and shoved Franz aside. Franz twisted like a spring and shot out a balled fist, but was clumsy with young-buck rage and winter clothes. Fritzie dodged and caught his hands; wrenched them back so that Franz shuddered with pain and came to his knees. "Learn you who's boss here." Fritzie knocked him from the load into a snowbank and made him walk half the mile home, legging behind the sled.

We nagged him; went out of our way, I guess. "You'll have to milk the kicker tonight, Franz," we'd tell him down in the barn, just to see him swing around, yelling, "I won't. She hooks and switches her tail."

"Keep your eyes shut then," we'd say, getting our stools. In the end he rattled the pail and shooed the heifer over.

The hours we put in riding milking stools, morning and night, endless with the patience of resignation; hours of lantern red and shadow gray slanting over the cows, and horned shapes moving on the walls . . . stink of horse wet, acrid and filling the throat, until smell became heavy on the tongue and left in the mouth a taste of manure . . . the white arch of milk falling from Walter's bucket . . . the heifer with the brush of her tail curled on her back like a snake . . . Franz crouched on his one-legged stool, dodging the hairy swishes and failing, no matter at what angle he crooked himself . . . endless. Once he battered her ribs with his fists and when she moved restlessly, caught up a slab of a broken box and splintered it over her hips. Walter came and ripped the pieces out of his grasp. The rough edges tore into his flesh.

"My hand." Franz whitened when Walter pushed him.

"Milk that cow."

"Cut open, Walter—"

"Shut up and milk. Learn you to pound the cows."

"It hurts."

"Git goin' before I break that board over your head."

He went to work and I remember how disgusted I was because he kept stopping to look at his hand. But when Walter saw the milk tinged red staining the foam, he jerked the pail away.

"Never saw such a stupid. Go to the house and put turpentine on." Franz stumbled out. He had this then to store and mix in with memory—pain and the slow rust of tears, eyes full and brimming over—pain overwhelming in its sharp immediacy but with its edges blunted by the forgetfulness that comes with a dog-tired hanging of the shoulders and palms rough and hard; with knowing sunset and moonup as something more than events in the almanac. There was anodyne in growing older alongside things that put forth leaf and stem quietly and with strength. A certain cheer welled out of untried blood as irresistibly as bedrock water out of a hillside, though laughter at our house was thin-bellied enough, a ghost of mirth. But all the laughter, all the arms of strength, could not take from his mind every scrap of the somber leavings. Some fell deep and lodged; lay there; seeds with power to bud in fierce and unpredictable shapes.

5

Squeezed in among the years like pebbles in a rock pile are days unimportant in themselves but taking on meaning when added to what came before or followed after. Such a day was the one that came treading behind the Pastor's visit, leaving us uneasy with worry we could not put our hands on.

In those days the Pastor had his white parish house in Mary's Hill instead of in the congregation, and drove ten miles to our little church at the crossroads, next to Toffmann's store and feed mill. It spired above the elms, straight over two sections north. He came there two Fridays in the month, his buggy severe and black, with mudguards over the wheels, and his grays a spanking team. The Toffmanns gave him bed and board. Were glad to, they said. Thinking they'd earn an extra pillow-covered seat in Heaven, I decided.

Saturdays he held school, using fist and willow stick to lay down the cornerstones of piety and faith. He troweled in doctrine as Mr. Mais did mortar, with a strong hand. Even the housefathers cringed a little when he spoke. They held him as a whip over their children, and threatened overgrown and ox-like sons. "You fellers, you; off to German school next week. We'll see if the Pastor can't pound some of the Devil out of you."

At ten or eleven years the unconfirmed came to him. They gripped lunch box and desperate courage together and went in behind his shepherding mercies. Fritzie howled when his turn came, Walter told us; tried to get out of it by smoking corn silk wrapped in basswood leaves and staggered in sick of face and wanting to puke. But Father made him go. Once he ran off and hid in the willows; for a day and a night. In the morning, hunger-driven, he came home and Father met him with the rawhide. He was confirmed now, as Walter was, and free, and used to plague Franz with telling how bad it became and the lickings that fell to his lot . . . unnumbered beatings.

"You got it coming yet," he'd say, with a sharp laugh; "a year or so, and you'll catch it. Got an oak club, the Pastor has. Thick as a wrist. Not afraid to use it either." Franz would listen with uneasiness wrinkling on his face. But once when Fritzie was hot with a tale of whippings, he turned suddenly. "I'll go, anyway. Can't be any worse than you, he can't." Meaning what he said and yet afraid and in the end running away. Fritzie stopped on a word, half-grinning foolishly. Walter, easing his wide bulk on the manger, drawled out, "Sure pinochled you that time, little Bull Calf did."

Whatever wells of energy the Pastor drained on Saturdays he had refilled brimful after a night at the Toffmanns' and long wrestlings with the flesh. But Johnny Toffmann guessed it was more than wrestling did it, the way the Pastor's breath stunk of wine. Sunday mid-forenoon, unimpaired, he trod sin and death underfoot again, and thrust sharp hooks of uncertainty into the tired minds of the congregation. They sat there, *die Gemeinde,* leg and brain weary after six days in the fields, wanting sleep—and were afraid. No one forgot the time Old Man Gerhardt, red-eyed and bleary with terror and too much whisky eggnog, crawled on hands and knees to the altar and hung on the railings, repentantly drunk. The congregation whispered awe-struck for days.

After services and handshakings all around, one family or another asked the Pastor along; nervous and uncomfortable with honor when he accepted. Or he asked himself. He came to our house sometimes; often, after the congregation bought him a house near the church and the way to Heaven became appreciably nearer. I remember how his long black coat filled our house with a kind of darkness, and Franz ran to Mother and hid his face when he came.

Father and he went off by themselves and we'd see them

talking earnestly. What strange threads drew them together I never figured out, unless Father looked for ease of disappointment in the Pastor's counsel; for patience and a distrustful sort of hope that comes with the sedative of promises made over and over again, but now wearing off.

There was a night in early autumn when we felt a vague stirring of things hidden behind our backs, a sense that we fumbled in mists thicker than those walling out the trees and hills on rainy days. We had just begun supper. Father paused to clear his throat after grace, and Franz clutched his spoon, one eye on Fritzie and the other on the small bowl of milk soup. Father took up the ladle and filled it, then stopped. Outside, wheels rattled to silence and before we knew, the Pastor stood in the lamplight. He took a step forward, trembling and breathless.

"Bruder Vildvogel—I can't—you must say. What do you know about Northland City jail?"

Even at this distance I remember how still the room was, how Father got half up, a grayish color like weathered ashes going over his face . . . how the soup spilled over the oilcloth . . . Mother crumbling bread and butter in her hands and Franz nothing but eyes in his fright . . . the feeling that I could never breathe away the tightness in my heart. Father stood holding to the table; words came slowly. "Minna, Minna, now they'll have something to talk about." Mother came to him then, unafraid, her arms half-raised.

"Tell me, Johan. This belongs to me, to both of us." But the Pastor came between. "Bruder Vildvogel, we have much to pray for, tonight." They were gone with the creak of hinges . . . the grind of wheels. We faced one another and the awful silence that pressed like cloths upon our lips. No one ate soup that night, for the dryness in our mouths. The bed blankets gave off a sticky chill instead of warmth. But Mother had the table left to clear and the dishes to wash . . . the soured cans . . . the milk strainer, stuck full of hair and the slippery drains of buckets . . . Martha jobs that neither birth nor death may put aside nor sorrow alter. With doubt and despair howling in her brain like hungry dogs. Finished at last, the house chores, for her to find what peace she could on the hard cot. The slow hours. Tomorrow he'd say what we wanted to know. Tomorrow. We heard Father come in late and go straight to the lean-to.

I remember how grim he looked at breakfast, daring anyone to hurl the first stone. Mother's eyes were red and she ate sparrow-little. All at once she lifted a hand; meaning to speak, I guess. But Father said as if it didn't matter, "No, Minna; this is not for womenfolks. I and the Pastor have spoken all the words. You and the boys put a hand to the mouth . . . from now on." He got up. "Get your mush down, kids," he said and went out.

Mother began to cry, Franz with her, for company. We sat dumb, knowing fear again and dread like a heavy ache in our minds. Mother held Franz to her.

"*Junge, junge,* for you there is this—this always." She turned from him. "Now is the black frost come in summertime, Fränzchen." So low, her voice, we hardly heard yet never forgot. Black frost in summertime and the crop dead on the stalk.

6

There was after all a sameness about this minute and the next and all the number of our yesterdays that would have left us sick of earth itself, had we stopped plow or wagon long enough to wonder. We'd stir ground feed into milk for pigs today, half-knowing we'd do this again tomorrow . . . and the next and God knows how many to follow. Until the pigs died or we butchered and ate them. Which ended nothing. We'd carry the slops out to the calves then, or Father'd get another couple of hogs, by trade or exchange of a week's grubbing.

But after that autumn in Franz's tenth year (it seems to me

now), days took on a kind of shape and meaning. At least they were something more than a space to hurry through between two sleeps; vague and confused at first but hinting at what was to come, as early frost is winter warning of deep death. More for him than anyone, perhaps. Though by now, knowing this as one who moves and moves restlessly on his pillow and cries under the breath, it seems plain that night and day are only darker or brighter lengths in a pattern of years, losing identity with the even shading of one into another. However, what happened on some days sticks up huge and bold in my memory like willow clumps in a level drift of fog.

We went to the Griebers' that night, all of us for once, even Mother. I think it was the way her eyes opened and shut quickly with a violet-blue light in them we seldom saw, that made us hurry with the wood and water and splitting of the kindling sticks—the last of the chores.

"She's like a candle, inside her," said Franz with an odd expression, almost old and wise, pulling at the birthmark on his cheek. He gathered eggs without protest that night though he hated it.

Fritzie laughed in his sharp way, "For a ten-yearer, you see too much. Get on egg hunting."

"Candleshine," muttered Walter sullenly; "God knows where she finds it here, in this forsaken place." He spilled the last of the slops into the hog trough. "Just like the little Bull Calf to see it, though," he added grudgingly.

Walter was sixteen at the time, Fritzie two years younger and I in between him and Franz; but it was Franz even then who noticed what we never saw and pointed out the silver on the underside of willow leaves while we were still gawping at the tree.

The last cob of wood crashed into the woodbox. We were yelling for clean shirts and overhalls, and Franz was complaining, "My pants got a button loose," when Father walked in, shouting, "Who left the haymow door open?" Dead silence in the room made the water kettle bubble louder. Walter sat with a shoe half on, oak-stiff, his lower lip caught back in his teeth, and Fritzie's lean face sharpened about his bloodless cheekbones. Franz began to snivel; Father made for him, his arms stretched out, but Mother flung a hand to his shoulder. "Johan, we're nearly ready," she cried, talking fast, "You said seven o'clock. Chores are done. And I've got potato soup—"

"I said the haymow door was to stay closed," he shouted, throwing off her hand. "Franz, would you like to stay home— alone?" Father pulled a chair to the table and began to lard a crust of bread.

"Little Bull Calf got his foot in the pail again." Walter pulled on his shoe. "Serves him right," growled Fritzie, breathing hard. I felt the blood moving in my veins again, and wanted to slap Franz for letting the tears drip on his cheeks, although no sound broke from his lips. Father hated snuffly noises; this might stir up the pot again.

Perhaps it was the soup; perhaps it was the candleshine Franz saw in Mother's eyes; perhaps none of these but a strange shift in the weather wind somewhere within himself that made Father show his teeth all at once and say over his last piece of lard and bread, "Get into your pants, Franz; I've got the mares harnessed."

Remembering that night from this peak overlooking the valley of years, I wonder that we buttoned pants and shirts and rushed out into the star-cut dark so light of foot. We piled into the platform buggy, Father and Mother in the seat front, the four of us in the box back, Walter in the blackest corner, Franz in the middle where he could see, though Fritzie pushed his face into the straw, with loud words. "See anything, Doughpan? Straw in your teeth will make you say nice things." Walter growled, "Let the little Bull Calf alone," but Father heard and shouted, "Shut up, back there, or I'll take a rawhide to you."

The wheels made an iron sound on the rocky trail. September, slanting down with midnight frosts that blackened the corn in hollows and unhooked the leaves of basswood, nipped our backs under our patched shirts. We crept together for shoulder warmth and watched the dark woods jolt past. Why Father took it into his head occasionally to go the meadow road we never knew—a wild notion he kept even from Mother, like the dim closets in the mind which we keep hidden almost from our own eyes. The way he turned down a pitchy side road brought us up with a jerk. Mother was crying, "Johan, not this way—in the dark," but Father roared, "I go where I damn please—and tonight I go the meadow road," and pounded the mares with the whip. Through the hog wallows and dry washes, along a broken trail only faintly marked by day, we lurched, tall reeds crashing against wheel and buggy box, now one wheel down axle-deep, now another, so that our positions were all on angles. Twice I saw the North Star shuttered out by the sudden upthrust of the box and felt sick at the way my head shot backward and down. Franz flattened in the straw, too scared to do anything but hold on. Even in the dim light I saw Fritzie's wild eyes and thinly drawn nose pointed like a hawk's against the sky and sensed the hate and fear that lay behind his lips. No word bored the dark shadows where Walter crouched, a hulk of the night itself. Once a tire threw flame from stone—we saw the flicker on the overarching willows. Father was cursing the mares and shouting, "Don't like it, do you, Ma? I'll show you how to put red meat on your hinder." The wheels flung against a rock and my head rattled on a board; dizzily then I realized that we were on smooth road and, after a while of riding, that the Griebers' house lights fell in a pale bar across us. As we went indoors I saw Mother put her handkerchief to her lips and tuck it quickly away, and that Walter had a red bruise on his temple. But Father was whistling *Im Kühlem Keller* with gusto.

How little we understood, or, for that matter, knew about one another, we who were slouching in chairs under the slant of the kerosene lamp bracketed out of reach on the wall—Father slowly and almost painfully telling about timber booms; Mother twisting her wedding ring over her knuckles and back again, wishing she had never come, although she answered "Yes" and "No" and smiled at Mrs. Grieber's rambling words. In a corner where the light didn't strike, Walter sat, touching his head, his jaw clamped tight, and not far away, Fritzie, his thin face alive with a foxlike expression, laughing shortly, sharply; Franz on his belly on the floor, his tangled head lifted and a distrustful pull at his lips, as if he felt that we purposely talked in riddles and half-sentences to keep him from knowing what we gossiped about, and hated us for it; until Mr. Grieber brought out the flute and began to play *Ich weiss nicht was soll es bedeuten.* Then Franz crept like a drugged animal to those oversized boots tapping the beat, and lay there, his long slender fingers quivering, his face washed of color, only his eyes moving restlessly.

"What's the matter, little Bull Calf?" grunted Walter. "Sick to your belly?" Fritzie laughed sharply. "Look at him—like a frog that a snake has hexed. Froggie, give the snake a belly-ache." But Mother suddenly spoke up in a voice I'd never heard before. "Let him alone. Can't you see it's beautiful to him? If you could hear what he hears." She stopped, breathing quickly. Father lowered his jaw to say hard words but laughed stickily instead. "That's right, Minna; stuff him full of notions. He'll fill the woodbox quicker." Mother twisted the ring backward, forward. As if he had touched a key that hurt him, Mr. Grieber lifted his fingers and laid the flute on a corner table.

How often in the quiet backwashes of thought have I pawed over what happened that night—and whipped myself with the lashes of futile regret. Some things stand out brightly—the flute in the corner, Franz, never pulling an eye from its silver length, cat-crawling closer to it until his fingers touched its magic, and, when every eye but mine was busy elsewhere, popping it into his shirt. I felt sick and started out of my chair but sank back at Father's loud voice. Franz hugged the shirt pocket where the flute bulged and crept into a corner, a white radiance burning on his face, to sing within himself. But I saw only the empty table and dreaded the Griebers' knowing it and Father's hard hands when he found out.

It was late when Father said, "I'll get the horses," and got up, all of us standing outlined with him, so that an elbow crooked out had a distinctness that was terrible. What is now a mere haze was sharply cut then, like tamaracks against the white wash of the horizon—Franz, betrayed into sleepiness, letting the flute slip thudding loudly on the floor; Father seeing, teeth striking teeth; all of us standing; Franz, eyes wide like a dog caught under a tree deadfall, full of desperate fear. I remember how Father struck him, so that he knickled to the floor; how Mother ran with an upraised arm against him; how Franz screamed and then grew still, lying crookedly; how the Griebers stood like posts, too neighborly to bend a knuckle one way or another. It comes to me now with a clarity that follows the settling of roiled-up water that always after this night Franz would remember beauty and pain as two that go together, balancing on the pivot of experience, like two buckets pulling at the ends of the wooden yoke Mother put on her shoulders when she carried water from the pasture spring.

The hollows and uplands of our ridges are torn and ripped and made over by the five fingers of God—the four seasons and the drought that slinks in with its lean moons. An earth change comes with each long swing of the sun. But our ways, and the wheels of our thought, ponderous and huge—these change slowly and with protest, after the length of revolving years; stubbornly, with rusty noises. It is clearer now, since the winds of distance have blown away the mist that hung before our eyes. But in the chill of that homeward ride, I felt only anger and the weight of Franz's misbehaving. That, and the relief of putting blame on someone. Else I should not have kicked out a foot against him, that gray morning when Franz crept under my arm, head in his elbow, for Father might hear, "It was pretty, the music—why did Father hit me?"

"You stole it," I snapped. But he cried against the covers, "I didn't. I wanted to play. Mr. Grieber makes pretty sounds."

But because he was one of us, as much as the willows down by the creek, and wearing the same overhalls and shirts, and sitting down to pancakes and coffee mornings like the rest of us, I shoved him away. "Get to sleep." And turned over on my side.

7

The last acorns fell in a swirl of red leaves, and wind scattered the bright feathers of summer into the corner places. Franz and I put our bread and lard in a Prince Albert tobacco box and black coffee in a sirup pail, and got ready to go on the path to school. Franz counted off on his fingers the places where late flowers might be found—the willows, the creek, the rice lake, the pasture which we cater-cornered, and the yard with the paint-peeled schoolhouse. "There's blue-spike there, in the south corner, if the grasscutter hasn't killed them," he ventured, but I pulled him up shortly. "Who's looking for flowers anyway, this time of year—unless maybe you and Tinkla Bauer."

For three weeks the morning bell had clang-clanged the nine o'clock hour and we no more than lifted our noses from grubbing and hauling stumps. Father put his foot down when Mother hinted that school was near beginning, and Franz looked eager. "Not till I say." A black look came on his face. "There's work here to be done." But I knew it wasn't work alone. He was thinking of the Griebers and how the neighbors were sharpening their tongues. He saved his breath about the flute but the way his eyes smoked at Franz when his anger burned deep, we knew that he hadn't forgotten; a worm turned in his brain then, and would not be stopped. Thereafter, when he had to choose between Franz and any of us to do a chore, he pointed at Franz with a crooked finger.

"Franz, you watch the cows today. Walter goes with me to the north meadow." Or he thundered: "I said Fritzie is to split wood. Franz can clean out the pigpen." Franz picked up the fork, the scar red on his dark cheek, knowing that Father purposely sent him, and biting back words, young as he was.

We went no more to spend a lamplit evening with the Griebers. They talked, or Mrs. Grieber did, and the congregation knew, and it came back to us, as talk always does, by the circlewise tossing of tongue and lips. "Hell of a queer lot, the Vildvogels. They say the old man keeps a gun under his pillow and goes spooking around his farm at two in the morning." Mother heard and held Franz close, and knew—or felt the shadow if she didn't know—that Father carried to her door the reproaches for that September evening. "Make me the slop pail for other men's spit, that's what my wife and kids do," he glowered, and stalked out to the barn. He was even afraid, I think, of what we might hear at school, and held us back. We helped with the corn and hauling stumps, until Father dared keep us no longer. Old Lafferty, the teacher, hated latecomers and last year the superintendent had the Mankins arrested for not sending their boys.

Franz nearly kicked off a heel the day Father grunted, "Monday, you kids better start school." He wasted an hour over the ruler Mother whittled out of pine and edged with tin for him. School meant singing and do-re-mi on the board. "And maybe Yellow Head will be there and you won't have to go up to Too Far Lake," teased Fritzie, eyes pinched together. Franz went back to feeding calves and splitting firewood with grumblings. "Near cut my knuckles off, fixing that old kindling. Why can't we have something besides elm and oak chunks?"

"Ax is in the woodshed and popple as far as your eye can see," Fritzie snickered. "Hop out and cut yourself a dry tree, Doughpan."

"You talk big, Bull Calf," growled Walter. "Guess you can stay home and take my place." Franz rammed the wood into the box angrily, but he let that be; he wasn't going to have anything keep him from "Last Couple Out" and the stories of Galahad like those which Lafferty read the winter before. He fretted through the hours till Monday and was up with the split of dawn, pulling at the covers I had sneaked up over my ears. "Get up; you got to slop the pigs before school time."

"Oh, shut your teeth. I wish the schoolhouse would sink to the bottom of Diemer's swamp." I envied Walter and Fritzie driving away with Father in the wagon, Walter slapping the lines down like a man. He had banged shut the covers of Jones's *Ninth Reader* and the doors of District 115 the spring past. "I'm through," he said, and ripped his spelling book in half. Fritzie, safely thirteen, and knowing that Father would find winter jobs to keep him out of Frye's *Geography* and Montgomery's *History* for an extra month of schoolless days, taunted us this morning. It puzzled Franz. "Why does Fritzie get so mad at 'rithmetic, and wants to stay home?" he asked, bringing in oats. "Don't he care what six times seven is?"

"Well, Old Lafferty licks him," I started out, when Franz butted in, "Fritzie makes noises with his feet and spits on the floor—tobacco juice last year."

"Oh, you and old Lafferty—good team, you are. Why don't you crawl up his pants legs?" I couldn't help growling, not in defense of Fritzie so much as in futility of having to go at all; even the thought of dropping a lighted match down a crack of the old building was tinged with doubt.

We did chores to the last forkful that morning, for Father had no patience with the waste of time in getting book schooling, and we never did enough to suit him, though the bell would likely catch us hustling along the rice lake halfway there. He grumbled when we needed things; had, every year, even though Franz wore the lead down to the metal band at the end of his pencil. "What? Paper again? Just bought some. When I went to school we wrote examples on slates with a white stone for a pencil." We knew he was thinking of the Bank again. Even a five-cent tablet put an extra rail on his shoulder and he hated us for the ant's weight we added to his load; and tried to shove it off. He had brought home a stack of old letter forms the last Christmas—a heap which the machine-shop man in Mary's Hill gave him free. "Use it for writing paper, kids." He threw the bundle on the table. "The other side is blank and good for pencil." Franz looked at Mother, that time, and thought how the boys would laugh. Mother pleaded, "Johan, *bitte*—the boys—white paper costs no more and—"

"What now?" Father shouted, tight and angry. "Ain't good enough, heh? Can't save, can you, you wasting money ankle over heels? Well, use it for school or the backhouse, I don't care. But paper you'll not get till it's used up." To this moment I can bring to mind the dirty-reddish paper, rough to the finger tips, wearing the pencil down like sandpaper. The words on one side—

"Dear Sir:
    "Yours of the————inst. received and beg to state that your account . . ."

are all mixed up with the spelling words on the other—long-legged monsters like "asafoetida" and "latitudinarian" which Old Lafferty called "terms familiar in every home." And there was one page on which we wrote from memory

"Hail to thee, blithe spirit,
Bird thou never wert,"

commas and all. Those sheets of paper were as leaves on the oak and fluttered in our hands all of that year.

Our first Monday of this term was one of Satan, fiery-eyed

in the east, and restless fury in the air tumbling the juncos on the oak ridge. We were in the middle of the pasture when Franz remembered, "The pencil tablet—you got it, ain't you?"

"You're s'posed to look after school truck." I put the thing off on him. "In your bundle, ain't it?"

"No," he yelled, "and it's your fault, making me feed all the calves this morning. I left it on the commode." His eyes looked as if he wanted to throw stones. "What'll I write on now?"

"Aw, use your tongue," I shot back; "it's big enough. Anyway, who wants to write in school?" Franz had it in his mind to go back but we were near the road and a Kloster boy, coming along, shrilled, "Heh! Starting in school at last?" We followed him, Franz crinkling with wrath and I wondering why the skunks under the schoolhouse couldn't push out their stink plugs today and empty the place, as they did once last year when the Biebers' dogs dug after them, and the whole school turned out skunk hunting.

When we came inside, the four walls and the slanted roof rattled with shrieks and boos and a loud voice, "I'll tell Teacher." The Kloster boy opened the door quickly; pigtails and towheads scuttled over seats and across the floor into their places, and silence fell like a stone from the ceiling. Eyes came over shoulders and saw us. "It's only Diah Kloster and the Vildvogels," somebody said and double seats squeaked under shifting buttocks. A girl squealed "Ouch!" and the free-for-all freshened up. But in the pause between rackets I saw two seats gaping empty, one beside Jonas Bluber and one just behind, where Clyterdale Mankin sat gnawing his fingers.

A boy at an uncurtained window screamed, "Old Lafferty," and the floor groaned with bodies plowing into seats. Franz slid in beside the squint-eyed Jonas, who put a shoulder against him, yelling, "Get out!" and pushed.

"I want to sit here," insisted Franz.

"Ain't nuther."

"Well," Franz tried again. "Seats are full."

"Not gonna sit with no stinking German." **Jonas crouched** pugnacious.

"I ain't got dirt in my pants," said Franz.

"Smells like it," and Jonas haw-hawed with a wide mouth. Franz bristled his feathers for fight but Old Lafferty, with a two-foot ruler and a nose like a clothespin holding up his eyes, rolled in. "What's the ruckus, boys?" He slid the ruler along the top of the seat.

"His paw hits his maw." Jonas pointed with a finger wound in a dirt-gray rag. "And I guess his paw's been in jail, too."

"It ain't so." Franz turned with a wildcat twist. "Father hasn't."

"An' his paw ain't brought the two cords of oak he's s'posed to bring for school wood, and my paw has," crowed Jonas. He felt he had the right. His father had a new red barn, though the house was log and hump-shouldered at the corners. Besides, his father ran a threshing machine, and so Jonas stuck out feathers of a higher breed. Franz turned away, not answering. But Old Lafferty decided with a short "Seats are all full; Franz, sit there with Jonas."

The days behind the desk carved with a teacher's head and half a hundred initials are fled with the rain; so are the days we spent with history and tales of adventure, noses stuck in the pages. This one remains, I don't know why, except that after recess there was sudden trouble. Franz shot side-first into the aisle as if pitchforked there. Jonas, gurgling in his big mouth, drew back a heavy foot, his squinty eye crooked. Lafferty ordered them both to stay after school.

"Better mind your own henhouses," I reminded Franz at noon.

"Ain't botherin' none." He tried to join the circle of blindman's buff but Jonas pushed him aside. "What you gonna bring for school firewood, Franz—cow cakes in a straw hat?" Everybody laughed, Tinkla Bauer the loudest. She pulled his shirttail out of his pants, shrieking, "Handkerchiefs for sale, handkerchiefs for sale," and added, popping her eyes, "His pa's crazy, walks after dark in the swamp, and he ought to be put in the bughouse." Franz shivered and the scar cut a red gash on his cheek. He watched her as if pulled by the crow-calls of her voice; fascinated, yet with a half-sick look on his face. Tinkla was eleven, with ears like clamshells in the creek, and a turned-under nose; a blue-aproned clattering animal. But she is a part of that day as a minute is a part of an hour. Remembering how Franz glared at her and how she slapped out her tongue at him, I wonder that a pendulum started swinging here that was to catch them both in its widening sweep, cracking the old ties that bound up Franz's life.

We sneaked home, late by an hour, and I felt rubbing up against me the edges of resentment and anger at whatever it was that made Franz look as if he wanted to hide himself from all eyes and couldn't. He left slopping half done that night and streaked into the woods, though Walter yelled at him, getting only the echo of his own harshness for answer. The dark brought him back, trouble pulling at his lips, so that Mother tucked him close. "Fränzchen, Fränzchen, *nicht so;* lift up the eyes. Salt only makes heavier the stone lying on the heart."

Before the week had run to seed, he put in words what was digging under his skin. "Why do they say such things about us? What do they mean?" he wanted to know. "Ain't we the same as they? Don't we plant potatoes and keep our fences up and go to church Sundays, just like they do? What do they mean, we're a bad bunch?"

Fritzie snapped, "Keep your face shut, Dough-pan. You want Father to hear?" But Walter shoved the black heifer's head out of the pail of oats he was carrying before he growled, "Just hang your tongue between your teeth and don't remember things, little Bull Calf." His voice was kind—kinder than I'd ever heard it. Franz turned away slowly. But it wasn't until the Saturday we went to the store for coffee that we heard in plain words what had long ached like a canker in our minds.

Mother didn't want Franz to go, I remember, thinking him still in diapers, I guess. "Such a long road, Franz. You'll ache in your bones." But he set a stubborn face. "If Jeppy can, I can," he said, and Mother gave him leave. "Don't forget, Jeppy," she called; "half a pound of coffee—the cheapest. And mind your eyes on Franz."

We were in the dim, kerosene-smelly back of the store, sucking horehound sticks Mrs. Toffmann gave us, when Mrs. Pilversack waddled in, fat as a roll of cotton bat with a red pumpkin for a head. Straight to the counter she went, guggling, "Mrs. Toffmann, those Vildvogels—that boy, now; and the old man is a jail sparrow, they say. Matthew Heiland was up at Northland City, and he heard—*ach, ach;* what will our good Pastor Sunnenbaum say now?" She laughed so hard her middle flopped up and down. Franz's white face flashed in the duskiness; he stood before her, yelling, "It ain't so, it ain't so, you— you old fat tub."

Mrs. Pilversack's neck burned red, like a turkey gobbler's. "See now, Mrs. Toffmann, already the boys sneak around like their father." Franz banged out of the store, I after him, bitterness welling like a salt spring up to our eyes. Not for a long time did we speak out straight what lay behind a shift of the eye, or a drooping head. Linked by the same notion, we would have had it out with Father at the supper table but his stern lips barred the way. Franz ate his hard-bread and milk without looking up. A new fear and strange was beginning to shove its roots upward, to lie alongside those already in his mind— the fear of what the neighbors would say.

8

We undid the spool of our daily jobs no more than usual— and no less. There was hay to be pitched from the stack and carried to the manger . . . calves jerking at the end of ropes, bull-mad at the smell of milk . . . corn bundles waiting the husker. We'd be out with the moon for light sometimes and with the frost coming into our gloves. The sharp necessity of never stopping. I suppose there is security in the anchor of a job steady at hand, in knowing that a length of work done today is enough and more than enough. But we grew restless and impatient, feeling the irk of changelessness like a shoulder strap rubbing the flesh raw on a hot and sweaty day. Franz chafed under this as much as anyone.

"Will it always be like this?" He wrinkled a brow and ripped the leaves from a nubbin. "Always like this, next year and the year after—husking corn and helping with the feed?"

I shook the basket down. "What did you expect? Sunday to come in the middle of the week just for you?"

"Pete Prinzing said they are going to Fergus next week. And the Maises take a day off and go visiting. But we—we just stay—"

"The Prinzings got money in the Bank," I snapped. "And you—you talk with flour in your mouth." He rattled a kernel or two on the dry leaves. "Do you s'pose there's people over past Jenny's Peak and the ridges—out there, that don't have to milk cows and wear eye-patches on their pants—and—"

"There's a bundle of corn. Try s'posing on that." I emptied the basket into the sack.

"We might as well be cows, all we do," he muttered, his eyes stormy. But that was before the hand organ came and the wood-cutter sang a fiddle bow across his life and left it forever different.

Father got the organ at an auction that winter, God knows why, unless it was to plague Mother, organ music making her day more sodden. But Walter said the bargain was too cheap for him to miss. Franz clapped his hands when he saw the organ, excited at the brown box and the shiny crank, so that Father looked as if he wanted to shove rollers and all into the woodbox. "No music for you, only when work is done."

Mother set the organ on an apple barrel in a corner and tucked

a curtain like an apron about the rot-eaten staves. Near it was
a box in which she put the rollers, each a hand's length of round
pine with brass pins like teeth set irregularly in rows. It
stood near the ladder to the loft, the slanted glass top showing
the wide grin of the nickel keys, teasing Franz when he back-
crawled downstairs mornings.

Cold drove down hard on us, the ice booming on Long Lake
in the creaky nights, but we were woolly-warm by the stove, forgetting when we could the black pump and the frozen cans, in
the round of song. That is, when Father shrugged a yes and
let us play. Franz cranked out the *Barcarolle* whenever he
dared—a dreamy, wine-sleepy waltz that brought Father
humped up in his chair the first time he heard it. "Franz, no
Walzers. Stop that." But he found a little time to play.
Mother saw to that, we agreed, watching as she came in, arms
loaded with wood, her torn fascinator laced with snow. She
put his daily chores on her own thin shoulders sometimes, so
that he could stop heart and ears with tweedlings. We'd have
to shout twice to bring him down to the barn.

And there were evenings when Mother was quiet about her
dislike of the music because Franz hung happy for a while over
the crank, though Father, patching up harness straps, growled,
"You like it too much. Devil's music, those *Walzers,* that's
what they are." Suppers when Father was away, we'd have
potato soup and bread hash and the *Barcarolle,* Walter yelling,
"Stop that stuff and come eat." We were half-proud, though,
over the way he could name what tune lay caught in the brass
teeth of the cylinders. One glance at them and he told what
piece it was, though we tried to hook him into mistakes.

"What's this one?" Walter would pick up a roller. "Don't
look at the end. I'll read the name, if you're wrong." Franz
bounced resentfully.

"I'm not spying. That one—that makes the jigger key peep.
That's *Washington Post March.*"

"Good guesser." Fritzie laughed sharply.

"I don't guess." Franz got excited. "That's *Old Black Joe* and that *The Girl I Left Behind Me* and that—"

"And that's the *Barcarolle*," butted in Walter. "We know that, smart aleck." It was fun, though, to parade Franz off when the Prinzings came or the Mankins, the only neighbors to come that winter. But with Father's step on the porch, the organ usually wheezed off breathlessly and the glass top came down.

The hills rounded off with snow. Trees bent down and the world sagged with the weight of winter arches. We slid on the Diemer hills, dragging our homemade sleds up the eighth-of-a-mile slant, feeling the cold, and the ice slivers grow between our lips as we shot down alongside the cliff and coasted far over the frozen swamp. Mother let us go with a kind of fear in her eyes, afraid of the cliff, that giant's handful gouged out of the hill, edged with a fuzz of bushes like hair on an upper lip; with its sixty-foot drop at the end of a short steep incline. We whooped with the Prinzings till the echoes brought our voices back; damp to our belts with snow and sweat; played like wolf cubs in the drifts, a Prinzing boy catching Franz and thumbing his ribs, laughing: "Going up to Too Far Lake soon? Bring her along sometime, your Yellow Head, and we'll ride double." And there was no handscribble on the dark wall of trees below to tell us that here one day I would be doomed to crawl turtle-fashion, chained to earth, and that Franz would forge another link, and fear like a ragged blade would scrape at his heart. We slid, and went home hungry, and the hard-bread cracked in our teeth.

Before we were ready to throw off the cloak of winter ways, spring edged the night with warmth and snow vanished in a rush of water. Bubbles quaked up through the mud of the fields, soggily and with reluctance, as if earth cleared her lungs of winter breath. By the day Father brought home seed wheat and scoured the seeder shoes, the furrows were dry.

We tore at our acres with iron and wood, flea-scratches on the vast hills; putting in brown kernels of wheat or straw-colored oats; seeding life back to death, hoping with the blind faith of moles that rain with warmth fail not in a quiet season and that fruit come out of the ground. We prayed sometimes, with a desperation beyond the folding of hands, knowing the uselessness of waiting for harvest until the scoop ran brown with the grain. The fear grew with wheat and corn; and Franz, after that day in the field, was gnawed at by worry.

The corn was jackknife-high, the stems dividing carefully and with diligence in the sun. Father went out with the one-horse cultivator, calling, "Franz, you ride the gray. The rest of you fellers come along and pile rock."

We followed him into the seven-acre patch, Franz climbing on the gray with a scared look. Not about the horse; he had shaken bridle lines and giddaped him a dozen times. But uneasy because Father was there. They turned into a row and went along, Father gripping the handles, the cultivator shoes plowing up new earth to bury the faint whiskers of pigeon grass and weeds spearing through soil. The gray was a jumpy brute, with a tender devotion to young corn and with wide hooves to tread the row. He veered abruptly. Father yelled, "Watch where you're going." Dirt flew as he jerked the handles. But at the end of the piece the gray took the bit and dragged the cultivator across the row. Three hills of corn lay broken from the ground, bared to the sun and as good as dead. Franz grabbed desperately at the lines, white-faced because Father was raging. "Turn that horse around, you ox-head. Stepping down corn. Good for nothing around here, that's what you are. Get down, and let Fritzie ride."

Franz came to the rock pile, shivering. He would remember that hour and what happened, and a hundred more like it, no different from each other than seeds in a rose hip. A part of him. Afraid to tackle a job because Father with angry patience would rip out the faults and cover him with red-faced shame. Time without end, until courage and faith wore thin as a shingle. Half-afraid all his days, I think, that Father would run up at his back, shouting; knowing how the red lightning of his anger crackled in the mind.

Fritzie rode the gray horse down the rows that summer, and Franz watched, hating us for the slow eyes we unwinked at him. The corn walled up green, flowered, and waved at last pine-top tassels above the ears sticking out stiff as arms from the stalk.

Autumn was in the air, and we were still digging at the calluses of summer thick on our hands, the morning Father said, "Get out the shocking buck and the twine, kids. Corn is nicked by frost now. Got to get something out of seed." He turned impatiently. "Don't know what I'll pay the Bank with, this fall; or next spring, either, unless Abel Kloster gives me a sawing job."

He cut the corn with the sickle, beginning to swing the blade a wagon-length down a row and widening a circle through the corn, wheeling about the cut-off stalks, which he set up against the shocking buck in the middle; the buck a large A, hip-high and with a long pole slanting to the ground. In an hour the wigwams of the corn pointed to the Indian-summer sky. The morning sun still threw long shadows when he came in for a drink.

"Where's Franz?" He wiped the sweat beads from his face. "I want him to help tie corn shocks. He can carry the string." No one had seen Franz. "Sneaked out of work again," grumbled Walter, mixing oats and milk for pig slop. "He went off with the spade," tattled Fritzie. "I saw him." Franz came out of the chicken coop just then. Father held back his words and said shortly, "You come with me; both of you. Jeppy, you pick up loose corn."

Franz carried the string, running the end around the shock and back to Father's hand, like a queer sort of shuttle. Father pulled the twine tight halfway up the side and knotted it—putting a bow in the apron strings, he said once; usually he kept his peace and we might tie a field of shocks and he not so much as clear his throat. We worked through the backbone of the morning up near the road. Until young Pete Prinzing rattled along in a wagon, up to his ears in news, with Old Jens Lindergaard in behind, half drunk, his fiddle in his hand.

"The Maises are giving a late harvest dance—pretty soon, they say." He grinned, wide as a pocket.

Old Jens mumbled soddenly, coughing till a suspender slipped over a shoulder.

"And me, I'm gonna be there, too; give 'em the seven o' my—"

"Jens is on a little toot," broke in Pete. "I'm taking him to the Blubers'. Goin' to help shuck corn there. He's all right when he's on his toes."

"Sure. I'll spit to hell 'n gone—sure I'm all right." Old Jens rubbed his long whiskers, coughing; swung the fiddle up. "Listen now, once." He slid into *Liebeslied,* plaintively, sadly, the trouble in his mind getting into his fingers.

Franz gripped the twine, bent forward, as if listening to something he'd heard before without knowing when or where; something that came with the *Barcarolle,* maybe; or the shine of yellow curls; wild strains singing under the wind, when he stood where a hill told off four valleys and a cowbell trembled in a lonely sound, far . . . far off.

Old Jens stopped with the bow lifted, staring calf-eyed at Franz. "You're a good kid," he muttered, wheezily; "good kid," and began to cry in his whiskers, hiccoughing sorrowfully. They drove away, Franz staring down the road.

"Late harvest dance," snorted Father at dinner. "Godless dancing, that's all—nothing but a man wanting to feel a woman's tits." He sopped up gravy with bread. "Ain't nobody going from here." Which ended that, or so I thought. But Franz squeaked in his chair, wanting to go, but daring no word to ask.

We finished the corn and left it turning gray-brown in the sun. Father hitched his belt impatiently across his hips, as if ant-bitten. He worried up and down his steep acres this fall, as every other, shouldering a horrid fear—he must pay the Bank. Nothing lay beyond the reach of the Bank. Butter, eggs, a cow. A penny squeezed out of a day's chopping wood for the Bauers. Even Mother's turkeys were tracked down. "With them I wanted to get shoes for the boys, and underwear." She was white and tired-looking. Father turned away. "It goes to the Bank," he growled. And Mother smoked the lamp chimney late, patching and sewing on our old things. Until Franz wondered, "Is it like John Bluber's threshing machine—you pitch in and pitch in, and it never gets full?"

"I guess you could throw in the farm and that wouldn't be half enough," gloomed Walter, cocking sloo grass that we pulled out of the swamp on sticks. "No, not by half." A vague uneasiness gnawed at us, like the fear we had when the Klosters saw a crazy man loose in the woods. For the Bank could put you off the farm—and we could not imagine where we'd go, once the turn in the road hid our blue-paper–covered house, with its one room and lean-to and the loft upstairs, the oak scratching at the only upper window; the barn, four walls of pine slabs set upright and boarded tight inside, where the cows and two horses stomped and blew steamily together, cold nights making whiskers of heavy frost along the cracks. A shelter for back and belly, this place, and now the Bank wanted it; would take it; in spite of any hand an honest man might lift. Or a dishonest one. All this breaking of muscle and bone over rock and clay—for nothing. It made one suspicious of goodness itself; ready to grasp at any sparrow-feather of luck drifting near. I remember how grimly Father laughed when Toffmann beat himself out of ten dollars on a feed bill. "Ain't giving it back. Toffmann got plenty." He grunted. "Anyhow, this goes to the Bank." As if feeling that he worked harder than he'd ever be paid for in this world.

But he sat down to supper one night, short but with a kind of dour satisfaction in his words. "I'm working for Kloster this winter. With logs. Three months or so. Starting in January." He didn't let on more, but we drew breath into our lungs again with less care.

There was a fierceness about this autumn that meant a hard winter, Mother said—after-dinner heat that stayed late and a sky in Indian summer so deep blue and unwrinkled it made the eyes drop. Sometimes for the length of days its curve slid down from the zenith to the pale wash of the horizon unstopped by clouds. After stormy nights there were mornings smooth with the quiet of valleys and what we could see of the creek a silver patch, the trees on the ridges undisturbed at last, still weary and bent forward from the hustle of wind in the dark.

Franz drove the cows to the meadows, herding them on the short grass, and, shut away for hours by hills and trees, stood tiptoe, his lean body uneasy, taunted by the wood voices of his own imaginings. Fritzie said sharply that he needed more watching than the cows. I remember how his dark face twitched when the smell of rain on the leaves rode the winds, and how we laughed at him for saying, "Don't you smell it—wild grape in the air?" But Walter stuck a pitchfork in his hands. "There's the manure pile. Put your nose in that for an hour." And when partridges rolled their drums from the hills, Franz tore outside, as if he had to get doors behind him and good drizzle-mist in his face.

"It's showering again," Mother'd say.

"I don't care."

"Franz, where's your cap? Rain in the hair—"

"Don't stop me," he'd yell.

I ran upon him among the willows where I thought the cows were—flat on his belly in an open space, thoughts lost in the branches of a swamp oak. And once when ducks whistled overhead in the wet cloudiness of evening, I came over a hill and saw him by the creek below, cap lost, his dark face torn with laughter that knew no bridle, running in wild steps, and screaming a song his tongue and the harpstrings of the wood made up for him. Before I put out a foot he was gone. I ran down the hill after him, following the path to the clearing; found him back against a tree. Fritzie rocked in front of him, cat-calling in a hoarse off-key: " 'I'm a little fairy, little primer fairy.' " He grabbed him by the shoulder. "Little school-girl, that's what you are. What's this, singing in the woods alone, you—" He gagged suddenly. For Franz, hard and curled back, struck out like a whiplash. Twice; and Fritzie went down on a knee, a hand to his mouth. Then he was on his feet and ripped into Franz. I came running to see Franz with his arm up but not striking back; his face wild and bloody but lips shut down on any sound, and a look in his eyes that made Fritzie stop all at once and yell, "Get on home, before I grab a club." Franz went, sidling but not beaten. His cut lip hurt less, I think, when he saw Fritzie slyly finger a tooth that was wiggly at the root. All that week and the next.

Why the *Barcarolle* should plague me, like a merry grin over the shoulder, these early October days, I don't know; unless it was that Franz dinned it into our ears. But I hummed bits of it, thoughts and fingers elsewhere, so that Franz, hearing, twinkled at me, "You too, huh? It's the fall and the smell of the woods."

"It's something I ate," I snapped; "don't be a fool," and finished my work. But Franz's teeth slipped out in a curl of his lips. "Hunh-huh; it's the dance tonight."

Fritzie came up, clanging the milk buckets. "The Prinzings are going. Pete told me. He's learned to dance."

"Well, you s'pose he's going to foot the turkey reel with you?" I couldn't help a sour look.

Franz squinted into the sun, setting now, and half gone in trees. They lived only a piece away, the Maises; we could see their barn sloping among basswoods just over the seven-acre patch and hear voices plain.

"Old Jens is going to fiddle." Franz spoke slowly. "I'd like to watch them." Fritzie laughed sharply. "Better sneak over then. And get your girl along. That's the only way." He added with a smirk, "Tinkla like you a little, Franz?" We heard the calf-bawls of greeting as the firstcomers came spanking up in wagon or platform buggy. A kind of Sunday excitement stole on the evening air, making the eye blink quicker. Franz, ear up, hummed the German waltz in his nose, but Father hushed him.

Father marched us up the ladder to bed early that night; but through the window which we pried open, we could hear pops of laughter and slow drawls uncoiling on the dark. "If we could only go, this once," mourned Franz, hunched over. The ta-te-ta of a tuning fiddle brought him up. "First round, now." Square dances and polkas reeled over the corn patch, one on another, until we lost count. Mist rolled in from the creek, and downstairs quiet was covered with night.

Franz whispered thickly, "Let's sneak down, Jeppy; the oak branch—we can crawl down."

"We dasn't," I said, but we did; one propping up the other when fright brought sweat to our hands; the *Barcarolle* all mixed up with *The Girl I Left Behind Me*. Though I think even now, he wouldn't have gone if I had said no. How we got down and across to the Maises' and through the darkness of their barn and up the hay chute to wriggle into the closeness of hay under a slanting beam is dim and hazy now, except that I remember Franz wouldn't lie still, and sneezed once and I poked him, but the polka and the whoops of the dancers covered the noise.

Franz shivered with hot joy at it all—the arch of darkness above the lanterns, the shadowy circles they threw on the floor, each biting into the rim of the other, like the beginnings of eclipses; the crossbars smooth and brown with the wear of hay, the dancers swaying and swinging under them, now yellow light in their faces, now the kiss of shadows.

"There's Pete Prinzing." I nudged. "Look how he's dancing. With Rena Schaaf." Pete was seventeen and tall, with starch-white teeth and a swing to his shoulders. But Franz watched Old Jens thumping the floor with a steady heel, loud on the beat—thump-two-three, thump-two-three for waltzes and thump-two, thump-two for polkas and square dances; his whiskers straying over the tailpiece of the fiddle and nearly getting mixed up in the strings, no matter how often he brushed them back, between pieces; once he skipped a bar in the middle of a tune, swooped the whiskers back, and came down on the beat with untouched calm. Franz stopped his ears to anything but the web spinning out from the bow, catching the dancers, until the end struck and broke the tightening strands. He stirred and a streamer of light caught him across the face and I saw how his eyes gleamed.

"Jeppy—someday—if I could play like that—"

"Shut up; they'll hear us."

"Jeppy, how could I get a fiddle?"

"You can't. Shush now."

Then we saw Father's back in the door—and froze until the man turned and we knew that it was someone else. But the bright arrow of fear fell on us and we crawled back, to slip down the hay chute. We landed on a pile of hay below, sprawling but silent. Until the dark split open with a man's wild yell, "Holy sapping son of a gun," crowded out by a woman's voice: "Dick! What was that?" I heard a frightened gulp and Franz brushing past me; we legged it for the door, and out, and for home, never hearing the ghostly creepings in the cornfield, and cat-crawled into the loft. Snuggled warm in bed, Franz turned suddenly.

"Jeppy."

"Don't talk now."

"That couple there—"

"Never mind that."

"I landed right squawk on top of them."

9

The strains of the waltz ran in the blood like ferments, with a faint warm fire, so that sometimes we whistled without knowing why. Though there was precious little to whistle for, unless we tried a funeral song, I thought at times; smiling when we could, but with wormwood on our lips.

Franz, more after the dance than ever, cranked away, hanging over the *Barcarolle* or a waltz sister to it, after school or Saturdays, whenever chores gave him a minute, as if he could never get his fill of it. Until even Mother wanted to throw it out on the woodpile.

It appears to me now, safe in this chair with wheels and with people instead of shadows in the corridor, that Franz, even when he could draw melody between himself and the darkness that rested on the rooftree, had little to count as laughter, and that, scrawny as a buzzard's throat. The taproot of his being, thirsty for good rain, grew up in ground salted with bitterness and insidious dread—dread that made him go with his head cocked birdwise against a step or an iron fist. Even with Father gone, as he was, days at a time, grubbing in a neighbor's clearing.

Fall chilled down and the basswood leaves, first to give up the green of summer, slithered away among the branches. We were glad to be inside, nights like this one, though noons sent the resin trickling from pine. Walter was notching sticks for a rabbit deadfall; Mother, patching in a chair near the stove, spoke out that snow would whiten down in the rag-end of the month. Franz laid his ear close to the organ, worlds off in dreams. Father was away at the Mankins'—had been for a week. But suddenly—I think he liked to startle us—he stood in the door, his eyes crackling at Franz. The organ squeaked off and was still. Walter's knife came to a stop deep in wood. Three long steps and a wrench, and Father had the roller and made for the stove.

"Always this, when I come," he shouted; "never a church song or a good German *Lied;* always this devil's *Musik.*" He poked up a stove lid.

"Don't; don't." Franz's hands twisted. Mother came out of her chair. "You like to hurt him, don't you, Johan?" She

touched his shoulder. "Hurt me instead; you like that better."
She covered her face. Father turned uncertainly. "You wait
and see, Minna; nothing good comes from *Walzers* and polkas.
Pastor Sunnenbaum says Satan is in them. You let Franz stick
his fingers in such truck and you'll cry plenty." He dropped the
roller as if it were something unclean. "I must ask the Pastor
about this, Sunday, when he comes here for mealtime." He
stood there, flinty-faced and with no more softness, even for
Mother, than rocks in the pasture have. Never asking her
whether there was bread enough for a meal, or meat to go
around. Never stretching his dark length beside her under the
same quilts. He hadn't since Franz came, years before. We
found out by adding whisper to word and turning them over
in our mind. We spent the week with a kind of prickliness
in us, unthreading the nerves, knowing with sureness how stiffly
we'd move, ice-proper when the Pastor came.

Father shouted Sunday morning, as he usually did, "Up now,
and finish chores. Nobody stays home from church today."
Sick or well, we readied ourselves and piled into the buggy,
songbooks making our pockets sag. "You got your penny for
collection?" he always asked, before he climbed in, making
sure everyone nodded.

Church had been called when we came, the hymn rushing
out into our ears as we opened the weather-dry door. The sun
and the window made a ladder of light and shadow on the
benches—we marched through it to find our seats. Father
bowed his head. Those already there nodded or pulled their
eyes away. I wonder to this hour that Father endured the
bench farthest back, among the graybeards. For he crouched
aside whenever the bead of people's glances was drawn upon
him. Perhaps it was something the Pastor said that brought
him, wind or wet. We boys sat in a stiff row, afraid to move,
or look at Mother, penned up with the wives and girls on the
women's side; shivered while Pastor Sunnenbaum pounded the
Old Testament and sizzled us with hell-fire. Franz trembled

with excitement over the torments in store for us; until Fritzie stuck a fist in his ribs to keep him from slipping off the bench. I cannot think of Heaven, even now, without seeing the Devil skulking near the gate.

We never stayed to join the talk after church; Father hurried us off. But this morning he slapped the lines nervously, wishing the Pastor would hurry, knowing that people watched. "There goes Sunnenbaum with the Vildvogels again. They say he prays for Johan's soul. Prob'ly needs it." Tittering; eyes screwed at an angle; until Franz didn't know where to look, and Mother hid in her veil; Father grim as the stones in the graveyard. The Pastor came, his lips wide in a bedside smile. Cheerful. Franz pushed into the farthest corner of the buggy and away from this lean and unfed-looking man with the spade-shaped beard and the drakes' tails curling up his neck. We all felt what was coming, deep in us, as an aching scar foretells rain.

No sooner was dinner off the plates, the Pastor finishing the pieplant wine regretfully, and Mother wrist-deep in dishwater, than Father said: "Franz, play." Franz lifted a foot and stopped.

"I said play." Franz snapped in *Sweet By and By* and watched the Pastor's suspicions melt to approval. "Pious, that song, my friends," he nodded.

"No sin there?" Father rasped his chin with a finger nail.

"Indeed, no. I always say, Christian folk must look out for instruments of darkness; but an organ and godly songs—"

"Play the *Barcarolle*." Father's voice rumbled in the loft. Fritzie slipped tightly into a corner. I saw Franz fall back.

"Father—you don't mean—"

"Play it."

"Not that one." The mark came red on his cheek. Mother bent forward beside the table. A cup slipped into the dishwater with a splash. Father shouted: "Franz." The roller clicked into place; the waltz hurt in our ears.

It all slips back now like the eerie happenings of a dream—Franz with an arm over the organ; the Pastor thundering, "Bruder Vildvogel—in this place—Devil's tunes—and you fresh from the house of God"; and Father raging, "That's what my wife and kids want—leading me on." I remember how hopelessly Mother sagged against the table; how the Pastor yelled, "Burn it; burn the wood of the Devil," an unholy twitching at his arms as he caught up the roller and carried it to the stove; Franz pulling at his arm: "How can the Devil be in a piece of wood?" and Father shoving him away; how the fire reared high as if sucked up, and the Pastor chanted: "Back to your Master, the Devil; in the name of the Father, the Son and the Holy Ghost," signing with the cross; and Franz running out of the house. He came back hours later, shoes muddy and shirt ripped. Time like a good salve healed and thinly scarred those wounds. But Franz would remember; remember sometimes with a hopelessness worse than dying. The *Barcarolle* tripped out no more in the evening and the hand organ grew sticky with uselessness.

Winds, ridden by the trolls of winter, sucked down the chimney and played pullaway with the blue paper. We came through woods, hard on the path to and from school, and watched the sumacs flame like fire over the hills and burn down to bare bones of wood. They were as prints on the hillsides to show which way the year went. Snow sieved through them in November, with scratches hardly audible, like mice in dark grass, as much imagined as real. Evenings and Saturdays we took up spade and fork to keep off the rough hide of winter; banked the house with manure and the chicken coop with ground; squeezed the light out of cracks in the barn walls with boards and rags. We grinned when we learned that the Maynards, a ridge or two over, waited for freezing weather and stuffed the chinks with fresh manure and old wool bat.

That winter is part of my memory, dim now and with outlines broken; for Old Jens came with a johnny of whisky and a fiddle, and Franz knew the shine of yellow curls again. January rode down on us, with drifts swelling over the hoghouse, eaves-deep, and packed solid. On nights gray with the watery rags of moon, the wind, with hunger in its moan, leaned stoutly against wall and door, and the hinges muttered.

We came in from chores one Saturday to hear Father say, "Kloster wants me to ride log carriage. He's got forty loads of pine and oak now." '

Mother put down the milk-pitcher hard, splashing on the oilcloth. "Log carriage—like Joe Kaiser—last year; she told me, Mrs. Kaiser, how he fell and was cut and—"

"Nobody but a fool like Joe would monkey around and fall into the saw."

"Johan—*bitte*—you—" Fear in her eyes—fear of what would become of her and us, alone and no one to turn to.

"I'm no lickspittle in short pants. Rode the saw before, up north." Mother wiped up the spilt milk, slowly. We knew what crawled in her mind—Father beside the log on the rack-like carriage, moving forward . . . the saw like a white flame . . . the scream of wood and the shock as a board tipped loose and fell . . . the carriage sliding back, Father at the levers rolling the log an inch forward . . .

"I've talked to Jens." Father slipped into his coat. "He'll help here, and cut basswood on the twenty. No drinking either. I'll be home, sometimes—maybe." The closing door almost shut off the last words.

Mother took up a plate as if it were something she'd never seen before. The pale grayness of a moth's wing was on her this winter, so that Franz used to watch her with a kind of fright on his face, puzzled over an ache he couldn't explain. "Now it begins again," she said wearily. "Nights with the saw in my ears, and no sleep." Father left that day and a kind of peace came with his empty chair. But it was a peace rotted and spoiled with all that had gone before. We sharpened the axes and waited for the woodcutter; Franz went with singing in his mouth. "You think he'll bring the fiddle, Old Jens?" But we set him to turning the grindstone and laid the steel helves down with firmness.

Old Jens came whistling and a little drunk, and with him the fiddle in the black hide case. There was no one to tell us, when he opened the door, on an afternoon of storm in January, that something mightier than a scraggle of snow came in with him. Came into our lives, into our muscles and minds, for that matter, lying snug with our bones. Something like a fever, I decided afterward, but a fever that couldn't be sweated out in a hundred summers of haying and harvesting. A tousled man, Old Jens, lopsided because a water elm had crushed him to earth years before and left his bones twisted under flesh and his mind spotted in places. Except for boozing and fiddling; there his mind was clear, they said. He straggled over the ridges, summers and winters, pegging off a tune at barn dances and shindandies; cut wood, when he put his brain to it, or grubbed, for the jacket on his back and the bread he crowded between broken teeth. He had rich kinsfolk in Minneapolis, Alb Hukelpoke hinted; but Jens never mentioned them. No more use than an old harness, Father said, but brought him to our place the months he worked in Kloster's sawmill. Because Jens was cheap, Walter grunted. You couldn't find it much cheaper than nothing a day. I remember that Father before he went growled at Franz, as one who needed last words, being eaten with sin, "Jens'll let fiddling be. And schnapps, too. Don't let me catch you monkeying away your time."

Franz was uneasy the first days after Father left, hearing the nails in the ladder squeak out when Jens grunted up into the loft. The hack in the old man's lungs—a horrible sound up there. He wondered, too, about the black fiddle case. Until one night of stars when we came up from milking. Jens was in the house, melting the cold from his toes. He had come in from work with a hangdog eye, and a bulge under his coat. A present, he said; from Hukelpoke; a little johnny of a present. We laughed about it, coming up the path with the lantern. Franz was ahead, I remember, the shadows of his legs pointers of darkness growing and widening into a part of night itself. He stopped, quick-short, and half-turned. Softened by boards and rafters the heartsick melody of *Liebeslied* trembled on the cold-stiff air. Ragged in spots, but quavering and catching Franz between the shoulder blades, so that he dropped his milk buckets for us to carry after and ran.

Jens was fiddling quietly when we came in, the jug near him by the stove, his eyes bright; Franz, coat off, down on his knees. When the bow slid its length and stopped, Franz prayed, "Jens—can I—will you show me?" Old Jens hid his eyes in the weed patch of his brows, watching him; then he put the fiddle on the untried shoulder. I was afraid Franz would drop it, he trembled so. And the look on his dark face when the bow sang on the strings. Screaky in his unfamiliar hands, so that Fritzie called out, "Pinching a pig, Franz?" But clearer after a while, and firmer. He would have played this night into morning, if we'd let him; and other nights, too, his deedlings broken and unsure, but growing in strength, until the room could no longer hold the thin melody of two strings.

I had a queer notion, wild as a tale of spooks, that the melodies he had shrilled to himself when he herded cows became in a strange way a part of the tunes that slid from the strings; as if he had known them before and his fingers knew better than he where to find each sound and went there without his say-so. A tomfool notion, I guess, remembering how he wheedled Jens to show him where the notes went up ladder-fashion from low to high; the nights he sat evening-long with *America* and *Yankee Doodle* faltering out but taking on shape and form with each try. He became fiercely impatient but angled his jaw solid over each tune; or sprawled on the floor, watching Jens play, eyes stuck to those humped-over fingers walking up the neck of the fiddle and down. Up and down. Like a twisted spider, weaving and weaving God knew what dark cords to tie about the heart.

We grudged him fiddle and bow, knowing that Mother dragged in the wood sometimes and pumped the water pail full. There was something unreal and ghastly about those days, Franz playing, and the music heady as old dandelion brew pushing into our heads, but under the round of work a deep dull pounding like a death call through thin and wakeful sleep, over and over again . . . Father . . . Father . . . if the door opens . . . if the door opens suddenly. Unbelievable that we washed faces and sat at three meals a day, without knowing change.

Father tramped home in the middle of February and the air tightened like a clock spring—almost rang with the tautness nobody put into words. Mother smiled when he came, we never figured out why, but Father had no eyes for her. We walked on tiptoe, keeping out of his way, so that he glared like a mink suspicious of bait, but growled sourly, "Kloster is giving a *schwat Suer* supper—for the men, with the neighbors invited; April, sometime. Damn fools, that bunch. We're not going." Even Jens stayed out with the basswood an hour longer, until Father went back, and Franz, when he played again, moved mouse-quiet. He left his school truck idle in the bag, careless whether the spelling book was written full or not; until Old Lafferty hauled him over a desk and slatted his pants with a homemade ruler. I haven't forgotten that day because of this: when Franz, his tail feathers dragging, slouched back to his seat, Tinkla Bauer suddenly stood up beside her bench and stuck out her tongue at Old Lafferty. Full-length and with venom in her face. "You oughta be licked yourself," she screamed at him. "My pa says you're gonna get fired one of these days, if you ain't careful. Right quick too." Then she began to bawl and slumped behind her geography book. Franz was beet-red and shamed. But I saw him glance at Tinkla. Eye meeting eye. As if he were grateful and thanked her, even in humiliation. The boys hooted in glee, that noon, Jonas Bluber the loudest. "Tinkla's feller, Franz's got a girl." He minded, Franz did, a lot, especially when she picked him out in games thereafter, yet he never said no to her asking. Shamed but going with her. I think he had no defense against her loud mouth and direct ways. He addled along, short-tempered over fractions. No one batted an eye less when mumps broke out in the district and school closed. For three weeks in February we let the paths lie buried in drifts.

Franz nearly wore out the strings then; and one night he played the love song so that Walter stopped with his face soapy and half-washed, listening, and Mother rose quickly. "Fränzchen, Fränzchen." Her voice was sad, as if she already knew what we groped for, in darkness. "Fränzchen, what is this that I have done to you?" She put an arm about him. But Walter grumbled, "All this fiddle-faddle—where's the good in it? All he cares, the milk can rot in the cow's teats." I guess he had a mind to tell Father but didn't. It was enough and more, this premonition making a noise within us like a rat gnawing loudly in a dark and empty cellar.

February blew itself out in storm and March swooped up the valleys with eastern winds before Father came home again. He rode over one morning on the Klosters' mare. A clear sunrise, warm after snow. Franz was up at the house with Jens. We were still in the barn, feeding calves, when Father opened the door and led the mare in. Silent and gripping the rawhide. He was grumpy, we could see, over something that had crossed him; hard words with Big Seelang, one of the sawmen, we found out later.

"Milking done?" he growled. "I want you—" he stopped then and went to the door. *Darling Nelly Gray* sang over the snow.

"Jens. Is he—didn't I say—or is it—?" Then he saw our faces, telltale with truth.

It is hard to say this, even now, years away from that late March, realizing that it had to come. Had to. As well try stopping a bullet with a feather, once the trigger is pulled. We stood there, in the barn shadows, Fritzie stiff as the pitchfork he held, watching Father stride along the path, fast but with grim purpose setting down each foot. I had a feeling that we were rushing to some awful doom, headlong forward, without pausing, without taking breath to think. We saw him tear open the door. The quick and dreadful silence that followed . . . Franz breaking from the darkness inside, the sun in his face . . . running, desperate fear in the way he hunched over . . . Father after him, the rawhide twisting in his hands. He caught Franz there, behind the woodpile. We heard the first loud cry Franz couldn't shut back and then a short whimper or two. We let the shadows hide our faces. Walter kicked the feed can the length of the runway. After a while we saw Jens with the black hide fiddle case stumble out. He humped down the road, coughing and in a hurry. We went back to feeding calves.

10

There were times that spring when I thought Father wanted to move hills and the shoulders of hills, bull-like in his anger when he couldn't, the gall in him rising, chin-high. Wanting to stop the crash of oak in storm. But it came to me as a strange notion that he couldn't even stop the fall of an acorn in its season. I got what sour comfort I could from that.

He let Franz alone but was still grouchy over his set-to with Big Seelang at the sawmill. "Kloster's giving the *schwat Suer* Sunday night," he said, one noon. "They butchered yesterday." It was the fore-end of April then and late for butchering and catching pig's blood for the black soup, but the Klosters were behind in work anyway, with the sawing at hand. "Hadn't figured out, going. Guess we will, though." Father helped himself to leftover pancakes. "They'll be there, the sawmen— Big Seelang, too; a blower from way back." But we guessed it wasn't Big Seelang or the supper that changed his mind, but Kloster himself and the fear of losing a week's pay.

I remember that Franz didn't care whether he went or not,

for once, slipping into the circle of self. He seemed older, in a queer way, as if something had added a finger-width to his stature. Something a rawhide had left, I thought—crusty and in red welts under his shirt. I saw his back stripped bare the night after that day in March—and wondered why I longed for a club to batter down walls. Futile. As well cry out against the grave, twisting the heart's agony over the clods. Father said our yeas and nays, even to our comings and goings.

We squashed through melting snow to school, wondering about the blood-soup supper; Franz in a hurry. Old Lafferty rang the bell with promptness these loitering spring days, and Franz disliked being late. He dug at lessons heatedly, finding a sort of balm in spending pounds of energy in work. Tinkla seemed less like a nettle in his path, I think, for he chose her partner in a game of "Last Couple Out" before the week ended. Her company was beggar's pay, meager and none to his liking, but more than he got from the hands of others.

It was long after dusk on Sunday evening when we rounded an arm of Too Far Lake and climbed a knoll. Our eyes had a kind of dimness on them from driving this road, dark with the gloom of valleys at night. We followed a bend in trees and came out clear, not far from Kloster's place, and the moon was suddenly above his sawmill shack, tree-high, as if bounced up from behind a hill.

The yard was strong with the smell of fresh pine dust tickling the nose, and the house bulged out with people, when we drove up. "Get right down over the wheels," Abel Kloster roared at Mother in a hearty voice; but he stood knee-stiff and Mother climbed down unhelped.

They were all there, the neighbors, the house rattling with laughter and the hubble-bubble of voices—the Maises, the Prinzings, the Bauers, Grossmutter Katzenhoft, wrinkled and dark as old shoe leather, telling stories from her squeaky rocker; Big Seelang, his nose scabby and sore-looking where a flying splinter had ripped it; Pete Prinzing with his lazy smile; Old

Jens, shaking with coughs, avoiding Father but eyes watery for Franz.

It is all smeary with years now, that evening, a blur of many pictures like Old Lafferty's magic lantern, confused and out of focus. . . . The men humped over on benches or store boxes, the old and cripple-boned relaxing in chairs . . . fingers hooked behind overhall suspenders. Here and there someone dragged on a corncob pipe or tongued snuff, pulling up now and then to spatter into a three-gallon can set in a corner . . . lifting their throats and gabbing, or letting off whinnies of laughter, chest bent to knees, over a joke. The women, flushed with the heat of talking after the months of tick-tock quiet at home, were well fired up now, shrill as a flock of sparrows . . . every married woman there heavy with work, a baby squawling in her arms or nuzzling at her breast . . . Maggie Gross among them, her second trailing at her skirts, a boy, fathered without ring or church. The young ones yelled and tumbled over the men's feet. The Bluber kids got into a scrap and pulled hair, and Mrs. Bluber borrowed her husband's pants belt and dragged them off to the outhouse. Far away and almost lost, those hours, dim as people walking in rain.

But some things stick in the memory, clear because heavy with a kind of dark portent . . . charged and waiting the spit of flames to set them off. Franz came into the house and stopped, face to face with Yellow Head; red-cheeked but with wonder in his eyes, he took her hand shyly, as if it were a kind of swamp blossom. Until Tinkla Bauer shrieked, "Hey, Franz. Let's play 'Numbers,'" and grabbed him by the arm. He said "Yes" to her and followed, but his eyes went back to Yellow Head—Liliem, he found her name was, Liliem Schoen. I had a notion he wanted to touch her yellow curls again. He put his hand in Tinkla's but watched shadow-eyed for Liliem; saw Jonas take her arm as if she were something belonging to him, and started forward, the scar sharp on his cheek, but trotted with the kids to romp in the bedroom.

These things, and Big Seelang unbuttoning his mouth and bragging about cutting logs, Father tight-lipped and dark, trying not to hear and squeezing into a corner; Mother twisting her wedding ring, hands ready to reach out; Pete Prinzing, eyes fire-coals behind sleepy lids, pulling Rena Schaaf down on the bed beside him, and Jonas blowing out the lamp and the kids shrieking . . . Grandma Katzenhoft squeaking in the rocker . . . squeak, squeak, forward, backward . . . spinning off stories of the old country as she knitted the hank of yarn . . . stories about the man with hooves under the gaming table; the minister's wife ripped to pieces by ghosts; the maid who called up the Devil; the E-string . . . the E-string. I remember how we herded around her chair, the boys with Fritzie coming up to hear, begging for the story; Franz beside Tinkla, long-lipped because Liliem stood with Jonas. Little beggar sacks, Grossmutter called us, settling herself solidly. . . .

It happened many Christmases ago (her story runs in my mind); more than the number of all our fingers. My mother's mother told it (she said) in the old land. She *saw* the man with the fiddle and the red cloak who came in the night. Slender as a pine he was, with a laugh like the gurgle of water under hollow ice. He came running to the village where the *Fest* was held and the dance, and put a bow of white hair to the fiddle and played— *ach,* so the ears rang and were sealed up with sound and the lights running together laid a blindness across the eyes. And they danced, *der Landsmann* with the peasants, the *Landsmann* proud in his long black cape; swirled in a mad circle, the fiddler in the red cloak singing along with his bow of white hair and leaping high; they danced, the men drunk with delight and wine, their boots lost in the folds of women's skirts, their faces lifted, as if the sky were no more than a hand's-space away. But the men who were bachelors, left over and without girls, felt the scissors-end of jealousy; their mouths went crooked and they put out their hands. And at once knuckles tasted flesh and fists knew the scrape of bone. There was a great cry and a scattering and in the snow they saw him lying, *der Landsmann* in his long black cape, and the red fiddler bending near, shaking with an epilepsy of laughter. He waved the fiddle, one string broken and dangling; jerked about, the red one, whispering, yet all heard, "The E-string—it got him—the E-string." There was a handclap like a sharp echo and he was gone. But the *Landsmann* kicked and kicked, a knife letting out his blood red in the snow. . . .

Grossmutter gathered up a lost stitch, and in the silence the rocker spoke—squeak, squeak, a part of the tale, it seemed. Franz squidged back frog-mouthed at the telling and edged toward Liliem. "Fly away now, *Kinda.*" Grossmutter flung the yarn at us. *"Mutta is' müde."* We were ready to pitch into a game of "Pussy Wants a Corner" when Jonas yelled, "Soup's coming."

Nobody said a word when Mrs. Kloster and Mrs. Mais between them carried the heavy black kettle to a low bench. Nor put out a hand to help, certainly none of the men. Too polite to be greedy, being right-brought-up folks. Yet hunger plowed deep furrows in their middles. You could tell by the way backs became straighter and fingers quietly unloosened belts.

It was my first *schwat Suer*—the black soup, made of new pig's blood and meat, butter-flecked and vinegary, full of potato dumplings and swelled-up prunes, and stringy pieces of chicken, heavy with a smell like sausage boiling. Mrs. Kloster ladled it out into bowls and we ate it with cracker bread or *Süsskuchen*. The men lined up first, getting their steaming portions and sitting down to work spoon and bread in earnest. The women watched, dulling their hunger with talk and waiting. But Grossmutter Katzenhoft, older than the eldest and great-grandmother twice over, moved in her rocker and shrieked loudly, "Don't get your feet in the trough, you hogs. Pigs, that's what men are. Somebody fetch me a bowl of soup, before they lick the bottom." The men laughed, going back for more. They slopped down bowls of it, hefting the rims to their mouths when spoons gave less than they promised. Franz got a second dipper-ful from Mrs. Kloster, and Walter and Fritzie two slices of hard flat-bread apiece. But the stuff set my stomach on end. I kept seeing our yard at butchering time . . . the kettle on a pole between two sawbucks and the fire red against the black soot . . . the deep smell of pine smoke and water with ashes boiling in it . . . the barrels propped against a platform of logs and boards, the wide mouth of each belching steam thick with the odor of scalded hair . . . the squealing pig, Walter astride it, holding it down and Father, all his weight against its struggles, a finger curved about the knife . . . and Mother kneeling with a bowl to catch the spurting blood, stirring with a spoon, her hands drippled, her face the color of old ashes. I was thankful for the egg-sized glass of chokecherry wine they brought out; swallowed it at a gulp because the rest of the kids and the women wanted wine, and glasses didn't reach around. The men gulped theirs from cups holding half a pint.

Jovial with soup and wine, Father and the sawmill gang drifted into the kitchen, when dishes were washed and the women strayed into the sitting room and the one bedroom. Night pushed thick and furry against the windows. Somebody shouted, "Get out your fiddle, Hans Bakken, and tune us one." My eyes jumped to Franz, half off the cracker box he straddled, as if pinpricked by the words. The kids, gathered around, screamed at the fun coming.

Hans scraped a merry tune but kept forgetting and stopped with a loud "Nope, 'tain't that," retracking his way and begin-ning where he left the trail. I heard Father's voice in the kitchen, and Seelang's, breaking over the music. Franz itched in his pants, eyes wide and the scar burning in his cheek. Hans tried again and gave it up. "Nope; ain't of much account; not since I got my trigger finger shot off." Old Jens, coughing a little, cried, "Give it to young Vildvogel—Franz." There were questioning laughs but Hans handed it over.

I saw how Franz gripped the fiddle, as if getting back what

was rightly his; coaxing the strings into melody. He tore off a tripsy jig, light as a dancing leaf, so that Mr. Prinzing, enthusiastic with chokeberry wine, called out, "Take up the hat, boys; young Vildvogel needs a fiddle; I'm going to have him play at my barn dance next fall." But Franz was deaf, ears over in playing. He drifted into *Liebeslied,* scrumpily at first, as if the fiddle were clearing its throat, but growing clearer with each swing, until silence hushed down and Grossmutter dropped stitches and yarn and closed her lids, dreamily, and Mother stopped pulling her ring; Tinkla at standstill for once; Liliem with her eyes hid in her yellow hair; quiet under the ribbons of forgetfulness woven among them.

Then there was a snap, loud as a kettle-clang in the stillness; a tight breathlessness; and striding on iron heels into the hush came Seelang's hard voice: "That's a damn lie," and Father's thick words: "I'll knock in the teeth of any man that says—" and Kloster speaking out, "Hold up, Vildvogel, this is no place for fists." Father's tones, giving in, "All right, then." The quiet broke; voices crashed down again and somebody wanted more music. But Franz clutched the fiddle with a queer laugh breaking from his lips.

"It broke—the E-string. Broke."

"We'll get you another," said Mr. Prinzing. But Franz watched the broken string-end dangling, jerking in the air, and looked as if a ghost had put a cold hand on his shoulder.

12

By the first week in May, most of the crops were in, the kernels buried in the hollows left by the seeder shoes—deep finger-scratches in earth, between the flat and sunken tracks of wheels. The harrow teeth rolled the clods in dusty confusion then and swept away even the reminders of the place where life was covered under; shaken and sifted, so that a hand went blindly to find a seed and the sprout of a seed.

Father came from Mary's Hill one morning, a plump bag in the back of the buggy. "Try beans this year, kids. Dickley, the seed man, says they bring a fair price. Put in a patch on the highland." We ruled the field into squares like a checker-board; used the corn-marker, four runners under a platform of boards, dragged lengthwise over the patch, and then cross-wise; and sowed the hope of an extra dollar with the white seed. We watched the beans we'd planted push up, long rows of thumbs breaking through soil; until they leaved and began to throw dwarf shadows at noon.

Father eyed us with a grim twist on his lips, a puzzled look for Franz. He said nothing about the fiddling at Klosters'. Baffled, I think, by that which he couldn't hold with his two hands; not knowing that there are some things worlds beyond the power of rawhide or fists to change. We threw words over the bean hills about it that summer, the four of us, backs arched to earth, the dry swish of the hoe-blade loud in our ears, and dust powder-thick on our faces.

"The way he came out of the Klosters' kitchen—" Fritzie broke a stretch of hoeing one afternoon. "Oh, he was mad enough there; madder'n a sheep-buck. Dough-pan had it coming, I guess."

Franz shifted, looking away. "Well, I—the music—it gets in my head—I—" He slowed down, needing words to say how he felt and finding none.

"It's a wonder Old Prinzing stood up to him," I ventured. "About taking up a collection, I mean."

"Father had it in his face to lick you, Bull Calf." Walter shied a pebble at Franz. "Would have, too, if—"

"It was the money." Fritzie propped himself up with the hoe. "A handful like that—silver, some of it; they must have emptied their pockets. Father couldn't let it go by. Not with the Bank and all." No, not with nickels and dimes, we saw. There was little that escaped between his fingers; though generally, as honesty went among the neighbors, he held to the trowel-mark dividing right from wrong; but where money opened a silver palm, he crimped his eyes and hung a rag of conscience on a nail. We knew that.

Walter chopped a milkweed with anger in the turn of his arm. "Father'd lick us too, give him half a chance." Thinking, we knew, of the black words Father spewed on him that morning. "All I can remember—since I was knee-high to a bull's hind leg; afraid of seeing him reach for a strap; and here I'm near twenty."

"Shut gabbing." Fritzie looked over his shoulder, rabbit-fast. "If he hears—"

"Oh, you've had your pants stripped down, too; more'n you had hankering for; better be scared." Walter set his lips. "Getting tired of it; damn tired. Got myself full of him and his ways—full and belly-sick." The fear slid in our minds again, crawly as the first snake in spring. We hoed for an hour, the sun a hot belt across our necks, burning below our hat-rims; finished our rows before Walter muttered, "Real job, this is going to be, threshing out the seed." He lifted the gray-stone jug to his mouth, the water sloshing down his shirt.

"Couldn't we have a dance?" Franz spoke up. "A good polka would get them out—quick."

"With you fiddling, I s'pose?" Fritzie pinched his lips. But Franz had a span-new idea. "Let's make a thresher; Jeb Bauer did; a keg with nails for teeth and—" He cut weeds with fury at the way Fritzie hooted, "Fiddler's thresher." Walter flung a rock half a field away. "Anything like a thresher you make, Bull Calf—well, it would set a she-goat laughing."

Father lowered his brow on Franz at supper. "Better you spend an hour evenings on your catechism. Pastor wants you to begin school in September. Jeppy, too." We dared no look at each other. The shadow of the Pastor suddenly lay like a burden on us. Father set his cup down with a bang. "Get that fiddling out of your head, you." He pushed the table back so that the dishes rattled. "Prinzing was over. Wants you to play this fall. I said I guessed no."

Franz looked at Mother; asking for a word to stand between himself and sick helplessness, and knowing by the tremble of her lips that the thews of her strength were frayed and salt-eaten; few in number (fewer than we knew, then) against the crag of Father's stubbornness. Franz pushed the last of the left-over mush aside and sneaked into the woods back of the house.

That evening he began to tinker with the bean thresher. I don't know why, unless it was to shape with his hands something he longed for, however vaguely, but couldn't find on our gaunt acres. Something inside him wanting words to speak, or a form to take. Real to him when he fiddled—so it appears to me now. No one bothered him there, behind hazel and plum thickets, off hours and the Sunday Father was away. Nor paid him any heed, except to twit him.

But Walter found the nail box empty and even the old and rusted spikes gone and wanted to know who hammered them up.

"I used a few," Franz admitted, getting red; "handful or so." He picked up the feed can.

"Did, heh?" Walter shot a look at him. "What's all the pounding for, you've been doing? Maybe I better heel up and see."

"You stick your nose in your own pants," yelled Franz; "keep it there too." He was stiff against the barn wall. "Let me alone."

It wasn't until Sunday evening that we saw. A wind-still evening, with clouds like lambs' tails catching fire one by one across the sky. Father hadn't returned from Mary's Hill but would in time for milking. And Fritzie, gone with the Klosters and their gang to drown out gophers, hadn't showed up. I came along the pasture with the cows, Lady's bell tinkling, and above it heard Franz hammering behind the house. There was a hush that went to the ribs of heaven, quiet as if the hills had enough of our ant's-scurrying and were losing no time to hang the night between, shutting out both us and day. Mother's chimney smoke lazed back on air. I pulled a twig to pieces, looking at our place as a hawk does, far and away. And a feeling drove through me, gentle and slow, that it ought to be like this always, safe and with no shadows licking at the door. For once I thought we'd let fear slip off with our weekday boots and pants. But it was there; piled up in corners where we couldn't see.

Fritzie came out of the meadow with the Kloster boys and Asa Sperry. He had the cunning of a fox large on his face, when I came along. "That's him, pounding up there," he was saying. "Let's sneak up and scare him." I felt anger in a black tide run over me; even this day had to be blotched; but followed after.

Franz was nailing at the last board when we crashed through the hazels and stood before him. He had the hammer and put it against the thresher—a square box with a keg revolving in it for a cylinder, bristling like a porcupine with nails in rows across, and two boards prickly with spikes set in parallel lines, fastened so that the stationary teeth fitted between the moving teeth without touching. Crude, I guess, and clumsy as the flail Old Man Rippey brought from Vermont. But something his mind and his two hands had made. He snapped back at the laughing and the scar ran crimson in his cheek. He gripped the hammer hard.

"What are you going to thresh out, Franz?" Asa Sperry asked, grinning derisively. "Squirrel-nuts?"

"He's aiming to run John Bluber out of business," jibed Fritzie. "Got a run of threshing—all taken, back of Too Far Lake."

Franz twisted, quick and like a cornered mink. "Get away from here, you blockheads." Suddenly, goaded and trembling, he lifted the hammer and sent it crashing into the machine.

"That's it; what you wanted," he choked; "spoil things for me; always."

Fritzie was making noises, a splinter-mark red across his mouth. "Throw things, will you," he gritted and came at Franz, arms flying.

I wonder to this day that a hot fork of rage thrust in my brain. I lunged against Fritzie, knocking him aside. Stood with Franz, shouting, "Let him alone; no more sense than an ox." Laughable, the way we crouched, the two of us, against Fritzie and the others, if anyone had been there to laugh. A tall Kloster boy came between. "Cool down, there, Fritz. Let's go."

We left off and began chores with thickets of ire between us, Fritzie racketing among the cows and Franz peeking at me when he thought I didn't notice. Puzzled. But when I came up to bed later than he, I found his pillow on mine; double-thick for my head against the hard boards; and him asleep with an arm curled about the heaped softness. The only way he knew how to thank me, then.

13

The barley over the hills whispered in its beards, silky green in July but running with golden threads before the month was counted out. We waited as if for a sign. Everyone within the circle of five miles did; until we saw Mr. Mais, stripped to his red flannels and pants, wading through the fields, his fire-colored undershirt startling against the gold of barley. We hitched up then and began. The grain was ready for the sickle and the shock.

Pete Prinzing rode over an evening during harvest, with the black fiddle case under his arm. An evening hot with the blast of noon still in the air. We sat on the step, Walter fixing a bridle and Franz whistling a two-step under his breath. Pete slipped off the mare. Father, tipped back on a box and cooling himself in the shade of the corner, nodded but didn't ask him to set.

"Old Jens kicked the bucket—last night," Pete said. "Over at our place. Hot sun the other day, I guess; took him. He wanted Franz to have the fiddle." Franz came half on his knees, the scar showing.

Father thumped down. "No," he shouted. "Get that Devil's gut out of here." Then came off his high G in a hurry. The Prinzings had money and jobs to offer, and he knew where his bread was buttered thickest. "Ain't really got time for fiddling much." His voice trailed away.

"Well, Old Jens said 'fore he died, Franz was to have it." Pete scraped a boot on the step. "Besides, Pa wants Franz to play—"

"Guess not." Father was angry again. "There won't—"

"Pa'll give him a dollar." Pete's voice had honey around the edges. Franz wanted to speak but didn't; just looked. Father stopped. "A dollar, you say—for one night playing?"

"Sure." Pete threw an arm over the mare's neck. "Course if you don't want—" Father came up quickly. "*Na, na;* put it down. Maybe, maybe."

Pete tossed the case to Franz, and jogged on. Father bent his eye after him. "Dancing and truck," he growled; "and hardly out of his diapers. Young he-dog running loose, nights." But Franz was deaf to his mumblings. The way he opened the case and lifted the fiddle, I think that some things of those weeviled years before were squared up.

Old Jens was buried two days later. In the Wiggin churchyard, not in the cemetery of our church. The Pastor wouldn't have it and delivered Bible text to show that God was on his side. "It is not meet to give the things meant for God's children to every heathen, Turk and Hottentot that comes along," he proclaimed and the elders nodded. The coffin passed the church at the crossroads.

"Jens'll be kinda—lonely," Franz ventured. He was slow

with thought, shocking the last of the grain. Thinking that without Jens he never would have got the fiddle, nor have had the excitement of two strings full of melody when he joined them with one draw of the bow. Nights and noons as fall ran on. . . .

Not that Father gave him a finger of encouragement. He had a way of tightening his fists when Franz was deep in playing, and of stamping to the barn or lean-to. Holding himself back. But there was silver under this; precious and worth the waiting. Though he'd come in after eating and yell, "Hitch up the horses; no time for squealing on the fiddle. Corn to be picked." Franz went and whistled *Liebeslied* among the corn rows—for tomorrow.

His first barn dance gave him a pleasure half-eaten by disappointment. A cloudy afternoon preceded night. We were in the pasture, splicing a break in the fence, when a shower blew up and we heard the rain like the feet of running mice among the leaves.

"Think it'll set in for a three-day drizzle?" he wanted to know, anxiously, pulling his hat lower.

"Oh, sundown'll clear it," I said. He handed me a length of wire. "Jeppy, will you come—tonight—with me? Even if it rains?" I hadn't intended to, no more fond of dampness than a cat, but guessed I would. Because of the look on his face, queer and pleading. The thought beat in my mind that he wanted me for more reasons than company. We went home, soaked. Toward dark, clouds sagged down to the hilltops, wet and soggy, and trees began to drip slowly and with dreariness. The smell of sodden fields was thick and as if pushed up the nose; heavier after night fell.

Father wanted to shout words, we could see, but let it go. Walter in a strange moment said, "I'll go with them, the loonheads. Ain't sugar." Said it to spite Father, I knew. They'd got into a row over seed corn that afternoon. Father grumbled, "You answer for this, you kids, if the Pastor hears you've been playing. Ought to be in your catechism. I scrub my hands." But it was the money, we said inside us; a dollar for a night was more than he got in a week of sweating. We floundered into the mud and gloom.

A dozen people milled about in the shadowy barn, when we came to the Prinzings'. Not enough for a good square dance, Mr. Prinzing said, and brought Franz to the players' stand, where Heinrich Muehlbank tightened a string, and a sad little man wheedled an accordion into gaspy melody.

A slowpoke time. Walter stood with Harlow Mankin, good friend of his. Talked gravely. I heard Harlow say, "Clear out. Damned if I'd let him boss me. You're old enough." Mr. Mankin was there, fatter than his fat wife; the floor creaked when they tried a preliminary whirl—a starter, he called it. Pete was begging for a waltz, his eyes lazy as men's are who do not expect to act today but will find time tomorrow; Rena not there, for once, and he sliding his arm about the waist of a girl from over Long Lake. The men ribbed him but he laughed.

Franz played the waltz, the scar flaming, and his eyes half-closed; second fiddle but not caring. For all of him, it didn't matter that rain sluiced down harder and the cave of night flared up in blue lightning. It struck me as an odd fancy, when I remembered how muddy he was that afternoon, that he had a fiddle in his heart and earth in his hands. A fool idea, I guess.

The dance dragged; no one else came, and the barn seemed empty and full of shadows, with the thunder rocking between the hills. The players stopped, and Franz packed the fiddle with trouble hanging his shoulder. Mr. Prinzing came. "Well, boy, good fiddling." He hesitated. "Only—you see, you didn't play all evening ; I can hardly—" Franz looked scared, so that he said, "What's the matter, boy?"

Franz bit his lip, silent, but I answered directly, "Father'll lick him—if he doesn't bring home the money."

Mr. Prinzing scratched his neck. "Yep, he would, the old— Here's your money. Come play again."

Walter left his friend and we set out. Rain sloshed in the dark and I grumped, trying to keep a trickle from adventuring down my neck. But Franz kept saying, low so that Walter ahead wouldn't hear, "I played, Jeppy; I played. The G-chord was easy." He squashed in the mud. "That first fiddler— Jeppy, wasn't he fine?"

"Stir your pegs. I've got a puddle on me—right in the middle of my back."

Father was waiting up for us, when we slopped in. "Where is it?" he asked at once. Franz put the dollar into his hand. "Huh," he grunted. "Get on to bed. Church tomorrow." But Franz hid his dream in his heart. He played only at scattered times that next year. Folks thought him too young, and besides religious instruction was coming on. But we knew they hedged aside, fearing the Pastor and what he would say. Charlie Abendsmeyer had been excommunicated for drunkenness the year before—and Franz wasn't even confirmed. The sin was doubled. "You wait till you're confirmed," wagered Mr. Prinzing. "Everybody'll want you, and you'll fiddle in your sleep."

14

It was in the time of late plowing that we started to walk the wood road north to Toffmann's Corners and the church. German school, we said, and there was doubt and uneasiness in the lift of our heels. "Get your Bible and catechism together, kids," Father had reminded us gruffly, the week before. "Monday is German school." Unwilling to have us go but forced to it. He waited to give his yes until we could go together, Franz and I. "Knows he'll pay only half as much to the Pastor," Walter grinned sardonically; two came to less than one. He could explain away our absences better to Sunnenbaum than to Lafferty. And pieplant wine fist-high in a glass moved hills with the Pastor.

The Pastor had a patch of corn and hay for his team and cattle now, and dug the sod. The Toffmanns would come on him in the pasture, milk pails slung over his arm, muttering in his beard, "The seed of sin is woman, and the man who lies with her in secret is cursed." Planning his sermons under the cows. He rushed down on the congregation with the jawbone of wrath, Sundays, and even the hard of heart cringed and came to quick and shivering repentance. He used to thunder at us crouched in the benches those days; stabbed with a bony finger at each one; brought separate guilt flying to the throat. "Sinners, you are, that's what: all of you. Slimy as a rat crawling out of a spittoon; born in the dirt of your mother's womb, the lot of you, and going to Hell; tomorrow, maybe; or tonight; when you sit down to eat. No hope, unless you repent. Repent. Repent," he'd yell. And the girls would cry and Franz turn a sick and haunted face to me.

We came to the white church, this morning, clutching our Prince Albert lunch boxes, a hollow gnawing under our belts, and inches short of breath. Others were there—the Dunkel kids, the Maynards, and some we didn't know; popping out of the bushes, frightened and stiff, and looking as if a "Scat" would send them dog-scared into the hazels. Matt Prinzing, Pete's brother, and his sister, Wilhelmina; Jonas Bluber, starting late, as we were, and at once under suspicion, for the Pastor had told him his father was a lie-abed and a drunken waster, rotting out his belly over beer kegs; and probably not even God Himself knew what Jonas would turn out to be.

But Franz, still blinking from the morning dusk in the woods, half-chuckled, as he looked up and saw Liliem; a wide smile moved even his ears. Liliem was staying at the Toffmanns'; for her father's place was a ridge over and the miles too many for a girl.

We waited for nine o'clock and the Pastor. Franz stole glances at Liliem's yellow curls and scowled when Jonas boldly wrote her a note. But she twinkled at Franz, whereat the scar burned in his cheek, and I thought the leaf-curl of her smile the one bright thing in the room.

Always, we saw the black hat first and then the Pastor—the black hat coming in, held by a pale hand, and then the frock-coated Pastor. We'd stumble among the benches, rising, and say, *"Guten Morgen, Herr Pastor,"* in unison. And he'd say, *"Guten Morgen, Kinder."* If we lagged he grabbed up a birch stick. "Nicely together, next time. I've got something to tickle you sluggards." He came in, this day, in a hurry, his nose red and his breath penetrating as skunk oil even to the last row of seats. Heated over something. He chased us through the morning prayer and, without more than a tweak at his beard, flung the bars of his irritation at us.

"Loose women, that's where sin starts; from Eve to here in Pockerbrush. You young ones—beware; certain folk in this congregation—up to their gills in drinking, and fat with eating; wallowing in sin like hogs." He thumped the desk. "I tell you, the grease of Hell is hot and smoking, ready to fry such as live so." His eyes flickered at the Prinzings and the two slipped down in their seats. Guessing he meant Pete. The Pastor finished us off with Joseph and Potiphar's wife; said grace in a high voice, and went to his house. He attended to things of God before dinner and the things of the world after; gave reading and figuring when he wasn't throwing the Tablets of Moses at our heads. He was awkward at sums, though; hawed loudly over a problem that stumped Hans Dunkel: "Albert sold 2/3 of 4/5 of the half-interest he had in a thresh-ing machine. What was the loss per cent?" He scratched his beard for the answer and told Hans the book was old and there-fore wrong. He brought out the readers, dust-grimy and nibbled by mice, and taught us spelling—*Buchstabieren,* he called it. Adding syllable to syllable like stitch to stitch in a knitted stocking. I remember that Jonas bogged down in "Afghanistan" that afternoon and that Diah Kloster droned it out for him: a-f, Af; g-h-a-n, ghan, Afghan; i-s, is, Afghanis; t-a-n, tan,

Afghanistan. Nobody as much as squeaked a pencil on slate more than necessary. We understood the language of a birch stick.

It was at recess, with Franz still in his seat by the window, that Liliem came to him and put a hand on his arm. "You look sad," she said softly.

Franz swallowed the frog in his throat desperately. "I'm—I'm taking my feed regular." He said it as Father would.

"You keep looking at me—don't you like my dress?" She curtsied with laughing graveness. For answer Franz reached out and untangled a lock of her hair. Touched it with trembling fingers. She winked her eyes at him. Franz was silent, dizzy, I think, with the wild honey of joy, sweet to the heart but heady and beyond his power to know, having had only leavings and little of them. It was enough to be still with Liliem there, watching Mr. Dunkel plow in the field across the road, and the furrows grow and fatten on the stubbles. Then Jonas Bluber clattered up, noisy as a sack of tin plates, and taking no notice of Franz.

"We're gonna play 'Last Couple Out.' Come on." He slid a hand over her shoulder. She regarded him without movement.

"Why do you do that?" she asked quietly, with a half-smile.

"You're my girl, ain't you?" Liliem turned away but Jonas caught her arm; roughly. "You be my partner for 'Last Couple Out,' huh?"

Franz dived at him, and there was a snarl of arms and legs. Liliem shrank back—and then the Pastor was there, pulling them apart. "Fighting, so?" He glared at Liliem, full of suspicion as an otter, and reached for the stick but said, "Both of you write: 'I have been busy with nonsense.' Three hundred times."

Franz was finger-weary for a day. I couldn't help twigging him. "Why do you get in such truck—fighting?"

"I—she's—she's like clean water—" he hesitated; then added

furiously, "Jonas is a dirty old skunk." Which didn't leave much that mattered.

Five days a week we followed the road north and watched blue-spike and goldenrod frost down to skeletons fuzzy with old shreds of bloom; slowly, with the inevitableness of decay. The shadows of rust fell across the oak leaves where the wood-smoke of the year curled and browned the leaves. And a kind of death-moan hung in the air, evenings, dim and sad, breathed by earth on the wind-harps of a ridge of trees. Franz sent up lonely melodies then, the lethargy of the Seven Sleepers getting into the strings. But Father wrenched in his chair at the way Franz sat, pulling at the bow, the room and its scanty furniture no more real to his mind than a cloud pile. Never hearing Father grunch off to bed. Eyes dusty with dreams. Thinking of Liliem, I guess. Liliem.

They paired off, a noon in October, and hid in the woods in a game of tag, and didn't return for the hour, although the boys ran circles around the brush, bringing the echoes out.

"They'll catch it, if the Pastor comes, and they not in their benches." Jonas squinted with a leer. "Wonder what they're doing, there alone." I tramped into the church with a gloomy wonder in me that here, too, a ridge away from Father and the farm, worry hid in the corners and uneasiness folded itself with the shadows back of the door. It came creeping behind, wherever we went, and stepped in our tracks like a dog in deep snow.

The storm door, put on against winter, screamed with rust, and the Pastor came in. Saw the empty seats. And a fierce and holy pleasure grew on his face, as if he needed an example and the Lord had provided. "So. Here we have it. Jezebel and the man."

The door burst open; Franz and Liliem stood there; rooted, the breath swift in their lungs from running. They slunk to their seats.

"So." The Pastor took up the stick. Gently. Goading anger

with restraint. "Can't wait, eh, you two? Young snippers that
you are; wallowing together; bulls and heifers." He flung the
words like something dirty into their faces. He'd cut the toad-
stool of sin back to stem with a blow. We heard the watch in
his pocket tick loudly. It is far away now, that moment; but
the thought of it returns like a remembered odor: Liliem, face
pale in the wild tangle of her curls. Franz with his head in his
arms. Until the Pastor stopped before her. Then he started up.
"I wanted to show her the pine spring. It was far and we got
late." His hands going out. But the Pastor brought the birch
down whistling. Across Liliem's shoulders. Again. Franz
came at him then, striking blindly with his fists. The Pastor
swung around. Franz fell under his hand, half-stunned against
a bench. The birch end splintered over his back. Liliem was in
tears but quiet. The rest of us crouched away, bodies hard with
the breath and the fear in them, the pulse bouncing in the throat
and a lie ready on the lip, should the Pastor swing the net of his
questions in our direction. He rolled back to his desk, clean and
virtuous; started the lesson with "Come unto me, all ye that
labor and are heavy laden . . ." I felt that which was hot and
spiny as a rose stick, move deep; so deep, I wondered that it was
in me at all. For Franz, and yet not for him alone.

"That's what you get, hanging around girls," I told him on
the way home. He looked sick; afraid Father would find out
more than anything else. Afraid . . . afraid . . . we ate fear
with our bread and milk. "Maybe next time—"

"Jeppy, you think—Liliem, is she like that—what the Pastor
said? You believe that?" He pulled at a bush, thoughts on another track. "Mother was a girl once; pretty, I guess. You
think she was what the Pastor says?"

"Whoa, there and pull over," I dodged. This was deep
water and over my chin. "Mother is different. She—well." I
headed the talk off fast. "Tinkla, now—you—"

"Oh, Tinkla; she's fine. I like her. She's—she's—well, I
can touch her. But Liliem—" He let it go at that, and I felt

a vague stirring of the shadows and a sense that Franz was headed straight for a quicksand bar; though how, I couldn't make out.

The feeling that things moved back of my shoulder stayed with me like a barb, under the routine of our crawling lives. I couldn't forget that first day of German school and the Prinzings' withering under the Pastor's hints, hang-lipped to run home and tell what they heard. Shushed into silence and sullen, they'd be, as we had been, time and again. Not only us, then, who found a kind of security in hiding what plagued us and pretending it didn't exist. Other people, too, were restless over the wrigglings in their own lives, felt more than seen. I wondered in a fierce moment whether I'd ever find a place, even in the hills, where folks didn't sleep with one eye on the neighbors; where men's lives were clear like sandy pools, uncontaminated by the belly-crawlings of things hinted at.

A kind of iron grayness crept over the land, the sun cold in the trees, mornings, and giving off bitter warmth at noon. Northwesters rubbed in the pines, and the wind side of furrows hardened to gray crumbles of earth. Then on a night cloudy with the foreboding of snow came a rush of feet and a hand at the door, and we saw a neighbor's life ripped wide open by the blade of shame, for all the hills to see; under our staring eyes the secrets they had hid like dirty rags under the rooftree. A swirl of dark and Pete Prinzing sagged against our doorpost, eyes wild with the desperation of a hunted rabbit, and lips broken, we didn't know how then. Half his shirt and overhalls torn away, one suspender barely holding up the rest, so that we saw the black hair on his lean and bone-marked chest and the red welt across a thigh, naked under the lamp. It was like a dreadful nightmare in which we said inside us, "This isn't true; not really happening here in Pockerbrush; not to us"; but knowing with the swift clarity of despair that it was. Pete was choked by gaspings, yet urged to speak fast by what followed him in the night. "Schaaf and the men . . . it wasn't my

fault . . . his girl, Rena . . . after the dance . . . she wanted . . .
God! That's them coming." Father like a black pillar stood beside the table, his voice unmerciful. "You come here, with your
dirt. No place in this house for he-dogs and whorers. Get out."
Mother with her hands over her eyes, and Franz half up in his
chair, the fiddle dangling, so white all at once, I thought he'd
fall. Pete crying out, "They've got a rawhide . . . and knives,"
and sinking back. Fierce eyes like hungry wolves in the dark . . .
Old Man Schaaf, flipping the rawhide, his face roped with
hate . . . hands grabbing at Pete . . . at his clothes . . . his arms
twisting and clawing, and his body suddenly white and naked
all its length there in the doorway; the darkness shutting him
out, but voices biting through: "We'll fix him . . . fatherless
brats . . . geld the bastard." Gravel crunching fainter and
Pete's hoarse cry, freezing on the air . . . "Not . . . the knife . . .
Not the . . ." Silence and the awfulness of going back to what
our hands were on two minutes ago, before this was piled heap-
high on us.

Franz climbed to the loft, trembling, and slept no more winks
than I. He moved closer and his hands fumbled over the
pillow. "Jeppy, it's awful to be alive; like the Pastor says,
always wrong. Is it our fault? Why can't we—just die—and
be done with it?" I longed for a tongue to say the words I felt
in me, but found nothing more than: "We'll know, someday.
Someday," I said, and believed it. As one to whom any gopher
hole is concealment from unwanted truth.

15

The years dragged themselves across our stony lives, as
cattle over fallow acres, leaving but a smear of dusty tracks
to show that here they went. With only now and then a hoof-
print cut deep to indicate where life was molded into a different
shape, by the setting aside of that which was, and the slow
crumbling of design. Or so it appeared. Mother would look

at Franz, the faded violet coming to her eyes. "Shooting like a weed, Fränzchen; half a head higher than your mother." But Fritzie'd snicker, "Coming on sweet sixteen, start girling next."

There was little about those springs and summers in between, that was different from any others; a frostbitten robin in April, dismayed at the snow lifting gritty banks in the north shadows; bloodroots wasting by the rod under the hazels, their perfume mixed with the heavy wetness of last year's leaves; slow rains of June and heat lightning of August, promising wet that came weeks after it was needed. We'd be shocking oats under the ponderous wheel of clouds gathering in storm, defying heaven and saving grain, until thunder with a sound like a heavy cloth tearing ripped the sky open from hill to hill. Or Franz and I'd be at the Maises', threshing time, pitching bundles and sitting down to supper of fresh-killed beef and spuds and gravy; to a large table, shiny with new oilcloth, above it a mass of asparagus bush, ferny and green, to drive off the flies. We'd listen to Mr. Mais tell how he shot seven deer back in the 'eighties, and hung them all on a tree near a lake, and the lake to this day is called Seven Deer Lake . . . his wife shushing him: "*Na*, Schneider, if the Pastor could only hear; such stories. It was five last time." A neighbor woman, in to help them at threshing, talked about Mrs. Maynard's baby: "A year and a half, and still sucking. I told her to put pepper on her breast; that gets 'em off." And there were evenings when I'd go for the cows along the creek, sweet fern in my nose, and watch a muskrat wedging upstream with a silver stick of water in his teeth; and come back with the cows to hear *Liebeslied* drift with the smoke layers into the pasture, and know that Franz had stolen moments to rest his work-sore body before milking. Familiar as an old glove, these things, and now lost as one who is dead.

Pete Prinzing was gone; left the hills—went in the night without asking for hat or coat, and the Prinzings braced their chins with stubbornness and chipped pride, when they came to the store or church; never letting on that their hearts were running sores. There was some talk about the sheriff, and Mr. Prinzing loaded his gun with B-B's; but his chicken coop burned one night, nobody knew how; and talk slid under cover. Rena Schaaf screamed herself into the dark, when her labor came, and never knew the life she brought from the shadows, or that she left with Old Man Schaaf a wormy cud to chew on, all his days.

Franz would watch him at church and knock my arm. "Ready to fall to pieces, the old man, looks like. Think Pete will ever come back?" It bothered him, I guess, this knowing more about a neighbor's back cellars than we had any right to. Mostly he twisted glances at Tinkla, and looked for Liliem; had a time of it, when they were both there, Liliem shy as a roan doe but with a slow meaning that Franz couldn't escape, beginning to show in her eyes; Tinkla no more quiet even in church than a shuttle box, and as direct in her ways as a slap in the face. She took on height but little dignity; came to German school and rattled her shoes under the bench, to keep something moving, for the Pastor had thrashed her once for jiggle-jaggling behind her desk. Franz turned to her when trouble brewed, as something he could depend on, I thought; and yet it wasn't that either. She dug a sliver out of his thumb one day; deep and long; used the small blade of his jackknife and never flinched a muscle, although Liliem, standing near, had a sick moment. Franz had a strange look in his eyes as he watched Tinkla, his hand tight in hers. They were partners at the next "Skip to Mallew" game, I remember; played with a guard at the window, for the Pastor had forbidden with a whack of the birch any games that suggested the dance. But his edict added spice to "Four in a Boat" and "The Needle's Eye," Franz laughing with Tinkla. He slipped over to Liliem soon, in spite of Jonas' hanging at her skirts.

We struggled with the Israelites through the wilderness and through the winters, and learned dogma by the pound, it seemed, weighty as sacks of grain; memorized pages of the catechism, text and verse, for we were to be confirmed in the spring, and the year moved tedious as a breaking plow.

But the noons and recesses of "Duck on a Rock" and "Nip" are not all blacked out by the heavy pencil of the years . . . shinny-dog on the ice, and Franz limping from a stick swacked over his knee. Jonas up to his neck in the pond, when he took a dare on rubber ice . . . the store across the road and the time the five drunks set a keg of beer in plain sight of the Pastor's house and let the faucet run; glass after glass they gurgled down, singing bad love songs in good German, soused to the eyeteeth. "Come on, kids, have a beer," they called, and Franz wanted to go, but the Pastor came, swelling with wrath and the Lord's word. He found them four too many, and shooed us into the church; his face the kind of blue-red we'd seen on a gobbler's wattles. He birched Jonas for nothing more than snapping an elastic at Wilhelmina Prinzing; scolded loud with a penny's worth of talk about drunkards and loose women.

Incredible, all this past, though it remained a portion of our flesh and mind; incredible that yesterday's knee-britches became today's long pants in a space short as a dream, and that Franz one evening fingered his chin by lamplight and began thinking about a razor. We'd say, looking back, "That happened the spring Klosters had a baby—a year ago; no, two; why it *is* two years; going on three. The way the years sneak on!" Those were the honey-gold years, if we had only known it; sweet with Jonathan youth and David strength, in between the gall-blistered years that went before and those that were to come, soaked with pain and dragged over and over again by the dark inching worm of fate.

Franz ran on to his fifteenth year and out, lean and tall, dark as Father was, with the scar red on his cheek when the blood was up. He split his pants with growth and broadened out the size of his shoes. He was strong in his way and shocked with us windrow for windrow across the field, for all we ragged his sapling slenderness. Hands like Mother's, that quivered as they

poised above the strings and stirred to life strange fires in those
who had maids in their arms and whirled in the waltz. He'd
fiddle hours into eternity, give him leave, though Father growled
that any man who pointed a plow as crooked as Franz did would
be crow-poor along his ribs, and that before many years. He
put on a dogged look when anyone asked Franz to play, and
gave his yeas only after argument, his unwillingness being as
soothing to him as the money Franz brought home. But Franz
cared less than a shilling, and played in barn and granary when
the doors swung open for the dance.

He was confirmed that spring, and I; he straight and solemn
in the trousers that didn't match the coat; giving the responses
clearly, though pulling at the wild rose Mother fastened into
his buttonhole; kneeling to receive the sacramental cup, the scar
flaring, and the hymn leaflet fluttering on the dark altar step.
People gathered around after services to say, "Well, you're
through with it now," and he nodded dumbly. He laughed at
Tinkla when she came.

"Next year it's your turn—and Liliem's."

"The way you faddled around," she said, "guess I'll get it,
all right."

"Sure, if you get your ma to sit behind you—whisper what
you don't know. Unless she forgets. The way Old Lady Ochstock did."

"Say that again—and no invite will you get." She flounced.

"You really going to have a confirmation party?" Franz was
suddenly serious. Thinking what lay at home for him.

"That's what I say—a big time. Pa says no, but Ma says
yes—that settles it." She poked at him. "You've got an invite, right now—from me. Oh. That's Ma yelling." She ran
off. Mrs. Bauer, plumped on the surrey cushions, was shrieking
in a voice like a pitch pipe full of water, "Tinkle, Tinkle, where
are you? Stop dragging your feet and hurry up." She didn't
care that the Pastor frowned and the people giggled, and Mr.
Bauer said, "Keep your petticoat down, Katinka. The dead ain't

gonna listen to you anyway." A dried-up little man, he was, with a weaselish nose and a wet-weather slump to his shoulders, but with eyes that were almost like hands, giving out friendship. He looked like a dwarf beside his barrel of a wife. Old Mr. Dunkel said that she could put three like him under her skirts and still have room. And it was tittered about that once at a granary dance, when Mr. Bauer became soberly and determinedly drunk, Mrs. Bauer had pitched him over her sufficient knees and paddled him black and blue.

Franz watched them drive off with a shadow on his face. Most of *die Konfirmanden* had parties at their homes today, riding off with buggyfuls of relatives and friends, hungry for goose broth and pumpernickel. Jonas waved his hat from his seat with Liliem and Mrs. Schoen, all bound for Jonas' house. Franz climbed into the buggy without much smile, even for Mother, though she drew him close. "Fränzchen, I was proud—so proud of you." We went home to our house and the dog, to fried potatoes and warmed-over pork, for Father wouldn't have any fuss. *Fixerei,* and nothing else; confirmation is confirmation, that ends it, he said. The way Franz opened the fiddle case and closed it again, and slipped out under the stars, I think the wine he tasted had turned with a bite of vinegar in it.

The autumn of his fifteenth year had a brilliance we'd never known before. Sharp early frost fell like a black veil over the melon beds and set the woods into patches of flame. The ravine beyond the creek, dark with maple and woody dimness in summer, was flooded with a strange yellow glow, as if each leaf were a candle and gave off light. Valleys burned with the fire of popple and oak. Until Franz thought there must be a special reason, all this saved up for us.

That year and the one following remain like a dark wound skinned over; stinging under touch as old cuts do, in hot or cold, unprotected by the toughness of scarred growth. The ending of more than we knew. The beginning of much more, until I wondered how the heart endured, and wanted to cry out with what voice I had left, "Enough! It is enough, and more. The pitcher full and slopping over." But I know now that only the tongues of the dead, wrenched with the final separation, have the knowledge wide and deep to wail, "This is the end." And they are wormholed and swollen and silent as dust.

I'd dog-ear the pages of Jones's *Ninth Reader* with a kind of wonder, the thought scrabbling itself in my skull, "This can't be so. The last reader—the last year." No more parsing of sentences and hunting for lost objects; no more running to the Dunkels' for a bucket of water, noons . . . or swinging in the ironwoods . . . or cutting knotholes in the boards of the girls' outhouses . . . the last harness on the old horse. This gray room, beaten by time and weather—I'd be away from it, hereafter; from the primer kids in front, near a stove that baked them, and the eighth-graders in back, shivering five months out of seven; the seats filled with newcomers where Liliem had been and Tinkla, both still away, under the rod of Sunnenbaum (Liliem taller now, with the grace of a fawn; Tinkla too big to romp, but romping anyway). Jonas was sitting there, clumsy in the hulk of his shoulders; Franz sticking his eraser into his mouth to make it more abrasive; the geography class memorizing state capitals, singsonging the verse with gusto but half-shouting the emphasis in the wrong places:

"Maine, Augusta capital is;
Concord, New Hampshi-ero;
Green Vermont, Montpelier town;
Providence, Rhode Island, O."

This year we talked about skiing, and next—but there wouldn't be next year. Not with school and laughing over lunches on the sun-side of the woodpile. We didn't know then that there wasn't to be much laughter this year either.

Smallpox rode over the hills that winter and far into spring.

We let it slip off our shoulders with a shrug, at first; went to school and pitched manure without care, thinking, "Well, it's over Tamarack Lake way, and that's a good piece off." We skated on the lake and skied on the Diemer hills and Matt Prinzing was jim-ful of an idea. "We oughta get a couple of bobsleds next year, when the hill is blown clear—icy. Or long sleds; eight-footers. I'm a two-toed bloodsucker if she don't ripsnort down that ice—like a bat outta hell." He had the satisfied look of one who has spoken like a man, with hairy-chested words. "And we could have a bonfire—and girls." We guessed it was a good idea, and whizzed over the swamp, clean of worry for once.

But the Maises came down with the fever, and the Prinzings, and the terror grew. Enoch Kloster, with shoulders wide as a door across, left his sweetheart one morning—left her with a song between his teeth, and lay stiff before sun-dusk the next day; frozen with an ice that all the glow her body held could never warm away. The sled with the black cloth tied to a stake moved slowly to the churchyard; faster after the first ones shrieked in madness and kicked against the covers for the last time. School went cold and unattended but the church was stuffy-hot, the dead buried with Bible text and tears and flowers that women snipped from their own window pots. The dark cloth on the stake drooped in awful warning, and the black crow of death flapped under the eaves. We longed for a sign to put on our door to warn the shadow away, Israel-fashion. Why our house was forgotten I don't know, unless we were spared for agony even greater. Though Franz crossed the heart over in us by coming down with a fever for a day. Mild and of no consequence. Mother hung asafoetida in bags around our necks, until we wanted to puke with the smell, clinging as skunk oil. She burnt herbs in the room, and told us, "Eat salt; that keeps fever off." We did, and drank buckets of water. Listened for a neighbor's team and news. "The Klosters are down. Jeb Maynard died at two. Grossmutter

Katzenhoft . . . they can't dig the graves fast enough; pretty soon they plan to bury them in the sandstone pits . . ." Franz had dolor in his fingers, nights when he played; a dirge under the melody. We might be next, and Mother none of the strongest. He played with a kind of hopelessness in his face, until she flung down the patching. "Don't, Franz; it hurts tonight; Mrs. Mais—they are afraid she won't last till morning."

It choked off young and old; left those alive almost in envy of those with whom despair had done its worst. Black mounds grew like unnatural sores on the snowy quarter-acre. Long-faced Mr. Bieber, twice widowed and now lonely shepherd of his three children, at sunrise carted his first-born to the cemetery; came back and unharnessed his team; and found the other two eyeless with death and the neighbor woman crouched over the bed. Before the hills dissolved in dusk he harnessed up again and carried them away. The Pastor found him tearing at the grave clods when day broke, and his place remained silent of laughter until he died. Liliem's mother went—one night in late spring; turned with a great cry and died, and left Liliem empty even of tears.

Franz, when he heard, held Mother's hand as if it were the one solid thing in all this bog of ache and agony. Got up and left the house. I saw him edging the creek, where the stream bent the willows like an archer; regardful of the mystery of water, the unpredictable shift and whirls no more explicable than the dark currents in his own being.

The funeral was held on a weekday. We drove over and so did most of the neighbors, the women black-veiled. They came with a kind of defiance, almost daring God to strike them down, but knowing that the plague had run its tether. Mr. Schoen stumbled along, autumn frosty on his hair, and winter in his face . . . Liliem dark in the folds of her veil, the last curl of her smile crushed and broken now . . . people among the gravestones, the quick treading the dead.

Liliem was sad-eyed but quiet, not looking at the fresh earth scattered around; quiet, until they gave her a rose from the casket; crying then with the abandon of one who finds even hope a moth-eaten comfort; wanting to smother pain with grass. Before we thought, Franz stood there, with an arm about her. "Don't, Liliem; tears like this; I'll take care of you." She turned, as if looking for somebody else, and leaned against him; he drew her away.

The Pastor pulled a scowling face; this outraging all decency; and Father pushed forward, muttering, "Franz," his face granite; knowing the neighbors had fishhooks in their eyes, observant if full of tears and hidden behind veils. He grabbed at Franz. But Liliem's father held him back. "No, it is better, this way. More than I can do for her." He sagged away, tired and shaking with the unsteadiness of too much sorrow. Franz was stone-blind to anything but Liliem; led her from the wide rip in the grass; out of sight among the hazels.

The neighbors shook hands with Mr. Schoen, dumb to their lips, or broke their hearts over fragments of sympathy. And returned to their wagons and buggies. Nothing they could do. They had the living at home. What was left belonged to the night and tears unshed and festering under the lids.

Father raged for half an hour, waiting in the buggy until Franz came, bringing Liliem where her father sat, bowed over his knees; but he ventured nothing when Franz climbed in beside Mother and gazed back, silent under the awful certainty of death. Father let him be, feeling that grief was sacred and not spoken of, but put away in the mind.

We came in sight of our place, not much changed under the shift and sag that comes with years, except that the oak under the eaves had a dead and shaggy look that betokened little sap for spring and less for leaves of summer. Father kept his head down, as if something in the way the wheels cut and sprayed the slush had a meaning in his own mind that was too dark for any one of us to guess. He looked up suddenly, watching

Mother, the lids of his eyes pulled down like a hazel husk half-closed.

"Begins young already, Franz; hugging girls, and still frog-wet behind the ears." He snipped the backs of the mares gently with the whip. "Must be in the blood; comes down from way back, maybe; wanting a woman between the arms. Or a man." His eyes clouded to fierce blackness at the way Mother hid her face suddenly. "Bulls in the spring pasture." Father's voice was soft and creamy, as if this were a joke and he'd likely break out laughing. But knowing him, and the stranger he was to mirth, I wondered what he covered up with kindness to hurt Mother, and knew that this softness was like a tomcat's purr-ing—woolly, with claws underneath. A thought wiggled in the back of my brain—something about a neighbor and a Bible and a soft voice—where had I heard this before? It got away, too slippery to hold, and I forgot it, noticing how Franz grew red and set his lips stubbornly, his eyes on the blur of flying mud.

Nobody had the heart for confirmation when May came around. Too many homes had Bibles on the shelf with a lock of hair or a flower from a grave pressed between the leaves. Let this year go by with forgetfulness. But the Pastor said grimly from the pulpit, "The Lord giveth, the Lord taketh away. And, brethren, we sin with the heathen if we grumble when the Lord lays His stripes upon us, miserable sinners that we are."

We had confirmation—a sad affair, with Asa Sperry's sister breaking down in the middle of the questions; Liliem pale as the dress she wore but answering in a low voice; and Tinkla with a flower like a young rosebush spraying from her shoul-ders. She mixed up the responses so that Pastor hinted broadly in his sermon about flighty brains and the necessity of bolting down to serious thought. "The Lord is a God of order and propriety," he finished. "Amen. We will sing hymn eighty-three: 'O Lord, I but deserve to die; and Hell for such a worm as I is none too good.'" But there was much rustling and coughing when he announced those who were confirmed and, coming to the Prinzing girl, read in a solemn voice, "Josephina Wilhelmina Cherubina Prinzing." But they needed a smile, Mother said afterward, those faces marked by the hen-tracks of worry, huddling within their black and somber garments.

Tinkla rushed up to Franz at the close of the service; pushed among people like a hoyden. "You won't forget," she cried, breathing so hard the roses moved energetically. "Your ma's coffeepot. And bring cups for you boys. We ain't got enough for the bunch. And—"

"Tinkle, Tinkle," screamed Mrs. Bauer, the surrey wheezing when she stepped up and sloping to the edge where she eased herself. "Tinkle, we're ready." Tinkla hurried away, and a scent of roses hung in the air. The neighbors hinted it was hardly decent, these shindandies, with all that had happened. But I guessed it wouldn't keep any of them from coming.

We talked about it, driving from church. Father was at the Klosters', riding logs, now that they could saw again, and Fritzie handled the lines.

"It's not so wrong, Tinkla wanting a party," Mother was saying. "After all the crying this winter—"

"Tinkla," snickered Fritzie. "Muddlehead, she is, like her pa. Answering like that—Cain is Abel's son."

"Well, she got tangled up," Franz defended her.

"Huh!" Fritzie pulled up before the house. "Empty, that's what her head is. Can't tangle up anything that ain't there."

"Why don't you stay home, then, tonight?" Franz unhooked the tugs with anger. "If you don't like her; it's her party."

" 'Tain't hers alone." Fritzie began leading the horses to the barn. "Want to see the fellers, too."

"Tinkla had a nice dress." Mother pried in her words. "Three rows of buttons on the sleeves. Don't know where Mrs. Bauer got the pattern. Prob'ly from Fergus."

Fritzie snorted and Franz stopped, turning to say, "She was fine—rose and all. Grown up bigger, seems to me."

But Fritzie smirked. "Dough-pan'll need a horse and buggy soon—sweet sixteen and hogroot green. Out girling Saturday nights. Too bad Liliem can't be there tonight."

Franz flushed, the scar red. "You shut your mouth about her," he yelled, and jerked at the horses. So that Walter, limping out of the barn, saw him and called, "What's the matter, Bull Calf; burdock in your pants again?"

15

We walked to the Bauers' that night, Fritzie ahead and fast, clattering the coffeepot, and Franz lagging. Walter stayed with Mother at home; had to, with a foot swollen black from a nail he'd stepped on. We cut through the heavy timber and skirted Long Lake. It was an evening to hold the breath— the ragged ends of cloud scarlet in the western sky, like dawn over broken ice chunks, and the dark swinging across the hills like a gate, wide and heavy, shutting out day; the moon a white lantern hung in the arch of the zenith; wild plum blossom, pale slants on the ridges.

There was a gray confusion of people in the yard; loud talking. The boys, stiff as laths in Sunday clothes, gathered around the pump near the house. The hen-cackle of the girls came from the porch where, on the railing, much bouncing and tossing of arms caught the eye. Jonas and Leff Sperry talked up a horse trade with the air of jehus old in the wiles of barter. Mrs. Bauer shrieked, "Tinkle, Tinkle, where's the butcher knife? I've hunted high and low; want to slice the cake," and Mr. Bauer, tapping a pony of beer for the older men, yelled out of the night, "Keep your petticoat down, Katinka, I've got it; I'm cutting a wedge for the keg." Tinkla herself called out, "Drinks served here, on the porch, boys," and stood with the lamplight flooding over her, dressed in blue and white, with a waist buttoned down with silver disks. We drank the small glasses of beer, sudsy and tasting strongly of malt. The older boys ducked back of the house to join the men in additional gulps, Franz sneaking with them, and returned, rubbing their mouths with their sleeves. The house inside was yellow with kerosene flame, the oil colored with a piece of red flannel to keep it from exploding . . . a baby howling and a woman treading the floor: "It's his teeth; got any watermelon seed, Mrs. Bauer? I'll steep him a brew, and he'll be right, short off." Diah Kloster and the Morton boy, younger than Franz and comrades now, full of pup-love for Etta Rippey, played tag, never dreaming that years away one night they would pull jack-knives at each other's throats . . . moon washing the corncribs with silver.

Tinkla's voice rose clearly. "Everybody get your partner for 'Needle's Eye'!" . . . There was laughter and tugging of hands, boys catching at girls . . . the circle singing, "The needle's eye, that doth supply the thread that runs so truly" . . . shrill to-do's from the girls with "No" on their lips and "Come on, I dare you" in their eyes . . . "There's many a lass that I let pass, because I wanted you." Hands capturing a new partner . . . Jonas lumbering and a little tipsy, mouth as wide as a box. Matt Prinzing said to Franz between games, "Old Lafferty can ring the bell till he breaks his neck, all I care. School's done. You too, huh?" Franz nodded. "You got time to spare for the bobsleds then; I'll be a two-toed bloodsucker—" Talk floated away.

Franz asked Tinkla for the next "Last Couple Out," but she tilted her nose. "Latecomers get second best. I've asked Jeppy." Meaning to goad him, I guess. Franz scuttled about, to find no one left but Wilhelmina Prinzing, plump as a watermelon. Jonas was "it," and without a partner, standing at the head of the line of couples. Franz and Wilhelmina hurried up behind us, and were the last couple.

"Jonas is an old sack of potatoes," Tinkla gabbled. "Can't catch a grubworm. Run now, Wilhelie." Jonas yelled, "Last couple out," and Franz and the Prinzing girl ran, one on each

side of the line, far down, trying to touch hands again before
Jonas could capture the girl. Jonas won, and Franz was "it."
Although he didn't run worth shucks, I think, knowing that
Tinkla and I were next.

"Thinks he's going to get me," Tinkla whispered loudly;
"I'll run his legs off." Franz called. We separated, Tinkla far
out at the end of the line, bent for the corncrib and calling,
"Circle him"; Franz in front of me. I pulled beyond him, but
he lunged toward me; stuck out a foot and sent me tumble-
saulting. I came up hard with a bushel of stars flying and a
lopped-over ankle; took a breath and humped around the corner
of the crib and upon them suddenly.

Not all of this is thrust from the mind and left to forgetfulness; a part remains, etched with the tracery of a needle . . . the
moon dashing silver over them, so that their shadows were
black like soil newly laid in stubble . . . Tinkla full in the light,
still now, after twisting to escape . . . her waist torn aside, eyes
big and a hand up . . . Franz holding her half at arm's length,
staring, his voice thick and choked as with slow-drawn breath;
"Tinkla, Tinkla—your breasts—white as milk in the moon."
The seconds dropped with the laziness of feathers.

Then they saw me. Tinkla gasped and pegged off, chin
down, and Franz lurched by with a queer laugh; unsteady with
a wild urging within him, I thought afterward; blind hunger
deep as a bone under flesh. Let the blood stir and the root start,
and only death, or what is worse than death, can blight it, as
alone the frosts of January can strangle the peat fires burning in
the big swamp.

Our days were paid out in a round of jobs—leaning furrows
against the slant of ridges; more stumps to grub than Job would
have the patience to try. We picked potato bugs from the vines,
summers, their spit yellow on our fingers, and killed them with
boiling water—tasks that linked hour to hour, and forenoon to
afternoon, endless as the bull-path around the corn mill.

Franz played sometimes as if he'd eaten snakeweed and gone mad—an unbridled intensity that ran like brush fire through his being; as if he wanted to forget that night behind the corncrib—or wanted to remember it. He had a kind of hangdog look and avoided Tinkla, coming to church, feeling that he meddled with more than his hands could heft; scared and yet drawn too, but not sure of himself. Tinkla let not even a hair quiver to show reproach, and took it as something to be expected, I guess, as one does the slow climbing of barley seed or a change of weather. "Going to a shindandy soon?" she'd ask, but knew before he spoke. Few wanted to dance, with the notches death had cut still fresh in their homes, and barn dances out of favor. Besides, he had a fork in his hands oftener than a fiddle bow. Times more. He'd go to the fields in the morning, his whole body walking, and a whistle mocking the blackbirds in the plum bushes. But by evening, under east dark, he'd stumble home, leaving the black curves of furrow on furrow behind, only his legs moving, silent, his shoulders a dead weight under his overhall straps. All of us tired to the bone, for that matter.

Walter left home in July; came in one morning with a welt red across his mouth. Mother ran to him, a frightened twist on her face. "Walter, Walter, he—"

"I've taken enough," he muttered, nearly crying with rage. "A dog gets it better than this. He's hit me for the last time." He caught her into the circle of his arm, half roughly, yet meant kindness. "Mütterchen, Mütterchen, I've seen—all these years—" Then he was gone and the pegs where his clothes had hung were empty. Until Fritzie slid his things on them. Father stiffened his back and drove us harder after that. For a month Franz had no more than a peck at the strings. I guess Father expected Walter to hulk back any minute. "When the snow flies, the kennel of the dog is a warm place," he said. "He'll come back." But he didn't. Not even at harvesting.

We trundled the shocks from the fields, piled high on the

wagon, and Father built the stacks with the fork, putting the bundles down clockwise in circles, layer on layer, like bricks in a chimney, mortaring each in place with a thrust of strength. He rounded them off at the top so that we had three overgrown beehives in the yard, Franz thought once; high as the barn and each capped with two bundles, butts to the sky.

Franz tipped over with the last load of wheat we hauled and near broke his neck. I shouted to him that he would, pitching up more bundles than the rack could hold, and piling them on the hillward side. Unbalanced. He climbed the load, his body swaying on the unsteady footing, and pulled the team downhill.

"Don't do that, you crazy fool, you'll tip over," I yelled, running. "Drive straight along the hill." He never heard me. Didn't have time. The rack bucked up like logs in a jam, and went over, his dark form disappearing among the flying bundles. I had a sawlike thought—Franz striking a rock, his bones shattering . . . or his eyes poked out by the stubbles as Moses Carney's were, two years before. But I found him crawling out of the wheat, shaken and holding his belly, scared wordless.

"Set your spindles moving," I told him, no mind to scold. "Wheat off and the rack on. Father's waiting."

He forked the bundles with his lips set, and the cords of his lean muscles were taut. "Lucky no boards broke; she keeled over easy," he said, a kind of sickness on his face from having the wind knocked out of him. We lifted the rack on and started loading.

Father was climbing from the stack, impatient, when we trotted in the yard; and gave us his lip about monkeying the time away. But we kept this between each other, finishing the harvest.

John Bluber came to thresh in September, his old engine snorting, and spouting chunks of cinders, the firebox a red cave of flame. We saw the dark windrows of smoke roll over the trees before the steamer shoved a blunt nose across our fields and drew the little red box of a separator into the setting of grain. Jonas came behind, God Almighty important at driving the water wagon. There was a scramble to find room for the teams, and a bellowing for straw to keep the fire up. The separator man yelled, "Where in double-H hell is the scoop shovel?" Bluber swore in good sonorous German. A peppery man, Bluber, with a sucked-in kind of face, and overhalls shiny and leather-stiff with grease. Loose-tongued and full of dirty stories. He waved his arms to hurry the pitchers; the stacks quivered like ground in the peat bog, as they ratted up the side. A moment and the engine began to puff clouds of dark smoke; the separator howled, and bundles, half-turning in air, fell into the feeder, heads pointed to the whirling knives. Straw arched in a yellow blur over the mounting pile and the blower roared . . . the elevator hiccoughing grain, half a bushel at a time . . . horses kicking at the noise and starting away, the owner jerking them up: "Whoa, damn your knock-kneed, two-faced hide" . . . chuck-a-chuck of the exhaust, the odor of burnt straw and steam bitter in the nose, and a mist from the smoke-stack damp on our faces, as if the engine gave off sweat. Bluber shouted to the fireman, "She's foaming again, the old bitch; turn off the water." Dust settled scummy on the water pails, and drifted into the house, though Mother had the door shut, even with the room steamy hot with things cooking. Platters of meat and bowls of potatoes waited on the shelf; there was a rush of white vapor when Mother poured water into the scorching gravy mixture; the soup bubbled thickly; Mrs. Mais, over for the day, asked, "Want to put my water glasses down, Minna? Though with all they've drunk, seems funny they'd want some at meals." Mother said, "They'll be done—soon now; they're cleaning up the leftovers. My, how the engine puffs."

And in the growing dark, above the engine, curves of winking fire drifted into night, and died like stars out of orbits and too near earth. Wildcat shriek of the whistle, long and determined, to tell the hills that Bluber had finished threshing for the day. Supper and the men damp about the gills from sloshing in the tin wash-dish, and sitting down to eat. "Shovel in," said John Bluber, and fell to, the same bulgy grip on his fork that he had on the throttle. They ate as if it were a duty they owed themselves; silent but with eyes cocked; suspicious of the depth of a bowl or the height of the bread pile. All Mother's raspberry sauce they spooned down their scraggy red throats. (I thought of her patient hands.) Somebody grunted, "Dusty bastard, that last stack. Nothing but weeds and smut." Scrape of chairs, as they set their cups back . . . tamping of pipes . . . Adam Kloots sticking a thumb and forefinger of snuff inside his lip, and the men ragging him because though married he hadn't fathered a child. And the cool dark under the trees . . . the fireman's lantern winking like a wind-blown spark among the engine drivers. Drowsy water-ripple of talk. "Hell of a man you are, Adam." Bluber opened his knife and sliced grease from a pants leg. "Married three years and nothing to show."

Adam sopped up his chin with a fist. "Well, John, I'm taking my time."

"Hell, yes; a fine chicken-hopper. Ain't you a man?"

"Well, John." Adam took another pinch of snuff. "Ya see, I'm just diddling." Said it so good-naturedly that Bluber dropped the talk and began to tell about his experiences with "a hell of a woman in Mary's Hill." But stopped when a lantern bobbed near, yellow on Father's face.

Father lost no love over Bluber and took a cat-and-dog air when he came around. Testy and all his spines out, but got along with the thresherman. Had to. There wasn't another rig between here and Jenny's Peak to knock out our grain. They came near words though, over a half-bushel of oats. "Four hundred, the tally shows." Father was stubborn.

"Hell, yes, but I set the tally late. You had a couple of dumps in the box, by then."

"Not more'n a bushel; and that, all chaff, from the last threshing." Bluber looked ugly but they sliced the difference finally.

The rig clanked away in the morning and there was the emptiness where stacks had been. Father said, "Hitch up and take the plow to the shop. Lays need sharpening, and maybe the beam is out of true. Went kinda funny, in the corn patch." We plowed, or ranked up dry wood, heads bent against fall winds that shook the popples bare, and slipped into an extra jacket on mornings keen with the pinch of frost. The school bell wasted its tongue on air, for all of us, though Franz looked with a kind of yearning at the path along the hillside, where brambles were starting to erase the print of steps.

There would be other kids lugging water from a neighbor's pump this autumn, and other bodies arching the ironwoods to grass. But we were glad, in an odd way, when geese wedged under the clouds blackening for winter, that the harness of class and lesson was thrown off. Freedom of sorts, we thought, as we ranked out popple rails for fire cobs, and Fritzie dragged home a couple of springy birch-runners for the long sled. "Ought to zip down the hill, with these; go fast enough to sail right over the cliff, like a skier," he said. "Sure," I told him. "Try it, and smash your bones if you want to." He snickered and got the ax. Freedom of sorts. Though, I ask sometimes, what is freedom more than the exchange of one servitude for another?

Franz plowed most of the fields, straining at the corners against the pull of the lines, his body an acute angle with the earth. He came in one night with sweat marking white rivulets across his cheeks. The sun was a great fire beyond the hill, like a strawpile in flames back of the woods, burning the trees into dark skeletons of trunk and crooked limbs. He walked into the house, dusting his hat, and found Liliem there. She'd come to see Mother about pickling meat, while her father went to the Maises' for a plow. Though Fritzie smirked and said afterward it didn't fool nobody. Franz's cheeks tinged rust under the dirt. Liliem said in a hurry, "I'm just going. I see Father getting into the wagon."

"Is it because I'm here?" Franz asked, surprisingly. "If it is—"

"Franz." Liliem came to him, her smile tremulous. "Can I forget that day—Mother—" She paused a moment; then more firmly, "Nobody thought to do what you—I can't—" She put a hand to his cheek; fingered the scar while he stood dumb as a sheep; caught at her hands too late. She slipped through the door.

"Well, Dough-pan," snickered Fritzie. "Your neck's as good wrung as a rooster's. When a *she* begins coming to the house . . ." Franz swung up a pail and went for water; more to be alone for a moment than because water was needed; seeing that a full bucket stood near the stove.

Late-October rain fell early, freezing before it soaked into the ground. We hauled the corn and hay, and came inside with a wet-weather crick in our knees. After the first snowstorm slashed at the oaks on the ridge and whitened the blue of the tamaracks, Father nailed down the winter windows and put on the blizzard door. And in the yard and about the fields, knee-high with drifts, we plowed a crooked way and left what no man can escape—the imprint of himself; imperceptible, or blurred, or white-stone clear; perhaps in mud or sand, or on the silent face of stone, but unmistakably there, under the stars or sun. Inescapable. Man, the dust-creature. It runs in the mind that earth declares his comings and goings nowhere clearer than in snow. I'd watch Father and Franz break trail across a meadow, axes on their shoulders, and dark against the brightness; an arm's length near each other, but farther than ridges apart, too, I thought. Like sleigh runners going side by side, never in this world meeting naturally.

It was a deadly winter. There were mornings when the sun and his four dogs blazed with a fierceness that crinkled the eyes. Mr. Mais swore he tossed a dipper of water into the air and it came down crickly pieces of ice. High winds came and the Diemer hills were blown as clean of snow as a cat-licked saucer.

We trudged to the barn one morning to find frost on the cow's rumps and the cat with snowy whiskers. Fritzie called, "Help me bridle the horses. Got to rank out the oak logs before they snow under." Our breath hung like steam among the rafter cobwebs. I jabbed a fork down, and saw how the warm manure stuck to the icy metal. Franz unhooked the bridle, and blew on the bit to take the chill off, the iron growing white under his breath. But Fritzie muttered, "Pussyfoot," and jerked the other bridle between the mare's teeth. She flung back, trembling. Franz shut his eyes, and then caught at Fritzie's arm.

"How'd you like it, your tongue stuck to the bit?" he yelled, and lunged against him. Fritzie in a black fury reached for a length of tug. But Father opened the door with a cloud of warmth, and they growled away from each other, hate like a wall between them, rubbing against each other's grain with the blind antagonism of sheep-killing dogs.

Winter crept over the hollows sluggish as an angleworm, and in no more hurry to measure its length. We heard about Walter—from the Maises, who got it in Mary's Hill. He found a job farm-handing on the other side of the flats. Not doing well. Work hard and little to be had. We went about with a kind of heaviness in us; sorry; except Father. "Any of you want to try it?" He threw the words at us spitefully. "Go ahead. You can come sneaking home, after a while—tail between the legs."

Fritzie finished the long sled and was proud, until Matt Prinzing dragged his two-bob over—painted red and striped with black, screeching in beauty over the snow. "Peachy, huh?" Matt capered (more like a kid than a sixteen-yearer, Father grumbled). "Saturday night'd be good for the slide. Full moon and the hill—I'll be a two-toed bloodsucker if a goat can stick on that hill." His eyes shone. "I'm going up Too Far Lake way—get Teena Dorset. Want to come, Franz? We go past Liliem's place." Franz stained the color of old beet juice.

"Sure I'll go. But how'll Tinkla—"

"Oh, she can walk." Fritzie was impatient. "Only a little way."

At last it was settled. Matt was to bring the girls, since Father would never let us have the team, and Franz and he would take them home.

For a wonder, Father let us go without words, though he grumbled over fools with no more horse sense than to waste the night sliding. Less grouchy because Kloster wanted him to come sawing on Monday.

The hill was a sheet of smoothness. We brought the sky down with laughter, the night icy with cold and moon. A giant's fire of brush leaped in witch's flames, tossing the dark back over the cliff, dusky with the shadows of space. Franz slid with Liliem whenever he could, though Jonas rumbled like a pet bull. We skidded sometimes, striking a bump, and a prickly slash of panic tore through us; we'd hang for what seemed hours, with a kind of prayer in us: "Lord, if she goes over now—" until the runner hit solid footing. Tried it again, and felt the wind like cold wet sand against the face. Rode two deep, lying flat. We were clumsy with coats and extra pants, Tinkla in her brother's overhalls and plump as a pillow, but Liliem slender and willowy somehow in spite of her winter cloak. She twinkled, her eyes full of the red of fire and the moon, there beside me where the wood crackled and smoke spun, and we thawed the frost from wind-bitten fingers. She moved closer. I couldn't help asking, "Want a slide?"

"Let's," she said, tugging at my arm. "Franz asked me, but he won't mind. He's gone for firewood."

I swung the sled around. "Sit in front?"

"Let's go two deep." I felt her breath across my cheek as she lay prone along my spine, holding to my shoulders.

"Over she goes," I yelled. Somebody shouted—I heard Franz's voice, but the light along the icy slant blurred and we plowed into the darkness in front of us, swinging down as if on the end of a string, down, down . . . spraying up loose snow at the bottom. The sled eased into a drift. We lay for a moment laughing, as victors who have escaped the sword.

Franz had a sourish look when we came back, and said "No" loudly when Teena asked him for a ride; as if he were chasing cows; so that Teena shouted: "Franz is mad and I am glad— and I know what to please him . . . a bottle of ink to make him stink, and Liliem to squeeze him." But Liliem whispered, "Franz needs a stirring-up. Ask me to, again." I did, with more voice than I intended. Franz came over fast.

"I'm sliding this one."

"What's rubbing you raw?" I asked him.

"Nothing. But you sneak off when I'm lugging firewood—"

"Don't butt in," I told him, going aside. "You've had your chance all evening." He followed me. Like a pair of six-year-olds and maybe needing a slat across our butts, the way we wrangled. Little words, like spider lace on common days, but slivers moving under the hide now. It comes back this moment, clear and firm beneath the fingers of memory. The fire adding crimson to the anger on Franz's face; Liliem close to the circle of warmth, the rest choosing partners for "Fox and Geese" and not paying much heed to us in their chatter; and I with a foot on the long sled, its runners pointed downhill . . . Franz lashing out; my head suddenly numb . . . the crash as I hit the bobsled . . . the fire and the hill spinning, and moving faster, I wondered why, dazedly; shouts and a scream from far off. Then nerves knitted into one piece of fear flattening me into the wood . . . the cliff . . . I must roll, I must . . . the crash of bushes . . . a long falling. I kept saying, "Father mustn't know; dear Jesus, it wasn't Franz, not his fault." Wild horses tore at me then, and I went to pieces, only my tongue left, stone-heavy, but wanting to speak, and a star singing in the empty night. A thin melody dying. . . .

It grew clearer in a moment, the star and the song . . . or it may have been worlds away in time. I saw, as from the highest ridge, our room with Mother there and Father and many faces,

Franz with Tinkla beside him and Jonas, but Liliem nowhere seen. Suddenly I was within, curtains of mist around me, driven by a blunt necessity to speak. Father . . . he mustn't know; and there was something queer about me. Mother bent closer. I heard voices . . . Father wanting to know how it happened, and I knew I must speak, I must move. Jonas blurting out, "Guess Franz pushed him" . . . Franz cowering before Father and Father yelling, "So—you again—God damn you." I think I shouted; tore aside the veils and silence. "Don't hit him. Jonas lied. Slipped—fell—myself." But I couldn't hold back the fear and sweat inside me.

"Franz, Franz . . . I can't move—my legs." It is bleary now and dim. The awful look on his face; his dark head on the covers, not wanting to see, not wanting to hear, all his young manhood tight in his throat.

Part Two

WIND IN
THE EAST

1

THERE is that within us, hard with life, which is fiercer than the sternest will to say yes or no, however strong the desire; something deep under flesh and bone that keeps us shoulder-high above earth, almost like those roots arm-thick under sod, burrowing firmly and neighbor to the worm, which all unseen hold the tree skyward and lift branches for summer leaves. A part of our breath and blood, I guess, as toughness is part of leather, stubborn to decay. Otherwise the yearning to shut eyes and give in would come down on us like sleep, and be as hard to put off. Or so it seemed, in those years before Franz's twentieth birthday, and after. I remember them as something we fought through, like smallpox or scarlet fever, with hard breath and a scared prickling at our heels. Especially those first months. Hard for all of us, but a kind of agony for Franz.

The days were long—years between the cackling of the first hen up in the morning and the silence that came after Mother blew out the lamp. Years long. But the nights—endless in their slow dragging; the clock on the shelf beat out its faint asthmatic tick, nibbling the minutes out of the hours with no more haste than water drops drip-dripping in thaw weather; the rustling of the corn leaves up above, where Franz lay un·easily at rest; the room boxed in with silence so thick the blood started at the crash of an oak-stick settling in the lean-to wood-pile and left a pounding in the ears. There was loudness in the sawing grunch of a mouse setting teeth to pine splinters.

Afterward this became a part of me; as much as a nail on a finger. But during that first month, when I lay bedded down on a pile of old coats and a feather quilt, near the stove, it was as unreal as a nightmare. Months that were seared with the

heat of pain, and all the snows of winter not enough for coolness. Hour after hour, before they lugged the bed into the
lean-to and Franz's things with mine, I'd watch them—these
figures moving as in a smoke-filled room. Fritzie would bend
close and then dim away until only his voice was left: "Flopped
down, Jeppy did, I tell you. I wasn't more'n a yard away; saw
the whole shootin' match. Jonas—what he knows—" Even the
voice melted into nothingness, leaving me only a sense that I
ought to do something—tell them about Franz—too tired, now;
I'd do it tomorrow . . . tomorrow. Sometimes I'd hear Franz's
voice lifted high and pleading, but far away, so that I wondered
if he were down in the barn calling and it chore-time. "Stop
yelling," I'd try to shout. "I'll bring them—milk buckets are
clean and all." But nobody heard. More than once I'd half-
wake as one dazed from hot and fevered dreams, to find the
stove-light flickering under the trap door and him crawling
feet-first down the ladder, moving through feathers of red fire.
He'd bend over me, bringing with him the cold of the loft and
the smell of old clothes, his hands twisted until the knuckles
stuck out, the breath a harsh rasp in his throat. Minute-long,
he'd stay while the fire snapped in the stove. Once I felt his
hand on my knees; then he was gone and I heard the ladder
creak and in the wavering light saw his eyes like black buttons
and his lip caught in his teeth. Silence then.

And through the murk, Mother's quiet tones would come:
"Jeppy, drink; cool you off." I'd feel her near, even when
thought crumbled from me like frozen sand and wolves howled
in my skull; night and day slipping between her tired face and
the windowpanes. Often the dimness curtaining my lids grew
darker and I felt words moving sluggishly like heavy bubbles
deep inside me: "He didn't; Franz didn't." I wondered dully
whether they broke on my lips, knowing someway that Father
stood there, an axle-space away, watching. He never came
closer, nor put out a hand to unwrinkle a cover. Once I heard
low sounds as if he mumbled to himself; cursing, maybe, or

praying, I never made out. And often I didn't care, digging vainly for sleep, with nothing to stop the aching cry running along the nerves: "Move; you must move; even a toe." Sweat came with trying. After a while a sort of blankness lay heavy as a stoneboat over mind and body and the breath went out; the heart empty and still.

Some hours were clear, and what happened then remains as sharply cut in my memory as dead oaks black against moonrise. Mother would shake the last drops out of the arnica bottle and eye the cupboard with worry threading her face. "More liniment, somewhere; behind things, I guess; it gets away from me where, though." Franz would stomp in from woodcutting, his eyes shifting catlike from mine and sliding to the lower part of the bed where the quilts humped a little; his legs moving uneasily, until he turned suddenly and stood near the stove, as if he needed to look elsewhere. "Gets in the bones, January does," he'd mutter, half to himself; and the cold that stiffened his mackinaw flaps came out, sweet and clean, mixed with the smell of popple chips new-cut. But he'd go soon; down to the barn or the pasture yard and stay hours; restless, and the last one in after milking, until Fritzie fussed, "What's got you, Dough-face? Lice in your underpants?" and laugh sharply at his own words. The fiddle strings cracked themselves loose on the bridge, untouched now, though more than once Franz made as if to put resin on the bow, but let the cover down slowly and headed for the door.

Father's jaw took on an extra angle of grimness, those days, working about the place or riding saw carriage at the Klosters'. He'd go off sawing for a week with curt words when he left: "Hans got his nose in the pot; Hans can get it out again." Or: "Got a pile extra to do, this winter." His eyes would frost as they jumped to Franz. "You. Keep your fists out of your pants, and move. Off the fiddle, too." He said little to anyone about the sledding party; took it like castor oil, Fritzie said; holding the bitterness inside with a quietness that was worse than cursing. Once he turned slowly, after dinner, and looked at Mother where she waited, holding his heavy overshoes. I think she knew what he had in mind to say, remembering how her eyes lost their color; knowing that he burned to throw the dirt of blame in her face, and make her feel that for this also she was at fault. He laughed in a sticky way and then almost roughly grabbed the overshoes, and went into the lean-to. In the silence I heard the table squeak as Franz steadied himself against it. I had the scratchy feeling again that I ought to know the why and wherefore of this but couldn't put my hand on it. Mother stood for a moment, still, as if a strange and dreadful load, forgotten for a time, had been shoved back on her shoulders. Her lips trembled and she half-whispered: *"Nein, nein, nicht so"*; then hid her face over a pot she began to scrape. Franz went to her, a kind of wildness pulling at his lips. He touched her arm but she shook her head. We had this, then, to worry in our craw.

Even when the neighbors, good will broad on their faces, came with a coffeecake or a bottle of liniment wrapped in an old pillow, Father had a resentful twist on his face. "Neighbor's truck; don't want it. Buy my own." He scratched his neck irritably. "Snoopers, the whole bunch. Eyes in back and in front, they have." He glowered, fastening a buckle. "Can't let a man alone." But they came, stumbling across the cleared acres where the brown stitches of the corn rows ran crookedly over the white fields; or drove in sleds, the bells jingle-jongling across ridge and valley long before the horses swept up in a shower of steam and snow; and at last Father accepted them, but with grumbling. The men stood with their hands in their pockets and chins lowered, stiff and uneasy, and as wordless as Father; the women gabby with tongues unhooked and shaking out the skirts of talk, but with lowered voice and henlike cluckings for me. Mother smiled, strangely wistful, listening to the remedies they had, all never-fails. A mustard-and-flaxseed plaster from Mrs. Hukelpoke, guaranteed to kill any pain; skunk oil from Mrs. Mais—"It cured Grandpa's lame back overnight," she chirped, and left a can full. Jars and jugs of stuff, spirits of this and essences of that, older than Adam, and about as useful. Mother tried them all, though, Franz helping her, his hands eager and somehow pleading; scared when they rolled me over and I yelled out not to touch me; the bones sharp in the flesh. The plasters did no more than half-skin me, and the house, stinking of skunk oil, smelled over forty acres. Until even Franz had to admit that all the stuff might as well be sloo muck, for all the good it did. The teeth of pain still gnawed, grating like a piece of steel on stone, eating away calmness and sanity, so that one longed to scream into black madness. There were days when tears would have been joy, had there been tears left to cry; when even the kettle rubbling and the swish of Mother's broom were sand grinding into my head. There was raging helplessness in the way Franz took the bottles to the scrap pile and broke them, separately and with words under the breath.

Mother was scrubbing the lean-to the afternoon Mrs. Bauer came over, with her baby bundled in layer on layer of wraps like a cabbage to keep out the cold. *"Ach,* don't stop moppin', Minna, 'count of me. I just let Tinkle keep an eye on the kids, and come; long as Pa's going over to the Maises' anyway." She settled herself firmly in a chair and rocked. "Run out of hay, and he wants to buy their stack—up in the west sloo, you know." Full to her gills with talk and advice, she was. "Hot water, that's good for a hurt back. Sweat the ache out, I say." She bulged like an overstuffed sausage. "You soak him, Minna. So hot, the water, you can just tip a finger in, but not burn. And then—" The baby yowled and began to kick. "Little hungry sack wants his mush, huh?" She fished a cracker from a pocket, chewed it carefully, and took the paste in a white ball from her mouth. "Open, now, Zacheria," she coaxed and fed the baby with her finger. Mother watched, scrub brush in hand, looking as if she wanted to put out arms. "Lard and turpentine," Mrs. Bauer went on; "gets the soreness

[123]

off; good for cold, too, and— Stop spitting around, Zacheria."
She chewed another cracker. "Brought you a bottle; made it
myself—flaxseed and a spoon of mint. Best way, though,
Minna—" She hitched her rump and the chair creaked. "You
get yourself three *Schimmel* hairs—not just from a gray horse,
like Albert Mais's boy got; but a real *Schimmel*—white hair from
his tail. Course, you can laugh"—her voice boomed, then
lowered to hoarse throatiness. "Put 'em in the turpentine, the
hairs; midnight before you rub it on, and say *'Vater Unser'*
backward—" Her eyes, bright as a woodchuck's, narrowed as
Franz trundled in, slop pails banging from his hands. A laugh
gurgled in her throat. *"Ach;* sure got yourself in everybody's
mouth, Fränzie, you have." Franz let the smile slip from his
face.

"You mean—"

"Course, I don't believe it; anyway, not more than a quarter of
it."

"Jonas—he—" The pails made a tinny noise like an echo
after his words.

"Tinkle sure sailed into him, other day. Told him off, all
right." Mrs. Bauer angled another cracker out of her pocket.
"Said she was right by you. So did Etta Rippey—Mildred's
girl, you know; and— Course, the Blubers and Mrs. Pilversack; *ach,* such people, sure try to raise a smell."

"Fränzchen." Mother came close, as if to stand between him
and what she feared in Mrs. Bauer's talk . . . the hints and
nods when neighbors came to spend an hour, and the shakings
of the head—like prickly hedges around her and Franz, and
no path opening.

"I had it from Jenny Sperry this morning." Mrs. Bauer
rattled on. "They came by, you know, with a load of wood—
oak chunks for the Pastor; the way *he* wastes good oak wood—
ach, say I. Well, Jenny says—she's coming down again; did
you notice? Her seventh; such a shame; ought to be horse-
hided, that man of hers; her with six now, and not one big

enough for long pants." I saw Mother turn her head, this way, that way, slowly as if looking for escape, holding the brush, her fingers curled in the bristles. "Well, Jenny she says Hilda Pilversack told her, and she got it straight from Mrs. Bluber herself." Franz had a trapped sort of look, wanting to speak and yet afraid; afraid, seeing how Mother stood there bowed and sagging, as if a feather would crumple her to the knees; Mrs. Bauer, unworried as a pumpkin head, meaning no harm, we knew inside us, but wide open, ears and eyes to tell otherwheres what she saw and heard. "Well, Jonas said you boys got in a fight and Franz—" That which was more than fever and pain broke over me in a hot sweat. From this cickle-cackle Franz should be spared, if I could do it, what there was left of me. Without knowing how, I found myself shouting over Mrs. Bauer's voice: "A lie; a dirty stinking lie." I tried to get a shoulder up but buckled, and wondered that the roof didn't fall and crush my words along with me. Mother came with cool hands. "Don't, Jeppy; you're hot again."

Mrs. Bauer rocked comfortably. "*Ach,* Jeppy; talk is slow, but it gets big when it gets around." Franz made as if to speak and didn't, letting his silence say more than a Bible of words. This we had between us, unspoken of, yet as understood as if written in black and sealed with hands.

Then we saw Father standing by the lean-to door, ax in fist, ready to begin sharpening; silent and watching us; as if what he heard was what he had expected to hear; spitting on the whetstone before he took sure, unhurried strokes across the helve edge . . . over, back, over, back. Mrs. Bauer fumbled among her things, her voice no more than a mutter; saying she'd better hurry, and be ready when Pa came by. Father moved away; we heard the slip-slop of the stone in the lean-to. I watched Franz pour swill into the buckets and guessed someway how he longed to jump fences, run wild and away, yet dared not, marrowed with doubt; and I thought, in a half-crazy moment, that soon now a thread would snap and the shadows under the table laugh out the fear they hid in their darkness; but knew also that the minute would never come. Not with a bed unmade or a foal half-born and needing help. For the heart does not break, being flesh, but the mind does—our thought pulled and stretched tight like an elastic, thinning to weak and dangling strands, insensitive at last even to hope. And afterward, in a kind of darkness, memory, uncertain and groping, comes back like an idiot stranger to haunt the grim and empty houses of the mind.

We stumbled in the dull plodding of routine; Franz trailing Fritzie, knee-over in snow, to the south hills, ax on his shoulder, and coming back with holes in his knitted gloves that kept Mother late under lamplight with needle and darning wool; a coltish swing to the ax, Fritzie said; as if Franz sought forgetfulness in splintering trees or ripping up hazel-brush; hours too full of ache to care.

Evenings when Father was away, Mother read to us, stories of the Bible, and we forgot the snow swirled into banks, lying over the weeds in the level space by the barn; forgot the drifts in the fields and along the shore, so crusty and hard that the ice on Long Lake was smothered to distant growls. She held the book on her lap: a thick volume, scrolled with gilt and full of pictures, a dozen to a chapter, of the torments laid up for the wicked. There was the Flood with a mother buried in angry water, only an arm visible, shoving a child above her higher on the rock of the last mountaintop—a slanting bit of solidness where a crowd fought with a lion for space and the child clung to a stump; the ark on a dreary sea, Noah on the deck, his hands to his eyes the better to see his old neighbors. Franz used to look at the child's face a second, shivering, before he flipped the page. There was a scene of Judgment Day, God on the throne, smiling at the saved, and the Devil, mouth crooked and torn with glee, rushing off with the damned and throwing them like cordwood sticks into the flames. The rich man squirming in a fire, his body twisted and his face cracked with awful pain, begging for a finger tip of coolness. Franz worried his shoelaces into threads, one time; broke out fiercely, "All hurt and tears and people crying," as if he had mulled this over for days.

I remember that evening because of what Mother read. A night of quiet after storm, cold snapping the solid meat of trees and the thawed places on the window incredibly black beside the white of frost; the day's pitchfork and dishrag put up for morning and Fritzie snoring gulpily in the lean-to. Mother turned to Luke with sadness in her, Franz at her knees, eyes up at her, wide and dark with longing. A kind of fear squeezed his heart, I think, the way his fingers touched her hands, seeing the thin shadows lengthening along the wrinkles in her face. "No laughing and fun left," he muttered; "not even in the Bible." She laid the book open. "Old already, Fränzchen, you are," she said. "Old inside—here." She fumbled at his breast pocket before she went on, her soft voice mixing with the crackle of popple in the stove. " 'And Jesus answered and said unto them, Go and shew John again these things which ye do hear and see: the blind receive their sight and the lame walk—' " Her voice sagged and dimmed to a whisper. " 'The lame—' " She stopped, held by something she couldn't put away. Franz sat cross-legged, still. But I remember how the lightning from the cracked stove flickered and flared in the shadows of the ceiling; and how Mother sat bowed, Franz beside her, the book slipping crookedly on her lap.

2

Spring came late that year, weeks late. January storms, undaunted by thaws or the slow lift of the sun, lashed themselves through February and a good piece into March. Trees knocked with cold and the hollows at night echoed with the rifle-fire of popping wood. The windows in the barn were furry with frost, inch-thick, Franz said; the edges tunneled with round black holes large as a little finger, where winds, screaming through breaks no larger than a hen's eye, drilled their way clear and into the stalls, turning themselves into spurts of steam in the warm horsy air.

I'd shiver, watching Franz rush over the step, his chin blue and his fingers knuckly with chill. He'd peel off layers of old jackets and sometimes look as if all the covers on the cot opposite the ladder, where Mother slept, wouldn't be enough to thaw the ice from his bones. But there was the snugness of a cocoon about this room, the kitchen stove turning solid oak into warmth genial to the blood. And in the lean-to the jugbellied heater crackled half the night, scorching Father and Fritzie where they snored together. Warmth to the rafters, we said, though there was little for the loft. But when northwesters whistled under the eaves and snow dusted over the sill, not even the fire could keep the water pails in the corner unfrozen. I'd wish myself in the loft then, burrowing beside Franz and adding my body heat to his, against the cold.

Father was away much of each week, coming back to whip the team to Mary's Hill on Saturdays for the salt and flour Mother needed. He rode in a lather from the Klosters' one afternoon in the middle of the week when a cow broke into the feed-box and bloated. He plowed through the snow, ready to blame someone. "Sick in the house and sick in the barn," he growled in exasperation, and ordered a rope and the sticking knife. Franz came in after a while, tired and grayish, his hands dirty from holding the cow and his mind bitten, I guess, by Father's shortness and the way he had sunk the knife, the blade falling in a certain spot between the cow's ribs, and the flesh opening like a rotten squash; the air pushing up in bubbles. Franz looked at me strangely, his thoughts spoken aloud to himself. "A sick cow; that brings him home, all right." With a lunge of the arm, he broke a thumb through the loop of his coat, as if in his thought he were standing up against Father.

On town days Father was usually in a hurry, coming into the house grumpy and sparing no words because a strap or a hame didn't hang to suit his fancy. He'd haul out his blue pants and shirt with no more than a look at me; but he let Mother know when she missed a speck of cow-dirt in cleaning his Sunday shoes; and make her get out rag and scraper. Once he brought a bottle of liniment for me. Red stuff and like fire to touch, so that the skin mottled and swelled where Mother rubbed it on. But it didn't get me out of bed overnight, as he'd hoped, I guess. Thereafter he left medicines in town, and took the half that remained in the bottle down to the barn.

The cold kept no one from church; except Mother, and even she went, leaving Franz or Fritzie to watch the house, especially at first. In summer we used to drive, taking the road, but in winter we'd often walk when cold lashed down, following the short cut through the woods, a Sunday quiet below as we shuffled along, but the air above full of the crash and bone-rattle of limbs, where the wind pulled at the treetops.

I'd see them go off, Franz taller now and with the beginning of a furrow between his eyes; the confirmation suit too small, tight as a glove on his muscle and bone; the red-and-green mackinaw gay, although the front never did return to its first brightness; not after the Sunday at milking time when Franz hung it on a nail and the heifer licked it wet. But it was alive with color beside the somber black that Father wore. All three plunged across the open space of the field. Father was stiff and bent forward a little and dark against the snow; Franz trotted beside Fritzie, who twisted in his best clothes and clawed at his collar, tight as a rope about his neck. Sometimes Mother went, faint pink glowing under the peach-fuzz white of her cheek, glad to let the stove-poker rest for once; her dress faded and sewed over until it was all seams, she said, but pretty still because she walked in it.

Before the clock struck one, they'd be back, cold, eager and alive with news, Fritzie strutting his chest because he sat upstairs in the gallery now, among the "fellers"; Franz tickled over something Tinkla had whispered, now that deep snow kept Liliem a ridge away from songbook and sermon; and laughing to himself while he clattered the plates around the table. We talked the morning over, adding to it other Sundays we remembered . . . about the time the organist began a funeral hymn at a baptism and played half the first verse, subdued buzzes around her but no singing, until one of the deacons told her in a loud whisper and she stopped in a groan of bass chords . . . about the Trotzweg boys, in knee pants and proud with button shoes, their bodies squirming with the seven years' ginger beside the father; until the Pastor bent his head after the first prayer. Then the two slid under the bench, pulling hair, and came up, eyes swelling and noses bloody, the whole congregation turning in the seats at the sound of blows; so that the Pastor, his beard almost straight out like feathers, changed his text with a bony finger and made reminder of the children of Bethel who had mocked the prophet and the "she-bears" that came forth and "tare forty and two" of them; although Mr. Trotzweg said mildly after church, "Kids can *ja* fight if they want to; good for their fists. But not when the Pastor is in the pulpit." Sunday things we could chew on the week after.

Franz had a grin when we spoke of Tinkla. "She's gonna crawl right into your underpants, alongside you," Fritzie told him. "Way she looks at you."

"Don't mind," Franz said, with boldness he hoped was like Matt Prinzing's; but he got red. Mother looked at him, quietly, and he hung his head.

"Leff Sperry's taking her; granary dance, at Klosters'."

"Ain't so." Franz came up, uneasy.

"Ain't, huh?" Fritzie's laugh was edgy. "Leff told me; himself."

"She's—she's too young; a kid." Franz shifted, finding himself in for more than he bargained.

"Well, she's confirmed," Fritzie said. "And a girl that's confirmed, she's old enough to say it, whether she wants to go with a feller."

"There is Sunday school." Mother spoke up, taking neither

side. "Another year; that much, the Pastor says." Fritzie muttered about the Pastor and his ideas. But Franz scraped a chair
aside loudly, not even half pleased, without knowing exactly
why, I guess, at the thought of Tinkla in Leff Sperry's arms;
wishing tomorrow were church and he could ask Tinkla about
it. For us, church was more than a place in which to learn about
the Ten Commandments and how to turn the slapped cheek for
more pain on the other side of the mouth. It was a meeting-
house for people, those near by and those who lived the length
of a ridge apart and weeks away from talk . . . Alb Hukelpoke,
renting in the valley beyond the Maises', new there this year,
bringing a sack of oats he'd borrowed from Heinie Grosbeck,
who farmed a ten-acre patch the other side of Too Far Lake . . .
Mr. Dunkel, grabbing the shoulder of a man from Turkey
Hollow: "When you gonna pay me my money, Hermann?"
Hermann, wheeling his size-eleven shoes slowly around, saying,
"Pay you?" his forehead in wrinkles to remember; Mr. Dunkel,
getting mad, "For cutting corn; two years ago; rotten stuff it
was, too"; Hermann, digging a pint-size fist into his Sunday
pants and bringing out a tenpenny nail and four staples: "What's
in the pocket is here; yours and welcome," turning away from
Mr. Dunkel with a shrug.

Mrs. Bauer pulled at Mother's arm the next Sunday after
services, Fritzie reported; fretting in the fat comfortable way
she had, though really anxious. "If he's bad hurt—Jeppy—a
doctor could give him stuff—"

It wasn't hard to figure out how Father answered her: "What
for?" stopping her in her tracks.

"Tinkle—and I too—we—a doctor—" She must have become uncertain under his stare.

"Kill him—like Arnold Kluth's brother, last fall." He el-
bowed his way, Mother and Franz at his heels—"and just let
Old Lady Bauer stand there," Fritzie ended, not without malice,
I thought.

Franz came home with a slump that was more than a week's

[131]

tiredness in his shoulders. He took down the box where Mother kept liniment and plasters, and pried at them, as if wondering whether healing had escaped from the red and white messes. They were the best on our ridges; better than any doctor, we said, shaking up Old Man Hukelpoke's liniment, homemade, and steaming at the oak-plug cork, so full of bite it was. To be sure, the Youngdahls, over near Turkey Hollow, down with the pox, we heard, had called Dr. Allbauch; from Mary's Hill, ten miles away, and that meant five dollars; but as Fritzie said, they were newcomers and didn't know better.

Franz shoved the medicine box up and came, looking down at me, his eyes hunted and all but lost in worry. "Jeppy, I—" he started out, shoving a toe squarely on the bed of coats. I heard the cloth whisper against leather. He swept a hand across his face, fiercely, as if brushing away cobwebs holding back what he wanted to say. "Jeppy, if one had words to say it— what hangs inside—" He blinked out of the window as if he didn't trust his eyes; got into his chore pants after a while of silence and shut the door behind him. He wobbled down the path, I saw through the low window next to me, until he came to the sled in a crooked drift, a runner broken from crashing stone and sticking above the snow. He kicked at it, wildly, with a sudden vehemence; lifted it in a cloud of snow, shoulder-high, and hurled it against the woodpile. He trudged along, knocking the brittle edge of snow, as if the hard footway were too narrow for him, or he walked unseeing.

It pricked in his brain, I think, whatever it was that crawled in him, days when a fork or an ax wasn't enough to keep his legs squared with earth; days when March dissolved in slush, the yard and the roads swimming at noon but slippery with ice at night. Fritzie began talking about getting the horses shod. The sun, warm in the south corners, cleared the barn windows of frost— the first time that winter. From morning on, the chickadees whimpered "Teeber, teeber"—"springtime," Mother said it meant. But doubt quavered in their plaintive notes; blizzards still wallowed beyond the ridge cutting a ragged slant into the northern sky. So Mr. Mais said, talking from the load of manure he was spreading next to our line fence. He had seen a reddish circle around the moon the night before, seven stars in it—a sign for those who counted things over twice. It meant a blast in the air, and that before the week went out.

Franz milked cows and slopped pigs with a kind of fierce tightness; spent evenings with Mother hunched over *The Confidential Family Doctor,* hoping to page out a remedy. His finger chased the kinky lines diagraming the body, with red dots for veins, and a brownish-looking mass like an uncooked blood sausage, which, the book plainly showed, represented the stomach of a drunkard, eaten by the fire of alcohol. Near by on the same page were the smoke-rotted lungs of "a victim of that fiendish and Devil-inspired dissipation, tobacco-using," the book said. Columns were wasted on toe-aches and cures for leprosy and treatments for Asiatic fever and Australian snake bite; but little for what we had, at home. Franz would scrog his shoes noisily, impatient, but Mother read on, her hand firmly clamped on the quarter of the book marked in red letters "Confidential: For the Married only and those seeking Congenial Spouses." Nothing for young ones to know, Mother told us, severeness rubbing out most of her smile, although we felt it wasn't far off. Not that Franz gave a fig about the Confidential. Years before, one day, we had pulled down the shoe box where she hid the book and read doctoring in the loft; by candlelight and with crabbed brows over the big words. There was a puzzled sort of wonder in learning that "a hard mattress, preferably of cotton and stiffened with hair, and linen sheets, are highly conducive to connubial bliss and felicity, especially on the wedding night"; a breathless though guilty pleasure in knowing how to tell, long before the stork flew by, whether the expected baby would be boy or girl; knowledge that was "indispensable to prospective fathers and mothers," we read. And a whole section about "insidious and shameful secret vice," with photographs, one of a young man who looked as if he needed a barber and a shave more than a doctor, but who, we saw, was a "pitiful and hapless victim; the parents of this young man ought to thank God if their boy escapes the dread corridors of the lunatic asylum: a dire example of the kind of man no decent girl will marry." We clapped the book to, feeling as if we had listened to the men in the blacksmith shop tell dirty stories; burning to our fingers with curiosity and conscious, too, for the first time, I think, of our bodies as more than flesh and bone; the dark and fathomless currents that ramped under our hides, stirring us to a queer sort of uneasiness. Franz watched for weeks to see on the faces of our neighbors the marks of "the unnatural and lustful scourge." But that was long ago, seeming longer than it really was, with all that lay between, heaping up our days and nights; far and away from Mother and Franz over the doctor book, these March nights, Franz slapping the page and getting up: "Nothing there; might as well look in the Montgomery Ward catalog." Even Mother left chapter forty-five—"The latest medicinal advice on aches and sprains"—and gave in.

We counted the days of April a month too soon, Father muttering: "Frost'll be out of the manure pile, top layers, long now." And Franz was ready to peel off his winter underwear. The sun, stubby of shadow at noon, unfastened the snow on the roof. It rumbled down one day, in a rush that rattled the dipper in the bucket. Icicles lengthened ring by smaller ring to poker points, opaque as a frosted eye. They'd hang beyond the window glass, barring the sun, rows of them; like stiff white carrots, it occurred to me; the tip of each brightening to a silver drop, wheeling with specks of rainbow, fading with each drip but glowing again a moment after.

Franz tapped them one morning, lightly, with a finger, and nodded that each had a tune, the short high, the long, low; hearing melodies we were deafer than stone to, with our ears lifted for house and barn noises. Fritzie yelled at him: "Can't find your way to the barn, huh? Get corn down for the cows; chop ice." Franz slouched off with the ax. The path slanting to the watering trough was hoof-packed deep in snow; an icy chute down which the cows stepped like cats, mornings. They plunged to their quarters with swiftness sometimes, their hind feet thrust almost ahead of the front. He gouged the ice up, lifting his head to say: "Need a machine for this; to chop the ice."

Fritzie's laughter shrilled to the eaves. "The way you moon around, Dough-face, ice'll melt and run, 'fore you get your ax down." His grin sharpened. "What you gonna do, someday— with a farm?" Franz threw the ax into a corner, and went to the ladder. "Think wheat'll sprout with a fiddle bow?" Fritzie's voice followed him into the hayloft. "Monkeying around, and work thicker'n hair on a dog."

Fritzie came in at breakfast laughing to tell us about it, Franz sullen and tight-lipped; bristling inside him, yet not knowing how to answer back; sure of himself, I guess, in the hour of forgetfulness when the fiddle lay under his chin, or he leaned head to catch a filament of beauty, spun out God knows where or from what. Rock-sure. It was in the lift of his shoulders, the twin shine in the well of his eyes, the cry torn from the strings. But it was harder, mountain-hard, to say in the cool breath of an afterthought what voices spoke out of earth. Father, home on a weekday, scooped up the last drops of coffee, Franz in his eye. But he put the spoon down carefully, as though it were a guard on his mouth. A time for iron on the hoof, he ventured, pushing back his cup. "Fritzie, get the mares to Wibart's today; shoes on them." He watched the horses plop-plop across the yard when Fritzie came riding, the other horse on tether. "Corn barrel's empty again, Franz," he said; "get your husking hook on a go."

Fritzie came in that night, stiff in his legs from riding. "Old Wibart shuttled around, all right—six teams to shoe." He poured water and all but dived in, to wash. Father, his knife slanted, drew long kindling splinters from a dry popple piece, his face in shadow. Franz, stewing over a rip in his pants, squeaked his chair. "Everybody out with horses, seems like—Jonas Bluber, too, with his pa's bays." Fritzie groped for a towel. I wondered why the fire lashed out in crackles suddenly and Mother stirred a pot with softness. "The Klosters came driving, and a man I didn't know—Tetzlauf, guess they called him. All jawing about dances and sledding parties—"

"It's the ice—this thaw weather." Mother broke in, not wanting to hear. Franz eased into stiff silence. But Fritzie had his head down and wouldn't stop.

"Learned him to shut his teeth—Jonas, the old wide-mouth." Father stopped, his head up. Fritzie rubbed his face. "Asked him, in front of everybody, how he came to see so much—him on the other side of the fire." I was weak with wanting to laugh—Fritzie, as ready to trust anyone as a weasel, but greedy for his share of that night's excitement, now that everybody else had sliced off and claimed a part. He nodded, made man with his own two hands. "I sure put a curl in his hair."

"Enough of tongue-wanging for one night." Father pitched the kindling behind the stove, and straightened up, anger in the set of his shoulders. "Laugh over me; that's what they do." Hard anger that came with taking everything as personal to himself. What was in his mind, those days, when the lever of the saw carriage thudded in his hands, and the logs screamed as they shivered into boards, we didn't know. Not then. That hour was saved for us, but most of all for Franz.

3

March was springing on his haunches, fixing to blow out with roaring, when Father, back from Mary's Hill, said: "Butcher, on Monday, before real warm comes. Get the pig hooks ready, kids; and the skinning knives." He still called us kids, as if we needed a safety pin to hold the front of our pants together; blind to what his eyes saw: Fritzie as tall as Father, and Franz measuring up to Fritzie's ears; lean but with more strength bunched on his bones than the slack of a trouser leg or a sleeve indicated. It cut no ice with Father. We were more expensive in potatoes and shoe leather, perhaps, growing older; but when everything was counted up we were still his young ones, to be told and not heard.

"I saw Alb Hukelpoke." Father unhooked his Saturday over-halls. "He'll come; and Mais will." Fritzie was already piling odds at a cupboard drawer, grubbing for a knife; but Franz took a long breath, as if bracing himself against the black kettle and the pig's squeal . . .

They had a fire roaring in the yard, handily near the pump, an hour before the two neighbors came on Monday; knotted ropes to the heavy limbs of the oak by the chicken coop. Father stayed to tell them what he wanted done, and went. Too busy sawing this year to take care of his own butchering.

The yard stirred with movement that day, as if forty instead of four split wood and filled the kettle; Mr. Mais dumped ashes into the barrel—"makes the water stiffer," he said; Alb Hukel-poke honed an edge on his sticking knife and tested its keenness with a hair he yanked from behind his ear, the hair falling in two pieces from the whetted blade. "Sharper'n a cat's knuckles." He tossed the knife into the air, the steel whirling end over end, the point a blaze of sharpness; caught it by the handle, easily, grinning. Franz drew back, his arm up, and even Mr. Mais couldn't keep still. "Fool kid's playing—man as old as you are. Never learn till you slice off a finger."

"Aw sheets!" Alb kicked into the snow. "Sharper she is, the easier she's to catch." He flipped the knife beside the others. "Well, chase the old sow around." A tough and low-shouldered man, Alb Hukelpoke, forty-five or thereabouts, and good for fifty more, he bragged; face as brown as the tobacco he shot be-tween his teeth, and with a head of thin hair, short and kinked over, like the bristles of an old clothesbrush. The best tenor in the hills at shindandies, they said, when he got in heat with a dozen snorts of whisky; and a tolerable baritone, though somewhat flat, on Sundays, leading what choir we had, at Christmas and funerals; a good eye with a rifle and an ear for the fiddle, but the best pigsticker this side of Jenny's Peak.

By the flip end of the afternoon, they strung the second pig up, white and faintly pink against the dark skin of trees, hanging beside the steer, which still quivered along the red muscles. The iron hooks were black under the tendons of the legs, swinging the animals clear of dogs or wolves that sometimes came, slat-ribbed with hunger, to claw at the oak where the meat froze, or lap at the blood spilt and caking in the snow. All done but the tail, Mr. Mais said, splashing the last of the hot water. Franz ran into the house once, arm streaming, his blood mixed with the steer's, to bandage a cut. The cows bellowed in the yard, mad-dened by the smell of raw blood; pawed snow over their backs and rumbled. Until Fritzie drove them away with a club, and, coming back, shouted, "Lunch is on the table."

They came in to eat, their overshoes loud on the step; looked at me as they would at a colicked horse or a heifer with milk fever—with a kind of pity at the waste of muscle and bone. Mother dropped the lid of the coffeepot, flustered at so many menfolk, and she alone, too. Hardly decent. Franz pecked at his *Kaffeekuchen,* not hungry, his nose full of the smell of scorched hair, but the rest stuffed their mouths, slices of bread with butter and cranberry jelly crowded in, four bites to a slice, Alb Hukel-poke making one in three. "Better fiddle us a tune, first, 'fore we dirty our hands again, Franz," he said, pouring milk for a second cup.

Franz shook his head, not to be coaxed. "Finger's cut."

"Aw sheets!" Alb swallowed coffee with disgust, paying no heed to Franz's quick look. "Mosquito scratch. Where's your guts?" Then looked at Mother, sheepishly grinning. She was listening to Mr. Mais's saying, "All summer; hay and harvest, guess."

"What's hay and harvest?" Alb broke in.

"Prinzing. His woman's coming down with a kid and—"

"Cat's knuckles; again?" Alb bit a cookie as if the stork were a stranger at his house.

Mr. Mais snorted in his cup. "You talk—you with six under your feet."

"Good for another six, too, by God." Alb winked at Franz. Mother hurried about, ruffled at this men's talk, and before us boys, at that.

"Well." Mr. Mais let it go. "Prinzing, now—tough, his woman going to be down sick—at harvest time, like that."

"Aw sh—" began Alb, but stopped, an eye on Mother. "Hire himself a girl, can't he?"

"Going to, he is." Mr. Mais got out his cut-plug. "Needs one, too; the Schoen girl is coming—Lily, or what they call her." Mother answered: "Her pa gets along without her, I s'pose; his sister there to do houseworking."

I wonder the chair back held, Franz leaned against it so hard, his face red and the scar dark. "Liliem—coming to the Prinzings'—"

"Yerp." Alb piled his saucer high on his cup. "Hired girl, Mais says. I'd believe him if he wasn't such a liar."

"Told me himself, Prinzing did," Mr. Mais started wrath-fully, but Franz chipped in, not able to hold himself, "All summer?" and sidled in his chair, so that Hukelpoke grunted, "What you so red for—face and ears? Just been scrubbed?" Fritzie chimed in, "It's a *she*, he's thinking about—Yellow Head." But Franz was lost to their gabbing, drifted in the what-might-be—Liliem at the Prinzings', only the Diemer hills and a patch of black oaks away—twenty minutes by the clock, walk-ing as a man does after a plow; five by crow flight. Liliem who carried gold like candleshine in her hair. There must have been a small patch of singing in him, that minute, among those gall-blistered days crusting the heart like a sore; a small measure, perhaps, gill-sized, but squeezed behind to give him elbowspace to sing again, the heart needing as much room as the body; more, knowing the cavern it is sometimes. It was a moment to hold to himself among the cows, milking, or splitting wood; even after the Pastor spread a witch's tail of shadow across it. I had an odd notion, watching him tweak the oilcloth in humps, that his face lighted with mirth when he spoke of Tinkla, all the laugh-furrows showing; but at the thought of Liliem his lips pulled at the corners, something knotting itself inside him, and his eyes crinkled into vagueness, mixed up with fiddle music, I guess, and a yellow shine on a dark collar.

Mr. Mais had just asked for "half a drop of coffee, Mrs. Vild-vogel," when a fist pounded on the door and the Pastor stood on the step. He stalked in, his hat ahead of him on an extended arm; a black bag in the other hand. Franz, torn from wool-gathering, half-rose, uneasy but hiding it. This might have been *Biblische Geschichten* day and the Pastor weaving down the aisle, switch at an angle, because the name of the third man in the fiery furnace ran with the love *Lied* in Franz's mind, and he couldn't answer straight.

Mr. Mais near split his pants, shoving the cut-plug into his pocket. Hukelpoke, scratching the smooth place among the whiskers, planned his next word. Mother uncreased her apron with nervous hands, and asked the Pastor to a chair and coffee. He shook his head, his greetings snippy; grim this afternoon, his horse lamed in a fall, he told us, and he without a team to visit his sick lambs; although the Toffmanns had given him a ride this far. He hinted broadly that he expected one of us to take him back; so many horses without halter in the pastures these days, before spring work.

Mr. Mais coughed and the Pastor looked him through and through. "Not well, last Sunday, were you, Bruder Mais?" His voice rubbed into the ears. Mr. Mais choked, mumbling finally, "Had to go to Mary's Hill—get a pony—"

"For Sunday night," the Pastor shut him off. "A round one." Mr. Mais nodded. "I aimed to have—"

"*Ja.*" The Pastor nodded. "About three gallons, that pony; with a faucet."

"I—huh?" Mr. Mais choked again, seeing what the Pastor meant. "I mean—"

The Pastor left him digging for his handkerchief; went on carefully. "*Walzers* and polkas on Saturday nights—a pony shines there. But Sunday mornings—" His eyes snooped around and landed on the black hide fiddle case lying on the shelf. The way his mittened hand curled made Franz scrape up in his chair. The Pastor looked at him as though he were a strange pig in the yard, a lift of a smile twitching at his mouth. Franz sank back.

"I see; the fiddle still. Godly music not in you, but tunes of the Devil and—"

"Aw sheets!" exploded Alb Hukelpoke in a burst, holding all he could; then went to slivers as the Pastor swung his beard like a pointer at sin.

"A clean mouth, Bruder Hukelpoke, is becoming to a child of God," he preached, a text of a sermon. He heard Alb growl into his shirt sleeve, "Use soap and water on your own tongue, then," but he only showed his teeth in a broken row above his beard. Let him wait; Friday two weeks would be *Anmeldung* when Bruder Hukelpoke would come to the Pastor's house to say he hated no man and was prepared before the altar for communion. Then the good brother would hear the letter of God's word, a whole alphabet of them.

Mr. Mais shuckled a frog in his throat. "Work ain't doing itself; there's pig's guts to clean," he said and rattled the plates, getting up; almost knocked the table over. They piled out noisily, Franz reaching for his cap with them, when the Pastor spoke. "Stay inside." He raised his best Isaiah voice.

"Getting cold for the cows." Franz pressed among the coats hanging from the nails; back against something hard. Mother moved pots and pans and set them down again. Not her place to say no to God's shepherd.

"Hard and unrepentant." The Pastor warmed up. "Fearing cold on your bellies, but what of your souls—your starving unprotected souls? Sit down." Franz unbent his knees. "The spiritual food for your brother is also given for you." The Pastor unpacked a book from the small bag and began.

There wasn't much left to add when he finished. All my sins—all our sins, in fact, were dug up and lay open like potatoes rotting on a frozen field. "Evil, that's what's at the root of sickness and accidents and the frailties of the flesh. Sin and the Devil, carrying you off to the torture chambers of Hell. Think about it." The snap of his closing book was a sharp amen. "You have time, lying here. Blessed hours of grace. A gift of God. Good day." A kind of shadow faded when he went; or maybe it was only in mind. Fritzie had the team ready. The walls seemed more friendly, somehow.

Franz sat a space of thinking, this bitterness slipping among the roots of his thought, cold and blighting the shoots of joy quivering at what Mr. Mais had said. Liliem—and now the Pastor. Salt mixed with his sugar, stirred in by the tablespoon; always so, I thought, with a weariness in me.

"You s'pose God is black? with a beard?" Franz jumped up, restlessly. "Like the Pastor, I guess. Scolding all the time. Wonder how they laugh in Heaven."

"Franz." Mother stopped pouring water into the kettle. "The Pastor knows the Bible by heart. Don't talk so." She gave him the milk buckets. "Warm yet, they are, from washing," she said. He clattered out, Mother looking after him as if he were pulling from her hands with growth and growing. And the queer notions he was getting—not something he got in this house with her pumpernickel and headcheese, but odd things he must have found in other people's closets. She sighed, wringing the dishcloth. The room settled into quiet. I watched the splutters of flame in the stove. After a while the openings of the draft, arched like church windows, reddened to cherry heat.

Days of grace! The Pastor's voice echoed in the mind. Days of grace. For what? To lie spine-crooked-up under covers until the skin caked to the quilts with sores? To clench and unclench hands in air for a cool palm? Or moan for a spot to lie, easier on the bones than these unyielding boards, the body cemented down by a weight of pain? Days of grace. No, not for us, I was sure; not for Father, scratching like a dog to keep the roof with shingles and his coat with buttons, his brain full as a rooster coop of hate and suspicion, hatched we didn't know then from what setting of evil in the years behind him. Not for Mother, staring at her wedding ring sometimes as if it were a chain binding her to that which wasn't dusted off like flour, but remained as the pits of smallpox; a part of one, not even put away with prayer; drooping these days, pale as potato vines in spring, winter-cellared and running with water instead of sap. And little grace for Franz. He left the fiddle case locked, though I saw him trail fingers over the black hide times a day; went to clump among the cows, or jaw with Fritzie at chores. Twisted growth, it appeared to me; but whether in my fevered thought or in reality, I couldn't make out. Days of grace. It was like an echo of empty promises, mocking the heart.

Franz came from milking, Fritzie with him, after supper, his clothes smelling strongly of the barn. He hitched from window to chair as though the next jump would get him out of his pants; until Fritzie let him know he'd better go heave manure, if the day wasn't long enough to make him tired; the calfpen full. Franz slid a nail along the scar, thoughts elsewhere. He took the fiddle case and turned the key; lifted the fiddle with a quick grasp and tuned it, heart in his fingers; softly, no louder than a whisper, a melody running over me like water in the creek over rocks, cool with moss twining green hair.

"What'll it be, Jeppy? Waltz or quadrille?" His voice plunged into my dreaming. I couldn't move tongue to answer, the Pastor coming between me and the music and a dull wonder crawling in my brain that the Devil always seemed a little nearer when the Pastor was around and Hell not far off; breaking the dream. I shook my head.

"No tune tonight?" Franz touched a string, but it jangled. He looked sick, all at once; shut the fiddle from the lamplight and headed for the ladder; seeing that I didn't care and nobody else would listen.

He had enough to grumple in his brain, dragging the shoulders; for the elders at church had vinegar souring their lips that first day he came, after the sledding party, and the benches snapped as the congregation twisted to look. He folded himself between Mr. Prinzing and Mr. Mais, head down and in a hurry, Fritzie said; and went to church only because of Father's "What? Heathen in my house? Get your songbook," and because Tinkla was there, I guess, two or three benches ahead on the women's side, and he could peek over the songbook for Liliem. She didn't come much that winter. "Snow's too deep, past the lake," he ventured one time. He longed to spite Pastor and congregation together and would point his nose north where the crossroads were, spitting fiercely, as if to get rid of a bad taste. I'd see him in the field, the sled under him loaded and high after cleaning the barn, the manure flying from the quick jiggling shake he gave the fork. He'd give the mares the bit, driving past the house, coat open and the ends sailing, whistling *Devil's Dream* as though wishing the Pastor could hear, the tune plain indoors. It was good for him, the wind pounding his face like a whip and helping him forget what lay behind house walls; even if for only a short while, alongside the nights he spent in the loft, pulling worry like cart-ropes through the hours.

April came, mild in its first week, and one noon Fritzie began hunting iron teeth for those lost out of the drag. "Be digging ground in a week," he prophesied, breathing in air as if he could smell the weather.

"Snowbank yet, back of the house." Franz was dubious but helped him saw new crossbars. By midafternoon the oaks on the west ridge began to moan, dreading what came over the lake, and the sun burrowed into clouds. Before dusk the heavens slanted down white and screaming and trees lost identity in a gray blur. It was a night when wolves leave howling and track for the nearest strawpile or brush heap. The wind was like a currycomb ripped across the face and the dark a kind of fur along the hand. Above the storm whimpering under the eaves, we heard the lumbering roll and lunge of ice on the lake, churning into broken chunks. I remember that the curtains waved gently, for all that Franz and Mother stuffed the window chinks full and dangling with rag-ends; snow in an icy vapor misted down. Mother touched my head and pulled the bed-pile closer to the stove. "The Evil One—unhaltered and loose, this night." She laid on more wood, her face sad in the sudden glow, but hooked the stove lid with a quick smile. "Just came to me; the old rain-cape I made years ago; keep you dry. I'll never wear it." She went to the closet and stopped, a hand on the latch. The outside door flew wide with a dull bang and the lamp fluttered, so that the room sank away into dimness, and rose again brightly, the corners washed of shadows. Out of the storm's roar came Father's voice, "The ax—who took it from the woodpile?"

Before Franz could more than pull his shoulders together, Mother bent to reach under the stove. "It's here; I used it for meat bones, Johan." Father was inside then, wind-shot snow like salt white on his clothes, his face grimmer because half-hidden by his collar. *"Reich's hier."* The wind, dully loud, sucked up the words and left us less than an echo. Except his anger; that stayed with us like a living thing. We remained still, put in our places like checkers on a board; Franz bent forward, uncertain whether running were wisdom; Fritzie in the corner chair; Mother by the stove, moveless, as if woven fast in a dreadful web. There was a smashing outside and Fritzie bumped the wall, his lean face sharper. And after what seemed a year had dragged its turtle-way across the crackling fire and the smell of popple in the room, Father came in, arms piled with dangle-ends of runner and sled top; breath heavy in his throat; needing to wrench something to bits, no matter what, I decided afterward; release of that which plunged and plowed in him. He flung the wood in front of the stove. Chips flew, striking Mother and landing on the bedclothes where I crouched. His voice was harsh. "Let anybody open his mouth again, about sleds—" The words hung, whipping in air. He came closer to me. I felt the augering of his eyes a moment before he drew a finger along the window sill. "Snow." A kind of stiffness melted from him and his voice went strangely flat. "Snow." His hands suddenly reached and before I knew, he had scooped me into the circle of his arms, covers and all. Red-hot irons arrowed their way under my flesh, under inner bone itself, and whatever strength I had to yell dissolved in a queer jumble of black and white. I heard Mother cry. Franz came running, as if he'd butt against Father. The hardness of Father's arms loosened; and in a dimness not altogether darkened with pain I saw Franz, face white and lips pinched leaf-thin over his teeth, giving Father eye for eye; putting his young and untried courage against the fear he had of Father, and for that interval of clash (I am certain of that now), standing firm and unafraid, though ready to spring. A long moment. Then he backed down, as willows do before the ice jams.

Father, hard inside again, shouted, "Put him in the lean-to. Room in the loft for me, when I sleep." He pulled at the door, deaf to Mother's: "Johan—the cold—why must you go—"

"I have work to be done." The words shuttled on a snow blast between the opening and the closing of the door. Stayed with us.

Mother took an uncertain step; looked at Franz like a wounded thing seeking a den wherein to crawl. Then she was in Franz's arms and it was he now who was comforting her: "Mütterchen, Mütterchen, *nicht so";* facing the door, straight and with waiting in the curve of his back—waiting for another day.

4

We slept in the lean-to after that, Franz on a cornhusk mattress near my bed, Father and Fritzie moving into the loft, Fritzie with splutterings. "What you think I am, a mushrat? Need fur, a foot long, up there." The way Franz cupped hands on his shoulders, I guess he remembered the nights we shivered, close together for body warmth and our noses steaming like water kettles under the rafters; the horse blankets we had for covers holding little heat but lungfuls of the sweaty smell of horses; the mornings we found mouse tracks in the snow near the steadings. He answered Fritzie: "Stay down, then; I'm used to—"

"Not you, Dough-pan." Fritzie elbowed him. "I ain't sleeping with him—yelling when you touch him." Meaning me. He stopped half-up the ladder, sharp with slyness. "Like a couple of burdocks, you fellers. Stick it out together."

It was spicy with drying wood, the lean-to; cold after midnight. Water spilt near the door froze cloudy white before morning, even with the small potbellied stove roasting red and scorching the stockings Franz hung a chair-width away. A place the dog liked, my bed close to the door leading inward where I could see most of the kitchen and Mother washing what we dirtied, plates or shirts.

Spring was earnestly here now, we said; rode up from the creek with a robin, Franz ventured, seeing things his way. Snowbanks, drawing up their ragged shirts, turned grayer in the sun, and sank finally, grit-disordered patches, into earth; and the buds of the cottonwood, pointed and curved, stuck from the twigs like the spurs of a rooster. We waited like men girded for a strong labor, gathering our breath and belly muscles to move; those of us that could.

With Mother's help I managed a pillow behind my back and sat straight, for once; a sort of dumb happiness in holding my head higher than my chest. I let the window northward be an opening into what world I could see . . . trees stepping from level to level of ridges until the last one barred a further view; a field all but slipping from a hill, so steep its pitch, with only a fringe of saplings to keep back whatever tumbled . . . Franz trudging past the willows, or Fritzie in the north patch . . . the Prinzing house-gable an angle of faded white among the greening trees, and smoke puffing high near noon or six o'clock—a sign of inner hunger.

Then on Easter Sunday, when Franz stayed with me, and we waited for the Bauers to come from church with Father and Mother, the door latch rattled and Tinkla walked in grinning, her hair sticky with warmth. "I'm surprising your ma," she said directly, at home before she got her coat off. "Where's Franz?"

"Watering the horses," I told her, but she was hunting for Mother's apron and didn't hear. "Finished my chores early and walked over. Ma gave me leave." She knotted the strings. "I'll get potatoes on and the table set, 'fore you can cross a stick and count six."

Franz whistled in by the lean-to door, coat off and a wisp of foxtail plastered on his sweaty forehead. "Saw a flock of geese; honkers, fresh this year." He sent his cap whirling to a nail, a dead ringer. "They dove into a cloud and—" He let words go, seeing Tinkla in Mother's white apron, the blue pan in her arms rimful of potatoes and a loud laugh tugging at her throat muscles.

"Helping your ma out," she explained, banging the pan down. He leaned in the doorway as if he found something solid and durable in her bluntness and the fisty grasp she had on the paring knife; a meaning to this all his own. He was glad she was here; cackled over nothing; swam in the wash-dish, Tinkla was sure, scrubbing off a week's settling of dirt behind his ears. He watched her stride from stove to cupboard beyond my sight, and back again; watched potatoes go into her hand gray and come out peeled and white; but never sharpened a knife to help her, any more than Father would, or Tinkla's brother, or any of us; Tinkla not expecting it, as Mother wouldn't or Mrs. Bauer.

He teased her about the time she shook Epsom salts by mistake into a boiling kettle. "We use common stuff here—for cooking. Did your pa like his spuds salted that way?" She fired a peeling at him, where he sat, a strange glow spreading in his eyes, smoldering like fire under ash. She plopped the last potato into water and took pail and pan to the cupboard, out of my sight again. I heard a rush of poured water and her voice, thick and creamy, drifting around the doorpost. What she said wasn't meant for me, spoken low and to other ears; but Franz thumped to his feet and with two steps brought the wall between us. There was silence; then Tinkla's giggle, "Franz; you—you'll spill the water."

"Plenty in the pump." He spoke with rough insistence.

"Don't; you—you clumsy ox," she cried, but her words warned no one away. There was a shuffling and then the quiet of a house made livable with stove-crackle and clock-tick; until the floor bumped and Tinkla yelled and potatoes, naked for the kettle, bounced over the floor. Franz picked them up with a foolish grin, as if he had been caught in his own mousetrap; his shirt wet where the water splashed; Tinkla scolding him.

The dinner would have been far from setting to table, if the folks hadn't returned then, back from church, the Bauers trailing the end-gate. The womenfolks rustled in, Mother slipping from her coat. She ought to have been in two places at once, really. Mrs. Bauer, baby on her arm, sighed into the largest chair, saying it was a good sign, sun warm on Easter Sunday; we'd have seven Sundays of clear weather, now. Father and Mr. Bauer led the horses to the barn.

Franz behaved as though the meal were something that didn't matter, asking for bread when he had two slices piled on his plate; calf-eyed and awkward as a yearling. Tinkla put spoon to dish absently, and trotted in to me afterward to whisper: "We've got it all planned, Ma and me; *he'll* come to help you." She ran off at Mrs. Bauer's shrill "Tinkle, come here; the baby's wet again." A Sunday to remember, as though we had risen from the dark rock of our hates and fears to laughter and the untwining of muscles tensed and vigilant—the small odds and ends that keep the brain steady and madness under iron and away.

Fritzie hauled the shocks of corn, heaping the basket. Franz forked at the bundles with slowness in his bones. Winter laziness thawing out, Mother said, as she wiped cobwebs from the sulphur box and prepared tonic, now that spring lay in a blue mist on the ridges. Drifts to the north melted on the knolls and rushed over stony ledges in white ropes of water, small and untwisting.

It was a queer spring, coming so late, and hurrying to finish in a week what it had dallied over for a month; cracking open the vaults of frost three feet in a night and warming earth like an oven.

Father went less and less to the sawmill. "Logs won't cut clean much longer," he said.

Then on an afternoon ragged with showers, Dr. Allbauch drove up the miry road. He jiggled in with his crumpled bag (a black dog with a handle, Fritzie called it), his wrinkling inquisitive nose smelling behind the cupboards, it seemed, even when he stood in the middle of the room. A peevish short-legged man, high of voice and reeking of horehound and sour brandy.

"This the Vildvogel—yes, of course." His voice sharpened. "You're Vildvogel. I'm Dr. Allbauch. Two l's."

I think a slab of ice drew between the sun and earth, there was so much of cold in the room all at once; chill, as if no fire in the stove could warm the covers on me. Franz clawed his pants, trembling. Mother let the broom pull from her hands. The tail of a rhyme crawled dully through my head:

> "Doctors and coffins, together they go;
> One goes fast, the other goes slow."

"I didn't order you." Father would have barred the way, flint-eyed and suspicious, but the doctor was inside, squeaking, "Ten miles of this damned ditchy road. Where's the boy? Where's the boy? The Bauers sent me. Dammit, ten miles. It won't cost you a shilling."

[150]

"Bauers?" Father straightened like a bent young tree whip-ping up. "I'll not take favors—"

"Not a cent. Women's doings." The doctor was around Father and popped into the lean-to; glared at me. "Hiding, eh? You're—yes, the cripple." I saw Franz jerk as if someone had hit him full in the face. "What you here for?" The doctor plumped the bag on the floor and kicked it, before he un-buckled the straps. "Ten miles, dammit, and near broke my—" His mumblings strayed to moving of the lips as he pulled the covers down and began to work. He poked and prodded, his fin-gers clumsy and blunt as the ends of rails. He flopped me over like the half of a butchered steer, so that Franz's knuckles whitened in a grip on the table edge. He dug heartily, his hands flattening now and then in a pause while he snarled, "Hold still, can't you—can't you? Body'd think I'm trying to kill you, way you grunt." His fingers slid off my ribs at last, the final tamping done. Father hadn't moved from his place.

The doctor peered froggily over his glasses. "Nothing the matter. Nothing. Women's fool notions. Ten miles, riding back, dammit. Roads like a plow-field." He buckled the bag. "Nothing wrong with him. Give him Epsom salts; and plenty of time—time. They're both cheap."

"You think he'll—" The scar burned darkly on Franz's gray cheek; his tongue failed. Mother made a sound deep in her throat. Fritzie thought aloud for all of us. "He'll walk, won't he?"

"Walk? Walk?" Dr. Allbauch exploded fiercely. "Nobody said he can't, did they? Nothing wrong. Sprained muscles. Where's my hat? Nobody said he *can* walk, either. Ten miles, dammit." He grabbed his bag and spluttered to the door, short legs moving like pump rods; banged the door, but thrust it open again before we had our breath. "Better get him crutches—crutches." The door slammed. We heard the iron of the rim crunch on the road.

Crutches! Wooden slats to rub the skin raw under the arm; like those Abercrombie Lafferty stomped around with; loud so you could hear him when he went about the house, cellar to loft. Thump, thump. It sent a scare shivering up the spine, hurting among the roots of hair at the back of the neck. More money to be laid into another's palm, penny by penny, and the pocketbook limp. Too limp for the price they'd ask for crutches. The Bank after us, winter and summer.

Father felt the harness straps of obligation again. But Mother said quietly, "I'll thank her—Mrs. Bauer; someway." I wondered in a bitter moment why even friendship must be wrenched into barbs to tear us.

Franz lifted his hands in a hurt manner; went back of the stove like a struck old dog, belly to earth and creeping to lick his wounds. He rolled as in a fever among the rustling cornhusks that night; got up, a gray form in the night, and pulled on his britches. I heard the shoelaces pluck-pluck into the hooks.

"Not morning yet," I called to him.

He came fast, bursting out, "Why don't you hit me?"

"Franz, you're sleepwalking," I hedged, but he went on, mumbling, "I could stand it, then." The clock added the silence between us; for a while. I pulled at the blankets. "This—this is between us," I stumbled. "Franz, we're—we're brothers." It was the only thing I could think of to say, that bleak moment.

"Brothers." The edge of bitterness was in his voice. "When all I do is—" He let it go; pulled on cap and coat, and crept into the night.

5

He came in late; hog-tired when Mother shook him awake, his shoes in a corner dripping mud. He hitched the team that morning as if he didn't know which end of a horse went into the collar, and drove Fritzie to yells by tangling the lines. And in the weeks following, he scrabbled weird bits of tune on the fiddle, without melody and without joy, I guess; though May brought hawks the color of old brick hanging under the clouds,

now and again folding their wings as boys do arms before diving
headlong; plummeting to end in broken earth, it seemed, but
sweeping up again, in a long sky-curve; floating north. And
the martins soared, all tail and wings, short and stubby, like
jackstones, sooty as oven-polish, hurtling through upper air.
He saw them with half a glance, without much pleasure, shuffling
along; although one morning I saw him just beyond the window,
rooted to wet soil, and staring at the brown fire running in the
branches of the elm, as bud cases grew and burst along the
limbs.

Liliem came to the Prinzings' the middle of May and Franz
needed a halter, Fritzie snickered; mooning up toward the
Prinzing farm. "What's the matter, Turkey Hen?" Fritzie
scruffed his heels clean of most of the mud he'd gathered that
morning. "Lay eggs up there and want to nest?"

"Pockets full of gab again, huh?" Franz stepped to the table
and pulled a chair between his legs. "Maybe she ain't come
yet." He knew very well that she had, that Mrs. Mais had
brought the news to us along with a recipe for Juneberry pie.
Fritzie chortled. "Been there a week. Saw her come down for
the mail. Yesterday after dinner."

Franz let that sink in, raking the beans on his plate, an idea
growing in his mind that made him scrape up food jack-quick.
Nobody guessed, spring work in our fists, that he hung around
the north patch where our wheel tracks lost themselves in the
main road, and the mailbox, of wood and fastened to a post-top
with a single spike, pointed the wind almost as well as a
weathercock; the Prinzings' box and the Maises' beside it. Waiting there when he could expect her. I saw him sneaking through
a break in the willows, headed north, and wondered why he
lifted his eyes back over his shoulders. I knew, when Fritzie
snapped at him later, "Hollered for you; I couldn't unload the
wagon rack myself," and Franz mumbled, "Went over to the
sloo; ditch needs cleaning." It was more than the ditch he
wanted to see, I thought, watching him. Much more. He came

in to lunch, a grin pulled almost under his ears, and it didn't take Solomon to figure out that he'd seen her. I wondered with a kind of ache in me why this was given to us, this sneaking around to snarl like bitches over the scabby ends of happiness. Afraid to stand clear and openhanded, before all men, but skulking in the underbrush of doubt and suspicion; Franz gnawing like one starved on what honesty and beauty there was. The hours stolen with Liliem—sweeter than wild-grape honey they must have been; carried home with him to savor in the dreamy warmth of half-slumber, sleep like a wind blowing over him. I wondered too (with shame for myself) whether he put hands on her as he did on Tinkla, but guessed the answer, though why, I couldn't say; a feeling more than a knowing.

Even when she was busy, with field-work lengthening men's stomachs and the cookstove a gray maw for wood, and she didn't come; or when he missed the hour, held away by the leather lines, he followed the corn rows with tunes on his lips and waltzes in his legs, as if a part of her remained with him. He left straying nights to wolves and foxes, and snored in the cornhusks. But one night he humped up slowly and with caution that was laughable, to step like a cat in a snowbank, high and careful; ear down, making sure I slept. He fumbled at the wall, his match firing in a thin parabola of flame and flaring over a palm that moved whitely out of dark; shimmering on what lay there—the braided gold of hair; a long strand. He wriggled a finger under it, only his two hands and the tip of his nose seen. Before the match singed his nails, he put the braid in his shirt pocket and vanished from sight in sudden blackness.

6

There were days when I envied the dead, the moveless dead, pressed firm and molded into earth, silence thinning them to bone and the dust of bone. They, at least, were unplagued by the weariness of flesh sagging into a crooked shape. The longing to walk and feel earth resisting shoe leather became a cry loud in the heart, if stilled on the lip. I'd stop peeling the potatoes Mother set within reach, or sorting bad beans from good, and shut eyes, numbed by the sharp necessity of putting teeth on teeth to crowd back what tore inside. And even when pain and bitter darkness had receded in a great slow wash, and I could do tasks to snip shorter the day, I saw that nothing had changed; nothing altered . . . the lean-to smelly with clothes hung on nails and souring with winter sweat; the rafters fragrant with bunches of caraway and camomile, fit now only to throw away; Mother grinding coffee or parched rye by cracking it in a bag, hitting with a cob of wood and catching the beans that time and again broke the threads and popped out . . . Franz rooting in the fields, his nostrils full of earth-smell and his shoe-prints, mixed with ours, crossing and recrossing the acres—the mark of honest leather, touching and overlapping and lying God knows how many deep. True, there were things to break monotony . . . a neighbor driving up with a sow in heat or a heifer struggling with rope at the wagon's end . . . a horse tearing away and galloping into freedom, all his tail not bone bent with hair streaming . . . Matt Prinzing, younger than Franz by a season but stocky and built like an ox, walking over to tell about Jonas Bluber's new buggy; a topper, with side curtains and a storm front. "I'll be a two-toed bloodsucker if she ain't got windows," squealed Matt; "glass 'bout as long as my foot, so you can look out." News passed like salt or a grinding of feed from door to door. But in the end, what change there was could not be traced with a crayon or a stick in mud. It was seen, if at all, only after the passage of years.

Walter came home that month. Opened the door on us one afternoon before lunchtime, haggard and sick-looking, more sullen than ever; his body lean as a popple rail and his pants more hole than cloth. Mother put another cup and saucer down quietly, asking him to sit, but Franz was wordless with raw doubt; seeing what people beyond our ridges could do to one of us—this brother of ours changed into a stranger, almost, with eating at other people's houses and sleeping in unfamiliar beds. I think he never forgot how Walter burst out: "Got to say it now"; his voice straining to a dry rasp. "Mathilda—she says we got to get married." Franz suddenly looked elsewhere. Mother put a hand on the cupboard door.

"Mathilda," Walter stumbled on: "she's Old Man Krueger's girl—he owns the farm. She's one of his girls. I work there." He shifted unsteadily at what he read in Mother's face; bent his head, shame-hung. "It's so—what you mean," he said, almost stupidly, youth burned out of him, leaving ash for the rest of his years. All at once, Mother went to him, a hand on his arm. He gripped her fiercely. "Mütterchen, Mütterchen, so long, it's been, away from you." For a moment, I had a strange fancy that he was a kid again, and crying before her with a hurt to be bandaged. But now it was more than a toe or a finger; deeper than her skill to probe. He pushed her aside and gulped water at the dipper.

"Don't know where to turn," he muttered, walking past Franz without seeing him. "No money or machinery; nothing to start up farming." Mother looked old and tired. "It is hard to give," she said. "Hands empty as they are."

Walter swung loosely to a chair. "Can't ask Father," he was sure. He jumped up fast when Father came from the barn. Father was almost pleased; as if he had a stall ready for the strayed animal. He grunted when Walter spoke, "Ain't staying. Drove with Mrs. Mais's folks—the Doppelts, Anna and her brother."

We took in this news with the stiffness of our bread; biting off syllables over mouthfuls. There was nothing we could do to help Walter, even if Father were told; not when a ball of twine or a hunk of salt was another stone on the rock pile of our own debt.

Walter went away, before dark, a heaviness left behind in his place, Franz peering after him, and then standing by the barn to regard our house, as if its squatness offered an assurance he had missed until this hour. The tin disks were rusting, yes; and the blue paper bulging; but solid to the eaves against what the neighbors might say or do. He measured its safety with a nod and twisted his shoulders, as though dislodging an irksome burden.

7

May drifted over the ridges with honeydew smell of crab apple and wild plum, and was gone. The Prinzing baby was born, we heard, and added its howls to the family wrangle. "Liliem must have her hands full," Mother thought. But Mr. Prinzing chuckled, "Busy, all right, she is; and tends to Matt as much as the baby."

Franz mumbled, "Not anything to see, Matt ain't; wide as a gunny sack." He said it half-jealously, lugging a bag of seed to the west patch and not waiting for Mr. Prinzing to say, "You folks have an invite; come over, at baptizing."

It was June and haying time before I dragged myself to the table one breakfast, hobbling single-leggedly and holding desperately to Franz, a broken rail to a post. "Easy he goes." Franz led me to a chair. Fritzie said in his sharp way, "Stranger to meals, eh? Another strawsack to fill." But Mother handed him the pancakes and hushed him. "We've waited long—for this, Jeppy." She put cream on the cakes. Father lifted his eyes dourly. "Cream?" The word had weight heavier than its own.

"Mixed with water, Johan; this once," Mother said quickly, raising the pitcher as if it were a shield. "Water, and more than half." Father waved it aside. "This once—let it be." I think his face was less grim, though. "We have place for you, *Junge*." He rolled a cake and reached for his knife. "It stands in the corner yet—your hayfork; the three-tined. I kept it for you."

Franz was all smiles. "You'll be hopping soon; can't keep you from the barn." And Mother's cheek, paler than usual, pinked a little. A moment as golden as the sun cutting the shadow of Franz's head cleanly on the table; a stone rolled from us for a space.

Father speared the last of the cakes. "Eat, now. The hay is waiting. Franz, the hayrack needs fixing." A moment for laughter, truly, I thought as Franz helped me back; thin as apple parings, maybe, but drenching away the darkness clogging the heart.

The mower clattered in the meadows, Fritzie's shouts to the horses mingling with the echoes the hills gave in return. Father joined him after dinner, driving a machine he'd borrowed from Mr. Mais, and leaving Franz to repair the hayrack. A patch-up job, I guess, for all the hammering he did. Father grumbled at milking time and Fritzie exploded, "Look at that, Dough-pan; tie ends with a sack string, you would, to hold them together."

"Wasn't many nails," Franz began, but Fritzie shouted, "Whole box of 'em; in the barn. Dreaming again, that's what you been." Franz set his lips and went to water the horses.

Two afternoons of sun and the hay was ready for the stack—timothy and, in the meadow near the rice lake, June grass, lush as pigweed. "We'll haul today." Father pulled his saggy straw hat down firmly. "White dew goes off early. You rake, Franz. I and Fritzie'll cut poles for the stack and get twine hangers."

They went out and the house settled back as if on haunches of silence from the rumble of menfolks' talk . . . the fire tearing at the pine cobs with a hungry chewing sound . . . Mother swishing hot water on the dishes before she dried them . . . a chicken by the door cla-cla-cla-ing with each scratch and throw of dirt . . . Fritzie shouting, "Where's the neckyoke, Franz?" and Franz answering, his voice lost behind the walls of the barn.

"You'd like to be there—outside." Mother leaned in the doorway, wiping a cup with twirls of the dishcloth. "And hay with them; I know." She put down cup and dishcloth. "Let's see how it goes." She helped me to the outer door where the sun lay yellow on the step, her arm stiff against my ribs. I felt the blood surge in a stream over me, straightening the back. Air in my lungs, new air, like wine; and sun shedding from my cheek—even the legs felt less like wood.

I stayed until dinnertime, sopping up warmth, and wondering why I'd never noticed before now the shouldering lift of the Diemer hills and the blunt line of ridges west, broken with trees and notched like dovetail joints by the slashed clearings.

Franz, humped over the rake seat, drove in at noon, the tines jangling, curved iron against rock. He waved and threw the lines. "Couldn't be better," he called, running. "Got a job for you; after eating." His eyes were brown with the light in them. "I'm taking the first load. Want to handle the team?" Eagerness leaped in his voice. "Make you a nest in the rack—one corner, where hay won't fall on you."

"Franz—if my legs'll hold. But Father won't—"

"He never said whoa yet, did he? To anyone working, far as I know. And I found a mallard's roost; sitting, she is and—"

"Franz." Father stood by the barn, his bellow tearing across the yard. "Horses not yet unhitched?" No, Father wouldn't hold up a hand to stop anyone; not as long as a wheel lugged on its thimble or a spade cut into earth.

Dinner was off the plates before Franz coaxed his idea out. "Warm, in the fields. I—Jeppy—he's going to drive; in the last sloo, this afternoon." Father gazed steadily at Franz and a long time at me, as if calculating the forkfuls I could heave. But Fritzie hooted. "All the belly and get he's got, might as well take a jug of tea along." Franz was ready to bristle but Father said, "Trying won't hurt." Which settled that.

Franz had the horses stepping over the pole before the noon hour was over and called, "Hitched and the fork sharp." Mother hastened with a crock of water, anxious over our going; fussing, "The heat and all—and your legs; like straw under you." Straw under you. More like a pile of old rags. I slumped down. "In the corner there." Franz unwound the lines. "Stuff won't hit you."

There was about that day a sweetness of sun and clover in timothy we wouldn't forget; either of us. The sky held a blue that ran deeper with the wind unraveling a tangle of cloud. The meadow was tumbled with windrows snaking crookedly from edge to edge, Franz having no eye for a straight windrow or an unswerving furrow. The rice lake was full of long stems in bloom and strong with the froggy odor of damp places. The rack swayed gently but pitched in the hog wallows, Franz avoiding the worst of them. His fists were balled around the lines.

"Jeppy—if I could tell—" He pulled at the lines and shouted "Whoa." We stopped short alongside the end of a windrow. But it wasn't until he had pitched a while, and I had felt the lines drag like chains at my arms in driving several wagon-lengths ahead, that he poked at what was in his mind. "Good to see you in the rack—wind in your hair." He squinted at me from the fork-end, his face puckered into wrinkles, hiding what he really felt; until he cried out suddenly, hanging his shoulders, "Coward, that's what I am; afraid to start anything." He jabbed the fork deep, his back to me. "You there, down and aching, all because—"

"What's the use of it—raking old ashes." I shoveled in my seven cents' worth fast.

"Brothers, you said." His voice ranted. "Straighten things that are crooked, a brother ought. If I only could—" He hid his face behind a forkful and giddaped the horses loudly. Which was as near as we got to spelling in large letters what heckled us by the hour, when we had time to think. The falling hay was a period to the matter.

Before the rack was full and swelling over the edge like rising dough, I felt a curious blackness riding the hills and a sweat that wasn't from the sun alone. Franz was quick to see the lines slipping in a wide arc to the evener pin. "Jeppy, you're—stick tight." He was up the rack with a plunging of arms and legs.

"Knees weak," I managed.

"Why didn't you say—" He threshed through crisp timothy

beside me, bitterness like flint scratching him. "Try to help you; all I do is hurt." Feeling, I think, that whatever he attempted turned like a twisting ax handle to strike and lay open where he least intended.

"All right, now," I told him. "Little low in the stomach."

He picked the lines from the center post. We jolted off, the stems prickly about my neck, and took a short cut to kitty-corner a stumpy piece that elbowed itself into the meadow; no trail but a wagon track and Franz in a hurry.

"There's a rock there, on the further side," I said.

"Pull it off, when we get that far." He jerked a curling twist down the line to slap the mare's rump.

We stopped where a rock, white and larger than a wash-tub heaped high, squatted beyond the wagon tongue. It was big enough to make the sweat start, budging it. Franz climbed to the ground and set shoulders hard, his legs slanted like a prop, earth gouging under his heels with every grunt, and the veins on his forehead swelling; lifted and brought light the width of a palm between granite and its nesting place, before rock drew back; rested, his shirt stretching with the pump of his lungs. Until Fritzie, jogging along with rails like a yoke on his neck, called, "Pebble, like that; stick it in your pocket, Dough-face." He came; heaved his load on a bank.

"I'll pry." Franz searched for a stick, but Fritzie snapped, "Do it myself." He tried a corner where the rock was lightest, his breath tightening his body to iron. The nails in his shoes scraped roughly on stone; he lunged and sank back, gathered force and lunged again, rolling the rock clear. A job; enough for Father to grunt over, but Fritzie made it. He rubbed dirt from his palms. "Easy; for any kind of a real man"; and loaded his rails, whistling. Franz climbed the rack and strapped the horses. We drove on without a word.

Father said little when we lumbered into the yard. He prodded a fork at the hole where I had crouched, while Franz helped me to the house; rotten wood and useless. I had the lean-to again and the pile of dry oak for company. Mother brought a drink, pump water and vinegar, sweetened and cool. How long (I dug nails into my palms) before the body dusts with the boards on the floor.

Franz kept still within himself at supper, chewing gall with his meat and potatoes. He brought a cup to the bed almost reluctantly, I thought. It was a quiet evening, the sun tilted like a red and fiery plate on the ridge, the trees a faint tracery of design on its lower rim, black and as if painted on; night sweeping down slowly. Quiet, for all that the horses kicked pads of dirt high as the eaves, free of the collar and chain; and the turkeys took wing into the elms, bickering from limb to limb. I saw Mother with the egg pail on her arm; Father closing the granary for the day. Muscle and sinew alive to walk and run—beyond walls.

"Get you another pillow." Franz came in, slow in his steps. "Old coat or two." His hands dropped, seeing the no in my headshake. He worried a splinter of bark to keep his eyes busy.

"Franz." What moved in me, deep as a well, began to rush out. "Franz."

"Jeppy, don't." The bark wavered to the floor; as if he knew, before I spoke. "I'll get you a drink."

"Franz, Franz, does it mean—I can't ever get on my legs again?"

His face jerked. "No. No. God wouldn't let it." Grief shook his voice.

"Jeppy, Jeppy—" I never smell dry oak even now without a prickle in me, remembering how he bumped into the door, going away; how I had the dark to myself and outside a robin quirled rustily, too industrious with nest and young ones to sharpen his notes. Then the fiddle joined the robin, softly and yet with a cry in the strings, carrying melody into the room and beyond— beyond the treetops to the sky. Wood-smell and the lullaby of

Liebeslied, Franz letting his fingers say aloud what was too deep to be caught and held to view by a mere net of words.

8

He helped scatter the hours often after that; all summer long. Fiddled at dusk, usually, with milking done, and bringing the barn to the lean-to in the odorousness of spilt milk and cow smell rank on his trousers. He played as if the music might be a salve to heal over hurts; restless when it thinned beneath his bow and the melody in his head remained clear of his finger tips. He was ready to throw fiddle and bow against the wood-pile, then, his body tensed with rebellion and the strings twang-ing under the nails. Though, usually, the tunes ended with Father's thumping the ladder, or Fritzie, head in the loft trap door, shrilling, "Cut that pig-gut, Dough-pan; get to bed." And Franz, rubbing the fiddle with his red handkerchief until it shone in the last faint radiance, would grumble, his talk rustling away in the cornhusks.

There was about that summer a beauty strange and hard to de-scribe, the air sometimes heavy with the smell of burning, re-minding us of Mr. Mais's apple trees, winterkilled and dry, smoking beyond the line-fence and bringing a smell different from oak or elm. There were afternoons when cloud-shadows moved like dark islands across a green sea of woods; mornings when Mother helped me to the step, and I felt strength growing in at least a portion of me, and saw mist tree-high, hot and muggy. Bad for the wheat, Father said. "Rusting red, these forenoons." There were hours around dinner with the sun throw-ing nettles of fire on our necks, a foretaste of July . . . the grain bending and bowing when the wind, like a hand passing over fur, rolled up the slants . . . Franz excited about a clutch of par-tridge eggs he'd come on beneath a brush pile, careless of Fritzie's hoots, knowing that Mother listened—beauty we couldn't escape, cloud our sight with work and worry as much as we wished. But mingled with it was a kind of sorrow, too, as if tears ran shallow under our walking routine. Like that morning near the end of haying. A wet morning, with an east wind slapping fingers of rain against the windows, pettish with anger that was to keep haystacks smooth with canvas for a week.

Father was impatient to put spoon into his oatmeal but waited to say grace—and for me. Franz kicked the chair under my legs. "Knees a little stouter, this morning, Jeppy." He slid into his own place, a hungry look for the small toast pile. Fritzie plumped down, a sleepy scowl wrinkling his forehead. Mother hovered like a nervous kingbird, now the coffeecan, now the milk pitcher, in her hands.

"Good rainy day—fix the leftovers." Father dribbled corn sirup on his oatmeal.

"Good fishing weather." Franz let the notion out slow and feelerlike. "A slip of fresh pike, with bread—"

"The pork barrel ain't empty yet." Father crumbled a slice of toast. "Waste the whole day, fishing; and drag home a couple of minnows." He jerked impatiently. "Fix-up day, this is. Franz, the calfpen wants new rails. And Fritzie—we'll see about the granary. Jeppy can dig a posthole for—" He clipped his words short, giving orders as he always had, but remembering now. He yanked at a chair rung. Silence grew thick and heavy as blankets. The sirup dish in Mother's hands clattered on the table. Nobody spoke. Franz gripped his spoon, tortured.

"*Na ja.*" There was sourness in Father's mouth. "Jeppy can— he can sit."

"No." Franz dropped the spoon. "He's solid and sound—if he could get on his legs."

"Sit." Father reached for the milk, accepting this as he would a colt's breaking a leg or a haystack uncapped by storm and scattered; swearing and grumbling, but planning to get the stud again and raise another colt, or figuring to build his stacks where trees would shelter them. Nothing to do about me. For no wheel stopped because a pair of legs balked and refused to carry a body; not on Father's farm; any more than a binder at harvest time halted because a song sparrow's nest lay where the bull wheel rolled.

Franz might have said more but left the table, neck stiff, not giving in to any man's say-so, in this matter; not even Father's. He brought a length of rope to me (between pounding rails and pointing stakes), old and frowsy-threaded but serviceable to run along my body. "Measure you for a new suit," he said, tying knots for exactness. A curious eagerness lilted under his laugh. "You need one. Even grass has that much." But he was dumb to my questions. Fritzie, in for a drink of water, shot a stone of bluntness. "New suit. Measure him for a new bed, next."

Franz lashed forward, the rope flipping in his hand. "That's like the heart of you. Dog down, dog dead, far's you go." Fritzie swung half a dipper of water splashing, "Keep your hind end cool and your mouth shut." And went back to the granary. The rope tautened in Franz's fists, but he brushed the water off, damp of shirt but not of idea. "Get you pegging yet, Jeppy. Wait and see."

He must have stared holes in Crummie Lafferty's crutches, that next Sunday, printing them on his brain. He hammered and sawed in the granary, until Fritzie got after him. "Clean up your messes, Dough-pan; I just swept the floors." By the middle of the week, though, he was dubious with doubt; kept popping in to watch me peeling potatoes or picking stems and rotted fruit from the basket of Juneberries Mother had gathered—jobs that fingers could do asleep. He was away till late, after chores, that evening, and I remember, before sleep swept over my eyes like a curtain, that the moon flung the bars of the window in a strange and broken cross over the lower half of the bed, where the quilts had knolls of bumps—a black cross on the gray-and-white covers. What hour he came, softly on balled feet, is ticked away and gone. But near rooster-crow I wallowed out of fog to a sense of weight on my legs. The lean-to was empty of strangers, the moon-patch silver on a corner of the bed, and what was there, plain to see. I hate to think of that night and how he must have stood at the bedpost, his work done, and who knows what uncertainty scrabbling itself in his skull. But in that moment of discovery, I reached hands to touch the wood lying there—dark in the moon, with a sort of praying in me—"Dear Jesus, let them be legs for me." Raw and brown wood fashioned into crutches.

9

I try to bring back, sometimes, here where quiet is folded in like an altar cloth with peace and the footsteps in the corridor are encouraging as if arriving with hope, that hour, when the wood of the crutches first pressed against the hollow of the armpits and the shoulders shoved up and out of place with the load of the body hanging on them. I try and fail; scrawled over with years, that hour. For it seems strange now that I ever went easy as wind along the ground, running with raindrops to escape a storm, feathers on my heels; strange and mocking as mad laughter, that memory, with these extra bones stiff at the hips and unbending; my shoes dragging in dust, one firm, considering everything, but the other wrinkled and wearing off at the toe. It is easy now to swing the stretch of the mosaicked halls on cushioned tips; even in sleep my fingers curve to take the round of the crosspiece. But during those first days, there was agony in every desperate clutch; sweat leaking from the forehead; and a staggering like a new calf, sprawl-legged and kinking knees all ways at once to catch the balance; Franz watching as if even this hope were to be thwarted. Days of trying and the sweetness of triumph that came with slow success. I remember as I do my first firecracker how Franz shouted when I stomped the whole length of the path from house to barn and found him feeding the horses. He grabbed me by the shoulders hard, so that I wobbled; opened and shut his eyes fast and rushed off between the mares with a can of oats. And how the heifers unlidded their ball-eyes, snorting at this newcomer with the unfamiliar pitchforks; how Mother's lips trembled and she planned a batch of cakes, wondering how sweet they'd be without more than a teaspoon of sugar. Even Father was less gruff, fixing a corner of the rack so that I would be railed off from hay and have a board low-slung for a seat to drive at haying and stacking.

Fritzie was scornful about the crutches. "Old bull sticks," he hooted. They were clumsy, perhaps; two strips of elm planed down, with nails and wire at the bottom, and spreading to crossbars, shoulder-high and at the hip. Rags wound on the end bar eased the underarm. Bull sticks, perhaps: but more than Fritzie's cunning ever devised; or Father's harshness, for that matter.

Thereafter the lean-to chained me less and I saw the back sloos again, Franz and I after hay, Franz thoughtful over an ivy roping up the weather-gray scar of an oak. Its leaves stuck out— "like hands," he said, pitching the fork so that it clawed into peat. These were hours sweet with timothy and clover before the time of harvest and shocking grain; hours that dribbled away like honey, sun-warmed, from the comb. We trotted homeward one evening with a basket full of "blue" grass, taking the short cut over the kitty-corner way and passing the white stone again. It had been moved two rods or so from where Fritzie had left it; a deep ragged groove like a tail in the dirt behind it. One glance at him, and I knew by his dark flush and foolish grin that he had been here, jacket off, wrestling with rock and the furies within him, to lug its weight. "Show Fritzie," he muttered, strapping the team to a run.

There were other evenings when the ridges brought our "Whoa, Methuselah!" back with clearness, and healing seemed to rustle from the leap and vault of overarching trees. Hours of peace, knitting together what had been ripped apart. Not all, though. There were days when ache tugged like a fiend at the body; the bed hard at night and all the liniment in Mother's box ineffective to rub smooth the lumps of pain. Days, before I caught the trick of swinging a space of three feet at a throw, when each try seemed the last and more than nerves could stand. The crossbar snapped once, Franz getting white when I plunged down. He put in a new piece with spiteful hammerings.

It was on the same afternoon that the binder brace cracked and Father sent him to the shop, Fritzie being too busy. He hitched the team to the buggy and shouted, "Get your hat, Jeppy."

"Better leave me so," I told him. "Be under your feet, that's all." He had a pucker on his lip, half of sadness. "You want to spoil this, Jeppy?"

"Franz; talk about spoiling—" I began, but poked a crutch in his direction to finish the thought. He helped me to the buggy seat.

We drove the road east, the wheels in a blur, going over, Franz saying, "This ain't the last time you're riding either; if I have a word." The shop was small and fire, spurting from the forge, yellowed the steadings and made blacker the tongs sticking in the tool rack; brought the whites of the eye out starkly in the men, half a dozen of them, gathered where Old Wibart pulled at the bellows or hammered iron into red-hot scales. John Bluber was there, bolting teeth in a new thresher cylinder. Mr. Mankin, full of grumbles about rust in his wheat, went on to say, "Prinzing's sure blowing himself on his *Kindtauf;* keg of beer, Matt said. About time they baptized the kid; he'll have whiskers, pretty soon." Adam Kloots, still a husband but no father, dug snuff from a box with finger and thumb, and the men, loud with desire in their mouths, poked at him and dragged hands across his pants. "Rooster ain't much good, eh, Adam?"

"Well." Adam's lower lip bulged with a thrust of his tongue. "Well, ya see, I'm diddling yet."

"Tell ya, Adam." John Bluber adjusted a wrench. "Why don't you try the hired man? Maybe he ain't so weak in the legs." The men scruffed their shoes in laughter. Franz in shadow hid his face, although his teeth gleamed. Young Heinie Grosbeck rolled a bull wheel down the road and into the shop, saying to Wibart with despair and sweat streaking his face: "Wheeled the damn thing two miles; binder broke and horses sick." The wheel clanged as it fell among iron. Old Wibart polished a hammer on his leather apron: "Sure, sure, Heinie; we fix 'em for you."

Sornas Tetzlauf strode in, with more belly than you'd expect on a farmer; a shifty glitter under his lids and ice in the way he talked: "I want four holes drilled in this reel; here. I've marked the places." Particular, he was; so that Old Wibart grunted, irked by his lordly manner but saying nothing. Tetzlauf complained that he couldn't find anyone to handle his stacking team; sized Franz up: "You got time, maybe? Give you a buck and a half a week and board."

"Don't know." Franz drew back, thinking of Walter. "We got our own to stack."

"Huh! That henyard; no bigger." He could brag, renting the two-hundred-acre Lexler farm over southeast. "I'll see your pa."

Franz let the lines sag, jogging back. "No fun, working out."

"Sweat your hide rough, Tetzlauf would," I said. "Does to every hired man, they say."

"Walter looked like that—sweat out and tired." Franz shivered, thinking. "I could stand that, though, I guess." But he was dubious. "It's—it's being unhandy with stranger's truck that gets me. I—their ways different; and what they might say—" He slapped the lines; unsure of himself; half-expecting that anyone he ever would work for would rush at him as Father did, anger in upraised fists. Both of us were conscious, too, that a new force was entering our lives—growing man-sized, we were, and away from home. A force like frost, it seems to me now, breaking up the sills and cornerstones of families; heaving them aside, broken and cast-off, but drawing the pieces like a magnet into new designs and the foundations of new loves and hates; holding them together with that strange lonely bind-

ing that drives women to faraway graves and men to poke among
the weeds of lost and all-but-forgotten homesteads.

10

We went to the Prinzings' the next Sunday, the five of us in
the platform buggy, Fritzie standing, as became a man, his head
above Father and Mother sitting in the front seat. Franz,
crouched on the boards, shelved the fiddle in the angle his
knees made with his body. For Mr. Prinzing had insisted,
"Bring your fiddle; sure now. I'm having Muehlbank come, and
Arne Fledermann; fiddlers. We'll have a little fiddling bee."

The Prinzing chimney-smoke was clear on any day, spuming
from the hill, a shade under a mile of fields and pastures between
us; but it was three miles by road. And today, since it was Sunday
and we were invited company to their house, we took the longer
way. It was a hot afternoon at the harvest's end, the robins with
beaks open for air, and the blue of haze above Long Lake almost
grayish. Bad for corn, Father said, touching the mares. "Leaves'll
wilter to straw, in this heat." It was a snake-twisty road, boring
through the shadow of hollows with trees like green-and-gray
walls, the branches within whip-reach on either side; still and
like an oven, the gloom bringing no coolness, only a sense that
the throat was buttoned against breath. The grain on the cant of
hills when we rode clear of woods, rippled into broken troughs
with wind, the wheat shocks strung in rows of tents athwart
the field. There was a tight brassiness about the sky, and a few
bunchy clouds like hunks of foam grew and then flattened away.
Thunder-weather, Mother was sure, as we started the last hill.

They lived at the top of a long slant; a hard climb, broken by
smooth and level stretches—thank-you-ma'ams, Mother called
them—where the tugs slackened. "Hot as it is, and hard to
breathe, I guess the horses like the thank-you-ma'ams," Mother
was saying, when we drove into the yard.

The Prinzing house squatted in a tangle of plum hedges, a

woodshed a rod or so to the west. The yard, we saw when we
passed the corncrib, swarmed with splashes of color; people
moving; the young fry almost under the horses' feet; the menfolk gathered in clusters, coats off and white or blue in shirt
sleeves, a half-dozen going to the field to mill out handfuls of
wheat from a shock, blowing the chaff in a yellow shower and
cuddling the dark red kernels in a palm. Others pitched horseshoes, and a great shout went up as Mr. Prinzing came to un-
hitch our team: "Hukelpoke—the son-of-a-gun—threw a
double ringer"; and Alb snapped his suspenders: "Aw sheets!
Ain't more'n any kid'll do"; but pleased.

We got down, Mother shaking her skirts, Franz sprawl-kneed,
gripped with shyness, big as he was. Mr. Prinzing waved toward
the house: "Go straight in, Mrs. Vildvogel; womenfolks are
most in the kitchen." He bent to Father with lowered news:
"You are here just in time; cork is loose for a little schnapps—I
got a bottle, special." Horses and talk went away with them.

Mother was at once lost in Mrs. Bauer's fat arms and led to
see the baby. Franz, sliding the black fiddle case under his arm,
received a hail from Matt: "Be a two-toed bloodsucker if I
wouldn't 'a' batted you one, if you left it home"; meaning the
fiddle. Dominic Morton—Minica, for short—whooped: " 'Up
to your partners right and left and all hands round'; I'm getting
Etta, you know, Diah." Diah Kloster, stuck on the Rippey girl,
hauled Minica to the ground, talking to Franz: "Fiddle music
stinks, Franz, the way Old Muehlbank plays it; when you gonna
fiddle next?" Franz, eagerness rushing in his arms and forgetting
shyness, answered carefully: "Any time, now." The boys ran
thumbs over the crutches, pity in their eyes, but stout words in
their teeth. Franz stood by me as though he were the elder,
bandy-proud, and I a yearling that needed to be hurried off to
the backhouse for a change of diapers any minute. Brays of
laughter followed one another under the box elders where the
beer keg spouted foam, and the boys, Franz with them, got their
lips frothy on a second glass. Mr. Prinzing, handkerchief red

against his neck, called, "Got a couple of calves in the pasture,
Vildvogel; three months old and you can't see a rib; like to go?"
A flock of men with Father and Fritzie joined him.

The girls shrieked on the porch, Tinkla loudest, her voice
plain to hear, and Liliem there, free from work for an hour, but
none turning our way, pretending the yard was as empty as a
sloo, except for chickens and pigs. Franz stared seriously at the
woodshed, the boys with him, and then, surprised and as if for
the first time, noticed the girls; eagerness for their company
brushing away the shame of a rip in his pants Mother couldn't
quite mend. But he ignored the whole passel of young women,
as a man should.

Leff Sperry, loose-lipped and pimply, yelled, "Let's play catch.
Got a ball, Matt?" And the leather smacked from hand to hand
with talk and crooked curves: "Watch this one burn between
your legs." Franz sometimes tossed it to me, where I haunched
on a board pile. Matt said: "Arne Fledermann is sore; Pa told
him you were as good as *he* was, fiddling, and Arne pretty near
wouldn't come." Franz missed the ball, fumble-fisted at the
compliment. Diah Kloster mopped sweat. The girls, suddenly
quiet, watched, upset that we didn't come running, I guess. The
yard swam in haze, earth mixed with air, it seemed, light
enough to blow at the next fierce puff. "In for a twister, the Old
Lady says." Minica threw a stick toward the barn where a litter
of pigs climbed a sow's red side, falling off and into the same
puddle that cooled her dugs. "Old Lady saw a cross in the fog
yesterday morning."

"Your gra'ma knows—" Franz began, but Minica interrupted:
"Too much; lacing a feller 'cause he didn't bury a dead cat.
Brings awful bad luck, she says, 'specially if it's black."

"Never had a gra'ma." Franz flipped the ball, pensive. "At
least to see; the folks don't speak of any."

"It's just as well." Minica scotched a sizzler that Leff threw
him, and sank down. "All in, fellers." The game died to a
languid bounce or two, the ball rolling under the buggies lined

by the barn and nobody going after it. Sharp clink of horseshoes striking the iron peg and a laugh dragged over the yard: "Another ringer! Alb, you got the Devil in you today." The boys perched on wagon tongues and leaned against wheels to tell smutty stories, heat in their muscles. They rubbed their knees, Minica saying, "Old Man Mankin—sure keeps his woman busy—a new kid about every year," and added with a thick laugh before anyone beat him to another idea: "Adam Kloots— think he'll ever be a pa? The hired man says he can hear Adam—tries hard enough." Franz was scarlet to his gills, chin in his collar, the other boys wriggling in the dust, delighted. Once Mrs. Bauer's voice burst from the house: "Takes after her ma; like cow, like calf, they say." A baby squalled. Franz almost crossed his eyes, moving from the men, finished with the pasture and *prosting* their beer, to the girls ringed on the porch railing. Screams came from the "Drop the Handkerchief" circle, the kids in tangles, brushing the heat back with their damp hair, little Jimmy Mayer suddenly shrilling: "I see London, I see France, I see Mary's underpants," and the circle breaking to chase him around the house.

We moved under the box elders with the men, where Mr. Mais was digging the hot summer of 'seventy-four out of his memory and shaking his head: "Ground so hard, you couldn't drive a nail in"; Old Lafferty nodding. A ridge of clouds piled in the west. The Dunkel twins sneaked into the haymow and squirmed out of their underwear, thick cotton and heavy, running airily for an hour in shirts and pants; their mother noticing soon and marching them back, scolding: "Rheumatiz, that's what you'll get; sun sweatin' you, like that." Doves under the granary roof-tree quarreled softly—"Lookit the coon, lookit the coon," Franz thought they said, and squinted at the porch.

Tinkla came bouncing, the girls with her, Liliem too; Tinkla taking the lead. "Everybody else is slow as sticks," she chattered. "Circle ready for 'Happy Is the Miller'; girl and a boy, girl and a boy, around the ring; odd man in the center. Franz knows the tune." She let a finger trail over his bare arm when he came with the fiddle, and Franz almost dropped the case.

The skippy melody danced with the heat waves under a sky brassier than ever; got in the blood:

> "Happy is the miller that lives by the sea;
> Bread for his wife and sugar for his tea;
> Hand on the hopper, the other on the sack,
> Ladies step forward and gents turn back . . ."

Matt Prinzing pulled Teena Dorset close and rested his chin on her shoulder. Diah Kloster, odd man, waltzed in the middle, eying the players . . . the girls hopping to form an inner circle, the boys curving the outer line in an opposite direction . . .

> "Sailing east and sailing west
> And sailing over the ocean;
> Say young man, if you want a good wife,
> You better be quick in your motion . . ."

There was a scramble of hands tearing at arms and the flap of dresses as the boys grabbed their partners; Diah Kloster, head down like a young bull, galloping for Etta Rippey and knocking Minica Morton off his feet; a fierce snarl of elbows and legs, the two parting, each daring the other to touch Etta's hand; Etta prinking and proud; until Franz proposed: "Wrestle for her; first man down keeps his mouth shut; rest of the game." He moved closer to Liliem, bolder now, with the fiddle under his arm.

The two boys squared off, muscles bulging against muscle, pebbles flying under the kick and scrape of their shoes. Diah won her fair, but Minica sulked, and I saw that he stole her away to be his partner as soon as he could; sneaky. Franz switched the tune to "Four in a Boat" and the game went on. Liliem said, eyes as much on Franz as on her partner, "It's a shame; Franz fiddling so the heels get loose, and he can't even join the promenade." Tinkla laughed. "Well, you can't eat cake and put it in your pocket, too. Come on," dancing away with her hair jiggling like the straggle ends of a scrub mop. All of them swinging down the hours of that afternoon.

A queer sort of darkness fell at the end of the piece, and we saw all at once that the sun had burrowed out of sight like a badger, a tail of orange streaks behind him. Clouds like a great smoke rolled their black bellyings against the dull reddish sky. "Gonna be a ripper," someone said, and the play scattered. An uneasiness that wasn't fear exactly, but half brother to it, wrinkled the faces with the beginning of worry. Old Lafferty started to explain: "The cyclone is a revolving tornado; currents of hot air—" but Heinie Grosbeck cut him short: " 'Tain't what it is that matters; it's what it does." Mr. Prinzing assured everyone: "No more'n a gunny sack of wind; been expecting this, though," and called to Matt: "Shoo the turkeys in, or they'll get the chill, rain on them." Franz put the fiddle away and went with Tinkla and the rest to the porch. A rumble that might have been a hill rocking, as much felt as heard, ribbled over us, and an east wind moaned futilely into the darkening west. The thunderheads, drawn in a solid rank, like mottled ice, hung over the nearest ridge, and the forepaws of cloud were on us. Mrs. Kloster hauled down a line of diapers with determined jerks, hallooing to Mrs. Bauer: "They'll get no wetter, out here; but I need mine." Mrs. Bauer nodded and screamed: "Tinkle, Tinkle, did you shut the bedroom window, the west one?" Alb Hukelpoke, his hand moving in an arc, pointed in prophesy: "Cat's knuckles! The way she's raring up." A dull flash, strangely pale on the windowglasses, left the slope and the road darker than before. Mrs. Prinzing's voice was heard: "Liliem, I've put the water on—for coffee." Mr. Mankin, suddenly remembering, shouted above the heads of people to his son: "Hermie, skin the harness off the bay horse; fast, and ride; the haymow door is clear open." The ash trees over the porch creaked in the hushing wind . . . dark over us . . . the eastern sky clear now, what there remained of it, eaten almost to the ridges by the teeth of storm, but washed with a strong light, faded rose, like the opening of a great cave—a cave of murkiness in which we waited. The hooves of the bay clopped on the road. Franz leaned by a pillar, his face oddly gray with the lightning flashes winking faster . . . grumblings felt in the wood under a hand. The kids were still outside by the woodshed, Jimmy Mayer "it" and tagging another boy, ears shut with laughter and deaf to parent cries: "You get into the house, you kids, or Ma'll come with a stick" . . . playing on. A long cloud, white and the color of dirty milk, elbowed its way downward. Wind slowed to nothing at all, the squeak of a barn door heard with terrible distinctness. The wheat shocks, firm with next year's flour, stood row on row, each topped with a hat-bundle. All at once the tin horse on the barn roof squealed out as a gust whipped it round to point the wind stormward. A low sick groan troubled the air as if forests of trees twisted in bitter agony. Jimmy Mayer cupped his hands for rain, the other kids coming in reluctantly . . . darkness hanging deeper.

Then, before we had time to unhook a button, a long snake of storm lashed out over the hills; a shrilling in the trees. The wheat shocks leaned, tumbled, and at last bumped their heads to the ground, a bundle writhing into air, spun by an invisible cord. Folks crowded into the house, Mrs. Bauer shouting, "Tinkle, get away from the window, when it lightnings like that; Jeppy, too." Franz, still on the porch, crouched back against a post, spellbound by this Egyptian darkness creeping over the barn . . . wind screaming onward.

Suddenly the sky opened cellar-wide with flame and crashed to earth in sound. Jimmy Mayer, confused, cried out, scampering in panic into the woodshed . . . a roar staggering the senses, a howl growing until the head could no longer hold it; Franz crowding in; Widow Mayer, shoving about: "Where's Jimmy? Where's Jimmy?" A shudder wracked the frame of the house and Mrs. Prinzing's water pitcher slid forward from the shelf and splintered on the floor . . . a scream, and the next instant a corncrib tumbled awkwardly among the buildings. A buggy, hitched to the wind-stud, ran backward across the yard . . . Widow Mayer's hoarse: "Jimmy, Jimmy," and Franz calling over his shoulder, "I'll get him; in the woodshed; it's not far" . . . leaping suddenly away, the first large drops pounding at his heels. The womenfolk huddled, Alb Hukelpoke's youngest hiding under his mother's apron . . . heads at the window . . . thunder banging up the steps of heaven . . . water falling like hail dumped from a rain barrel . . . Tinkla crying out for no reason, "Franz, Franz," but Liliem near the door, silent, her hands over her face, shutting off fear . . . sheets of wet showing in the grass and spreading, the yard streaming in a lake of water, licked to red and angry flame with each burst of fire . . . a faint shriek, childish and high, nearly lost . . . the thank-you-ma'ams melting away one by one . . . Mother twisting her ring, this way, that way; Father grimly watching a straw rack crash into view.

There was terror in the way the lightning forked just beyond the window, close to the door, where I crowded. I saw Franz jump from the woodshed, Jimmy in his arms, head lowered against rain, his shoes splashing as he ran . . . somebody shouting . . . the woodshed rising as if on legs, huge, a monster waggling in the bushes; a wall hinging out like a giant's arm to catch Franz; Franz going down, a knee scraping earth, but shoving forward; the wall missing him and, in a burst of windy rage, it seemed, firing a board that ripped through air and caught Franz along the head. He lurched, pushing Jimmy in front of him; crawled on hands and knees.

They came up the porch, Mr. Mais helping, Jimmy swallowed in his mother's arms, Franz sagging on the doorsill, face bloody, dirt and wet in his hair. He looked at Liliem in a strange pleading way, as if he wanted her hands pressed to his cheeks. Liliem screamed and drew back, almost disgust in her pale face. "Don't; you're dirty; don't touch me." Franz slumped, hurt deep and wide in his eyes; as if Mother had slapped him.

People thrust forward, Mother before Mrs. Bauer. But Tinkla slid an arm about him; yelled: "Worse than stones, you are. Get water, quick; and cloth." She pushed them aside with a swing of her wrist, as though she carried a wand and magic dropped in a white mark on the floor; dabbled blood with a steady swabbing, though her lips were smeary red in her white face. The lightning's constant fire glared on her. "It's only a cut," she said, low, a hand on his shoulder. "Shallow, too." Franz breathed in short gasps, but became easier; closed his eyes and put his fingers near hers. "Tinkla, your hand—it's warm." Glad for that moment, at least, to be with her out of storm.

11

It is years from me, that late afternoon of roaring, the cold ice of panic melting to let us act natural again and speak without clamping the teeth. I remember how the wind passed and the water had its way, the barn after a long while emerging weatheredly from rain that was like a tangle of gray reeds. Franz was on his feet again before the last thunder strode over the hills; pale, but nothing harmed that a good supper wouldn't mend, Mrs. Prinzing said.

Liliem was sorry, her face wan among the curls, stopping, milk pitcher caught by the handle, near him. "I—it scared me." She was cryptic. "Such a racket and coming so—well, all over me at once." Her thumb followed the curve of the pitcher handle. "I thought my heart would jump out of me—beating so." She glanced at him shyly, and Franz quit shuffling his feet. "Don't, Liliem," he said, eyes on the floor. "I was scared—more than you, I guess. Don't blame yourself."

"And you won't think I meant it—what I said?" Her voice was soft. Franz met her eyes, half-eager, the distant lightning a flash in his own. "You know that." Her smile uncurled and blossomed slowly and what was left of a furrow folded on his brow was dragged away in a grin. "Come to supper." She teetered the pitcher and went into the kitchen, where Tinkla was loud among the pans.

A strange quiet that was tranquil with sound rested like a blanket over the valley; and the rush of water falling from leaf and roof and hill to the creek was a part of that quiet, as the drums of thunder were and the chuckle of drops in the barrels; the wind standing still, nowhere felt, as if hammered flat as the corn in the fields. It made supper a queer meal, hurried over with. Afterward Franz stood by a window, open now that what had showered down lay close to earth; half of him caught by the storm's retreat, half-watching the folks gather up wraps and kids, supper eaten and time for chores. "Cows'll be at the gate," Mrs. Mankin was saying to Widow Mayer. "Hate to think of the garden, though." She skewered her straw bonnet with a long pin. "All washed into the sloo, I s'pose." A kind of worry was mingled with the buttoning of a coat or the shushing of an awakened child: "Going home, now, Peter-boy; big man like you, bawling so." Home, when, for all they knew, home might be a junk pile of lumber jutting into air, matchwood of the wind; the bricks and blue paper sodden with moisture. Franz made a quick movement, as if our chimney, faintly seen in the oak, were a pledge of strength and security. But he didn't know where to look when the Widow Mayer shook his hand, wordless as he was; winked at Jimmy, carrying him to the buggy.

We saw the storm resting like a dark wall on the distant ridges. Lightning knotted the thunderheads with ropes of fire, or zigzagged four ways at once like the strands of a cord untwisting and flying wide.

The folks left, most of them; in a great rattle of wheels, buggy and wagon, to see what the fist of heaven had done to crib and cow; staying to milk and slop calves. "We'll be back," shouted Mr. Morton, waving lines.

"Pound the team, then; got another pony yet, to tap," returned Mr. Prinzing. "No good, poking at home. Corn'll raise again; shocks dry out."

"Yerp." Alb Hukelpoke climbed in, among his six kids. "Git your fat end over there, Ma; need a little room myself." He pointed at Franz: "Don't go home; you ain't fiddled yet," and answered Mr. Prinzing, "What's down is down, and a feller'll sleep better laughing than crying. We'll be coming soon. Git along, there, Jerusalem."

We stayed, Franz and I, because Matt asked and Father gave his grudging yes; had to, knowing that Mr. Prinzing would pay him higher than anyone for the grubbing job that fall, and not daring to refuse, even when his mouth was ready to; especially when Mr. Mais promised: "I'll bring them along, Johan; safe as can be." Fritzie went with Mother and Father, not sure how he'd feel after milking. Mother was glad, I think, that we could stretch this hour.

A few of the neighbors remained at home, counting with a dazed wonder the chicks and pigs drowned in puddles; or pushed with a toe at a steer, mauled and shapeless under a battered tree— finished with mirth, that day. But most of them splashed back, many while the sun yet burned the clouds to red ash. The yard stirred again, the Mankins jingling up, and the Hukelpokes, the Mortons, and the Klosters; the Bauer boys, Tinkla's brothers, whooping from a ridge, cutting across two pastures and a field. Not much damage done on their place, they said; hayracks tipped and corn flat; bundles scattered by the acre; but little rents, these, and of no consequence; easy to repair when a man is strong with singing and his neighbor's laughter.

Heinrich Muehlbank, jumping down, fiddle · case tilted, chortled to Franz: "Give you a run for your money yet, *Junker;* even if Arne Fledermann ain't coming. He got bad hit; barn caved in." Franz was all awkward with too much body; for Mr. Muehlbank, playing first fiddle at dances on Saturday nights, stood next to the Pope in importance (except to the Pastor, of course), even with rheumatism beginning to stiffen the limberness in his fingers. The folks moved restlessly—Tinkla and Liliem dashing at the newcomers . . . a wagon tongue clanging out of the neckyoke iron . . . Otto Krunz, a bachelor, driving in, red-eyed and crazy-haired, milk in cans and jars splashing the wagon; his barn gone up in swirl of flame, lightning-started, and no calves to suck the creamy pails: "I milked; every damned drop; but I wouldn't give it to the fire. Drink it, you fellers; drink it," he suddenly yelled, tearing at his coat; then sobbed, head on the wagon seat. Franz crawfished away from him, white, fear gripping his throat; raising his chin to see the earliest twinkle in the sky, as if doubt-riven: death falling from heaven and no strength in any farmer's thighs able to withstand the bolts of thunder. But he had to grin crookedly when Matt Prinzing rode the old black boar straight at Etta Rippey, who fled shrieking to the house.

We giggled and grieved, that night, the two shaken together like yarrow and mint, and poured brimful into our lives. Darkness grew, the wick of day screwed down slowly to the last glimmer. The storm was no more than a flibber of lightning beyond the stars; and suddenly we saw the moon riding clear of ridges, incredibly large; the grass shining with oil of silver wetting each blade.

There was a stomping of feet on the porch where the beer keg was fenced in with men; and a running through bedroom and pantry, big and small mixed up in the party. Mrs. Bauer, in a corner, had her shoes off to ease her bunions. Old Lafferty, gabbling politics with half a dozen from Turkey Hollow, announced, "Better schools is what we need; and education. Why, they have telephones, way over East; talk from house to house, miles apart and—" The men straightened in their chairs, mouths puffed with laughing and disbelief: "Smart, he is; tell the old mare how to pup, next"; so that Old Lafferty shuttled off, grumbling, "Old turtlebacks; so much moss in your ears, you'll sit and dry up," and going to start a set of charades, his favorite game. He corraled Franz and Liliem and the rest, though the group was reluctant, with the night and the moon beyond the door. He struck a snag the first thing, trying to act out "amble." Diah

Kloster sniggered, "Ain't no such word," and Lafferty got his bristles up: "Guess there is." Diah wanted to know what it meant. Lafferty, tightening his vest as he did at school, declared, " 'Amble, a noun; a method of progressive motion in quadrupeds, with the same sequence of foot-fallings as in the— the walk . . .' " He paused; then wheeled ahead firmly at the giggling: " '. . . but in which a hind foot or a fore foot is lifted from the ground before its fellow hind foot or fellow fore foot is placed thereon, and—and—' "

"Kick the horse in the tail," somebody shouted, and no one heard Lafferty further, all cackling, and meandering outside. Mr. Muehlbank called, "You got an extra G-string, Franz?" and Franz stayed behind.

The night was prickly with stars, but cool enough for coats after the rain. We had just begun "Light in the Window" when Jonas Bluber spanked along in the new top-buggy; a surprise, since he wasn't invited. The dashboard was black where it wasn't spattered with mud and the side curtains jetty triangles, the moon striking on the metal rings. Jonas waited for an excuse to hook fast the storm front, if anybody asked; showing off, we knew; strutting about, a whip with a ribbon at the lash snapping in his fist—like a he-dog with a new bitch around, Alb Hukelpoke said afterward. He raised his nose in derision. "You fellers, with your tin fiddles; ring around the rosy." He snorted. "I'm going to a real dance."

"Where, Jonas?" Liliem spoke, low and a bit breathless, but clear in the silence.

"Mason's Resort; on Pike Lake." That was the new place we'd heard about; the one Pastor had proclaimed another Sodom and Gomorrah.

"Tonight, Jonas?" Liliem, near the wheel, put a hand on the rim, and drew away.

"Sure; hop in, and I'll take you." He stuck an arm in her direction. "Show you some real pepper." She hesitated, half-rose to take his arm, glanced at the house, and turned aside. "No."

Then she took her partner's hand and joined the circle. Jonas laughed, a smucky sound, and lashed the team down the road.

"Yerp, the young blow-tight," we heard Alb say; listening, he'd been, on the path to the barn; too much beer. "Feller ought to take a skinning knife to him."

We shut him off, the song drifting high, half the faces plain in the light, the other half dusky; the ivy on the house like dark ropes, the leaves distinct.

The verse petered to girl's tunes and died. Leff Sperry, scratching at his pimples, listened to Wilhelmina Prinzing's account of a new schottische. The screen door slammed and Franz came, Liliem dropping her partner's hand fast, and Tinkla calling, "Watch the lowest step; it's broke." He hesitated, and found a place on the railing. I guessed he didn't care about Tinkla's babying him. The crowd eddied to the porch-end, where Franz sat, moon washing the house wall; Tinkla below him, but Liliem running up the steps and coming to perch at the corner.

It was a night for homely things, witch-spelled and re-fashioned as they were by an odd moon-change to lace and cloud. The barn was gabled in shadow and the granary windows lighted with a glow paler than any we ever saw flaring from a lantern wick. A night to chain the tongue and let silence whisper. Tinkla lifted a hand to brush the ivy, but Franz, catching her, said, "Don't; I've been watching them." His fingers slipped from her arm. "Ivy leaves; they're—they're like hands." He paused, unsure of himself but finished the thought in his queer way. "A pinch of silver, they've got; in each hand." It felt strange, his saying; suited to star-winks but silly here at a baptizing, I guess. Tinkla's laugh was earthy and strong with scoffing. "Franz, Franz, such crazy ideas; sounds like the Bible; you'll be preacher, next." Minica Morton chanted: " 'Roses are red, vi'lets are blue; I spit poo-etry, too.' " Franz looked at Tinkla; a long space of gathering laughter, it seemed; the furrow deep again between his eyes, and a bewildered helplessness

beyond measure sagging his chin; Tinkla making fun of him.
The dark fell blacker where his face had been.

But Liliem, dreamy-lidded as he, faltered, yet we heard her,
"I know, Franz; it's—it's like when you take wine—at Lord's
Supper; you feel good inside and—" She stopped, a shadow not
thrown by any substance we could see clouding her face; and
was still. Franz moved into light, swiftly, as if he wanted to test
her words with hands. "Liliem, you—you *do* get it, don't you?
Like fiddle music in the head and—" He was almost trembling
with eagerness.

"It's—" Liliem spoke slowly. "It's like that; something. But
not—not the same, either." I had a feeling that the two might
have been on a rooftree high as the zenith away from us. Heels
clicked and Matt sang in glee, "By the two-toed bloodsucker,
they've had more beer'n they ought to, both of them." The
group shifted, broke; went to the yard, where we tried "Drunken
Sailor." Liliem came with Tinkla, and Tinkla slipped an arm
through Franz's: "Don't be mad; it was nice, what you said."
Franz answered: "Ain't got horns; why should I be mad?" He
swung toward Liliem: "Lady partner goes to the left." But
Liliem wouldn't, strangely wayward of mood, all at once:
"You skip with Tinkla. Please," and gave him a slow smile. He
stood there, irresolute when she went with Leff Sperry, squirming a little, as though he had needles in his pants; until Tinkla
whispered to him, and he turned back, stiff and not very warm.
But she thawed him in a round or two, and when the set ended,
I heard her wheedle: "Guess I'd go to the granary dance—if I
was asked." Franz's voice was husky as if speaking and swal-
lowing near strangled him: "Would you, Tinkla? Really?"
Her answer escaped under Matt's bull roar, beginning the verse
for the circle:

> "What shall we do with the drunken sailor?
> Put him in a boat and sail him over,
> Sail him drunk and sail him sober,
> Fall of the year comes in October . . ."

Leff Sperry stripped off shoes and stockings on a dare, running white-footed and bold, Liliem's laughter inaudible in the loudness of the next stanza.

We had lungs for song aplenty, untired, when Mr. Prinzing yelled through the window, "Come in, all of you; Muehlbank's got tuned up; and the fiddle's warm, Franz"; adding, "He's ripe to beat you." We went inside and sat in corners. The chairs were occupied by the older folks.

I think it was the night and the storm, now gone; the moon, hardened to silver in his eyes; Tinkla's hands and Liliem's dreaminess—all of these, bundled together in him, and a great loneliness stuck lumpishly in his throat and crying down his fingers into the strings, that made him play so. The room, dim in spite of two lamps yellow-flamed behind glasses and high on brackets, became thick with sound, and small . . . the folks forgetting even to drop a toe beating time. Old Lafferty, unwed these thirty years, but happy in a young wife once, got off his chair, as if he'd lost something and thought he knew where it was, but sat down again, sober with regret. Tinkla stood motionless in duskiness for a moment, and Liliem, back of people, was hidden except for her hair. Old Lady Morton pushed restlessly in her rocker . . . the fiddle singing, singing into silence, a queer choked-up silence. Then the folks shouted the rafters into noise; so that Mr. Muehlbank smiled crookedly at his gnarled and rheumatic fingers and put away his fiddle: "No use me making a fool of myself. The beer is yours, Franz." And all our begging was futile to open his music case. The beer went around, schooners of it. Franz grinned lopsidedly, as close to tears as laughter; the fiddle twanged in his grasp when Mr. Muehlbank raised his glass: "First fiddler, next fall, *Junker;* in my place. I'll tell the players." Before anyone moved, Alb Hukelpoke bawled: "Yerp! he did it. Old Jens would be proud of you, boy. Fill another schooner and let's celebrate." The floor creaked with assent; until Old Lady Morton shrieked through the clamor: "Shut up! And don't puke in the beer, Alb Hukelpoke; you're pig-eye drunk now." Alb protested: "Ain't yet, Ma

Morton—" but the old lady snarled, "Don't you Ma Morton me. I know you, kid-up; 'fore you could use flaps in the front of your pants." She pounded her chair: "Shut up!" and pointed a thin knuckly finger at Franz: "You got a toad's wart? or a bat's foot in your pocket?" We laughed her into a rage, although Franz was a little scared at her fierceness, and hauled the ends of his pockets into sight to show emptiness; at which she snapped: "Don't pull your guts out. But the fiddle stinks after *hexerei;* stops the blood, like a cross made upside down—"

"Aw sheets!" Alb Hukelpoke drank disgustedly. "Take the old tomcat to bed with you, Ma."

The crowd clapped hands and shifted, groups splitting to gather into new ones; Mrs. Bauer telling Mrs. Kloster: "Anna Doppelt—Gina Mais's sister, you know; she's coming, Anna is; to live with the Maises"; and Mrs. Kloster: "She's a sharp one, she is; couldn't get along with her brother, huh? Don't know who could, with that woman."

Franz played again, but the young jacks milled around, inattentive; all this waltzing scratchy as an itch on the toes but no dancing; not on Sunday night; anyway, not among godly folk. Franz locked the case, not very easy in mind. He went when Mrs. Prinzing said: "Come and see the baby, Franz; I tried to get you and Jeppy, all afternoon," and blushed red as the skinny face on the pillow at what he saw; said anxiously, "Gosh, he's small; no bigger'n my fiddle."

"Bigger'n you were." Mrs. Bauer came in and kitchie-cooed the baby. "Ain't he pretty, though? All mine were scrawny."

"He cried and cried, this morning." Mrs. Prinzing tucked in a blanket. "Such a baptism! When the Pastor poured water on his head, he gave one squawk; just one, and was still."

"Good sign, Ma Morton says." Mrs. Bauer leaned against Franz, easing her bunions. "Might be a preacher, holy water washing his head and he quiet, like that."

Franz wiggled with all this woman-talk; babies and truck. He gulped and hurried off, I with him. He was still disturbed, I could see, over Old Lady Morton's bony finger pointing at him; until we played "Post Office," the whole pack of us in the kitchen. Franz stared at the way Diah Kloster smacked Etta Rippey. Minica Morton purpled with gall. Matt almost doubled Teena Dorset—looking for a likely spot, he crowed. Franz shifted, knowing more about fiddle bows than kissing; in front of folks, too. He held a Kloster girl in his arms gingerly, as if she were a bundle of sticks, and messed a kiss on her cheek; flustered but liking it, his forehead burning; bolder with the wine of enchantment; kissing Tinkla with a sudden mad fury that left her without breath and a hand at her throat. But when his turn came with Liliem, he hung back a moment, his eyes big and the scar fiery. He bent down and lifted her chin as he would a rose; held her so a space and leaned forward, but slowed up all at once; caught her hand and kissed it fiercely, though the crowd hooted and Matt scorned him: "Franz's got a baby-lip, Franz's got a baby-lip, can't kiss a gur-rel"; like kids at school again, but with difference, too.

He didn't have much to say in the next "Pleased or Displeased" game; poked at his chin like a puppy scratching at an affectionate flea. He was mostly "pleased" and thus out of the play, or imposed such light sentences, when he was "displeased," as, "Make Etta sit in Minica's lap," or "Teena—let her sing *Yankee Doodle";* though you could see he didn't mean it. "Nubbins and rat-tails," Leff Sperry howled; "I'm displeased; I want Tinkla to balance a butcher knife on her nose."

We shouted, hours full to the striking of the clock, the heart and the head dizzy; sealing this laughter up like honey in the comb against the winter of our agony and the shadows under the cellar door—the manury pants stiff as boards rubbing the skin . . . waiting . . . waiting at home.

When Mr. Mais went to hitch the team, Franz put the fiddle under his arm as though shaking hands forever good-by; wishing this night could be lengthened like a belt and wondering (as we all did) why Sunday was the shortest day in the week. There was a queer sort of excitement in him. I remember that we played "Full Show, Half Show, and No Show," and he and Liliem were partners, closing the pantry door behind them to select the next couple. Tinkla, losing her chatter as the door narrowed to nothing, leaned forward a little, as though the shut door barred her from secrets rightfully hers; knowing suddenly, I guess, that this was different from pigtails and calico dresses at school, this pain, woman-sized and man-large. She chattered almost wildly when the hinges squealed. They came out, flustered-looking, just as Mr. Mais called: "All aboard and the wagon's ready." The party broke and we scuttled up ladders of spokes and buggy steps, Alb Hukelpoke seeing two wheels where there was only one and getting snarled in the lines: "Yerp, I'm getting her; move over, Ma."

Franz gabbled one moment, was silent the next, riding home. The night was so still we heard dogs barking miles away. The chir-chir-chir of crickets rose from earth, it seemed, thin as the dark. Franz jiggled and fussed; wanted to tell me something, I could see, but doubted how I'd take it. Once the fiddle strings whispered faint jangles when we bumped a stone; the wagon's rumble mixed with the crutches' dull thudding.

"Jeppy," Franz said, low and eager. I let the wheel grind past a dozen rounds before I answered: "What now?" The moon, broken in the basswood overhead, threw a faint spark beneath his brows. We clattered over rock on the slanted grade, protected by trees, and a hill curved gently against the sky, its line round as though it were a saw blade, the pointed shocks of grain upthrust like sharp teeth. Franz ruffled his hair and burst as if ripping a shirt to tell me: "Jeppy—I—Liliem—she's going to the granary dance—when it comes—with me."

12

We finished cutting the wheat—the last of the harvest. Father's shouts of "Giddap" rang across the bundles still to be lifted two at a time and set together—"grab'em by the ears and plump their butts down," Fritzie said. The binder rattled, and the horses, crazy with the flies sucking and swelling on blood, switched their tails and cracked their heads against the pole-end to brush away the stingers, until Franz took old machine oil and daubed it into their ears, though Fritzie snapped: "Give'em the ear-pox, Dough-pan. What you doing?" But he admitted that the team appeared easier.

Franz gathered the bundles scattered by wind, less resentful than Fritzie or Father at sweating twice over the same job because memory lengthened his step and Mr. Muehlbank's promise oiled his bones many a creaking hour. "First fiddler," he'd say, biting half-moons out of the sandwiches I brought to the field, and forgetting to chew. "Lead the players, next fall."

"That's a year away," I'd remind him, pushing a crutch into the stubbly ground.

"It'll pass; and I can think about it." A little drunk, he was, and pitch-proud, I guess, with all this, the way he patted Mother: "You wait; I'll play the folks under the benches, see if I don't." And Mother smiled with sadness about the mouth: "It is good, Fränzchen; such happiness to sleep with." Not knowing then how undisturbed her sleep was to be, all Franz's playing neither sweet nor loud enough to wake her.

Father was quick to blurt his thought about wasting time fiddling, but Franz smoothed his hackles down: "They'll pay— dollar and a half a night; two, if the crowd is big enough," and Father growled off, unsatisfied but won by the silver tune of dollar against dollar.

Franz whistled the shocks into place; wrestled with the "grandmothers," those heavy bundles doubled by the binder when a cogwheel slipped; so large that two arms could scarcely circle them to touch finger tips. He was hog-tired, stumbling in to chores, and would slide a thumb over the calluses beginning to thicken his palms as if they were marks branded deeper than flesh. But he'd wash weariness with the dirt he scrubbed from his face; get the fiddle, and sit under the oak until dusk wove into the strings. I stomped in from the pigpen one evening and stopped with the crutches tight in my hands, at the way fire seemed to dance on the strings, but knew it was the sun and the flying bow.

He had more than a little water to dampen his coattails poured on him the next Sunday when we went to church. It was my first time that year. The crutches scraped on the boards, each thump a jar felt to the head. The congregation rustled to see, but Franz, rigid as a starched collar and with a hand at my back, kept close to me; chin level; for once bold and giving Mrs. Pilversack a steady eye when she twitched a waspish nose and then nodded poisonously in our direction. I saw her flouncing beside Anna Doppelt, black and spare in the bench by Mrs. Mais.

We sat down among those we knew, Father taking a place three seats behind us; Franz next to Mr. Muehlbank, and settling his pants carefully, as a man should, sitting with important people and perhaps becoming important himself. But Mr. Muehlbank regarded him dourly and with a graveyard face; Mr. Mais saw beyond him, dignified in his greenish suit and shirt without collar but with a gold collar button tagged to his Adam's apple; and even Alb Hukelpoke was so chastened and stiff with sobriety and sanctification that one forgot the "Alb" and said "Mr. Hukelpoke" without joking. Franz perked himself down, puzzled, but with suspicion growing; especially after he whispered to Mr. Muehlbank under cover of the organ piece: "Prinzing kid sure was baptized right, schooners of beer and all." Mr. Muehlbank looked sour and thrust out the songbook: "Sing; this is church," muttering the words with solemn awfulness. Franz let his pants alone, done with prinking.

He was thoughtful on the way home, beginning to realize that a man under one skin could be two persons, as unlike as dust and water; that Mr. Prinzing, on a spree and with a mug of beer in his fist, who yelled, "Allemand all, and back to your partners," was not even blood-related to the Mr. Prinzing, deacon in the church, who paged the prayer book with his thumb and droned in the song:

> " 'A child of God I surely am,
> Abhorring sin and shame.' "

Different, there in the deacon's bench, up front, though you could see he wore about the same hat and shirt, only Sunday pants instead of Monday overhalls. Franz muddled over this, getting the wagon fixed for stacking; troubled but coming to know that some things (like the sudden way the blood grew lively when a girl pinched your arm) were for weekdays and week nights and did not exist for Sunday—at least not for Sunday forenoon and church. "It's—it's like telling a lie, almost," he'd say to me. "Mr. Dunkel, looking so holy and—and praying he'd forgive his enemies; all the while his cheek cut from fighting at the dance." He came to know, too, that laughter and fiddle music stayed outside when the church door banged; and was bothered by that which wouldn't figure up right, no matter how he added it.

Sornas Tetzlauf drove over to see about help at stacking. He walked from the buggy in a stilted manner, lines under the thumb, and snapping the whip, the horses tense and lifting their feet. A man few trusted and then only halfway. He called to Father, who was on the stack, "Last bundles, I see; all done." Father nodded shortly and climbed down; suspicious of this rich farmer from over east; not our kind.

"I need a kid to drive my team." Sornas spoke every word as if giving a speech. "You're through stacking; your kid—Franz, there—ain't doing much. I want him."

"My boys—they work." Father was beginning to get angry at Sornas' tone. "Got jobs enough."

"You send him over." Sornas snapped a beetle from his coat

and crushed it into the ground, carefully. "I'll give a dollar fifty and keep."

Father clamped his jaw. He'd have no man give him talk about running his farm, though the wage was high. But Franz burst in: "Let me go; I can do it"; his words loud, so that he side-stepped a bit; almost sorry he spoke, I could see, but not backing out. Father looked at Franz, surprised and uneasy. In the end he let him go.

"Get you tomorrow night." Sornas clambered into the buggy. "Got fifty acres of barley to stack; in a hurry." He snapped the lash while he spoke and the horses jerked nervously. Sornas smiled. "Whip keeps 'em dancing; that's my motto."

Franz was jumpy as a rabbit the rest of the day. Dubious, now that he was hired; the fear crawling again, remembering Walter and how sick and starved he was. He wished that Fritzie *would* go in his stead, but kept this to himself. For Fritzie bit his lip when he heard; a kid brother beating him to a job. What the fellers wouldn't say. His tongue was acid. "He'll make you stir your behind, Sornas will, I bet. No music there."

Father let Franz know how he felt, and before bedtime. "You bring the money—Sunday at church." He was glad about the silver, we knew, but afraid that Franz would follow Walter and leave another man's work to do; knowing that Fritzie was more like a bull every day, itching to run and hard to handle.

"You work, Franz." Father locked the door for the night.

"Won't need the fiddle, that's sure." Fritzie crawled the ladder. Franz sat straight, unbelieving. "But when bundles are hauled and the team unhitched—"

"No fiddle." Father clumped his shoes with firmness. "When you hire out, fiddle stays home. Earn the bread with a fork; we all do." Mother hung the dish towel with quietness. Franz went to the lean-to.

I found him there, head hanging. "Guess I can handle the job," he said slowly. "Feel better, though, if I had the fiddle along; put it under my chin now and then." He stripped off his pants. "Wonder if I'll ever have money—my own. I wanted to use this—for things." He unbuttoned his shirt. "Lots of things. Store crutches for you, like Crummie Lafferty's, and Mother needs—" The corn husks buried his voice.

He went away the next evening beside Sornas snapping the whip; looked at us as though he were going to a sick man's house and dreaded the hour. He was back before the week wore down to the shank; wobbled in at supper time, a purple bruise on his cheek; eyes heavy with shame and tears unshed, man's tears, acrid as brine; walked the long road home. He slipped into a chair as if in the arms of one beloved and precious, these walls home and sweet with comfort.

Fritzie egged him, eaten by curiosity, but Franz didn't move. Mother drew him close and said only, "Fränzchen, Fränzchen, *nicht so;* it is best at home." Father gave him a hard stare, at first, and let him be; waiting. The story drifted around like seed on the slow wind of gossip, and dropped at our door soon enough. . . . Franz at the Tetzlaufs' sweating over the pitchfork and trying to whistle since he couldn't fiddle the homesickness out of his body; uneasy when Sornas with his snapping whip was near, but holding up his end of the stacking, even with a skittish team. Until that afternoon when the Tetzlauf kid brought his flute to the stackers and Franz, waiting his turn to drive in, jumped from the load to listen, leather tight in his fist but ears open to the flute's call. What scared the team Franz never knew; but suddenly the lines were jerked from his grasp; the wagon rumbled down the road, rocking wildly and scattering bundles at every lurch; Franz in its tracks too late; the Tetzlauf kid after him. . . . The team crashed into a gate, shoved onto the barbwires by the heave of the load. Sornas, when he saw the bleeding horses, pulled in his lip; swung and grabbed Franz, twisting the shirt collar like a rope about his neck and jammed him against the splintered rack. The Tetzlauf kid watched his father's fingers wriggling over Franz's chin, and ran screaming.

("I told that Vildvogel buck a thing or two," Sornas bragged at the shop when he brought the twisted wagon braces to be mended, we heard from Alb Hukelpoke. "I told him, 'Get out of here, you lazy, cow-eared fiddle-scrimper,' I said; 'ain't worth a shot of powder around here,' I told him, and—"

"Didn't snap the whip, did you?" asked Alb, at the shop with a broken hub. "Keep your team stepping?"

"What's that got to do with it?" Sornas caught up an iron rod and hefted it, his eyes unsteady with evasion. Alb stood braced and his fists balled: "Cat's knuckles! I'd of hit him one," he told us later; but Old Wibart shouted then: *"Verdammter machen";* took the braces and threw them on the floor. "Young Karl—he's starting a blacksmith shop—other side of Turkey Hollow. He's poor—you can have him finish your junk." Sornas froze to ice; gathered up the iron and went.)

Father grumped in a temper, often; that a son of his should give him a bad name in his neighbors' ears—a jack of a worker, fired from a job. He was gruff when people came and stiff in his answers.

Franz didn't forget, groaning in his sleep sometimes. He knew, now, himself, what people could do to one. Bad enough with kin and congregation; worse with those who were strangers and stemmed from other blood, owing you nothing. For hours, that week, he'd stretch the awful moment in his thought, pinching the bruise gently, the breath slow, as if he felt hands on his flesh and couldn't escape.

It came out one day when Father and Fritzie were in Mary's Hill; in the middle of dinner and over a spoonful of noodle soup. "Pastor says about loving your neighbors." His voice was bitter. "I don't see much, around here; this cat-and-dog fight; somebody always in somebody else's hair." He captured a noodle that strayed over the rim of the bowl. Mother sliced more bread. Franz said: "Walter, too. Ribs sticking out, almost, when he came home. Mütterchen, couldn't we send him a bundle?—handful would help some." But he knew we couldn't, being all bone and no meat to spare ourselves; knew this even as Mother glanced over her shoulder, as if the knotholes in the floor were ears, listening; and shook her head.

Thereafter Franz walked the acres beyond our line fence with a kind of misgiving in him. He was diffident, even at the Maises' or the Prinzings', closest neighbors, when he was asked to spike-pitch, threshing time, or handle a knife at butchering. Those gall-cankered years, flowered in a mist of hate, were starting to show their wizened fruit; bitter for him, soaked to the bone in the red shame of never doing a job properly, at least to suit Father, and beginning to hear in a neighbor's command, I think, the crackle like an echo of Father's rage and faultfinding; until he became suspicious of friendship itself at times; except when the fiddle lay like a cherry-wooded bridge from chin to palm and his long fingers quivered over the strings. Then his glance steadied and his arm tightened and what he did fell with a sure stroke. The bow ran with a sirup of witch hazel, it seemed; lulled to silence the curse on the lip and stubborn retorts; or begot new ones.

The fiddle quavered with an alien note, these evenings before the granary dance; a sadness so intense I wondered that it came from flesh at all. It brought Mr. Mais and his family over, Anna Doppelt with them, Mr. Mais saying: *"Gottes Willen, Junge;* you bring the heart up. I heard you, clear down in the hog pasture." But Anna Doppelt sniffed and scraped dirt with a toe before she went inside.

I remember that evening because it was the first time she came along the path to the house; but not the last. A tall woman, spare as a rib, and put together at angles; a primness about her that lay deeper than the black dresses she hung on her bones; with a long fox-nose and a mouth like a snapped-tight old purse; more vinegar to the square inch of her than any woman I ever saw. She examined our house in one broomy sweep, her eyes spearing into every crevice of the place; into the cot where Mother slept alone, and the lean-to's litter. She gauged the strength of Mother's whiteness with a sniff and a mumble she

didn't bother to hide: "Pindling away; no iron in her blood."
She wasted no sugar on Franz; you could see that; nor on the
fiddle either—make good kindling, her glance said. Even Father
winced under her stare, cold and laid on with the suddenness of
a spring uncoiling. She looked him up and down and overside,
that first time; poked into his hind pockets, I guess; while he
stepped about, all at once, prodded by a gimlet eye.

"H'm." Her nose wrinkled. "Good worker, but poor manager; all calluses and empty bins."

Father's neck reddened, and he got angry, hearing such words
in his own house. "Lay my seed underground," he growled.
"Good as the next man; better'n most, I—"

"What's to show?" She snipped him off. "These years you've
grubbed; except cockleburrs and your shirttail out behind." Mrs.
Mais was scandalized but Anna bobbed her graying head stoutly.
"It's so. You can't squeeze wine from a slop-rag. Hill over there
south—why use it? Sour and worn out; dead soil and hardly fit
for pasture." She waved her hands, long and drooping, loosely
threaded to the wrists. Father clawed at his suspenders, jaws
working. Mother sat stunned by this woman's talk, bold against
Father.

"All back and no head work." Anna fired another barrel at
him. "Those sloo-patches spoiling your hay. One ditch dug
over the knoll—the water's in the creek; and you got five acres
of good hay land."

"And break my corn-patch in two pieces—" Father began,
but Anna broke in, "Ditch and have hay; or don't, and have
nothing, I don't care." She turned flatly from him and scolded
Mrs. Mais for idle fingers when visits were made for knitting
and crocheting, even in summer. "Not that I do it; can't sit still;
but people should, with nothing to do." She caught Franz watching her and glared at him; flecked a glance at Father and Mother
and folded her hands primly.

Father couldn't answer her, and sweat because he wanted to
throw words and none were within reach; knowing that she was

right and admitting it, though grudgingly, to himself. His lids
dropped first, I'd noticed, in the battle, and I had a swift notion
that for once Father met someone who wasn't afraid of him;
who had only contempt for the lean and sullen tongue he had
and could measure him back word for word and a little to boot.
A shrewd woman, he could see, patient as a hen over the hatch-
ing of an extra dollar; more than he, perhaps. A kind of unwilling admiration sprouted in him and grew, that summer—the
admiration he had for an animal he couldn't quite break to the
yoke. I think he was almost pleased when Anna said, as they
left, and loud enough for us to hear, "Prickle ash, that man; but
good, in his way; needs his britches snaffled up, though." A
shade of a grin flickered on his mouth. But Mother sat as one
who feels the last and final agony not far off.

12

The fields were hauled and empty of bundles, the hillsides
marked with spaces of lighter straw among the gray and
weathered stubbles to indicate where shocks had been; and the
granary dance lilted on every tongue. "Ought to be a ripsnorter,"
said Matt Prinzing, and Franz agreed; thinking of Liliem, I
guess, and how he could snare Alb Hukelpoke into playing
second fiddle while he footed a waltz or two. He warbled again
but plugged up his whistle when people came by. Trouble
knitted his brows together after a Sunday at church, the services
over, when Tinkla stopped him with a rustle of skirts, noisy but
a tenseness about her, and asked without waiting, "You're—
Liliem is going with you?"

"Going—where did—" Franz stumbled in speech, as though
caught rifling a penny bank. There was less rustle in Tinkla
now.

"Franz." She spoke in earnest. "Don't; not from you." Then:
"Is it Liliem?" Wanting to hear him say what she already knew.

"Well, I—" he paused in confusion. Never before had it

mattered whose hand he took in a dance, joining the circle together, Liliem and Tinkla and he; and in his man fashion, it never would matter. But this time, in the queer shift of heart and mind, and the odd life-change that comes unbidden and unpredictable, it made a difference to Tinkla, he saw—peaks of difference, shrouded in mystery.

He answered softly: "Yes, Tinkla; it is so. But you will be there and—" And it will be the same, he might have said, but didn't, realizing that it wouldn't be the same; never from this day. There was a silence, stretched and hurting, the crowd around but miles away, too; the Pastor's jeremiads shaking through the hum of the folks. I had a feeling that the clatter in Tinkla was pressed flat and motionless; or all gone from her. Then she laughed, a chuckle good to the ears: "Well, swing a polka for me. Pa and Ma are going; but the kids'll keep me home." She was hidden by the crowd then, and Franz had dolor in the strings that night—and for many nights; sensing that it wasn't the kids that kept her from the dance.

The dog-days plodded over the ridges, loggy and lying on the bones like spring fever. We boarded the bins high in the small corners for the oats and wheat still in the head, stacked and drying in our meager settings; the year's flour and feed and kernels for the next spring's sowing gathered there, in heaps curving up like a dome. Tinder for spark, I thought; flames shouldering skyward for an hour—and empty feed barrels for the winter. It was frightening. I'd wake, hearing Father creak the ladder to prowl like a sick and distrustful wolf among the stacks.

There was a fierce and unreal beauty about those months that brought agony to the throat: dawns when the ridges seemed to leap with the red-pencil streaks of the sun, the yard strange and full of weird shapes in the fading dark, and needing broad day to make it safe. But I wondered whether any beauty out of heaven or earth were compensation ample for the load that weighed us down. There were days when I thought breath must fail if only to stop the slow falling away of flesh from bone; arms chained to the crutches, and the mind running like a hound far ahead of the body. It was long before I learned to slide onto a milk stool and under a cow; longer before I could safely clamp the handle of a water bucket to the crossbar of a crutch and move gently forward . . . one pants leg flapping more and more with emptiness, it seemed, though the other was fair enough . . . the quick lunge of fear that struck like a blow when a crutch slipped, and the awfulness of crumpling to the ground, no strength solid to bolster rib or thigh; feeling the dumb despair of a trapped and moaning animal. Franz would watch me sag in, and play no more that hour.

Then on an afternoon three days before the granary dance, Liliem stood in the door, Mr. Prinzing having brought her; and Franz chewed the yarrow-end of disappointment. It was a hot day, the willows by the creek green except where the wind like a breath blown on fur revealed the silver on the underside of leaves. Mother was sorting eggs for Saturday's market, a pail with oats in it beside her; pushing the eggs into the grain and covering them with a palm-width of kernels; adding layer after layer of oats and eggs—"to keep the hen-plums from smashing," Fritzie said.

Franz had just brought in a hatful of eggs and was dusting the straw when Liliem came in a hurry of steps. The blood moved a tiny place in her cheek with running. "Franz," she cried, breathless. "Excuse, Frau Vildvogel, please. Franz, I— I'm going away."

"Away." Franz dropped the hat and, without knowing, took her arms, paying no heed to Mr. Prinzing in the wagon outside. "Not far, though. You're tired."

"No." She slipped from his grasp. "Aunt Middie is leaving for Fergus; doctoring her rheumatism. And Pa needs me, home."

"Way up Too Far Lake." Franz said it as though it were Asia; then brightened: "I'll come and—"

"No, Franz; it's a long piece." She shook her head.

Franz couldn't hide the yearning in him. "Long, you say; but there's no road long enough that—"

"Franz." She wouldn't listen. "Please. I have to ask—you won't be mad?" She came closer to him and curled a finger under an overhall strap. "Give me the braided hair—the keepsake, please."

Franz put a hand to his breast pocket as if the golden hair like quicksilver might escape through cloth. He shook his head. "It's mine; for always. You said—"

"That was another day, Franz. But if I keep it for you—" Her lips begged like a child's. Slowly he took the braid from his pocket. She made a quick motion but he closed his fist.

"Give it; don't pester me," she cried in a sudden flash that brought a furrow to Franz's brow. He let the keepsake go with reluctance; troubled at the way Liliem casually thrust it from sight. "Save it for me, Liliem," he said, his voice low and as if forced out. He took her in his arms then, gently, yet determinedly; not caring if anyone saw, though I had a feeling that Mother and I were no more to them than the eggs scratching into the oats. He held her in spite of the arm she put like a bar across his breast.

Then I saw Father striding to the house; guessed in a cold and awful rush of thought that he had spoken with Mr. Prinzing and knew what brought Liliem here—farewell to Franz; the spleen packed in him venting itself. I wanted to shout but a thickening like wool stuck in my throat. It was a dreadful moment—Franz bending toward Liliem and Father suddenly beside them, pulling at his shoulder. *"Na."* His tone ripped into them; into all of us, into Mother most of all, shutting off a cry; Liliem back behind Franz. *"Na,* Minna; your dirt comes out now; your kid—already in the neighbors' pastures." He fired at Franz and Liliem, but it seemed to me that his words were meant for Mother. "They said right; you two—not enough to lie in the bushes—by the mailbox, but come here and—"

Franz struck him then; with all the young oak strength in

him. Father staggered, fingers to his lip. Not believing what had happened; incredible, flesh of his rebounding against him. His head lowered. Franz crouched, his eyes propped open, and fear webbing across them; his mouth no longer firm but beginning to be unsteady with little jerks. Before anyone moved, Mother stood between: *"Nicht,* Johan; not your son's blood on your—"

"My son?" Father's voice was sticky, his hands dragged away smeary from his lips. "My son." Liliem screamed and ran, and Franz, buckling at the awful look in Father's eyes, crabbed to the door, fast, and as though a squealing board would smash the roof-beam and let the walls tumble.

I wonder to this moment that Father kept the blackness in him from leaping clear; something stronger than the screen door that shut between them, stopped him—Mr. Prinzing outside, perhaps, and neighbors' gabble; or the thought that a hard fist would be excuse enough for Franz to follow Walter, and Fritzie after him; our farm empty of help. More than that, it seems now, remembering the heavy way he said: "My son; if I could believe that," disregarding Mother's wan face and pitiful words: "Johan, Johan, if I could change what you think." Something locked up with the past and whatever haunted his troubled walkings. . . .

The stickiness in his voice more than anything lodged like gravel in my thought, the scratchy sense of familiarity rubbing again. But it wasn't until the crutches were laid aside and the body melted out of stiffness into the ecstasy of going limp, muscle by muscle, that it came to me; all at once, it came, while sleep was beginning to mist the consciousness. It was late then and Franz not yet home; hadn't been, for chores that night, or supper; head bowed over God knows what rutted path, chasing worry along the mazy rabbit runs of doubt and uncertainty. I knew later, though, that he'd ridden with Mr. Prinzing and Liliem a mile before he left them to thresh this through by himself. I had a notion to wait up for him, but didn't; and was drifting away when it forked itself into my half-sleeping—dim and misty at first, but clearing . . . that day, years back there, spilled out of the torn envelope of memory, when Franz was bulky in short pants and I was no taller than Father's hind pocket. I was running to the house with a split finger and bawling along the path, but closed my mouth like a clam and stayed motionless at Father's loud: "*Stille,* Minna," his voice growing sticky as sirup and terrible in its gentleness. Most of his words are gone but I recall that he growled something about Klosters' hired man staying at our house, years before my remembrance; in a night of storm and snow, before Franz was born; Father himself caught in the blizzard, plowing through drifts on the road from Mary's Hill and putting up at the Bauers' . . . the hired man staying beside Mother's stove; a sprightly blade, I guess, with the Devil between his shoulders and talking too much next day . . . Father hearing, all the wild bulls of jealousy loose and roaring in his skull.

I don't know how long I sat there, chilled with fright. He threw words in her face—about mixing the seed of a dirty tramp with good blood; no better than a town woman. . . . It is all daubed over and smeary with many days; but I remember how she cried it wasn't so—Franz was a son of the house and no interloper; she'd get the Bible and swear. She *did* get the Book, it comes to me; said the words slowly. There was a silence then, as if Father looked at her, clawed at by distrust and hating her because he doubted her and had nothing but his own heated and stone-gnarled suspicions to support his doubt.

It was a day that should have been plain and unforgettable, if it weren't that new pigs and a bowlegged colt and my bloody finger were more important than all the scoldings Father ever gave Mother—common as pigeon grass. But it took on significance now, after these years, when Franz was going on his eighteenth year, and I was lying awake this night, sleep dissolved; significant, remembering how Father regarded Franz and barbed his words with blame. . . .

It was false dawn when Franz trudged in. I needed no match-flame to see how low his shoulders dragged.

"Franz."

"You 'wake yet?" He spoke gruffly.

"Mother saved a roll of *Kaffeekuchen,*" I told him. "I brought it; it's by the window." He said nothing, his teeth champing wolfishly into the *Kuchen.* Then: "She's not going, Jeppy." I didn't have to ask who. "Says her pa don't like it, going so far. Wants me to take somebody else." His voice was tired and lost.

"Tinkla?" I put in, spiteful in my help.

"Oh, Tinkla; she's fine, but—" He was half-angry, rustling to sleep.

I think he would have run away, those next weeks, if there had been a place to go; seeing Mother's white and torn face by the hour; avoiding Father when he could and swift to obey when he couldn't. Father acted as though his cut lip were a rusted badge of shame. Franz fidgeted. But the dark corner-posts of his being were eaten into insecureness by all that had gone before. He couldn't forget how Walter sagged in the chair, I guess, worn and abused as an old dog; nor Pete Prinzing's yell the night Old Man Schaaf and the men rushed from the house; nor Tetzlauf's fingers like bony knobs raking over the mouth, searching for the eyes . . . neighbors that were strangers, really, and worse than strangers.

13

The barn dance arrived and, in the end, Franz did take Tinkla; that is, if riding in a lumber wagon with all the Bauers, Pa and Ma, Tinkla and her eight brothers and sisters, could be called taking a girl. Tinkla was happy, though; her grin wide with teeth, and slopping over with talk. Franz was grumpy, at first, but glad to hear her friendliness; hungry almost, with the meager fare he'd had. I went along because he wanted it so. "You're going, if anyone is." He put the fiddle in.

"Much use I'll be," I said glumly, wriggling into my coat. "Skirts and sticks ain't likely to mix."

"Jeppy made a rhyme, Jeppy made a rhyme," sang Tinkla; "going to get a letter, kisses would be better; tell her so next time."

"*Ach, katzenjammer,* Tinkle." Mrs. Bauer slid a little lower on her side of the spring seat; watching us. Franz helped me up. "Jeppy, when you have to stay home, then more will stay, too," he said in his queer fashion. Father had merely grunted over my going, since I didn't do a lot of work anyhow. But Mother had waved cheerily. I went more willing than I knew.

Abel Kloster shouted when he saw me: *"Hüpscher Junge";* and Diah almost grabbed me from the wagon. "We got a new blade for the sawmill; over there. Big as a steer." We went along, the two of us, and he ventured, for no good reason: "I knew you'd be here, this night. Franz said he'd bring you."

It was a lively dance; a knee-tickler, Matt Prinzing whooped. The dancers swayed, girls laughing, their pink cheeks pinker with waltz or polka, the men stamping heels and blaring, the blood steaming in them. A boy swung his partner high in a flutter of skirts and the girl screamed, "Joe, Joe, you're wicked," but liked it. Franz was excited, his tangled head against the fiddle-end as if on the breast of one he loved; his cheeks tight over the bones; lazily smiling at no one in particular—someday he'd be first fiddler, singing the melody; next fall, Mr. Muehl-bank said. He started up now and then to glance swiftly over the bobbing crowd—Liliem might come after all. The dancers milled in circles under the lantern-flicker yellow on steading and sidewood, and the spike-holes were black where the bin boards squared a place for the grain. From floor and wall the dust of last year's wheat and oats rose to dim the lantern. Diah Kloster waltzed dizzily, all giggles when he promenaded Etta Rippey, knowing Minica's fume, but walleyed when Minica kicked in the heel-and-toe polka with her. Beer by the dipperful was ladled into tin cups from a pail which Mr. Kloster bore around. Mr. Prinzing stopped his schottische with Mrs. Dunkel to say to Franz, "When I build the new barn, year or so, I'll baptize it with a dance; and you play the baptizing waltz." Franz grinned, drinking more than was good for him, I thought. Tinkla, dancing, lifted her face like a ruddy flower over a partner's shoulder; to Franz, it seemed to me; coming to stand by him until he two-stepped with her, a kind of glory catching her lips at the tight way he held her, though his eyes roamed. . . . The crowd promenaded. Faces peered in at the door, the boys without girls timid as spring calves at joining the circles. Young Sam Bauer, teased out by a Kloster girl and all elbows and knees, tripped over his button shoes in a rye waltz. Franz left Tinkla, to pick up the fiddle again.

I saw Jonas Bluber among the wall-hangers, sporting a red-and-black diamond tie. "Not dancing," I heard him say. "Got a party outside and a long drive ahead. But God—has she got the pepper!" Franz's grip on the bow lessened with Bluber's retreating back.

Waltz followed polka. Somebody wanted an old-fashioned mazurka. Alb Hukelpoke slapped his wife's rump with a wild yell. Lunch was brought in, cakes in slippery pans, slices of bread and sausage, coffee like a burning coal laid on the lips, so hot it was in the tin cups where beer had flatted into foamlessness a minute before. Then the good-night waltz, promise of wild honey for another time, and we rolled home, Tinkla beside Franz in the seat; Franz gnawed at by wanting to take her in his arms, I guess. He pushed close to her, in spite of Mr. Bauer's wakefulness, guiding the team—half-forgetting Liliem in the nearness of Tinkla.

14

It was a strange autumn and winter, I thought afterward. A sense of tightness waited in us, the back held stiff for the next hour; as if we'd already blundered like flies against the web of that which had been spun wide for us, unseen but there, and felt the dread. The thresher tooted his machine into our yard and the bundles we'd sweated over with fork and fingers were heaped, stem and chaff, in a pile of straw and the grain poured like a slanted drift into the bin. The thresher clanked away and we got the plow sharpened, and whetted the sickle for the corn, Father storing the tallest stalks and the ears with the brown smoke of the silk flowing away at the tips; saving them for the Harvest Festival we had at the church each year.

I'd herd the cows on pigeon grass and clover and the thin blades of barley, up late and out of season in the stubbled fields. The heifer's tongue was pink and like a finger curling about the wild oat clumps, deep green capping the dried earth of gopher piles. Hour after hour the cowbell would clung-clung-clung in my ears, and I'd be caught in a valley of quiet. The blood dallied and slowed with the clouds lazy overhead. I'd see Fritzie mauling new posts in the ground, or Franz with the plow, laying the black ribbon of a furrow across the yellow stubbles, his blue shirt a target between the horses; laying another dark ribbon beside the first. The horses bowed heads with every step and the hame tops threw off sun-sparks; tugs were taut the width of the field. I'd see Father sickling the corn into shocks, or talking over the fence with Mr. Mais, or Anna Doppelt sometimes, when she marched boldly into the corn. He said at dinner once: "Guess I'll fence the south hill patch; pasture it." Not his idea, we knew, but Anna's; and Mother would find the meat saltless and the potatoes ashes, the way she picked at her plate.

I wondered sometimes; about the farm enclosing us like a pen in which to run our scraggly lives; and was plagued in dubious moments with a great Why—the why of fiddle tunes and laughter, and the grimness Father alone understood, looking at Franz; the patience of Mother's hands; the crutches, no flesh and bone, but walking as legs . . . Why? Why? Wondering how it would end and suspecting it never would; unless there is finality with sight and sound stopped up with death.

It was in the fall that Mother went down sick; stayed in bed one morning, weary and as if she'd swept her last floor. There was something awful in her white helplessness, lying there, that morning, and all the mornings that were to come. She hid in the covers when Father strode in from chores. He stared at her almost stupidly. "*Na,* Minna; what is this? No fire in the stove?" Said it as if incredulous that she dared miss breakfast when he was hungry. Franz was scared and empty of thought except for her; crept about the house like a whipped dog that day. He opened the door a hundred times to peek in, and ate the soup and stuff I slopped together as if it were partridge and turkey, though Father would have little of it, glancing with angry impatience at the cot where Mother lay.

It was the season of branches stripped bare by wind, then, and leaves scraping over the roof; autumn in the day's heat, the ridges and the noon-sun cooling with slowness, like a great oven. Warmth faded from rock and field. The Maises walked over and the Bauers drove, with jelly in jars and laughter in their teeth, hands clumsy with kindness. And Mother perked up; so much that Franz whistled again, his eyes often to the north, as though, by wishing hard enough, he could sail his yearning kite-fashion over the ridges to Too Far Lake. But Anna Doppelt met Father by the fence and told him to get medicine, if not a doctor.

Mother kept to her bed, and, with the table spare as the oil-cloth, Franz got peaked as a feather stem along the nose. He fretted even when Mrs. Mais trotted into our house to help us, those days, when the moon took on an icy flame and all night mist blew down from the ridges, cold and wet, jerkily in swift puffs, or easily in long gentle pushes. In the morning we'd see the white of frost in whiskery juts on straws that dangled from the cracks in the hayloft; and come upon the spruces in the upper pasture, silver on the windside and green on the lee. Mother'd ask, "Are the sparrows roosting yet—in the straw pile?" And we'd tell her, "Not yet; but will, soon," knowing that when they did, the snow would be deep, and that she dreaded white heaps piling over the flowers and cold freezing into the house; her strength growing slack. I'll not forget the day we said, "They hid in the straw, the sparrows, last night," and Mother sobbed brokenly; Franz by her, desolation in his face, crying at last, "Mütterchen, Mütterchen, let me play for you—*Liebeslied*, or something." And in that hour—and many thereafter—he lullabyed her to sleep, softly; played melodies so sad, I'd put on cap and coat and stump to the barn to get my ears empty of the fiddle.

He stayed indoors much now, in spite of Fritzie's grumbles. For Father was not tardy to notice that Franz didn't use the whole loaf in thick slabs for sandwiches, as I did, but sliced evenly, and that his coffee had flavor, and was not, as mine, either dishwater or brine-thick—"The coffee," Fritzie snapped at me more than once; "strong enough to go pitch manure"; until Franz took a hand. He played often, mostly the sad old love song for Mother, whistling it while he scrubbed the floor, awkward as a bear cub on his knees.

We banged pails to get more water at the pump, one time, Franz wet above the ankles; crossed a fresh fall of snow in the yard and looked at the marks we'd made, his tracks firmly cut and molded, mine crushed—holes in rows punched by the crutches and trails of two feet, one uncertain, the toe waggly, now this way, now that; and the other rumpled snow, as if a bean sack had been dragged there. Franz pumped slower, until a pail brimmed over. He swung away, speaking in a tired voice: "It's poor feet I am for you; even when I try." He swished off to the house.

Then on a December day, when we had shoved back chairs from a meal of scorched potatoes and black bread that Mrs. Mais had baked, Anna Doppelt unlatched the door and shook snow on the sill. "Minna's sick; you need three meals, you and the boys, to keep the place going." She spoke with directness that couldn't be avoided. "I'm coming to cook for you." Mother raised a white arm to say no and Franz stood between her and

Anna. But Father said quickly, "Let it be, Minna." Mother's arm lay limply on the covers. Too worn now to struggle against the bit and bridle of a will she'd obeyed meekly most of her days, even though Franz was desperate to protest. Thereafter, Anna peeled potatoes, feather-thin, at our house, and laid the oilcloth. She wore a path across the seven-acre patch, going home to the Maises' in the afternoon and after supper, since we hadn't a spot for her to sleep. Early in the morning, sometimes before Father had pounded into his shoes, she'd return to rake the coals and set the kettle to boil.

A kind of darkness swinging with the black skirts about her feet crept into our place the day she crossed the oak-sill, I think. It hung with the cobwebs under the rafters, this darkness, shadowy as a cloud falling on the bridge of the fiddle—and making Franz grab bow and endpiece with a fearful grip. But she cooked well, less acid in her gravy than in her tongue, and tended Mother with a gentleness in her fingers that I never found in her voice or in her silence. She had a way of pitching food as if it were straw on the table that made Franz draw back, at first. "Eat," she'd snap. "Ain't poisoned," and sniff grimly at her own joke.

Father was pleased to have her with us, especially with sawing at the Klosters' not far off; glad without probing further than that his pants were washed and dinner did not fail. Beyond what was woman's truck, he didn't care to go. But Franz was shut from the house by the hour, for Anna hated music, even church hymns, and didn't mind letting him know it, either; flounced out and home in the middle of washday when Franz wanted to fiddle; so that he had to go to the Maises' and beg her to return. It was mildew in his mouth, you could see, and he did it only because Mother began to cry, the clothes unwashed and Father loud if he found out. After that Franz fiddled when Anna was away. He wanted to join the shin-dandies on Saturday nights; was pucker-lipped when Matt Prinzing drove by and said he had room for another fellow.

He longed for the feel of a yellow curl, I guess, but didn't go.

Tinkla followed the swamp-path to our house—to visit Mother, she hallooed, but Franz grinned so broadly, going to the barn to sling manure, that Mother sent her down to be with him—a minute, she said; though it was an hour before Tinkla found the path back, breathless as though running hard and chattering she didn't know where time flew. Franz warbled like a song sparrow, happier than he'd been for days; Tinkla a kind of solace for Liliem's absence.

But on a January day Anna wallowed through the snow to the barn, where I was helping Father mix feed and Franz was whittling on a fork handle; banged the door and said shortly: "You might as well know. It's more she's got the matter with her than any man here can repair. Send for the doctor."

Father scraped the mixer, dripping with feed. "Doctor—with his truck. I'll not send for that old—"

"Don't, then." Anna sniffed scornfully. "Better send for her coffin." She stormed out. Franz let the wood slip, his face dead-white. Father got up, muttering angrily, but didn't need Franz's word to see that Anna was right.

Dr. Allbauch came, smelling sourer than ever of brandy and horehound. He fussed and cursed under his tongue, and wouldn't answer squarely, but hinted of this female weakness and that, each with fancy names; which would be higher priced, of course, but didn't help much. Not much, when we knew in our hearts what ailed her—worn, she was, and frayed as the dress, old and the color of light apple butter, she'd sewed and tucked to threads, loose and parting. Father counted four dollars and a dribble of change into the doctor's palm, and promised him a calf in the spring. We sat down to supper that night as to a meal of bones and snakeroot, Father silent and Fritzie glum, both leaving soon to dicker with Mr. Mais about a stack of hay. We had the silence then, and the smell of wood burning. The pain in Mother's eyes grew as she watched Franz thumbing a string; a quick moan brought him running to the bed.

"Is it worse—the pain?" Agony was in the slump of his shoulders.

"Lift the chin, Fränzchen. And hear me."

Her voice made Franz go to his knees. "You are worse. Shall I run for Mrs. Mais or—"

"*Stille,* Franz, and hear me." She put a hand on his. "Stay with Jeppy; always, Franz. Promise."

"Mütterchen." There was reproach in his tone. "What could I do else?"

"It is good—to hear you say it." She sighed. "It will be better for me—resting all night and the whole day, too."

"Mütterchen, Mütterchen." He hid in the covers and the hurt in his cry left me hot and cold and weak along the spine.

15

I wonder about hope sometimes, remembering how Franz was crowfooted with disquiet—hope that sprouts like the wild oat blades, new each season, plowed under and harrowed though they are with iron teeth and the curving share. Never dead, it is true; as if an eternal resurrection lined the furrows and no seed rotted; but cropped always, the blades, by horse and cow, and bitten to the root until the stems thicken and become stubby with sourness, so that cattle nose but will not eat; bitter, as the rag-ends of hope are, cherished but unprofitable and more like a burden on the heart than anything else. Or so I thought, regarding Franz that spring. He'd walk up from the manure piles in the field smelling forty yards away, when the wind was right, his fork on the shoulder and bloodroots, white and fragile, sprawling over his fist. "In the lower woods," he'd say hopefully to Mother. "The ground is snowing them." He'd bring a glass for them, blind to Anna's disdainful manner. "Jack-in-the-pulpit's there. Not very big; ain't lifted his cellar door, yet." Anna nearly dropped a plate once in exasperation. "Such notions rattling in your head—two beans in an empty can." Franz would have answered her, but Fritzie yelled from the barn, "Load's full and going out," and we went to the yard, just as Alb Hukelpoke swung his white horses and the buggy to the granary, waving his willow whip.

"Whoa, there, Jerusalem 'n Jericho." He pulled up. "Hey, you fellers. My old woman sent you some black currant wine—for your ma." He handed the bottle to Franz, scratching his head regretfully. "Had a hell of a time—the cork's loose and some spilled out. It got in the nose and I almost took a drink. Cat's knuckles." He shifted a cud. "How's your ma?"

"Well, she's—" Franz began, but Alb switched the talk, untwining his gossip. "Mrs. Dorset is abed. Pee-monia, they say." Alb chuckled suddenly. "I sure drug the underpants off of Old Toffmann—on a seed deal, yesterday. The old wood tick, I fixed him." He squirted between two spokes, a bit off side, and after a wink at Franz, tried it again, with serious determination. "Yerp. And Jonas Bluber—did you hear? He had a runaway with his new buggy. Team got scared at Buckman's Corner. Cost him ten dollars in repairs. I near ripped up my guts laughing when I heard; he knows such a hell of a lot about horses."

On any other day we would have spent hours stretching this news to cover the pull of work. But now the heaviness in us crowded out mirth, though Franz laughed, a squeaky kind of a sound that made Alb prod him with the willow stick.

"Where's your backbone?" he wanted to know.

"Got plenty." Franz rubbed a splinter of wood on the rim. "But I—"

"Aw sheets, Franz; all women get sick. My old woman'd be on her butts all day long, if I—"

Franz didn't look at him. "It's—it's the tiredness of her; and so white." Franz said it like a kid, almost. Alb Hukelpoke grabbed his lines and without reply drove down the road, slowly, the willow stick over the dashboard.

Mother died that summer; gave up breath as a flower gives perfume, gladly and without struggle; tired of putting two and two together and coming out three, I guess. I remember how Franz stood watching her, without tears, grief too deep for crying white on his face; as if he felt stirring for the first time the core of death that each one carries hid in his body, and knew how pitiless life can be, lying in wait like a robber, and careless of us as winter of a sparrow falling stiff-clawed and frozen from the eaves. And I remember, too, with a pain neither day nor night will entirely erase, the evening when waiting became a log on the shoulder; the evening when Mother spoke, calmly and as if closing a book, "It is the black frost—on me, now. Get the Pastor, Johan." We were at supper and Franz had a spoonful of soup at his lips but put it down without tasting. The heaviness in me was so great that the mind clouded and I could think of nothing except sleep—the opiate of forgetfulness.

Father, leaden in thick shoes, moved toward the cot, crying, "Minna, Minna," with more regret in his voice than I'd ever heard. He stood beside her, his hands too clumsy to offer tenderness, even if he had it in his heart—corked tight all these years with the hard wood of suspicion. There is only a mildewed comfort in the thought that his regret was less sorrow than loss of something on which he depended—as a well-matched team, or a full-eared stand of grain.

Father hurried out and we had the clatter of plates in our ears, Anna fumbling in her haste. Franz, by a window, let his head sink and put finger and thumb to the ends of the scar, measuring it over and over. Then we heard Father go in a racket of wheels and harness, and the loud swish-and-snap of the whip; the wilder rattle of hoofs in the gravel. The awfulness of waiting, not sure for what, or being able to touch the shadows that might be creeping through the door. Anna was silent now, work finished, and only the crickets grated under the floor. Mother lay so still the covers stayed smooth, and Franz came to her quickly, with terror, but she opened her eyes and smiled at him.

Even to this moment, I can smell that night, sweet with summer-warmth—clover and bush-rose drifting in when the wind swayed the curtains; the odor of the barn and the cows, warm and sweatlike, and the taint of medicine inside.

Then Father was back, and as in a dream I saw the Pastor standing by the table, preparing the confessional, the chalice burning with the dull fire of reflected light, and the wine filling our small room with a fragrance no flowers in our flinty hills ever gave. The Pastor's voice droned on and on. ". . . and if any matter lieth between thee and a brother or a sister, go to him first and—"

"Minna." Father's cry was hoarse. "Between us—there was one in our house, years ago—"

"You can ask that now, Johan? You, alive and well?" She sighed but with no rebuke, her eyes on Franz. "Flesh and blood given to you only; yours; all. You know that, Johan." Her lips were unsmiling and suddenly tears welled down her quiet cheeks.

I think Father believed her then; stunned into acceptance, seeing that what he had made into falsehood was still truth on her lips, near as she was to last words. Bitterness must have rolled over him like a snowslide, for he put hands to his face and sat hunched. It was awful to see him shaken. Then ashamed of his weakness, he arose and walked the floor, his mouth set.

The Pastor lifted the chalice but Mother shook her head. "No; this hour is mine. Johan—tell me. Those years, up north— you never said—" Her breath came faster. "The jail—it has hurt me, thinking and thinking, and never knowing."

Father stiffened as if phantoms he'd bound behind him swirled free into his brain. "Tell me, Johan," she pleaded. He would have refused but the Pastor said: "Before God, Bruder Vildvogel, this must be done," and seeing Father's grimness, added, "I'll speak, then."

It is not easy to say this, even with all these months ridged between me and that night; Franz at the table, head in the circle of his arms, beaten there; Father with his back to us and jerking, feeling Anna's spearlike glance as she stood by the cupboard, listening; Fritzie in a corner shadow; and the Pastor eager with duty to tell the story, his beard sharper than ever.

"There was a fight," he said, "over drink and a woman who was bad—a woman Bruder Johan took to dances; fighting, he and the other, a jealous man, over her. And the man fell in the fight and lay as dead; but was only hurt. And the marshal of the town stuck Johan in jail and the crowd yelled—"

"*Nicht,* Pastor." Father half-turned, a fist upraised. *"In Gottes Name."* Franz lifted his head to stare unbelievingly at Father. But the Pastor, as if hoeing weeds in God's vineyard, cared little where the blade fell; going on with the story . . . about the crowd jeering and breaking down the bars, Father lost in a mad tussle of arms and hands; how they tore his clothes off to the last button and threw buckets of machine oil on him and rode him naked through the town—along the street and the pine-planked sidewalk, raising their beer mugs and beating kettles; took him to the woman, who laughed and spat on him; how the crowd drove him to the wood's edge with ropes lashing at him and stripping the skin from his back at every blow. Drummed out of town and worse than a skunk in men's eyes . . . never forgetting, never forgiving, hate growing with the years in his heart . . .

It was quiet in the room after the telling, the wine and the wild-rose smell strong, and Mother taking the cup; Franz, both hands fisted, and eyes half-pityingly on Father. But the pity vanished, and all his days I think Franz remembered how Mother cried out: "Johan, Johan. You could tell so much to others; me you told nothing. And I waited—waited to hear." Franz crouched at the edge of the table, as if Father were a stranger; ready to leap at him.

It was late when the Pastor went, Father taking him, needing

[215]

the staff of his words, on the drive; and Anna going with the promise to return early. Franz shut the door on the night and what had gone, and, as if commanded, took the fiddle and began to play *Liebeslied*—played softly, a part of him slipping forever away on the strings, lost and leaving him lonely; tears in the melody but none under his lids.

It came when the bow was no more than whispering its thinning sadness. "Franz." Mother's voice, at first hidden by the music. The awful numbness when he stopped. "Franz, the sparrows—" Her lips scarcely moving yet we heard—and knew. We knew. And in the room silence like a curtain rolled down slowly and the crickets tore at it with the dull shears of their chirps.

I lived through that next week as one whose brain is nerveless as a finger struck by a hammer; moved and was well, but felt that what was happening to us would be forgotten, once sleep absolved us from care and morning brightened into another day; but waked with the numbness still heavy. I stumbled through chores and meals, trying not to see how Franz crept about the place, the crutches in my hands swelling the veins with every lurch. I went to Mary's Hill with Father and Franz and Fritzie, leaving the house to Anna and Mrs. Mais's tending gentleness, and the Bauers. There was dismalness in the thought that it took this to bring the four of us here together, bent on this grim errand. I heard Father haggling over the price of the coffin—"No better than if it were a sack of oats," Franz muttered, "instead of the last he can do for her." I knew that Mother would want it so; nothing expensive to add to the total of our debt. But Franz ran a thumb over the wooden box and touched the handles insecurely nailed—this pine like paper against the mold of darkness and the crush of earth. His knuckles grew white under the skin.

People stopped in front of the house that week, gruff with sympathy, the women with a bowl of salad or a batch of cookies. We answered, unable to recall what we said a moment later. A cow fell into the creek and we pried her into safety and warmth again. Walter shuffled in, home without his wife, lean and ribby as a vulture; had no reply for Father's growls about the crows finding the old roost when the corn gave out. Alb Hukelpoke came by, his spade and pick still grubby from digging at the church. Franz touched the clay but wiped the blotch off fast as though it were blood. Rain and wind burst in a white spray over the hills, the anvil of thunder ringing in the dark forge of the storm; and Anna nodded. "Another will go to the churchyard, soon; before the week ends; rain in the grave like that." Confused, to me, these things, as a pile of sticks.

It was a large funeral, our yard black with rows of buggies and wagons, many of the folks already haltering their teams to post and tree by ten o'clock. Carley Sperry, Leff's crazy brother, hung a chain of dandelions first on the wagon seat and then on the harnesses, talking to the horses in a senseless chant, "Jinny, jinny, jinny." Mr. Bauer brought a jug of grape wine so that Father could dish it out in small glasses; to the men only, as was proper. The people ate hugely of sandwiches and potato salad at noon, on boards set up outside (they could, their throats free of the lumps of grief); our house being too small for the crowd. The day was cloudless and hot.

Tinkla was there, squeezing my hand but beginning to cry when she saw Franz. And Liliem, tremulous behind her veil, turned from me and whispered to him, "I know; don't grieve, Franz. It will be better." The yearning in Franz's eyes was almost like a voice begging. Then she stood face to face with Father, and shrank aside, remembering that day when she said good-by to Franz. But Father took hold of her veil, awkwardly but kindly. *"Bange dich nicht, Mädel.* It was good of you to come now." Asking pardon in his gruff way. Liliem, as if she understood, bowed her head, her cheeks suddenly wet. I thought she brushed his arm as she ran to her father.

When the Pastor raised his great voice in the hymn, the folks filed in, the women bringing geraniums and bleeding hearts, or wild rose and fern, green and lacy from the woods, to heap on the bare pine; Tinkla a sheaf of yellow orchid and blue lady's slipper, and Liliem a wreath of honeysuckle and silver grass; until Mother, sleeping without dreams, was lost in flowers.

The Pastor's voice fell on the rustling like a cold wind. He began the sermon, a long one, drawn from the Old Testament: "Number your days," he trumpeted, counting on his fingers. Franz twisted, and I wondered what would happen if his trousers split, there among the people, so tight the cloth was; and no way to get a new pair. The sermon ended with stirrings of seats and planks.

Then the long procession moved to the church, the Pastor leading in the black top-buggy, stern in his black silk hat and white gloves, the horses waving black crepe hanging from hame and forelock with every step; next Mr. Mais and the platform buggy, slow with Mother in it; ours the next, and the neighbors behind.

The church was hot and sticky, and the Pastor ripped our sins bare again, a second harvest of iniquity. Patiently Franz measured the scar over and over. His eyes seemed to store up in his mind what he could see of Mother's face. With a great wheezing the organist began *Nearer, My God, to Thee*. A bench thumped as someone pushed it. Outside Carley Sperry sang his crazy "Jinny, jinny, jinny" to the horses, heard between the Pastor's Mosaic thunders. A baby lay in Mrs. Grosbeck's arms, asleep and safe, its tiny fist like a rosebud beginning to uncurl. The congregation started loudly on the hymn, relieved that it was the last.

Slowly and as if to unseen drums we walked to the graveyard. The crowd parted to follow us, Franz beside Father. Six neighbors with ribbons on their arms clutched somberly at the handles . . . then—an iron handle tearing from the rotted pine . . . Franz stepping forward to help . . . the sun hot on my lips and a dull agony in my heart . . . even this final hour spoiled for her. Franz glanced at Father with hate striking from his eyes; blaming him that this day was made harder for all of us. I remember that Mr. Toffmann's windmill squeaked noisily in a dry gust; that when the flowers were swept aside and a rose (for memory) was given him, Franz put out a hand as if to catch at something. Black soil from the Pastor's fist dropped on the pine wood . . . we shuffled away . . . the cemetery seemed miles long to walk. I saw Liliem and Mr. Schoen find seats in Jonas Bluber's buggy and Franz pull the rose to pieces, watching them—the rose to remember Mother.

We drove home, dreading the emptiness there and mute with memories, to Anna's gruff: "Eat now; lean arms make an early grave, say I." Home and the center gone, a wheel with the hub smashed; home wherein *she* had tied us to the very ends of her love. What chores there were, we did, the sun still tree-high; and returned to the house—to emptiness that sent Franz from the door.

I found him, his back against the barn wall, poking holes in the ground with a fork. The sun burned like a red lantern in the window above him. He glanced at me, dully and with eyes that spoke like words. I felt suddenly naked before him, down to my pindling foolish legs.

"Jeppy, Jeppy." His voice was less a voice than a tortured tormented sound. "What is it all good for, living?" He put the fork aside. "Like grass in the sloo—standing one minute and black the next—after fire." He straightened, head hard on the boards and his face lifted. "You first, broken like . . . and then Mother; Liliem, too." I longed for darkness to hide the look on his face and the tears brimming. "God has forgotten us, I guess; nothing, now; nothing. No music left in the fiddle bow, Jeppy." He turned away; his shoulders, bright with sun, parted the blackness of the doorway for a moment, and were gone. I heard him gather the feed buckets and wondered whether I'd ever have strength for words again.

15

Those next years were such a strange mixture of light and darkness, of noon and midnight, that we walked in shadow, it seemed to me. I remember hours with beauty like a star falling, a slant of glory burning in the dark; and hours with bareness, too, like a field dead and sinking into ashes under drought, no green thing alive; as though bareness and beauty were frost and sun to sweeten the crabbedness of our lives. There were springs when earth cupped herself in acres of anemones, and autumns when another leaf would have added too much red to a hill of maples. Beauty to heal the mind. But Franz couldn't forget Mother's cry or the pine wood, crumbly as bark; and started up in dreams, nights, mumbling as though earth fell and choked his mouth.

He became prickly as a bull thistle, sometimes; sullen over the milk bucket or hayfork; snapping back at Fritzie and once whirling on Anna even, whanging his tongue with as sharp an edge as she did—the lean fire of hate, never extinguished, beginning to feed again under the ash of broken hopes and shattered dreams. Slow embers, these, not breaking loose in rolling flame—not yet. But they popped out in a word, or a crinkle of the lids, or in the sudden tenseness of a muscle under a sleeve. More than once, I caught his glance wandering from his shoe tops to Father's shoulders as if he estimated the inches necessary for a hard leap. And a blind dread began to move in me; slowly, for this did not happen in a day or a month, but was like a disease carried under the rib bones. I think even now that we would have grumbled ourselves into gradual though inevitable change—into the grave itself—without a thumb lifting, if Franz could have forgotten the iron tearing from wood and if Father had not tried a gnarled and belated sort of love.

We began going to dances again the autumn after Mother died, riding with neighbors mostly. Franz was second fiddler still, and threw the silver he'd receive on the table when we blundered in late, so that Father would have it in the morning. I was glad he wanted me, glad to leave the house and Anna and the pigs squealing in the pen.

[220]

The congregation had its say, and gossip hung on the ear. "Those Vildvogel boys," Mrs. Sperry told Mrs. Toffmann, we heard; "dancing and raising Cain, like that, and their mother's feet hardly cold in the grave." Mrs. Pilversack grabbed my arm one Sunday at church, her voice ominous: "Jepthah Vildvogel, you listen; what would your ma say, such goings on, and—"

Franz wheeled on her: "You let Mütterchen alone. What we do, we stand good for. A sour face—what does it bring?" Mrs. Pilversack clicked her false teeth and hurried to the Pastor; the Pastor, making a sucking noise through his lips and patting the drake's tails on his neck, shook his head. *"Ja, ja;* God moves in His own way; another cross to bear; and poor Bruder Vildvogel has many."

He pounded the Bible the following Sunday, on a text about stubborn and rebellious sons. "What did the men of God do?" He shouted to the rafters. "They threw the disobedient ones out of the church—out in the cold where there is gnashing of teeth; so did they put evil from among them. And all Israel feared." The congregation went home to chuckle, "My, the Pastor scolded today; somebody we know, too." And felt better all Monday.

Franz led the horses to the barn, trouble in his gait. "It must be awful—kicked out of church," he told me. "No forgiveness; no one to bury you; burning for hundreds of years, as the Pastor says." He expected Father to rage, too, now that the neighbors were huzzing again. But Father said nothing, though his lips tautened, and one Sunday evening he rose hastily from milking, wrath stiff in him, and shouted from the yard. And we had to finish his work. Generally, he took the silver and that ended it; hushed Anna once when she plumped flapjacks in front of us as if they were henbane: "Dance to the fiddle, dance to the Devil's hoof, say I."

"It is enough," he growled that time. "More than enough; biting and scratching—like dogs." He ate his food quickly, annoyed at this betrayal into garrulity, I guess; a weariness about him that was odd, his tongue less like a wire brush in its harshness since Mother died. He'd stop full tilt in a stride of work to watch Franz, a strange expression plain on his face. But the very next week Sornas Tetzlauf used a buggy whip on one of his boys, and the congregation, like snake-hawks, flew to another carcass and let us alone.

We wore our work pants to threads six days a week and forgot sweat in going to shindandies on Saturday nights, a bulky knot in us untying itself in the rhythm of polka and two-step, in the whoops, Franz wild in his playing and getting Alb Hukelpoke to fiddle while he stomped through the clapping and shuffle of "Birdie in the Cage" and "Fiddle in the Furrow." He danced with Tinkla until she was breathless, her mouth wide and her hands clinging; or swayed in a brief waltz of forgetfulness with Liliem in his arms, the world singing, I think, for him; though she appeared rarely enough, and always, it seemed, Jonas Bluber hung in the skirts of the crowd. Jonas took her to dances otherwheres, we heard, though Franz growled and wouldn't believe it. "Old woman's stuff," he'd say. He used to miss the beat when he saw her, the music awry, until he left the players and slid an arm about her waist.

But it plagued him that folks talked. "They think something is wrong—whatever we do," he'd say. "And that makes it wrong, I s'pose." But he doubted it, tossing in bed, I could see, and I'd hear his hopeless: "Mütterchen, Mütterchen, is it wrong—to laugh and be happy?" The love melody sang no more from the strings; not during those years before the Prinzing barn dance. "I'll fiddle it someday; when I'm first fiddler." He'd smile in refusal when the dancers clapped, and let imagination run ahead to the time when he'd stand in Mr. Muehlbank's place. "I'll show them," he'd say after a round of tunes, his whole body trembling and the scar vivid. "They'll shout when I finish; and want more. I'll make them."

"Franz," I'd warn him. "The nose—don't hold it so high;

might get a kink in it." He'd laugh and the fiddle would mock the strangeness lying deep in me.

As always, Father pounded the team to Mary's Hill on Saturday, rain or shine. There would be a pail of eggs or a stone-jar of butter in the buggy for the Wienlanders; only now it was Anna instead of Mother who wrapped the cool grass, lush from the sweep of the scythe, about the jars to keep off the sun on the trip and to be used as hay for the horses in town. He rode carriage in the sawmill each winter; the best man in the hills, Abel Kloster said; sliced logs by the inch into boards, the unsawed logs a roughly slanted wall above, which a wrench of the peavy would send crashing. He had time enough to mull over what had happened—admitting error in his own hard way; and would have taken back the wasted years, if he'd known how, his distrust of Mother going like scraggly ice crusts in spring, reluctant as flint; but gone now. It must have shaken him to find that he could be wrong; as though the multiplication table had cheated him—he who had mangy pride in being right when he gave every neighbor a just exchange of borrowed hay or muscle. He jerked with obligation when he found himself in debt to Mr. Mais, or Mr. Toffmann at the store. It wasn't easy for him to give in, and he'd throw a milk-box the length of the barn when something riled him.

He was wary of rebuke, I noticed, and took the lever himself when we pried stones in the field: "It's heavy, Franz: too much for you." And himself mauled the fence posts that Franz was to do; until Franz muttered, "Drives a man to swear-words; nothing suits him any more," and slouched away, remembering the times without number Father had brought shame on him by yelling about a piece of work—blind to any tenderness Father might have offered, seeing this as another form of scolding. The day of the funeral was like a burdock clinging in the folds of his memory. He never understood (I know now, years away from those winters and summers) that this was Father's manner of penance and showing that he was sorry. Father would peer cornerwise at him, when both were pitching hay or busy at this and the other, as if any minute he'd reach out and say, "Franz, such blockheads we are; acting like this," but didn't then, and never would in his awkwardness; not knowing that it was too late, and that all his efforts were rooted to failure, ineffectual and worse than madness.

What change there was on our farm—on the ridges, for that matter—came slowly; almost imperceptible to the eye, so closely did we regard each present moment and the labor of each day. The field south went to grass (Anna's idea), the cowbell ringing from its pastured sides. The drained sloo added acres to the hay land, and a stumpy patch to the east lengthened a piece of grain (this, too, Anna's idea, we said). She came to live with us the fall Mother died; told us she wasn't going to soak up dew any more, humpling from the Maises', or get her stockings matted with beggar's lice. If we wanted a housekeeper, she'd pack her stuff and come. Father grunted, uncertain, but knew we'd never get the dishes washed or the slop pails emptied; and that we could soon grow wheat on the floor, with our bachelor's dirt and litter; as bad as the Diemer boys living in a dugout over north.

"Why don't we get Mrs. Kloster's sister—or somebody else?" Franz spoke up, determined that Father should know how he felt. Fritzie nodded in agreement. Anna glared, forgetting to sniff. But Father said without anger: "She's a good worker; knows the house"; which cut the knot of the matter. Anna brought her things, and the first night she slept in Mother's bed, Franz prowled about the lean-to like a homesick dog, uneasy, and far from rest, hearing Anna snore.

There would have been scandal but Anna settled it with venom when Mrs. Sperry cackled at church and the womenfolks had sly grins. "Pigs resting in the swill, that's what you are." She nearly spat at them. "Old Vildvogel sleeps upstairs and I down—anything else you want to smear on your snouts?"

Thereafter the women avoided talk about Anna when Anna was around.

She was up before the turkeys gobbled and gipped from the trees, rattling an old milk can like wild to get us out; had the house shingled when she found the flour in the loft mildewed, though we couldn't afford it, and Father grumbled that one crack didn't make the whole roof leak; but had it done. He was wheedled into it, we could see; until Fritzie snapped: "The rest of you fellers going to crawl under her skirts too? I ain't; not me." But he kept still when she trotted to the barn one evening after we'd finished a hard day of shucking corn, to milk the cows we felt too tired to touch. She sat down under the kicker. "You're short a hired man," she said in explanation. Fritzie laughed in the feedbox, but Franz shouted: "Not that one; she kicks." Anna sniffed: "Milked worse cows than this—before you ever sucked a tit, too." The kicker didn't stir a hoof that night— one thornbush understanding another, I thought.

She had small patience for the slowness with which I stumped along, and one morning (Father and Fritzie were already in the barn) when I said, "We got to rank out wood today, Franz," she turned on me smartly, her sniff acid. " 'We, we, we,' " she mocked. "Tongue's handy, ain't it? If your legs were, maybe you'd get something done." She banged out with the water buckets.

Franz started up to shout after her, but came to me quickly. "Don't, Jeppy; don't look so." He clapped my shoulder. "It's 'we'; always 'we.' "

"No, Franz. What she says—it's true. Even a fork—"

"Don't care. It *is* 'we'; all of us together."

I was glad he went then; afraid of the unsteadiness in me and that he would see it, or Anna would.

She tied Mother's things in a bundle and wanted to cart it into the cellar, but Franz cried: "No, it's dark, there," and piled the few leftovers in the lean-to near his bed of husks. I found him once with the bundle undone and a dress in his arms—the one the color of light apple butter. He knew I was there but made no move. "Do folks marry wrong, sometimes?" he asked, as if of himself, taking out his jackknife. He cut a length of ribbon from a sleeve. "Jeppy, you think Mother married him— in Heaven, too, as the Pastor says?" His tone was queer. He put the ribbon in his breast pocket where Liliem's braid had been. I had no answer but mulled over it, as he must have—wondering what hour of agony and desire brought and planted them together, Mother and this silent man—kernels alien to each other but growing in the same hill like corn and oak-seed.

It was in both our minds, dammed up, for when we drove to the Bauers' to return a dozen bags of oats we'd borrowed in July, and sat down to coffee with Mrs. Bauer, I burst out, "Why did Mother marry him?" The words were at my tongue's end and gone before I knew why or how, or that they were foolisher than kid's questions. But I heard Franz say unsurprised, "Was Father different then?" as if the two of us had one notion.

Mrs. Bauer eased her bulk, her eye on Tinkla hovering near. "*Ach, Junge,* what you want to ask! How should I know? Fire burns and—and the mother-sheep finds her lamb—even in the flock—" She waved her thick hands at Tinkla: "Run and pick eggs, Tinkla; Pa's going to the store tomorrow." Tinkla went, banging a door. Mrs. Bauer patted her knees.

"*Ach,* she was a mousy one, your ma; from north of Mary's Hill; her folks dead. She was adopted, and her step-folks— bad farmers and hard drinkers. She ran away, she did; to Mary's Hill. Such good times we used to have." She cleared her throat. "And when your pa saw her at Sunday school—*ach,* the way he went for her. We had a shivaree all fixed, but they got married—by Pastor Sunnenbaum—and went. Some more cookies, Franz?"

We drove home, Franz with his fingers curled in a shirt pocket. At bedtime, when the kitchen door shut off the lean-to to ourselves, he pulled the ribbon free—a ribbon that once meant laughter and youth but now was only a souvenir of faded hope.

He smoothed it over a palm and lifted his hands to his face, saying with softness, "Mütterchen, Mütterchen"; lay on the pillow, the ribbon close to the scar.

17

The hills changed no more than the farm. I'd look toward Long Lake and see blue haze dimming the walls of pine and tamarack—thin blue smoke we'd noticed since we were six years high. But there were bald spots on the ridges now—clearings seeded down or cutovers left behind the ax. Fences were put there, and a cow or a deer could no longer run miles along the hills, finding the woods barred by steel wires, strung to posts instead of trees and barbed like thorns beside those old rails, weathered on their rusted spikes and broken, that had once secured the cattle. Only the gully was still gloomy. A machine shed went up on the Bauers' place and we talked hours about it, the neighbors inspecting wall and roof on Sundays. Mr. Prinzing even marked off the corners of his new barn the year Franz turned nineteen, and said he'd build a cupola on it with a red horse vane; he'd bet his youngest heifers would calve in the new stalls, he'd have it ready so soon.

Old Lafferty finally jaw-beat the school board into buying a new dictionary, the old one coverless since the day he'd fired it at a Kloster boy and missed, hitting the blackboard instead. They bought a new rope for the school bell, too. The last one had been lost three years before, at Hallowe'en, and we still grinned at the prank—how Mr. Dunkel, on his usual constitutional to the outhouse after dark, had paid no attention to noises at the school building across the road; and amiably secluded himself behind the narrow door; when suddenly he found an earthquake pitching through our hills, he said afterward; the backhouse tumbling and Mr. Dunkel yelling German cusswords, so that his wife heard and came running to release him. There was the school-bell rope wound about the little house, but nobody in sight. The bell remained silent, mornings, for no one had the nose to fasten the rope in the tower. Mr. Dunkel was black and blue for a week and swore he'd load his shotgun, next Hallowe'en, but nothing occurred. . . . And the Mortons were stuck-up because the graded road slashed a yellow width through the hills within forty acres of their front door. But beyond that, the ridges suffered little change.

With us it was scarcely more than the picking up of fork when we laid aside the hoe; working in harvest time like sparrows, and hard pressed to save grain. We'd get up mornings with dawn a gray blanket over the fields; still worn from yesterday's exertions, our eyes torn red by the foxtails of sleep. I'd wash the separator and slant the milk cans against the wall to get the breath of sourness out of them, for Mother used to say that sun and sky would sweeten anything. But no sun or sky could ever draw the taint from us, it seemed to me, tightening my grasp on the crossbars of the crutches, the knuckles sticking high and bony like broken cogs on the rim of a wheel. There were nights under stars when I'd come to standstill after egg-hunting in the dark, the blur of the Milky Way over me sliding two directions down to the black ridges; the Beggar Man's star bright as a lamp in a neighbor's window, so close it seemed. All that glory there—for what? For just this moment while I let its vastness dwarf me into sad humility? or sweeping forever in a mighty wheel, its inner rim the four-and-sixty winds of space? I remember one night, when I blundered along with the egg pail, and the riddle of why and wherefore and the dark Self was like an iron question mark heavy in my thought. There came then to mind another spring—the spring before, when Franz and I were in the calf pasture, mending a gate, and the kingbirds were early in the oaks. We snaked a length of wire among the old milkweed stalks, Franz leaning to pull, when he cried: "Don't move, Jeppy," and pointed. There on a stalk was a gray blur of moth wings, and not far away, the broken shell of babyhood; vibrant and strange to life, this creature, not long born and yet eager to test upper air. It maneuvered awkwardly and flew in an unsteady circle above the low trees, both of us watching. What followed is clear even now—a rush of feathers; the king-bird swooping, and the click of bone on bone, swift, like nippers. And suddenly Franz was throwing rocks into the air, madly and without direction. "Did you see?" he cried as if he couldn't believe his sight. "Alive and wanting to fly—to taste honey; never got a chance; kingbird's belly." He became speechless with excitement. Then the stones rolled from his hand and he looked foolish and silly; but said: "Worth no more than that, Jeppy; a whole life getting ready; over in a minute." A whole life caught up in questions, and where were the answers? In our bones, or beyond the skyline of a star pricking the dark, as these did this night?

The egg pail clinked, swung by a hook to the crossbar in my left fist, and I stomped on.

But there were other evenings in the cowyard, when I'd more fall than slide (after bitter practice) onto the stool and feel thankful for things ordinary as pebbles in a wall—cows that didn't kick but had patience in each hoof . . . sun hurling light through the interspaces of the trees . . . Franz, elbows in rhythm with the white jets boring peepholes through foam, and sing-ing—ta-ta, downstroke; taaaa, upstroke; taaa, downstroke on the beat of *My Old Kentucky Home;* until Pitcher, the black cow, raised a foot warningly, and fetched him a swipe across the ear . . . the puzzle of Self and the universe gone, and the tin cups of milk steaming from the cow more important than any-thing I could think of.

Fritzie left the summer before the big harvest dance at the Mortons'; sneaked out in the night after we'd stacked the last meadow of hay, his clothes gone in the morning and his milk stool vacant when we came to chores. He joined a group from Too Far Lake, we learned, going across the state line to pitch bundles in the Dakotas, at threshing time. Father raged, venting the steam he'd held back; suspicious of Franz too, though he didn't press him, in spite of all the labor that fell on us; on Franz and Father, really, for there was little I could do. It was terrible, the despair that made hours sick and miserable when a crutch slipped and the pail of milk I'd try to carry splashed and trickled scummy with dust among the grass roots at the edge of the path. The awfulness of being useless as an old coat and pup-helpless to drag a sack of grain, when Franz slaved at two men's work and a thunder-bank threatened the ripe wheat. Anna, fork flying and as good a worker as Fritzie, pitched like a man, this harvest; as though the farm were hers—would be, Fritzie had growled, if we let her boss us much more. But Father drove himself from hour to hour as if lashed by a gangmaster we could neither see nor understand; taking Franz's jobs, sometimes, along with his own. He'd shout across half a field: "Look what you're doing; no sense, shocking like crazy. Get sunstroke." Meaning kindness but lacking words, unable to shuck off the barbs of crustiness. And Franz would follow the bull-wheel tracks home, the muscles along his jaw flecking; Father staring after him, the binder whip limp in his fingers. I had a feeling that dreadful shapes were beginning to form just beyond my reach.

Cold whitened the north side of corn rows early that autumn— the autumn before Franz was twenty. By the last of August the geese were wedging south, though Mr. Mais predicted a warm winter: "Mushrat houses are small, this year." The har- vest dance was posted for a Saturday—the night before the *Erntedank Fest* at the church. Father had the largest sheaves prepared and the heaviest stalks of corn. Anna polished two pumpkins and a basket of yellow cucumbers; and Franz and I had a peck of potatoes between us, scrubbed till the eyes shone, although he gabbled as much about the dance as the festival. Bitter nights threw a net of blackness over the melon beds and flung white bridges from edge to edge of the puddles by the barn, the handfuls of water swept up and fastened in icy spans, held in place by the bolts and screws of frost.

It was on a morning after such a night that we discovered the black steer ripped along the ribs, trembling near the barn, and a young cow with bloody horns. Father jangled the buckets. *"Na;* hooking again. We'll have your head smooth—and soon." Franz chased the steer in. Father said: "We'll get Schoen—he's got a saw; knows how to saw horns. Next Sunday, maybe; won't be busy, then. And Mais'll come; Prinzing, too." Franz straightened when he heard Liliem's father named. A widening grin hauled his lips back and red swept up his neck in a rush. But he was pestered by doubt. "She won't be 'long," he mourned.

"You don't know," I reminded him. "She might take a notion."

Anna wrinkled her nose when she heard. "Snooping women-folks; noses long as a pitchfork," but Father said, "Cows need the horns sawed off—all of them. I can't tell people to stay home." Aware that they'd talk, if he did. Anna baked cookies and a cake—"There'll be vinegar in it," Franz was sure. "I saw the jug on the table." He flung manure like a hopper-bug the remainder of the week, banking up barn and chicken coop against the frost thieves of winter; was restive when Father helped. He angled a leg over a chair, laughing, when Matt Prinzing came by to tell him that Liliem had slapped Jonas' face at a party the night before—something Jonas had been comical over. "Served him right," said Franz.

Matt was in a jubilant mood; full of giggles; bursting out finally: "Gonna get married, I am; me and Teena Dorset."

Franz's jaw slacked. "Matt—you—get married?"

"Sure; near nineteen." Matt hooked thumbs around his suspenders and lifted himself taller. "No yearling any more. Pa was only eighteen when he hitched up double. And me and Teena figure we can make it and—" He goggled at the future.

"This summer, you and—" Franz was still groping.

"Naw, not yet; not for a couple of years, maybe. But I asked her pa—last night. It's right by him. And my old man says to me, 'Yup, you might as well sleep double now as—' " Matt stopped, red and sheepish under Anna's glare. Franz clapped the heavy shoulders. "Matt, I'm—I can't say it, but—"

Matt broke in, "We'll be neighbors, almost. Gonna clear the eighty west of Pa's; just a piece over. And new buildings—a decent set. And a garden for Teena—" He gripped his trouser straps, blown like a bubble with excitement; whooped, "I'll be a two-toed bloodsucker—" and tore from the house.

Anna sniffed: "Young sprouts; ain't tried it yet. Wait till the paint wears off." But Franz watched from the door, fiddling with the screen and silent.

The Bauers were first, Sunday afternoon. Mrs. Bauer wheezed from the wagon, *"Ach,* my; Tinkle couldn't get here fast enough," her back to Tinkla's shaking head and scarlet cheeks. "Near busted my hooks and eyes." Mr. Bauer cast as thin a shadow as his buggy whip, I thought.

Franz was in his best manners, attentive to Tinkla but in a joking way, sneaking glances at the road. "Got yourself a new hat," he said.

"You noticed." Tinkla jiggled, glad. "Ma made it."

"No; really? With that big bloom and all—sunflower, is it?" He crinkled at the mouth she made. It was a warm and sleepy day, Indian summer weeks late, the air pungent with the smell of fire and smoke, and a burning that was less flame than dying; the corn beyond the yard standing in pointed shocks. We sat on the step, waiting for what others might arrive.

"Guess they'll have a crowd—the Mortons, at the harvest dance." Tinkla put the notion out, carefully, like a kitten pawing at a beetle.

"Guess so." Franz leaned against the wall, pensive, and thoughts elsewhere.

"Going alone?" Tinkla shook her pinkish dress indifferently but even her eyes were listening.

"Nope." Franz was cautious. "With Jeppy," he answered unsmiling. "He always goes; won't go without him."

"I mean—" Tinkla scratched her elbow, confused. Franz shouted, "There's the Hukelpokes," and the moment was lost.

The Klosters rattled along and the Prinzings, the Dorsets with them, Matt all grins beside Teena, and the girls crowding around him. His shoes teetered, now one toe, now the other—"like a rooster with a flock of hens," Alb Hukelpoke drawled. Franz stared in Matt's direction often that afternoon—the hefty shoulders and legs of him, and the arms heavy in the shirt sleeves; a skinful of potency for a field or a saucy woman. And a kind of woe troubled Franz, feeling that he'd never dare challenge desolation and beat the woods from the clearings.

The Schoens drove up, Mr. Schoen climbing stiffly from the buggy, and Franz lifting Liliem over the wheels. She was in white and hatless, her yellow hair loose over her shoulders, more shining luster in one curl, I thought, than in a meadow of marigolds. She smiled slowly for Franz, and shook her head so that her hair drifted like a bright cloud over his face. He held her longer than the height of the wheel made necessary—a reckless moment for him, I guess. But Tinkla's lips quivered and she picked at the flower on her hat. Chattered excitedly with Teena Dorset.

Alb Hukelpoke selected the oaks below the barn as a good place for the sawing—two trees, thick as stovepipes and slanting to form a V about cow-high. He fastened an elm piece to make an upper bar and closed the V. Mr. Schoen tested the saws. The men gathered round and some of the women, Tinkla among them and Liliem on the fringes of the group, saying she didn't want to see.

Franz led the cows one by one struggling at rope's end to the sawing oak, Father encouraging them with a birch, until their heads were maneuvered between the tree trunks and the bar was clamped down. A steer lowed from the pasture. Mr. Schoen, ready with the saw, began, the blade raspy with a zaa-zaa-zaaing sort of noise; steel on bone. Franz set his teeth and Liliem went to the house. Pawing earth and throwing their bodies sidewise, the cows struggled, bellowing futilely, their heads caught firmly, and the saw zinging. The silver teeth came out stained and dragged with them the dust of flesh and bone. A sharp crack hit our ears as the last fragment of horn broke under pressure. The horn fell and bright jets spurted on the scarred oak and were oddly red on Franz's brown hand; so that he whitened, and thereafter let Alb Hukelpoke hold the animals. . . . The sawing ended and Mr. Schoen wiped the blade on the grass. At the pump the men lifted the rusty dipper, drinking.

Anna shrilled, "Coffee's poured," and the men forgot duty and dirty jobs in devouring plates of food. Alb Hukelpoke washed his hands a second time when Anna rapped his knuckles and pointed sternly with the bread knife: "God's sake, man; where do you stick your fingers—getting them so dirty?"

Franz hoped for a quiet corner with Liliem alone, but she perversely brought her cookies and coffee where I sat by the pump.

"You're quiet today, Jeppy." She balanced the plate on her knee, then set it beside her on the planks, away from the moisture of the dripping spout. She moved a crutch softly, with a tremor of her lips; remembering the night on the Diemer hills, I guess. "Jeppy, you're—you're brave and—"

"Sure. Like a calf sucking; the cow might kick," I muttered, knowing there wasn't much sense in what I said. She smiled. Franz clattered up, peevish because he was in a hurry and Anna had made him wait for the cookies.

"Harvest dance—next Saturday," he ventured after a while, biting into a sandwich; as if she didn't know.

"They give a good time, the Mortons." Liliem tossed a crumb to a cautious hen.

"I'm going," Franz began eagerly but she countered, "Old Lady Morton is stewing—claims nobody'll show up for the Thanks Festival, on Sunday."

Franz chewed a moment, baffled; then started again, his eyes begging. "Liliem, if I drove, would you—"

"Gracious, there goes my coffee." Liliem jumped to avoid the brown stream. "Clumsy, I am."

"I'll get some more." He took the cup but Liliem refused. Before he could plead again (it was in his mind, I could see) Alb Hukelpoke rolled near. "Kinda damp place to spark—ain't it? Pump dripping, wet-like." He snickered at Franz's expression, and Liliem threw the last of a cookie at him, running into the house.

The sun was pointing the long shadows of the corn shocks over the yard when Mr. Schoen closed his whittling knife, though the others were in no haste. "Guess I'll hook along," he said. "I got furtherest to go."

"I'll get the team." Franz was off the step in a leap. "The colts, Jeppy; come along and watch, will you? They'll run off when the gate is open."

We were in the barn, the smell of clover and timothy sweet in the nose, and Franz was wishing he had a span like Mr. Schoen's. Suddenly Liliem's voice rang in a soft call. "Franz." He stepped forward. "Franz, I want to say—" She saw he wasn't alone, but Franz laughed. "He's a good horse; and knows things." Meaning me. Liliem poked at a feather waving under a splinter. As if he knew what she wanted, he went to her, and took her in his arms.

She tried to draw back a little, glancing at me. "Franz, should you—"

"Liliem, Liliem." His voice was shaky. "It—it hurts inside me, to say your name; so—so like a fiddle tune." He kissed her hungrily, blind to everything except this sweetness in his arms. I think he would have given all the crow-pickings of eternity for this moment.

"I'm coming for you, Liliem," he cried, exultantly, after a while. "Saturday night."

"Franz, you—"

"Long road or short road. I'm coming—"

"But how, when you—"

"I'll get a team—someway." He was suddenly rough. "Steal it maybe."

She squeezed from him. "Pa's waiting." Franz's laugh was throaty as he buckled lines and straps and trotted the horses through the gate, Liliem with him.

That week stretched endlessly, until I clenched fingers, waiting, waiting, the crutches intolerable, unwieldy and like burdens of scrap iron swinging beside me. Franz marked courage with courage in order to ask Father for the team and buggy; half-knowing how Father would tighten his fist and yell. But he was determined, this time, let anger blaze where it would.

Thursday night—a rainy one, with the curtains of dark shoved back by lightning, but a chill in the air promising snow—Franz kicked the milk stool under the manger, after chores, his mind set. He was pale and in a kind of despair at being put off from that which gnawed in him; hungry for Liliem.

Father was bent over the kindling when Franz started, slowly as if chewing wool: "Ought to have the buggy, Saturday; long way, Mortons'; half over to Too Far Lake and—"

I could see the breath, deep and full, swelling Father's chest. The stick in his fingers wiggled with the anger that rose in him. He guarded himself, though, saying loudly, "Horses need rest, nights; walk, if you want to go."

Franz buttoned and unbuttoned his trouser strap, the hook tinny against the metal disk. "There's Sunday for rest." He tried again. "Riding with neighbors all the time—no fun in—"

"No," Father shouted, breaking the stick. "No team leaves the yard."

Franz hooked the trousers with a snap and his fist shut with carefulness.

He ripped his pants off viciously at bedtime. "We'll go, Jeppy," he said, his voice thin and gaspy with rage. All at once he hit the pillow with a hard lunge—like a kid; as if something

[236]

had to come out; something even the fiddle was powerless to release. "We'll go. And the team *will* leave the yard." I pulled the quilts over me with a numb sense of fear . . . Franz taking the horses and Father rushing from the house. . . . Nothing was safe any more; nothing.

But a night of sleeping on it changed Father's will. "Won't need the team tomorrow night," he grunted at dinner. "Use it. But there's church, Sunday; no snoring late." Said it as though against his will and grudgingly and with a harsh edge that ruffled Franz. But he meant kindness if we'd only known. Franz was perplexed for a moment, not understanding; nor I, then; but both of us forgot the why's and wherefore's of Father's behavior in a rush of excitement over the trip. We'd drive in style, going to the dance in our own buggy; as good as Jonas Bluber, almost. And we'd puzzle over Father another time. "Besides, he owes it to us." Franz's words seemed fair then, though I know now that they were thoughtless and blind. "All these years—hog-leavings for us; and other kids driving their pas' teams."

I'll not forget that night nor the ride to Too Far Lake—the slant up Deedee's bluff and miles of timber below reddened in the sun, the ridges like great knotty fingers dividing the land; the clearings squared off like postage stamps in the blue, fire-tinged distance, ours lost in woods and nowhere seen. Depth and beauty for the hawk's eye and ours to behold. The wheels twinkled, for Franz had pulled the buggy to the creek, and washed spoke and hub. He was dreamy, Liliem not far now, though Father's grumbles over leaving the corn unhusked grated in me. But I forgot that, too, when we began to straighten to level acres, and Too Far Lake sparkled between us and a thin strip of woods far on the other side, the sun tilted on the farther shore and a wake flowing toward us like a scarlet river in a dark land. I wished we'd never go back—back there where Anna was rinsing the strainers and Father switched himself over God knows what bitterness hid in his skull, and the farm waited to suck our strength into its stony acres. I wished then with a fierce longing that we might stay here with doe and rabbit, put head on moss, and forget—forget in a green sleep.

Liliem wasn't ready, Mr. Schoen told us, when we rolled into his yard; but would be. And sooner than we thought, she was between us in the buggy, a yellowish coat matching her hair and making her dress whiter. Franz stared until she asked, "What is it? Have I got measle marks?" He quavered, "You're—you're— I can't say it, Liliem."

It was a broken sunset, the east scattered with clouds, and the tufted horns of night, blue and feathery, over the ridges and growing wider with each blink. Before the wash of gold and green had faded in the west, a glow as of fire beyond the ridges made a hill and trees blacker, and as we topped a knoll we saw a house and windmill—the Sperrys'—move with us across the rising moon like figures cut from inky paper.

But Franz saw nothing but Liliem. He twisted in his seat, the lines dragging and the horses taking the road; restless and stirring with that which ran like a current beneath the skin, making the breath hard and uneven; wanting to whisper those scrappy half-words which have no meaning in broad daylight but are inflectional with silence and soft dark. Bitterness suddenly soured me and I wished myself an earth away, hearing him mutter, "I—I wish we were going home and—" I could have filled the pause for him: going home and Jeppy anywhere but here. He said it almost violently. Liliem eyed him in a startled fashion, as if this in him were new to her, but said, with slow emphasis, like a promise, "It will be nice—a long ride home," and hid her glance. We drove on. The crutches leaned heavy as posts on me.

The dance at the Mortons' is distinct in my mind because of Liliem and Franz's queer saying; unintelligible then, but clear now, with thinking in long nights and probing to understand. It was the last of the barn shindandies that season, and the crowd roared without halter or chain. Beer sudsed from the keg. Franz, glass in one hand and the fiddle in the other, asked, "Jeppy, Mr. Mais—if you—" but let me finish his thought: "I know; I'll ride home with him," a dull ache in me I couldn't explain. Franz poked my shoulder with the bow-end to thank me; his lips puffed the foam as he drank. Tinkla polka-ed up to stand near, Franz smiling at her and nodding at Mr. Muehlbank, as if to remind him: "Ain't got many tunes left to play; my turn, next year," and Mr. Muehlbank thrust his jaw forward to curl his rheumatic fingers on the strings. Liliem waved over a man's shoulder, a question in a little wrinkle on her forehead. The barn was shadowy. . . . Etta Rippey laughed at Minica Morton. . . . Jonas Bluber hulked, quarrelsome with drink and glowering at Liliem. He got Diah Kloster unsteady in his shoes and fighting mad with jealousy, hinting about Minica and Etta. He beetled when Franz had Alb Hukelpoke play second and waltzed with Liliem (Tinkla passing them as if unseeing and stumbling over her partner's feet)—waltzed with Liliem, ribbons of blindness laid on his eyes, and toes finding an insistent path over the floor. Franz held her so fiercely, his lips close to her chin, that she pulled away and said her ankle hurt; wouldn't join in the square dance, though she polka-ed with Matt later. Franz brought the fiddle to his chin, frowning, Liliem more of a mystery to him than ever.

It was near midnight and the supper waltz when he put the fiddle in Alb's hands again and said, "Play," in a choky sort of manner; his shoulder set. He caught Liliem's arm possessively. "Let's go home." His voice was thick, demanding and pleading together.

"Why, Franz—" She twisted aside. "You're—too much beer."

"No." Fire, long smoldering, gleamed in his eyes, so that she turned away, reddening. "Liliem, the road will not be too long, tonight." Said it eagerly. But her chin went up and a strange laugh rang from her lips. "You're drunk," she cried, her tone sharp.

Franz stepped back, not at her words but at the hard way she uttered them. "Liliem, I didn't mean—I'm sorry; I thought—"

"Thought I'd hop to your whistle?" I had a notion that she was enjoying this, holding the whip of mastery over him—over any man, for that matter; a crazy notion.

"Please, Liliem—" People were beginning to stop, itchy-eared, and suddenly Franz was angry with a blind unreasoning anger at being thwarted—this happiness snatched from him. "I'm not begging you. There are others."

"Others; Tinkla, I s'pose." Her laugh brought the blood up. "Tinkla; why not?" Franz was white, seeing the crowd leave a space for them. "As good as anyone, Tinkla is." His voice was harsh and, all at once, Liliem tilted her head with a slow smile; laid a hand on his arm. "Franz," her tone soft. "Forgive me. I'm—I'm wild tonight, I guess." Franz was stiff. "The Mortons want me to stay and go with them—tomorrow to church. I must stay. Another time, please, Franz." She glided away and Franz muscled a road back to playing, still angry. I heard Jonas Bluber's bull-laugh and Liliem call to him.

Franz shut the dancers from him with belligerent sawings. The supper waltz came and went. Franz ate alone, Tinkla among the girls, without partner, but Liliem gone from the barn. Jollity slipped over the rocks of this incident, hiding it. Tinkla stopped to brush the faded smoothness of the black fiddle case, not even peeking at Franz, although I think she knew that he grinned at her.

Diah Kloster, heavy-lidded with drink, lurched ahead when Minica, in a tall mood and bold, said loudly, "Listen, girls; here's a riddle for you"; nodding at Etta, at his side in the backwash of a polka, close to the players' stand: "When does a maid have the most foam between her legs?" He rolled his eyes to his brows, explaining before anyone could spoil his joke, "When she's milking the cows. What did you think? Shame on you—" Diah hurled himself on Minica and the crowd shoved, fists flying before they were separated. Diah threatened, "I'll knock your teeth in, one of these days."

Franz played a while before he asked, in an odd tone, "Did you hear it, Jeppy?"

"Hear what?" I settled a crutch.

"Before the fight; I thought a string broke." He added strangely, "Guess it was something inside me snapped—snapped off."

He took Tinkla home that night, partly out of spite to Liliem because she had rubbed him up the wrong shoulder, partly because Tinkla asked, finally, and he couldn't refuse her directness. But he said to me: "Ride with us, Jeppy," as if he didn't trust his hands to anyone, alone. I left them, Tinkla shy as a wood hen, all at once, even with second-best joy; and stomped off to tell Mr. Mais I wouldn't ride with him, but couldn't find him, until Matt Prinzing pointed. "Saw him going to his wagon—over there; a piece ago."

The night air was good after the warmth inside. The sky was sickly yellow in the west where the moon dipped earthward. I wove among wagons and carryalls and the black humps of top-buggies. Laughter floated dimly. I nearly pitched over a crutch when I heard Liliem's voice, low and pleading, but plainly: "Jonas, you're so mean," and Jonas gurgling, "What do I get, if I make up with you?" Silence then, broken by Jonas, triumph in his manliness. "Little devil of a pepper pot." I wobbled from the place, longing for a stump to cling to, fast and safe, in the whirl and confusion that ran like swollen waters in my head.

How this snarl would untangle itself, except as the short end for somebody, I couldn't see, climbing the buggy wheels and using the crutches as a boy does stilts, that early morning. I stretched my bones on the horse blankets in the buggy, going home, and watched Franz and Tinkla in the seat; lay there, disquieted, knowing that Franz would never believe me, if I told him; torn by indecision and resentful that anyone could act so, weather-wise, blowing now this way, now that, as Liliem had. I was aware, too, that Tinkla must be tasting sourness, near enough Franz to feel his arms jerked against her side by the lines and yet ridges apart, too, some ways. He guessed how she felt, I think, for he put an arm about her; so that she cried, her voice trembling, "Franz, is it too late? If you could only—" and rested against him.

"You are sweet, Tinkla," he said, and kissed her. But he did not expect the anguished wildness with which she clung to him, hard and as if shoved toward him by a will stronger than her own. He caught fire from her vehemence and responded in blind madness. The horses dragged at the lines but he let them slip; then struggled for calmness: "Don't, Tinkla. We mustn't; I—"

"It is Liliem, then—for always?" She began to cry dully.

"I don't know, Tinkla; I don't know." Franz pulled the lines with a kind of despair.

I wondered if there were surety in heaven or earth for hope. This blind staggering, for all of us . . . Father hitching about in exasperation, recognizing his wrong but not how to make amends, even if he could . . . Franz remembering Father's heavy fist on the rawhide and Mother's trembling lips; seeing the meagerness, as he grew older, of the bitter years past and aching at their emptiness, feeling that whatever Father offered was payment long overdue—rightfully his by every token in youth's almanac, and therefore to be accepted as Matt Prinzing accepted his pa's steers and span of horses; with no reckoning for the pain it cost Father to give an inch to anyone. All this did not burst in the mind at once in a blaze of thought, but grew slowly, added stick by stick to what was there before, as ants do to build their squat cones; easier to see now. But in that homeward ride, I dreaded tomorrow and the day after, with the blind dread of an animal.

18

"Wind's changed," Anna called the next morning. "Warm out; Indian summer's lasting." Harvest Festival Sunday—*Erntedank Fest,* we called it. But I remember that morning with a kind of fear. Father growled among the cows at the way the horses hung tired over their timothy and oats. Franz milked with short angry strokes, so that the cow stepped about uneasily. The sun was clear of vapor and bright, casting the shadow of old cobwebs on the white heifer's rump. Before noon the junk shack Father had erected a year before grew brownish with resin. Mr. Mais darkened the barn doorway to tell us, "Did you hear? A telephone line, that's what they're building; south of Mary's Hill." He reached for his cut-plug but remembered that it was Sunday. "Tall poles in a man's fields, so he can't turn around; not without hitting one, leastways." He ran his tongue along his lips. "Got your *vegyables* and truck loaded?" We hadn't, Father said, but would. Mr. Mais nodded and tramped on home. We busied ourselves with the last of the chores.

Franz bent to lift a sack of corn, Father observing his struggles a moment silently; then said gruffly: "It's too heavy for you—let me."

Franz tugged and grunted: "Let me alone."

Father took a step. "Franz." His voice was curiously brusque, as though he were afraid to trust himself to words. But Franz jerked up quickly, his mouth burning reproaches. "All my days—all I've got from you—lickings and calling-downs." He flung this at Father, the floodgates at last torn away and the torrent rushing. "Blockhead and fool—that's what I hear—all the time. Nothing I do is right."

"Franz." There was a sort of gnarled anguish under Father's harshness, if Franz had ears to hear instead of being deaf with rage. Father was stiff and still as the barn post beside him.

Franz shouldered the sack with a sudden upthrust. "Done this before—can do it again." He wobbled through the door.

Father balled his fists slowly. I think he knew then the futility of taking back what had been given and had been made a part of us—stubbornness to resist his way like a hide covering us, especially Franz; as well change the shape of a tree wrenched out of place by ice-storms. There was left only anger and his will. He'd let no flesh of his thwart him; not while his arm was sound. Unaware that it was too late, the word spoken and gone, marked by an eternal period.

Every hitching post at the church had halter-ropes fastened in the cross-holes when we turned in. Father tied our horses to a tree and gave us collection money, a nickel each. The church-yard was black with people, many loaded with bags and jars. Mr. Dunkel heaved a huge sheaf of grain, dwarfing any I'd ever seen, though Anna sniffed, "That never got through a binder; bound it himself, he did; to show off holiness to the Pastor. Thinks God don't know, I guess," and clanked her own jars of jelly.

That was the Sunday Franz and I, for the first time, climbed the stairs to the gallery and sat among the "fellers"—those out of Sunday school, but unmarried, male and female. We looked down as from a barn-roof upon the men, women and kids in the pews below and saw the altar, dressed in black but gay now with the yellow pumpkins, two side by side supporting a third on the lowest step; the red of tomatoes from slanted baskets; squash curling its greenish horns over a box; a sheaf of wheat at either end of the altar table, the candles whiter against the faded gold of straw; corn stalks arching their gray-brown tassels and sagging with harvest weight of ears, the husks ripped, red and yellow kernels bright beside the pale-green leaves; carrots in bunches stabbing out their points. Pine boughs hung everywhere, the green splashed with the rusty color of winter-killed limbs.

Mr. Sperry brought a rooster and a hen, for he'd had the best year yet, raising chickens. Mrs. Pilversack, proud with an arm-ful of rutabagas, made eyes over her nose at Tinkla's rope of bittersweet vines, the berries scarlet. Alb Hukelpoke twiddled his fingers or scratched a spot on his cheek, nervous in his baggy trousers, for he was to lead the choir today, and he could never tell what the choir might do; not since the time the sopranos from Turkey Hollow got mad at the altos from Loon Lake. They threw songbooks in the middle of *A Lamb I Am of Heaven,* that Sunday, because the altos fell over a low note; and all of them became sopranos, screeching, and the congregation was scandalized for a month. With flutterings of paper the choir got into seats now. Behind the walls of a little cabinetlike enclosure with crossbarred window and curtained door, the Pastor remained hidden, waiting for the first note from the organist.

Tinkla tripped up to the gallery, to sit on the girls' side, Liliem not long after. Franz grinned at Tinkla but acted chilly toward Liliem, in spite of her smile; though I knew he'd have gone to her for the beckon of a finger, and she was aware of it, too; which irked Franz the more.

The organist settled down, stacking music, a quick glance shot over her shoulder first, to see whether any boy had a frog or a mouse out and ready to shove at her on a stick. Diah Kloster sat sheepish, but glowered still at Minica. Squaring his jaw in a businesslike manner, Deacon Pilversack planted his feet firmly, his stool slanted near the head of the stairs and his look sharp for *"Fix-foxerei."*

Old Father Buckman, shaky with too many years, rose to begin the service. The floor cracked as the congregation stood with him; for nobody stirred until our old father of the hills pulled himself up, with difficulty, and led the way. The Pastor roared out the hymn, ahead of the organ by half a step, no matter how fast the organist played, until it became a kind of race, though the Pastor usually won. The little kids in knee pants scoogged around in the benches, peering up at us, their faces fresh and rosy as an autumn apple; full of wonder, this young crop of our scraggy hills, their lips quirly at the corners with questions. Franz winked at the Prinzing boy—Eddie—and the boy waved back; until Mr. Prinzing hauled him into the seat with vigor and glared at the gallery.

The hymn was loud, Jonas Bluber's bull-bass vibrating the plank under my thighs. The hen, startled, began to cackle, and Mr. Sperry lugged the crate down the aisle, his ears red. Diah Kloster sang by heart, "In a cross-eyed Christ I glory," getting the words mixed. And in the hush before the sermon, while the Pastor gathered his sleeves ominously, kernels of wheat from the overripe sheaves on the altar fell and gently clinked on the communion plate. The Pastor thundered about sin and the worthlessness of all our efforts. Even these gifts were putrid in the sight of God and fit for pigs, he said ("A fine way to talk," Anna snorted on the road home. "He gets his share of them, and not a cucumber lacking, either.") The sermon was long and a Dorset boy, restless, slipped off one of his small shoes and threw it at Mrs. Pilversack's flowery hat. Mrs. Pilversack quivered with anger and Mrs. Dorset jerked her young one out of the church to the backhouse near by; and soon yells and wails drifted through the open windows, to punctuate the Pastor's secondly and thirdly. Around us the boys slid to ease their butts, Deacon Prinzing's false teeth adding to the ruddle of his snore.

The Pastor dragged the tail of his sermon through a fourthly and fifthly and three conclusions before he snapped book and Amen together; then dived from sight into his cubicle— "ashamed of himself," Mr. Prinzing said once. "Ought to be, too, scolding like he does, sometimes." Then the choir rustled among its papers, Alb Hukelpoke, with a "Now-I-lay-me-down" sort of expression on his face, getting the tune for *Heavenly Gates Ajar*.

They started bravely enough,

> "Heavenly gates ajar
> Longing of mortals . . ."

But by the time they got to

> "Shining above us afar,
> Open thy portals,"

Alb was staring wildly, half the choir "shining" on the scale, the other half whooping up "the portals," Abel Kloster, tenor and dull as a fence post to melody, six measures behind; until Alb stamped a foot and yelled: "Aw sheets! Let's sing *Jesus Knows Me Inside Out*." The whole congregation sang with gusto.

Everybody rose during the collection to march around the altar and lay his gift in a basket. I was going to put my nickel into Franz's hand when I saw Crummie Lafferty hitching along in line and went downstairs myself, Franz ahead and little Eddie Prinzing squeezed between us. The procession shuffled into the dimness behind the altar. There was a sudden clank and the Prinzing boy pushed against me in a scared way, his fist empty and the penny he had, gone under the altar; frightened and his eyes large with tears. Franz swung around and understood; grinned at the boy and crowded his nickel into the grimy fingers, rattling the coins in the basket loudly a moment later to give pretense of liberality to his empty hand. The Prinzing boy was all smiles.

There was a final hymn and a great sigh among the pews, everybody standing and pushing to be away; Franz going in a hurry to avoid the girls, though he couldn't help a sneaking glimpse now and then, talking to Diah and Leff. He gripped the tattered songbook when Jonas' fat shoulders hid most of Liliem from view.

He was sober-mouthed, riding home, as always after the Pastor's thumping and hell-fire; the uneasiness sinking in. "Is that all there is to it?" he wanted to know, when we took the horses to the barn. "Sour-faced here, trying to live and get along; burning when you die?"

"Pastor says so," I admitted. "He gets it from the Bible, they say."

He hung a bridle on a nail, shaking his head; plagued by a swarm of doubts, as much by the girls as by anything, I guess. He was baffled by Liliem and her tantalizing unpredictableness, always beyond his reach, just when he thought he understood her; disturbed too by Tinkla's violent hands and insistent body.

19

For once Mr. Mais and his muskrat piles were a sign. That autumn the hills cooled no more than to receive frost, wet on the grass by nine o'clock, and what snow fell was closer to rain.

Mr. Prinzing hallelujahed over his barn: "Get the foundation walls set; by December, if this weather keeps up. And rafters and shingles on by spring." There were days when we threw windows open to take in warmth, and the perfume shaken down with dusk was as of wild-rose and frosted grape, stirring the blood, fierce and untamed, as if spring with apple and sweet clover had come to the middle of November. It was weather to set the teeth of ire on edge; Franz jumpy as a colt and Father blowing the hidden coals of wrath. I'd go to the junk shack and monkey with brace or saw in the dimness there, or pick up the hammer, only half-seeing the rot-eaten handle that needed fixing before Father raged again; and wondered why the shadows fell black-etched and sharp with angles. Until that afternoon in late November.

It isn't easy to say this, even with knowing that it was inevitable; nothing to stop it, iron or flesh, any more than trees will hold an avalanche. It was an afternoon out of season, the sun bleary with haze and autumnal heat. Father was jerking at his overhall straps, itching his shoulders as he straightened old bent nails to build a new front on the hayrack (nails at the store too dear per pennyweight). He was in a hurry, having a job at the Prinzings' stacking fodder the next morning. Franz hammered, sweaty of face and restive under Father's curt: "Watch what you're pounding; the handle's weak, as it is." Franz was careful with the hammer on lumber loose at the knots and spike-holed—a pile of splintery stuff Father had brought home after Mr. Mais tore down his old pump house.

Father was grumbling, "Always broke when I want to use it, fork or hoe," when it happened, snarling into my ears like a buzz saw. Franz brought the hammer down and the head snapped away, the wooden handle, weakened with use, cracking off. He had a blank look. Father started up. "So; didn't I say—"

"Old stuff," shouted Franz, goaded to fury. "I've heard it before. Why don't you buy something that will hold?"

"There's another handle—in the junk shop," I broke in, and they looked where I stood. A sickness moved in me, even as I spoke. "I'll get it." I hobbled off, thinking in a childish fashion, "It's only a hammer handle; nothing to fight about," but I had a queer sense that one slender length of oak held back rivers of hurt and agony; went as I could, almost pitching, the crutches clinging to sod as if earth-bound. I was scared, for there wasn't another handle between us and the store and I knew it. The dimness was good to hide in, if I could have stayed hidden under the sun-slash that brought the dust-motes dancing a window-width across the place. I rattled among the tools, wasting a minute, thinking: wait; let them cool off, waiting. Then heard Father yell, "Jeppy, hurry up, there." A moment later Franz was with me.

"Can't find it, huh?" he asked, poking under a bench and kicking a box aside.

"I—we never had another," I said, shivering as if it were cold as an icehouse here.

He saw what I had in mind. "Jeppy, without you, I'd—"

Then Father was there, shutting out half the door; face grim and tight. "Two big loafers; must I wait all day?"

Franz jumped around. "Find it yourself then," he howled. I shoved against a corner bench; heard the soft hiss of air between Father's teeth; his slow, "You misbegotten—"

They ran like bulls together, shoulder to shoulder, numb to anything but desire to tear and rip, fury smoking them into insanity; the thud and bumps of fist on bone and hide; the rip of cloth; fingers clawed into skin, bodies thrusting through the slash of sun, now in it, now out of it, lost in shadow; Franz in a wild moment seen, blood like a crooked nail red on his white cheek; silent both, except for hoarseness of breath loud and deep; Franz half to his knees once, the redness on his face growing and his bare shoulder marked with dull bands; holding his end against Father, the fierce strength of youth maddened by taunt and jibe, stored up, barrels of rage, and now as if spewed out in a great spurt; dust in a gray cloud dimming the sight, a box of shingle-nails crashing and the shiny pieces as though sparks in the dusk; Franz twisting aside and ramming his fists like clubs against Father's mouth, so that Father, off balance, lurched and fell under the bench, striking his head.

He was on his knees again, wobbly, and then on his feet, a kind of death-lust hooding his eyes; rushing at Franz but, deceived by the sun, missing his reach, his lips stiffened by the quick jabs Franz mauled at him . . . both lost in a blur of light and shadow on raw meat and flapping shirts; Father swinging his arms like a scythe and Franz breaking away to avoid him. Suddenly, so that I yelled and grabbed something hard, Franz was falling; one moment I saw his brown tangle of hair bright in the sun; then he was gone, a moan wrenched from him as he hit the box on the floor. And Father was there, sun splashing over him, his face awful out of shadow, his shoulders hulking and his hands curved downward like talons of a hawk, poised; below him Franz unmoving.

My hand gripped; was chilled by iron; and with swiftness but without thinking, I flung it. The iron bar struck Father's neck with a soft sound like a fist hitting a pumpkin, Father staggering into dimness . . . my brain thinning to threads that would snap, one by one, soon, very soon, now; the world slowing to eons between seconds.

Then Anna stood before Father. Fearless and like a man she threw him back, shouting, "You fool; jail—jail; ain't once enough?" and shaking him. I think it was the word "jail" that drove an arrow-length of sense through the red fog of his anger. He was deaf to Anna's sharp: "Kill him, would you? You fool; pen you up, they will, and you can rot behind bars." He pushed her aside and slouched out. Futile, I thought, watching Franz stagger to his feet. Anna went with a bitter glance at him. Nothing done; no fangs drawn for either of them; no venom spilled. . . .

It was awful to see them the space of a table apart, after

that fall day—stiff-legged as stranger dogs. When they hauled manure, they held forks like spears in their hands. I'd wake Franz at night with my yells, sure that the tines were stabbed to the curve. This was not end for us, only prologue to madness; a crazy notion, haunting me.

But Father learned this much, I think. He had measured the stripling and found him good oak, not yet seasoned to toughness with years, though hard in the grain. But he did discover that which must have lashed him sleepless from bed: the whipcords of his own strength no longer supple for leaps from log to log, as they had been in years past, but fribbled away with squandering himself on hopeless distrust. For when Alb Hukelpoke came to get a load of the gray rock that jutted in our pasture, Father called Mr. Mais to help and let Alb hoist the larger ones—something he'd have shed blood rather than do, five years before.

He began at the sawmill early that year, Abel Kloster setting up a new rig; and stayed weeks at a time, in no rush to return home. Franz was not far from glad to have him gone; would have run wild otherwise, I think. He suspected even Tinkla and Liliem of God knows what and dodged them at church; all that winter. He'd ride off alone in a clatter of pebbles on wheel sometimes, to a house dance. Got sousily drunk at a birthday party, we heard; and joined the Diemer brothers, hunting coon in the hills north of Long Lake. He'd be splashed and short-tongued when he got back and sullen the next day, careless that the team was hang-weary in the harness. Once he was gone two days and Anna let him know, "You wait till your pa hears about this." She did most of the chores that time as if she belonged to the farm, sniffing at my share of the work: "You help? I might as well have a three-legged calf around."

The shindandies were few, that year, the mild weather heavy with wet and foreboding of fever, and the folks in no mind to gather and spread the pox. It was strange, a black Christmas, the fields lead-colored and like April, and Mr. Mais's crab apple swelling with buds. "No good in this," snapped Anna; "dry fields in January, short heads in harvest." But Mr. Prinzing crowed: "I couldn't have struck it better. You get the fiddle tuned, Franz."

We hauled hay from the sloos in wagons, and the rims cut into the sod, limp as in summer, without frost. Trees were stringy and hard to chop, the ax almost dull against the sap-moist wood, soft with warmth. And swamp elm was so tough we used a wedge and the maul to pry the halves apart.

Franz peeled off his stockings one night, a sheepish grin on his mouth—some of the wild brush burned out of him and more like himself than he had been for days. It was March then, rainy, with lightning, and the lean-to roof pattery with drops. Anna mumbled in the kitchen, her thought like an almanac about "thunder in March, snow in May."

He stuck a thumb absently through a hole. "Well, I've had my spree," he said at last.

"For the winter, or the week?" I asked, with more acidness than I realized.

He hung a stocking over a chair. "I wanted you along; but—"

"No need," I told him, and could scarce believe the words my own, so like a stranger's they were. "Cripples—they don't dance much."

I couldn't have hurt him worse if I had slapped him. He turned to the window, slowly, as if I'd played false with him; his voice sad. "What is between us, Jeppy—that no one can take away; no one but you." His head, bent forward, was plainly seen in the lightning's flash. "It tears me, Jeppy—inside; boiling up." He pulled at his shirt. "Like to run over the ridges and—and—" He stopped muttering and blew the lamp. As he passed the bed, I felt his hand for a swift moment touching my shoulder; and I wished my tongue were out for the words I'd said.

Winter and spring were so like acquaintances, we hardly made changes in our routine when April and May came. The fields

were rid of frost long before Franz borrowed a disc from Mr.
Mais and spread darker earth over the winter gray. He'd flap the
dust from his hat sometimes with gladness that another wheel
track had been made across the ten-acre patch and another day
was dusking; would slip bridle and harness from the team and
stand listening to the splashes the horses made in the creek,
pawing water before they drank; or call to the mare rolling on
the soft earth and shuddering dust from her side: "Feel better,
don't you, Florie?" and lead her into the barn. "Feel better
myself." But the measuring of oats into the feedboxes and the
slimy mouthings of calves sucking his fingers before they would
drink from the pail—I saw how these things irked him. He'd
finish work with a tight breath of relief and bump pails into
corners with no gentle throw.

But he'd uncover the fiddle with eagerness as soon as his
hands were dry after washing; even while Anna was slamming
meat and potatoes on the oilcloth. There was a loneliness about
his melodies that made the crutches bulkier somehow; especially
after Mr. Muehlbank told him, "Well, *Junge,* first fiddle it is,
for you; at Prinzing's new barn dance—if he gets the barn built."
Franz let me know it at milking—neither excited nor sober, but
restless and driven by a necessity greater than any barn dance to
cry out in the strings what was hurting in his mind.

"Play *Liebeslied?*" I ventured later on.

He shook his head. "Can't; too close to the skin." He rubbed
the flies from a cow's legs. "Jeppy, if they don't like me then—
they never will; never." He might as well have said, *"She'll*
never like me," for he meant Liliem, I thought; guessing that
he'd have pounded the trail over the ridges a dozen times the
winter past but his pride wouldn't let him.

But a loneliness akin to sorrow lengthened the strings, noon
and night, as fields lay harrowed down and earth lifted itself in
green sprouts. I'd notice how his lips moved at church, pretending he sang the hymn, when his eyes were really on Matt
Prinzing and Teena, as near to each other as they could get with

an aisle and Deacon Pilversack's expectant glance between them. Franz envied these two, I think; yearned one evening, "It must be like—well, like Heaven, a woman in the house." He split kindling while I gathered the sticks before he went on: "You—you shut the door and you're alone with her—glad, too; not like Mother, looking so scared every time Father came in." He chopped the ax fast in the block and we left the woodpile to the night.

He met Liliem unexpectedly the day we had a load of feed ground at Toffmann's mill and were starting off, our clothes grayish and our neckbands itchy with the dust of grain. Liliem waved from her father's wagon; stepped down in a swirl of dress, and an ankle stockinged black visible among the rims of petticoats. Franz pulled to a halt. She stood by the wheel, a rogue under her lids.

"Franz, you're so mean." The words and their echo stung in my brain. "Jonas, you're so mean."

Franz frayed the threads of a rip in his coat. "Mean?" He put it up to her. "I'd better ask, are you a friend, or what?"

She wove her fingers into a tangle, her eyes down. "Franz, need you ask me?"

"Well, you have others—" Franz began, but she broke in, "I have many friends."

"Jonas Bluber?" Franz was curt with directness; wanting to know for sure, I guess.

"He's a neighbor—a friend." She smiled slowly, uncurling her lips, and I felt Franz uneasy beside me. Her voice was soft. "But there are friends one likes better—you know." Her smile perked a reluctant but answering grin on his mouth. I hated her for what she was doing to him. "You will polka with me? At the Prinzings'?" She poked at the wheel gently.

"I'll polka with you—anywhere." He was tense with eagerness. At once she played sly puss. "You say it nice; like all the boys—such an easy tongue."

"All?" Franz exploded on the word, his grin lost. But she

rustled away with a flash of a smile and a hasty: "There's Father; good-by."

We lumbered on and I had a mind then and there to tell him what I knew; but didn't, seeing how the furrow dug in his brow. And wished futilely afterward that I had.

The week before the dance we heard that Liliem had gone to Mason's Resort, partnered by Jonas. Alb Hukelpoke brought the news, more than a little malice mixed in the telling. "Cat's knuckles! Off with every rooster that flies the coop," he said; which was hardly right, but Alb didn't care. "If she was my girl, now—I'd haul her over my knees and swipe her a couple— good ones so she couldn't gallop around for a week, anyway. That kind—"

"I don't care what she does." Franz was vehement. "Don't say any more, Alb."

Alb scratched his cheek. "Course not, if you want it so. Only—she lets you sit like that; makes me sore." He couldn't make Franz out, shaking his head. But Franz ripped polkas in a frenzy, burning with the fire-leaves of jealousy; wild tunes, senseless to the ear. *Devil's Dream* became a nightmare of un-tamed fingers. Sometimes he fairly threw the fiddle in exasper-ation; and clattered loudly in the barn.

20

He took neither Tinkla nor Liliem to the new barn dance; said, "You're coming, Jeppy," and I was ready. We rode with the Maises, for the horses had finished corn-plowing and even Franz saw they needed a rest. Father didn't go. Prinzing could baptize the barn without him, he growled. Anna was wrinkly, hinting that the Pastor ought to do more than he did about such goings on; Mr. Prinzing an elder, at that.

The loneliness was on Franz again, all that early evening ride. I saw how he edged in the seat, as we came to the long slant. The Prinzing barn, paintless and pine-yellow with unweathered lumber, poked a gable-end among the green of oak and popple. The hill was red with setting sun. He remembered the last time we drove this road, I guess, and was sad at the thought—Mother with us then, glad for the level "thank-you-ma'ams"; Fritzie home and safe, instead of facing summer in the Dakotas, we didn't know where ... Tinkla and Liliem, Matt and Jonas, Diah and Minica and Etta—all of us, neighbor boys and girls, just out of pigtails and short pants, and no more than on the brink of growing pains—those growing pains that tear friendships apart and comrades, ripping old designs to pieces with the levers of desire and jealousy. All that past, we didn't know how, but gone. The fiddle case and the crutches lay side by side, rattling dully with each jolt of the buggy bottom.

The air was fresh with new-mown timothy and clover and strong with wood shavings and the dust of pine; the cupola a dovehouse by itself and the red horse brave, pointing the wind with prancing grace. Piles of lumber were stacked against trees—leftovers for the calf-pens, Matt said, hearty in his greeting. He'd sloughed off kiddishness like a pair of old pants, now that the farm next door was taking shape under his ax and grub-hoe, and Teena waiting. Franz regarded him with an admiring shake of the head. Mr. Prinzing took the fiddle case with tenderness. "I'll let Ma take care of it, Franz—in the house, until you're ready," he proposed, and Franz nodded, coming to walk with Matt and me to the new barn.

There was a kind of glory in the airy arch of rafter and rib, a duskiness along the rooftree not quite dispelled by windows at either end, or the big door below; pride in the shouldering cross-bars, the beams new and untried against the settle and push of hay and the solid strength of storms; and the knotholes were like black eyes peering. We took a share of the pride Mr. Prinzing had in building these steadings, staunch as our hills. Downstairs the stalls were wide and "clean enough to eat off of," Alb Hukelpoke said, arriving with his horses, his tones hollow in the emptiness of feed alley and manger. "Get your hind end

over, Jericho." The harnesses sagged like webs, dark and heavy,
from their pegs, and a draft, lifting the hair, rushed from door
to door, filling the nose with the smell of pine resin and hay
and the mustiness of sweat pads.

It was in the powder-grayness of evening that we wandered
to the yard, where buggies and wagons were rolling up, the
"thank-you-ma'ams" dim and the valley dark, but the ridge
above a mile over, ruddy with the leavings of day. The yard was
running with the movement of wheels turning and horses stepping from the evener and pole; iron thump of a neckyoke
falling; jangle of a tug chain dragging; arms waved in greeting
and kids jumping from the boxes; twos going here and a half-a-
dozen there, the elder sedate in black and sober-threaded cloth,
the younger in shirt sleeves, open at the neck. Tinkla hardly
more than raised a hand to Franz, hurt by his coolness, but she
sneaked glances at him, I felt sure, in spite of her loud talking
with Leff Sperry. Minica Morton pranced by, slender and as if
poured into his tight pants and coat, his black shoes fancy with
white bird's-eye buttons. He handed Etta from the buggy with
a flourish and a bow that drove Diah Kloster to the beer keg
early, moody and dark, his coat pockets bulging with his thrust-in
hands and moving with the opening and closing of his fists.
Liliem was late and Jonas absent—a two-and-two that made a
large four in Franz's mind, I think, the way he hitched his
trousers. Dark slid overhead and westward to the ridges, held
in place by the half-button of a moon. Squeals and giggles
broke on air, the boys with boldness in their fingers already,
early though it was and the beer passed around only twice . . .
Etta shrilling, "Quit that, Minica; you keep your fingers to
home" . . . Franz meeting Tinkla in the rounds, oddly stirred
by her wistfulness, saying with more earnestness than usual,
"You're pretty tonight, Tinkla; like a flower"; her lips tremulous.

Then more lanterns were added to those throwing shadows
from the beams. Two great kerosene flares at either end of the

barn tossed up horns of fire, disturbing the sparrows, and a flurry of wings in the peak brought a feather or two floating. Franz mounted the players' platform, where four chairs stood. Mr. Prinzing handed him the fiddle: *"Junge, es gibt was,"* and slapped his shoulder. The crowd pushed in, boys hasty with "Can I have the waltz?" or "Lena, for God's sake don't trip over my corns again." Diah Kloster lurched past, steps uncertain, muttering, "Dirty old pig-sucker." Mr. Bauer cautiously approached his wife: "Were you thinking—ah, of a dance, Katinka?" and Mrs. Bauer nodded with a gurgle. Humming a schottische, Matt walked in large circles, knife in one hand, a bar of wax in the other, shaving white curls to the floor, a herd of small boys after him, skating the wax into slipperiness with their shoe soles. With a gait made lively by a little schnapps, Mr. Prinzing marched up and caught his wife firmly: "Come on, now, Bertha; forget your old bunions."

Mr. Muehlbank stopped beside Franz and raised his arms. Silence spread like a wave from where he stood to the edge of the crowd. He shoved a chair out of the row, ahead of the others by a foot or two; waited until Franz sat and then took his place with the bull-fiddler and the accordionist, playing second fiddle tonight. No word was said. Franz's face was a little pale and the scar burned. He touched the strings with hard intensity— first fiddler at last. (I thought of that night at the Maises' when we hid under a beam.)

"Baptizing waltz," trumpeted Mr. Dorset, Teena's father, the caller for the dance. "Get your partners and circle round."

Franz brought the bow flying to the strings, blood sweeping like a shadow over his cheeks; every note falling true. The crowd clapped and yelled, each man getting a partner and a mug of beer, and milling in the circle; pressing into the curve of his partner's arm, drawn back of him, her fingers caught at his hip with his left hand, the right free and lifting the mug. Mr. Prinzing and his wife were in the center. The dancers went forward, swinging a step around and coming back.

[258]

"Sing," called Mr. Dorset and the birds fluttered again, with the chorus welling high:

> "Drink to the hammers, drink to the crew,
> Drink to the rafters, bright and new;
> Drink to the stone walls, sturdy the walls;
> Drink to the neighbor, good and true."

A great shout rumbled to the rooftree at the last line. The couples advanced upon Mr. Prinzing and his wife; the men, stepping a little in front of their partners and raising their mugs above their heads, shouted again, *"Prost,"* and retreated, blowing dribbles of foam and beer to the right and left, drinking half of the mug and offering a sip to their partners. Then they tipped the bottoms to the roof, drinking again, heads back, and spilled the last foam to the floor in a large sweep of the arm.

Mr. Prinzing began the waltz, the circle joining. Franz looked my way and never saw me, lost in melody; winking slowly, as if this happiness were too much, a seal on his heart and an enchantment on his sight—squaring up some things. He smiled in a dreamy manner when Tinkla came; smiled so that she turned red and pale at once.

Then Liliem walked into the barn, every eye on her, Jonas behind, a smirk on his lips. She was in white again, the curls like gold fire. Franz trembled, the bow scraping raggedly over the bridge; played again, the crowd sweeping on. . . . Mrs. Bauer folded Mr. Bauer away in her fat arms until he was nearly lost, and one couldn't tell whether she had a partner or not. . . . The dancers swayed. . . . Beer turned sudsy in the pail.

The barn downstairs (when Sam Bauer and I groped through the gloom) was a queer darkness full of scratch and scrog overhead; the music unheard but shoe heels and soles rasping on wood rhythmically . . . the horses nervous and snorting now and then, and Carley Sperry mumbling, "Jinny, jinny, jinny," hiding in the manger.

We went back to find a waltz finished, partners separating with sly and knowing looks. The girls tangled fingers and went into a corner to fix mussed hair and waists, and pretended no one heard their gabble: "Wants the next square dance. I won't let him, there's that; time after next maybe I will." Etta Rippey squealed, "Ain't he wicked? Holds you so hard—I felt his ribs, he squeezed me so tight" . . . "Muscles in his back—like big lumps." Talk drifted away.

Franz gnawed a finger between pieces and nodded shortly to Liliem's wave. Sudden anger touched her thin smile at his brusqueness. Somebody trotted in to tell Alb Hukelpoke that one of his horses had broken a halter and run into the pasture. Hooking his partner closer, Alb laughed, "Aw sheets! Let old Jerusalem go; find 'im in the morning."

The sets for the square dance formed and Mr. Dorset called "Birdie in the Cage":

> "Up to your partners, gee and haw
> And all hands 'round and 'round
> *I ain't gonna bach in the hills, I'm bound,*
> *A shanty, and a bottle, and an old gray hound.*
>
> First couple up to the couple on the right
> And four hands round, and round you go,
> *If you don't get married, you sure are slow,"*

chanting the last lines of the verse in a wavery tune to the beat of the fiddle. Tinkla stood near Franz to watch. . . .

> "Birdie in the cage and the hawk outside,
> Three hands round and the hawk outside,
> *If you ever come a-kissin', I'll tan your hide.*
>
> Birdie fly out and hawk fly in;
> Three hands round and the hawk fly in,
> *Your old man's gone and I'm here agin . . ."*

The circle stomped, the men leaping high as their partners' waists, cracking the floor flatly with their soles. . . . Diah Kloster was stiff by a wall post, coat off. His hand twisted in his pocket. . .

> "Grab that lady across from you
> And swing her hearty and swing her true;
> *Your wife ain't lookin' and if she do*
> *Spit in her eye with a good brown chew.*
>
> Swing, swing around your own, your lady small
> Till her skirts fly out; and swing away all;
> Promenade your partners round the hall."

The caller began all over again: "Second couple up." A wagon-length away, Mr. Prinzing talked with Liliem and Jonas, neither dancing, I saw. A sparrow became blinded and fell halfway to the crowd before it fluttered against the beams.

The set ended and Mr. Prinzing waved for quiet: "Neighbors, here's a go; just found out. Jonas is getting married—to Liliem here—Liliem Schoen." Jonas blurted: "Not yet, for a year or so; we're engaged," but Mr. Prinzing, unabashed, chuckled: "Well, a month or a year, what matter, so long as you're minded to have one bed between ya." Liliem blushed and Jonas swallowed hard.

Franz made no sound; sat so quietly I could see the blood pounding in his neck. The fiddle slipped down over his knees to rest on the floor. Only his eyes moved, winking slowly, and the scar flamed in his cheek. As if this were faddle and not truth.

Tinkla touched his arm, and would have gone, thinking even this futile, when he caught her hand a moment and cried: "Stay, Tinkla." Then he thrust the fiddle into my arms; crossed through to where they stood, and searched Liliem's face for denial.

"Not this, Liliem." His voice was curiously choked. "The dream—our dream—that you told me about by the mailbox; you smash it—"

"What's all this?" began Jonas truculently, but Franz twisted on him like a bobcat, his eyes frosty. So that Bluber cringed back.

"Liliem, is this true? Tell me." He spoke more bluntly, and something in his tone angered her again.

"Didn't you hear? Jonas told—"

"I want it from you—the words." He was suddenly harsh. Her face sharpened, the leaf-curl of her smile broken.

"You, Franz Vildvogel—you, bragging about so many others? Must you go begging?" This was her hour, a taunt under her mirth.

"Others?" Franz brushed his cheek stupidly. As if to goad him, noticing how the crowd surged about, she leaned her head against Jonas, the curls bright on his shoulder. "Take the words from Jonas, Franz." Her voice was lazy. The smile returned, slow and unfolding.

Franz let the breath go, his hand creeping to his breast pocket where the gold braid had once hid. He shoved back, heels clicking, to the player's platform. Grabbed the fiddle and began *The Girl I Left Behind Me* spitefully and as if he hadn't a care in the world, sawing with a fierceness that was hot as a fever; the crowd catching his mood. You'll never know, you'll never know, the rhythm of the music seemed to sing. He pulled Tinkla nearer with a swift grasp, at the end of the piece, his eyes probing hers like knives: "Tinkla, you're sweet"; pleading with her, almost. He waved his bow, lost in a kind of frenzy; yelled for beer, the brown liquid curling like a mustache beyond the corners of his lips and spilling down his chin. He saw Liliem waltzing with Jonas, an odd expression wide on her face, and caught Tinkla about the waist again; released her quickly. She was flushed and reckless now, rigid with excitement. He laughed queerly and took from his breast pocket the ribbon—Mother's ribbon, colored light apple-butter, and tied it to the fiddle-neck.

Then without anyone's asking, he began to play; gently, needing elbow space, cheek on the fiddle; so that those close by thought those farther away could not hear. But no one missed a sound—the sad, heartbroken cry of *Liebeslied* wailing between them, joining them. He played, a sadness deep and lonely as desert places quavering in the strings; something inside him going to pieces; an inner grief, plowed and harrowed with the implements of fear, and wild surgings tearing in him like untamed colts, bridle-free and stranger to a furrow; eyes blinkered with shadow and his hair more unkempt with every leap of the bow.

The shouting among the dancers died; quiet grins changed to the ghosts of smiles. They waited for him to fling into a two-step or polka. Etta and Minica stood arm in arm near the side door, Etta pulling him nearer the door. Men pressed closer to their partners, and arms that had been slack grew tight with yearning, with a kind of fear of losing what they held. Tinkla refused Leff Sperry with a mute shake of her head. The musky pungence of hay and wild rose gave off fragrance with dew, drifting in to become part of the melody—hay that tomorrow or next week would pile high where now the dancers listened, forgetful of calluses and the hard mornings and afternoons waiting for them; conscious only of softness in their arms and the wild honey of madness leaping under the skin. . . . Etta's mouth close to Minica's ear, as if she whispered but her lips were still; Liliem frowning and with a shadow on her, watching Franz; puzzled that he took her scorn this way. Diah Kloster, dark with jealousy, lowered his jaw, his arms crooked, a fist in his pocket, moving . . . moving. . . . Franz played for no one now, with Mother and Liliem lost . . . swinging faster, the fire of the lanterns slipping the length of the bow . . .

Then—it clangs in my memory even now like a bell stroke—there was a snap, loud as a wire breaking, it seemed where we sat. Franz stopped and unclosed his eyes, dazedly. . . . Minica and Etta moved through the side door, unaware that the music had died brokenly; vanished outside, Diah fast at their heels, his fist at his hip and steel glimmering brightly.

[263]

Franz stared at the fiddle wildly, as if a ghost mocked him in some empty corridor of his mind; cried, "Look, Jeppy; the E-string—broken," and laughed without reason. He mumbled all at once, "Tinkla, Tinkla"; threw the fiddle from him so that it fell on the platform edge and the three strings snapped and jumped from the bridge like Devils' fingers curling up.

Franz was blind to everything before him, ears plugged to the calls of the crowd for a tune. "Tinkla," he said, bending over her; "don't be afraid; not tonight. Not any more"— Tinkla half-fearful at his wildness, but yielding to his low in- sistence: "Tinkla, Tinkla, kiss me. Morning is yet far off. Come." He caught her up and carried her, shoving through the people to the big doors; deaf to the bewildered questions of the dancers; deaf to the long scream curving over the barn—a woman's scream. He plowed a clear path outside, heedless of my stomping after.

It was like a dream of slow falling where a moment seems an hour—Franz lifting Tinkla into Jonas Bluber's buggy; untying the horses and leaping in, his yell wild as he whipped the team . . . my shout, "Stop, you fool," unheard. A crazy thought began to scrabble itself in my brain, persisting even when I stood at the side door a minute later and looked down where Diah Kloster, face sick and the color of ashes in the hasty lanterns, stood, wobbling his head and his hand, staring from his fingers to Minica kicking stiffly on the ground. . . . Don't think, don't think, I told myself as I gathered up the bow and fiddle (the dance over and the new barn baptized). I rode home with the Maises, the strange notion mixed with the stars overhead—that night at the Bauers', years before, and the game of "Last Couple Out"; Tinkla behind the corncrib and Franz saying thickly, "Tinkla, Tinkla—your breasts, white in the moonlight."

Part Three

WIND IN
THE SOUTH

1

THEY were married that autumn, with a wedding dance at the Bauers', which was proper, for a man really ought to come for his woman and fetch her from her father's house, we said. Not like some folks. The neighbors still slid their eyes when they mentioned the Grosbeck wedding two years before, the Muehlbank girl marrying Peter Grosbeck in his own house; coming to his place a day before the wedding at that—almost like a woman who couldn't wait but had to hurry to get herself alongside the hard ribs of a man.

Mrs. Bauer waddled and heaved about, excited; must have driven Tinkla nearly wild; cackled in church like a laying hen, but really, Anna sniffed in a sour tone, without sense in her speaking. She shooed Mr. Bauer from the corn he was cultivating and pestered him into going to the Abendsmeyers', who lived by the river, to see whether fish were still running, so that the men might spear half a dozen gunny sacks full for pickling—a plate of spiced fish would go good with the wedding meat and potatoes, she was sure. "That's right, Katinka," Mr. Bauer nodded crustily. "And the whole wedding bunch will eat it in jail, the way the game warden has been nosing around." But they went, Mr. Bauer and the Abendsmeyer boys, nervous and unsettled though they were, with the sheriff and his posses and the searches in the woods for Diah Kloster giving hot tongue. They spent three nights pointing a small boat into the shallows and backwashes of the river, the gasoline torch at the prow flashing the mossy rocks and weedy bottom into view and the slender pickerel weaving shadowlike, the bass and the clumsy "red horse" hiding there; bringing the catch shoreward at last, a fish flipping a tail in spite of jagged spear wounds. But one night of heavy clouds and wind wet to the cheek, they had a fright. They bended a curve in the stream and the flare lighted the bank so that a shitepoke in the reeds was clearly seen. Mr. Bauer was in the darkness behind the shield of the torch, and poised his spear. Suddenly, there was a crash in the bushes and a shout, "Hold up, there, you," and the splash of a muskrat diving panicky from his feeding table. Mr. Bauer admitted afterward he felt the game warden's fingers closing on his shoulder, right then. He gave a yell, tore the standard and the flare from the fastenings in a single wrench and was cloaked in night with the last fizzle of flame and heated iron. A slipping and a sliding in the boat, and the next instant the Abendsmeyer boys, pitching spear and pole wide, and swearing heartily, half dived, half fell into the stream, Mr. Bauer not far behind. That ended the fishing. Mr. Bauer crept home wet and bedraggled to his whiskers, and Charlie Abendsmeyer swore he spit river water for a week. No one ever learned whether the game warden really shouted, or a neighbor, bent on fun and laughing to split his belly over the Abendsmeyers, spluttering their cusswords into the river.

By midsummer even those of the folks who weren't wise in their own hints and imaginings knew, and the whole congregation giggled at Mrs. Bauer's pickled wedding fish. She didn't let it bother her, but scraped scales and pulled fins, hot as it was. Mr. Mais said there wasn't a fly, house or barn, at his place; they'd all flown to the Bauers' and the fish-heads. She could laugh, now that everything was settled. But there had been tears and bitter railing that morning after the Prinzing dance, when Franz came and took Tinkla in his arms, straight from the breakfast table, and said she was his wife. I think Mrs. Bauer was glad, as Franz was and Tinkla, and all of us, that the huzz and halloo over Diah Kloster whipped the attention of the neighbors into such uneasy speculation that they had only a sly grin to give us at church—most of them, at least. But Jonas Bluber stuck his underlip full of words, we heard; about getting the constable on fellers that stole buggies at dances; till Matt

Prinzing snorted, "Two-toed bloodsucker, what's graveling you? He brought your old buggy back, didn't he, all safe?"

"Sure." Jonas leered. "When he got through with it. I've a notion to pound his nose so flat—"

"You want I should tell him that?" Matt was getting heated. "You can have it out, you two." Bluber growled, but he always locked up his teeth when it came to squaring off man to man, Matt told us. Most of the folks chuckled that it was a good joke on Bluber, he so high-toned with his rig anyway. But Leff and Amos Sperry, taking the short cut through Mankin's Ravine, that morning, had come on the buggy and the horses quiet by the roadside. And had seen more than an owl's eyeful, they said, wriggling in their pants and slapping rumps when they finished the story. And the news, stretched out of this man's memory and that, along with plugs of black twist and "Chewers' Delight," became a mouthful before long. Though Alb Hukelpoke grabbed Leff one day at the shop, tightening the slack of his overhalls and shaking him till his ankles swung. "That clacker of yours—keep it in your mouth and your mouth tight." But the story was too juicy to hold; even Alb grinned with the rest of the men gathered near the flicker of the forge. "A feller can't hold 'em, the little squirts; like young studs jumping a neighbor's fence."

I wondered at church sometimes, watching those earnest faces, grave over hymnbooks and singing the verse—

> "Despising worldly joy and pelf
> I God alone adore,
> And love my neighbor as myself . . ."

—Mr. Sperry's, Mr. Mankin's, Mr. Dunkel's, the Pilversacks'— knowing how they'd begin to rip a man or a woman to pieces almost before the Amen grumbled from the altar; and I wondered too, with a helpless kind of ire, from what brand of malice they drew this desire to snicker in enjoyment over what they

could find in a man's life to twist askew according to the crookedness of their own fancies. A special cussedness inherited from
the old Adam, I thought. Though I can see now that a man's
good name (or a woman's) is a kind of taunt to our own limita-
tions, and praise to another is something we take as a warped
sort of criticism of ourselves. That seems clearer than it was,
when I call back the hours in which we ourselves laughed at
error and gossiped over this and that half-truth with a grim "I-
told-you-so" kind of satisfaction—gossip being no more than
the self-justification of our own faults. But I couldn't see it so,
that summer, and certainly not in the dawn of the day after the
Prinzing dance.

I had scarcely dropped from fretful tossing into troubled
sleep when Franz opened the door. As if blind to me, he walked
to his bed, a strange and almost sorrowful heaviness on him. He
undid the lace from the hooks and yanked off his shoes; lay full-
length face on the quilts and slept as he was; a helplessness about
his limp body that brought anger welling in me. He was ready
at Anna's call and changed to work pants; had little to say but
anxiety in his glance. He dressed with us for church and hitched
the horses; but said, "I'm going to the Bauers'; maybe I'll ride to
church with them." Before Father had time to decide, Franz
stepped down the path, soft dust instead of road gravel under his
feet. Father curled the lines about a fist and cut the team a
savage lick with the whip. We jolted ahead with a rush of
pebbles. I turned back but he was gone and the trees grew between us.

The Bauers were absent, I saw, Mr. Bauer's favorite oak
hitching post empty of horses. Not that anyone missed them,
with all the talk loud outside.

"Dead, all right," I heard Mr. Mankin say. "Didn't need no
doctor for him." I humpled along to where Alb Hukelpoke and
Matt Prinzing exchanged news.

"I can't get it through my head, Diah behaving like that." Mr.
Dunkel slid his hat over the bald spot and hooked it on the rim

of hair behind his ears. "Solid kid, I thought. Never ran around much, girling and drunk, late nights."

"The quiet sort." Mr. Grieber was solemn. "That's it; the quiet sort. Got the Devil setting right between their eyes, seems like."

"Sure takes it hard, young Morton does—Dick, his brother. Thought a lot of Minica." Mr. Dunkel settled the hat firmly.

"Cat's knuckles!" Alb Hukelpoke nodded at me; scratched his cheek and whistled. "The skin of some folks—thicker'n bull's hide. Look at that."

Etta Rippey stepped from a neighbor's buggy, her head bowed; crushed, it seemed, and sniffing into a mouse-sized handkerchief. The men parted and she walked as through an aisle of shifty glances. But her dress was frilly and she wore beau-catchers in her hair.

"Two-toed bloodsucker." Matt slid a hand along his belt. I thought, "Liliem might be going here—instead of Etta." Alb said surprisingly: "Fine pair, they make, her and that Schoen girl—Liliem." Read my thought, almost. "Nothing but a little armful of hell, them two."

"And for something like that Diah went and—" Matt stared hard at the ground. "God, what a feller won't do—over a woman." Said it so seriously I didn't laugh, though I wanted to, the way he sighed, as if in his nineteen years he'd known enough of woman's waywardness to last him ninety.

"If there's women in hell, the Devil ain't no man." Alb pulled at his baggy trousers. "Nope, they'd 'a' run him out long ago."

"What you say!" Matt was shocked. "If the Pastor hears you—"

"He won't; if he does, and got any sense, he'll say, 'Amen, my boy.'" But Alb shot a look at the church door, just to be sure. "A woman'll skin you every time—more ways than one, too." He laughed knowingly.

"Not all." Matt grinned, but meant it. "Teena wouldn't; not her."

"Young rib, you; wait till the corset begins to pinch," Alb teased him. I listened to Mr. Prinzing, who was telling Mr. Mais, "Dove right out of the window; about five o'clock, this morning, they say; soon as he saw the sher'ff." He scraped dried manure from a heel. "Abel couldn't 'a' stopped him with a club."

"Hiding in the swamp, likely. Sticks close to the ground." Mr. Mais's fingers worked nervously. "Grass and bushes— nigger-high and thick; you could walk past a man a yard away; never see him." He fumbled for his plug of black twist and absently nipped off a slice; began to chew, forgetting it was Sunday and that he couldn't spit for the next two hours.

Mr. Prinzing nodded, and quit jabbing his heel, listening when Mr. Sperry spoke.

"Hang him, I guess. That's what they do—murderers, like that." Nobody spoke further for a dozen seconds—a heavy period. Matt became very still. Mr. Prinzing said casually: "Hay looks good, there by Long Lake—the south shore. I figure on getting my mower on it."

Talk wove and interwove. Matt touched my elbow and jerked his head for me to come aside. "Seen him." His whisper was harsh. "Early, when I hunted the cows. In the swamp." He edged uneasily. "Jeppy, if you could have seen him—scared and shaking." I was glad for sunshine, and air free and mine to breathe, even if my legs were chained.

The Pastor might as well have shouted at the slivers in the benches, his finger of doom for once disregarded and his testament lost on the altar steps; for people pushed along the aisle out of church, anxious to shake their heads and crow over what they had gathered here.

Anna swished her skirts and rubbed her nose almost triumphantly. "What I said—a neck-stretching—it might learn some folks which side of the fence to stay on." We climbed into the buggy. Father shook the lines.

"Diah's not bad." I couldn't hold back. "Young; no older than Matt or Franz—"

"The wages of sin"—Anna paused to nod prophetlike—"is—"

"Giddap," shouted Father, with suddenness that blocked the syllable in Anna's teeth and sent the horses into their collars. Anna glared but said nothing.

They were in the yard when we passed our house—Mr. Bauer's lean mouth pinched and sober; Mrs. Bauer heavy on the springseat, the iron squeaking as she moved; Tinkla in the back seat, head lowered, and Franz standing beside the wheel, watching for us. He had a queer expression, when we stopped beside them—relief that we had come, mixed with tenseness, now that the worst was here at last. They all had the hushed air of those who wait for another's sentence before they speak for themselves; ventured no more than Sunday greetings. Anna stepped down after Father and asked them in. Mrs. Bauer shook her head, gabble all gone. Anna's key rattled loudly in the lock. Father pried loose the thong fastening the tug to the singletree and slipped the leather from the wood, Franz helping him. The horses stepped free, heading for the barn.

Father started in their tracks but Mr. Bauer wound his lines about the willow in the whipsocket and said, slowly: "Let them go, Johan. They'll no more than eat grass."

Father, mindful of barn duties, swung round in surprise at the weariness in Mr. Bauer's tones. "They'll roll and break the harness."

Mr. Bauer shook his head. "Chores'll keep, beside what I'm here for." The crossbars under my hands became sticky, my head loud with scrambling thoughts. Mr. Bauer gave Father a steady eye but Mrs. Bauer was afraid. She pressed a fat thumb so hard against her loose chin that the flesh remained white long after she shifted position. Franz straightened the singletree, eyes half-shut, and hands fumbling. Father gouged a button through its hole and stopped, neck stiff with suspicion. I heard Anna's steps back at the door. The oaks were hanging their leaves in heat that wrapped us in sweat.

No gentleness in us, I thought afterward; not in our bodies,

closer to wood than flesh and bone; not in the words of our
mouths, blunt and harsh, being unpracticed in speaking what the
heart feels, but long accustomed to the hardness that goes with
handling rock and iron and stubborn animal-strength. We used
words as one does a hammer, striking home soundly what we had
in mind, careless of blows falling wild and hurting; or so it
seems, as I remember how Mr. Bauer blurted out Franz's name
and Tinkla's, with slow emphasis, as if this were prologue to
barter; how Franz drooped, the red of shame mottled on his
cheeks; helpless to stop ears. He went and almost timidly
reached to touch Tinkla's arm where she sat, hands over her
face. Father was straight and silent, taking this with dreadful
calm. Until he shouted, "Franz, you—" anger choking his utter-
ance. But when he saw Mr. Bauer's glance and Mrs. Bauer's
stare and Anna at the door, watching, listening, he groped as if
blindly for the step; beaten, it seemed to me; all his rage so much
clashing of dried branches in winter: "*Na ja;* this too; on top of
all else."

He came to his feet at Anna's shrillness: "So, Vildvogel; a
fine young rooster you hatched out." He waved her to silence
and said unsteadily, older by years in that moment, "It is bad
enough—to think of this. Let done with your talking." He
nodded somberly at Mr. Bauer's quiet statement: "This stays with
us, Johan; between our houses." He answered gruffly, "No
shame to me, I guess; that mine should join with yours." But
he looked away when Mr. Bauer extended his hand. What
needed doing must be done, and fast, he said; and would have
had the Pastor come that very hour, hasty to hide this fault under
the coat of respectability promised by book and sacrament. But
Anna, when she heard, asked stridently: "Married? And live on
this place?" As though this, being a new idea, tumbled into
dire confusion whatever plans she had fiddled over. She slammed
the door on us, without waiting for a reply.

Franz scraped dirt with a toe, wishing the hole grave-deep
and himself in it, I guess. But Mrs. Bauer clucked again, a

wilted sort of joy lifting into smoothness the worry-creases about her jowls. She mentioned after threshing as a good time for the wedding. People always had a spare day to leave the plow for a shivaree and dance. Franz listened and said little, as if he doubted that it was about him they were talking. But Father was quick to exclaim: "A whole barnful of ears and eyes—you think I'll stand for that?"

"*Ach,* Johan." Mrs. Bauer poured sirup to unruffle his ire. "Let people come and sniff around; that'll shut their mouths quickest." And Father agreed at last but with grumbles.

So it was settled; the broken pot mended, if sticking pieces together haphazardly can be called mending. At least for Father and the Bauers, their pride saved by letting honor sneak in at the cellar door. For Tinkla and Franz, staring at each other now, with a kind of startled surmise, nothing was settled; for them, only a great beginning—Tinkla blinded by a love she didn't hide and yet knowing as a wild thing recognizes danger that Franz was scarcely half hers; accepting even this. Franz turned his head from side to side as if encircled with bars and no gates to open; already feeling the irksomeness of obligation and fearing with cold sweat on his palms what tomorrow—a year—would bring.

A long moment for them. Then Tinkla leaned forward and Franz patted her cheek, Mrs. Bauer so full of approval her hat rocked like a hobbyhorse. They wheeled off. Father strode after the horses. We changed Sunday shirts for weekday blue-cloth, Franz saying as he drilled arms into shirt sleeves, "You brought the fiddle home. It is good, Jeppy." I laced shoes, half-imploring that this was only a dream and that I'd wake soon; wake to anything but this.

2

The Prinzings cut the wild-hay meadows beside Long Lake— shore land and a part of the swamp, belonging to nobody, Mr. Prinzing said. It was a dry season that year, the bog shaky as new jelly but holding firm under mower and wagon rim; although now and then a horse knifed its hooves through the layers of peat and mired to the belly, tearing the harness to a tangle of broken leather.

Matt came to tell us: "More hay there than we'll feed up. Besides, we're shorthanded. You fellers help put 'er up, huh? And take half the crop. Suit you?" The plan suited even Father.

He was like a hawk, these days, suspicious of a neighbor's smile and hasty with explanation: "Smart one, that Franz; to pick a hustler like that Bauer girl. A wedding in the house, this fall." What he really thought, no one guessed. He was as bearish as ever; but in a quieter way, it seemed; hoping, I guess, that he might yet make up to Franz the years that had been wasted and were behind.

We went into the hay, the rack bouncing and weaving on the bolsters over the three miles of ditchy road and corduroy swamp trail, morning and night. Glad for once to put the house and yard behind our heads, and to listen to sounds other than the echoings from floor and wall. Glad also to be rid of Anna's scorn and sharp snicker—the sourness with which she'd dump potatoes on Franz's plate, whether he asked or not, and kick the stockings and underwear he left scattered on the floor in his hurry to dress: "Slop your things around—under your feet. Worse than a pig. Maybe your wife'll pick up after you. I won't." Her snicker must have been like salt in an old cut for Franz.

She'd sniff knowingly when Saturday night and Sunday gave him time to go to the Bauers'. "Huh. First tooth in the apple—sweet to the taste." Once as if stuck with needles and pins she burst out to me: "Bauer's got land to throw in the swamp—plenty, over past North Goose Lake. Why don't Franz ask for a piece? He'll get ahead faster by himself."

"And live off his wife?" I wanted to know, snippy myself at her meddling.

"Living off his pa's hate now, ain't he?" she demanded flatly, and I could only be stupidly angry, realizing that she was more than right, but that Father and Franz were of different minds.

She couldn't leave well enough alone and hinted to Father, keen with malice: "House is like a chicken coop for room—all squeezed into corners. And the loft—kind of short-legged for the wedding night."

Father settled the water kettle with a bang. Franz, at the wash-dish, cleaning up, hid his face in a lather of suds. Father spoke harshly: "There must be added another room. I'll not have a woman crawling up walls—like a squirrel," he added unhumor-ously, and nobody smiled, being far beyond laughter. That week he saw Mr. Mais and Abel Kloster, and with them planned a lean-to on the north wall. Mr. Mais flung his chest of tools in the shade; a Kloster boy carted a pile of lumber near by; and the walls arose—walls to shut Franz in. He muttered, hooking the neckyoke strap: "Wonder how many boards Father means for me?" And how many to nail tight the neighbors' mouths—I finished the thought to myself, guessing what was on his tongue. He listened to the beat of hammers for a while. "A room for two of us," he said, in a wild sort of way. "Jeppy, it's wrong—wrong spiked into the walls"; then picked up the lines. "Git dap, there," he called.

We hitched the team early after milking, bound for the meadows, with the sun not yet untangled from trees; the racket-ing rumble of our wagon loud between the tamarack walls on either side and the coolness of wet grass and peat-smell spinning the blood faster in shoulder and arms. Matt's rousing "Hullo, you fellers," and the wave of his broad straw hat lifted the back straighter above the heels, somehow. And on mornings when Teena was along (she was helping out at the Prinzings') Matt whooped and strapped his team until the wagon careened like a drunk uncertain on his feet among the ruts, and Teena clung to the rack boards like a bird on a stick. With the flick and bulge of muscle we dug like ants at the hay piles, Franz and Matt at the forks, and Teena and I on the loads; and all that had happened seemed to ooze from us along with the salt of our sweat, leaving us clean; in part, at least.

Song bubbled in the throat, mornings when the kingbirds slanted up high over the tamaracks and shot down again in sheer singing joy; even Franz hummed, pinch-mouthed and aloof though he was, sensitive to chaffing. But he grinned at Matt's wobbly bass, hoarsely off key:

> "Marry me, my freckled maid,
> Oh, marry me and take a chance;
> But if you marry me at all,
> Marry me in underpants";

and Teena's outraged: "You get me right down off this load, Matt Prinzing, if you're going to sing that song. The idea!" Her cheeks were crinkly with trying not to laugh. Matt whooped again. But at lunch, with the stack thrusting its bulk high to throw shade where we munched, he'd sit dumb, the sandwich in his fingers dribbling to crumbles, hungry as he was; filling his wants with Teena's quick smile and easy-coiled-together body (like Franz turning to Liliem for what Tinkla could never give him). His gaze flickered with eagerness—some moment now he'd reach and crush her in his arms, the way he looked at her, I thought.

The mower rattled by the hour, laying the grass in swaths wide as arms outstretched, the sharp clink-clink-clink of sprocket against cog echoing from the green cliffs of the tamaracks and the hollow emptiness of the swamp—the swamp, where the sheriff and his deputies beat the willow clumps and edged cautiously around the pine windfalls, and avoided the sun stabbing through the branches and striking the blue-steel of rifles, cocked and ready. Rifles for a farmer's boy who was lucky if he had a twenty-five-cent jackknife in his pocket. But it was neighbors' talk (and meant for the sheriff's pendulous ears) that Diah had somehow got himself a double-barreled shotgun, and wouldn't stop a wink to pepper the hind end of any snooper that trailed through the bogs.

Wherever he went, the sheriff found the flat hand of stubbornness hard against him. He cussed and swore and spat out questions like bullets, for which he received answers by the yard without an inch of sense in them; except from the Mortons and their kinfolk. The rest of us didn't want to say, this side, that side; not with the deer taking to the higher ridges and the hills beyond; not when it became clear that by night and under shadow the fugitive was getting help. Soon there wouldn't be space large enough for a coon to hide a track; not in the hilly woods.

Franz would let the team idle at the turn and peer at those dark and shadowy undergrowths and the green steeples of pine towering yards above the rough wallows of leafy branch and treetop. Somewhere behind that duskiness Diah Kloster was skulking from copse to thicket, every stump an enemy to his frightened senses; a neighbor's boy, and fear turning him animal. Franz shivered when he told me about it.

Once when the hay was down and drying, we saw the sheriff break from a thicket of young hazels. Franz stared as if hypnotized at this huge man with the bone of hawk in his face and the steel in his hands; this man whose trigger and lead had the law with it, to plunge a man, vibrant on his heel-leather one moment, into bloody stiffness the next.

Franz's head wobbled, pulled by the strings of dread, as he watched the long stride of the sheriff cut into the woods again. "Hunting a man—like an old hound," he muttered, untying the lines. "Like a toothless old hound." He slapped the mares into a slow walk.

"Two-toed bloodsucker if I'd leave my trail around here." Matt stopped by to mop sweat and gurgle water from the jug. "No siree; I'd 'a' lit out for North—"

"And have every farmer ready to sick his dog on you?" My words sounded big and almost like gospel. "Got friends here; up there, nobody. He'll stay."

Franz chewed his thought with a timothy stalk, realizing better than any of us what strange cords knot a man to his home place and pull him along familiar paths. I'd watch him from my perch on the load and see him walking beside the team to the next bunk of hay, veering sometimes a rod to the side to catch on his fork a wisp of hay lodged in grass. And the ache in me lengthened. Not our Franz any more. True, his overhalls were the same, the new cloth Anna patched into the rips bright against the fadedness of leg and bib; and his shoestrings all knotted to repair breaks and half-untied, as always. But not the same, either. Not easy to say *how,* but it was on him, the difference; a mark on him as on those who have sojourned in strange places.

They pitched, and the wild grass that lately swung on its roots and hid the song sparrow's nest was forked into long loaves of stacks, bound to earth with twine-strings flung over them and weighted with stone on either end.

Matt settled the twine with a tug and grinned at Teena. "That'll hold 'er," he said, turning to Franz; "cyclone or snowstorm." He sucked a mouthful of water from the jug and swallowed, his Adam's apple jumping. He was merry these days, whistling like a meadow lark, strong as two men, with Teena near him, his muscles tight under the wet shirt. "She wants to help," he said when she first came driving his team. "Says it's— it's our hay; us together"; said it as if it were nothing new; but the red in his face wasn't from heat alone. He gurgled more water now. "Ain't cold, but it's wet," he shouted to Teena and climbed the load, jug under his arm. "Want a drink?"

Teena lifted the jug. "Hey," Matt yelled. "Rinse off the spout. Might catch something from me." But she giggled and drank. "Guess your bugs ain't stranger to me," she said after a while; and, shamed by boldness, hid in her floppy bonnet. Matt called her a hussy, his laugh ringing; hoisted her in his arms, and, for all her squeals and the sudden tight clamp of her hands on his shoulders, threatened to drop her into an ant heap.

Franz regarded them with sadness, screwing the corners of his lips. That was the way it should be—and wasn't with him. He let Matt rag him with no more than a tight smile and a scratching of the nose. "Smart ones, you and Tinkla, huh?" Matt poked at him with a thumb. "Acting like you was just hatched and the shells still hanging to your ears. Beating me to it." His grin broadened at Franz's stammering. "Kinda smelled something in the air, you sweetening on her." But said no more. And Franz was grateful. He saw how quick Matt was to run at Teena's voice; eagerness in the lift of his heels and the outstretching of his arms; how he dug at the hay tumbles as if each forkful were a stone laid in the foundation of his barn or a clapboard on the house—new and with hope and laughter mortared in with the plaster on the walls of bedroom and kitchen. The ache deepened in me, observing the hurt in his eyes; remembering how slowly sometimes he put on his Sunday shoes and pants to visit Tinkla on Saturday nights; almost reluctantly, duty-bound rather than whipped over the hills by those fierce inward proddings which lovers alone understand and obey. He'd step high, once beyond the door and in sight of the window, but his whistle must have had vinegar in it to pucker his lips; and he'd swing away, but not—or so I thought—as he would have if Liliem had waited at the end of the path.

Three stacks grew by the shore and were topped off—huge rounded heaps, gray-green now, but weathered yellow before the snow would whiten the tamaracks walling them in. On days when Teena baked or scrubbed at home and what wind came was hot to the skin, we'd pitch our forks and rakes in the bushes where afternoon heat curled the wild-potato stalks, and run for the lake; stepping white and naked from piles of trouser and shirt; kicking sand and shouting as the spring-fed cold water splashed over tender spots, Franz a stripling beside Matt's bulk, both their bodies flour-white except for mittens of tan to the elbow where the forearm had been free of sleeve-cloth and bare to the sun. I'd lurch slowly in their rippled wake until the water bobbed me corklike. Waves slapped my underarm with chill tips. I'd dodge the arched spray Matt shot from his cupped hand, and follow the bubbles when he dived, his kicking legs out of focus beneath water; suddenly feel his cool arms about my waist and the lake in my nose as he dragged me under. We'd roll out at last, moist and clean of wild-grass seed and the dusty salt of stacking, our feet molding prints in the sand, our legs prickling as the hair dried in the hot wind and sprang from the flesh.

Then on the day Franz pitched the last sloo grass on the stack, fear walked boldly from the shadows. Matt had a face as long as a rail, that morning; he let the team lag in the tugs. "Sher'ff nabbed Abel Kloster last night," he told us. "Says there's a trail to the swamp where Diah's been to get food and stuff; Abel's aiding and abetting him, he says. The sher'ff's got dogs now— from Fergus."

Matt topped the stack. Silence was made heavier by the squeak of calloused palms against the fork handle. The sun roasted our shoulder blades before ten o'clock. Once we heard a long howling that mingled and grew with the echoes of the swamp—worse than wolves at midnight. It brought a chill under our sun-hot shirts.

"Not much hope—with them on his trail." Matt hefted a bunch into a low and unpacked spot. I scarcely heard him. That jungle of young trees above which old and gum-scabby tamaracks pointed their sharp tips not two rods away—the scaly dead-limbed lower trunks guarded from sight—I had an odd notion that a company might stand there in frozen stiffness; and who but the fox could tell man from tree, or tree from man?

Franz heaved a forkful and let the tines slip down slowly, his gaze woodsward. His fist gripped suddenly. I had never heard a cicada buzz with such metallic noisiness. We knew before sticks crackled that Diah Kloster tore from the brush, a shoulder and chest bare, the flesh caked with sores of cut and scratch; a curved branch clawing at him as he ran. The fork that Franz held remained in hay. He stood as if empty of life, except for a quickening of the muscle-throb in his throat. Unbelievable that this was

Diah, our neighbor—this running animal, fright bulging his eyes, his hair straggled, and his mouth yanked crookedly as though he shut back screams that would soon shrill from his lips; half his chin rough with man-whiskers, the other down-white with boy's fuzz.

"Franz, Franz." Diah staggered to the wagon. "Get me in the rack—under the hay. Quick." Franz quivered at the hoarseness in his voice—wild and unhuman. Before he could free his fork the deep and hungry baying of the dogs rushed into our ears, filling the meadow with clamor. The kingbirds whirled and vanished. Diah stumbled headlong, his fingers curling into the soft peat—wanting to burrow badgerlike into the safe earth. We stood like elm blocks, unable to bend a knee, watching him. A moment, then he was up; held out his hands despairingly, doubting our strength. He jerked around and legged it for the tamaracks. The green brush swallowed him eagerly, erasing his crouched body from our sight.

"He's—he's crazy-mad; headed straight for the dogs." Matt could hardly speak for hoarseness. He shuffled in the hay and nearly plunged from the stack; pale as Franz. "Shall we holler him back?"

Franz shook his head, without hope, a coldness on him, as on Matt and me, in spite of the heat that brought sweat on our bodies. "The dogs—near now. And the sher'ff behind them." His shoes rustled the dried stems as he moved. A web of tiredness made him sag. What was there to do but wait and round off the stack?

The dogs belled fiercely after a while—then silence swept on buzzard's wings over the swamp. A quarter-hour and the wall of tamaracks splintered into limbs and branches shoved violently aside. The sheriff marched forth with the deputies, grim and hard-stepping, Diah struggling between two of them, lunging back fiercely (as a steer at the halter's end does, smelling the blood on the chopping block) and being jerked forward without gentleness so that flakes of peat flew at his heels.

It was an hour large and out of shape with that which was still unborn—one we would remember, especially Franz. But our eyes like the young wolf cub's were sealed against what was to come. We saw only the meadow sickled into grass short even for a handful and quiet now, except for a meadow lark; the horses bending their long necks to see and the collars squeaking; Franz like a post mauled into the hay; Diah with the fear in his eyes, as one who sees in every looping grapevine or creeper a black noose dangling. He mumbled over and over, hopelessness in his throat, "Don't . . . don't . . . don't." A phantom of what was coming already darkened his mind. He cried brokenly with every jerk at his arms: "Don't . . . don't"; until Franz's lips were sucked white against his teeth.

3

The sheriff took him off; first to Mary's Hill, then to Fergus; beyond the ridges, finally, to Stillwater, some said. And we saw Diah Kloster no more; Diah, familiar as we were to the length of a valley and the clean sweep of ridge and ravine, waking now to a three-foot patch of sky laced with cold ribbons of steel. It was worse than a double funeral, almost.

We talked about it, adding nothing to what we'd said before, only a baffled wonderment. "Not much he wanted; not in this world, he didn't." Franz slipped a faded tie under his Sunday collar. It was midsummer then and the wedding a month away. "Not more than Matt—or anybody. A farm to raise his wheat and pigs and a house to come to."

"And a girl." I brought a shoe nearer with the upper end of a crutch.

"And a girl." Franz's voice held a tremor. "A girl to work his thumbs raw for, and not care; sweep his place clean. No bachelor's house—with dirt on the dinner plates. Not much to ask for."

"Skimpy wages a man gets, for fifteen hours a day, year in, year out."

"Now they'll choke the wind out of him—black in the face." Franz circled his neck with a finger as if his collar were too tight. "That's what he gets."

I stomped into a shoe. "Seventeen girls, at least, running loose around here, and Diah and Minica both had to hit on the same girl. Neither giving in."

"You—you can't give in, Jeppy; or give what ain't yours to give." He spoke as if the words came from outside and not from him at all. "Something wrong with second best; always, I guess." Liliem in his mind again, though he would have chewed pincers rather than admit it. I slung my coat on. We set off to church, girding our minds with a shield against the Pastor's axes of God.

The Klosters were attending again, boys and girls downstairs beside Father and Mother. They acted as if they didn't know that Jonas Bluber sat in Diah's place. But Abel Kloster looked so hunched and bowed of back, I thought of an oak split by the ax and left to dry. Two nights he'd spent in jail before the big-wigs found their evidence against him fribbly as buck's wool and about as valuable, and let the iron door clang him into sunlight. He'd nearly bawl, shaking his fist in trembling anger before services, while people gaped their mouths, listening. "Four by ten, that jail room," he would quaver. "My oats bin is bigger. There they penned me in; cramp a feller to death, they would." And Franz, ears rubbing Alb Hukelpoke's shoulders and jealous over a lost word, would scuff his heels, wavering; sure that Tinkla upstairs waited with a smile for him, but held fascinated— as most of us were. One of our congregation behind the bars of a jail and smelling of iniquity; the Pastor roaring to squeeze guilt from our souls with the tongs of the law—we made the most of it. But in a month or so it was a tale five times told and raggy with telling. We gave our backs to Abel Kloster, intent on the new and the tingling, except a few old weepers to whom a story was as ageless as their seamy hats and coats.

We'd tramp upstairs, my crutches loud on the boards, so that I wished often we'd stay below; Tinkla waving, frank in her possessiveness, although Franz reddened at the titters from the boys; irked by her triumph in showing that soon she'd be a married woman. But when Liliem passed by him and sat near the organ (rarely this summer), he was busy as a tumblebug searching as for gospel in the hymnbook; disregarding her smile haughtily, as if this lent truth to his pretense. But the old yearnings were not yet trodden into the ashes of forgetfulness. I saw that, the way he peeked over the hymnbook.

It was a season jumbled and out of order, the weightiness of dividing the calf feed or slapping a sweat pad on a collar for once less important because of what lay shelved in the mind. I'd wake blinkered with sleep to a thought neither shadow of dreams nor flesh of reality but something of both; and yawn owlishly until fact could not be denied: "Not long now. Tinkla'll be here, Franz with her; and the bed gone from the floor." Franz, the baby of our scraggly brood, unable until he was seven to say which shoe was right or left (insistent, though, in spite of Father's or Fritzie's jibes, that the trumpets of the morning-glory could be blown, if tried in the false dawn); Franz, the boy, plucking God knew what bright dreams from the fiddle strings—and soon now he would pillow a woman beside his own head. Tinkla—dependable Tinkla, solid as a ledge of stone; plenty of common bread-and-milk sense in her, but blind to a curl of ivy under her feet and deaf to the loneliness in a kildee's cry—no wonder Franz'd come home early some nights after seeing her, and rip off his clothes with impatient jerks: trying to make Tinkla understand, I guess, and failing. I'd peer at him sometimes where he snored, his body sprawled from corner to corner of the bed and humped in the quilts, one leg upthrust, whitely bare and an arm twisted in the pillow. Hogging the bed, man-fashion; unused to woman-softness and the necessity of reckoning for two instead of one—lessons he was soon to learn, page by page. And the worry-wrinkle lay like a flaw between his eyes to mar the serenity of sleep.

It grew deeper, that furrow, the day when we fixed the swinging gate with tamarack poles. It was late Saturday, Father being in Mary's Hill. I stopped at the pump for a bucket of water. Mr. Mais, his tools packed, shouted across the yard, "The last nail hammered, Franz. The room is all ready; waiting for your paint brush. Wish you happiness." Franz waved in answer. Mr. Mais lifted the hammer. "Peace on these new walls," he said, tapping a corner siding. He flung the hammer down and locked the tool chest; took a chew of black twist and spat before he shouldered the chest and went home across the seven-acre patch.

Franz was idle-handed when I stomped up. "New walls. Wonder what'll happen inside them, before they're old and the knots fall out." He dropped three crooked spikes into the nail box. "It scares me, Jeppy."

"Alb Hukelpoke says he was scared, too." I gabbled to change the look he had, yet wanted him to speak. "Says his ma-in-law invited herself—first three weeks after the wedding. Mrs. Hauser, you know; weighs two-fifty, anyway. She brought a blacksnake—said she'd lick the hide off Alb if he didn't treat her daughter—"

"Scared." He wasn't heeding my talk. "Scared to wake up and find her worse than a stranger beside you; not getting along decently. That's the worry in my craw." He hadn't spoken before about this. I was almost glad that words rushed from him, dammed up who knows how long. "Hate to salt your potatoes with and chew with your meat. And she scared, like Mother, when a step rattles outside. And Father—gall in his teeth, so black he was against her. If that happens to me—"

"Franz, don't." I gouged holes with a crutch. "Getting yourself sweated. Tinkla's a good girl—"

"Tinkla—she's—a man's a fool to want better. I know that." He slid the hammer handle in his closed palm. "No shirts will need patching, as long as she's around, I guess; or pots left dirty, far as that goes." His gaze was steady. "Don't ask it, Jeppy; what you have in mind. I am *promised* to her. That is settled.

Only—only—" His eyes flickered and breath seemed knocked from him by the word. Only she's not Liliem; not Liliem in the house. It was plain as a barn door. I dug at a piece of bark. "It scares me, Jeppy," I heard him say.

Anna shrilled, "Coffee and lunch," just then. She was stirring a pot when we entered the door, her cheeks crimson. "Well, it's ready—the room." She pointed with a finger she'd just dipped into the kettle and sucked to test the soup. "Door to lock and all—Franz's bedroom."

Her giggle sent him into lightning-swift rage. "Poison to you, that's what I am." He regarded her a moment to cool off; then asked quietly, "You want the farm, don't you?"

She glared, her grip on the kettle so firm I expected the soup to fly. But it startled her that he guessed, I think; pricking her crabbed honesty, so that she yelled, "Who wants stones and thistles except a brush rabbit?" The spoon splashed down; all the sourness of an uncivil nature twisted her lips. She bounced from the room and left Franz to tend the boiling kettle, if we wanted soup for supper.

4

Matt Prinzing rushed into the barn and nearly upset the cream pail, one milking hour, so excited he was. "Franz, Franz." His big chest pumped. "Me and Teena—two-toed blood-sucker—we're getting married—two Sundays after you. I asked her. No use waiting."

"I knew she would." Franz was suddenly all grins, as if he welcomed a brother into his own company.

"We're gonna live on the Beckers' farm—just across the fence from my yard; all winter. Me and Teena—godalmighty, Franz." He jiggled in his pants. "And they're gonna have a shivaree dance the Saturday before. Will you play?"

Franz was dubious. "Haven't fiddled much, this summer. S'pose I can though." He nodded.

"That's talking." Matt was jubilant. "The old man's ordered half a barrel of beer."

"There's something else, Matt." Franz pulled at the scar. "Could we—let's make it double—two weddings at once—if the Pastor can stand it." He was eager as if with Matt and Teena together there, he could outface what he dreaded to discover in people's faces. But Matt refused. "No, Franz; I want my own wedding," he said simply. Franz drew back, as though slapped for cravenness. And straightened his back, Matt's reproach an antidote for cowardice, perhaps. But when Matt was gone, he stared in an odd manner and for a long time at the knob of the new door beside the ladder—a door opening inward.

A strange time for him, waiting for a Wednesday and a wedding day; happy in his own fashion, I guess. He whistled and played again—tunes with the pull of yearning in them. And though he avoided folks whenever he could, he trailed the path to the Bauers' more and more; holding Tinkla as a shield against dreams that vexed him most; her ears patient for his trouble. Solace of a kind.

He hadn't spoken to Liliem since the barn dance; kept out of her reach at church but couldn't hide from her smile. Once she called to him as he passed, and there was more in the way her voice trembled than mere greeting. He took Tinkla's arm and hurried downstairs. Tinkla was high with victory. The folks laughed. "Did you see? Franz giving her the mitten—Liliem Schoen? She's a wild one, though; too wild for her shoes." Defeated victory for him, I thought, remembering how he stopped the bow, the evening afterward, still as the chair he sat in, running a finger along the crack under the bridge—a split in wood from the fall when he'd thrown the fiddle. He touched it as though it were a break in his own heart.

The wedding was announced for Wednesday, and in the seven days between, Mrs. Bauer dragged ten pounds from her fat body and got another bunion, trotting from cellar door to staircase, Mr. Bauer told us. He was excited over a "bossy" coming fresh soon. "Her first calf, too," he said. More excited over his cow than over his daughter's wedding, Anna scolded. Mrs. Bauer drove Anna to swearing almost, borrowing cups because most of hers were handleless, the kids having dropped them so often, and begging a pinch of this and a snuff of that. She poked into the bedroom and prodded the new bed she'd bought, quilted and pillowed in a corner; until Anna banged the kitchen door and shrilled: "Take everything; house and all; scoop up the cellar, too."

"*Ach,* Anna." Mrs. Bauer was comfortably unabashed. "Got every fork and spoon marked—black string for you, green for Mrs. Prinzing, red for Mrs. Mais—"

"All she left me was a toothpick and a hank of horse-radish," Anna grumbled that night.

Father grunted. "It will be over soon. And we can sleep again."

"Over?" Anna was short. "It's over now, for me, Vildvogel. I'll let the new wife boil your coffee."

"What's this?" Father thumped the table. "Who's leaving? There is room for all in this house."

Franz started to speak but Anna broke in, "There's room for only one woman in a house." She slapped the pancakes down. "The morning she walks in, I walk out."

"Anna, shame," Father lashed at her. "A young one, this girl; what does she know of baking and—"

"Twenty loaves a week," Franz shouldered in. "So much bread the Bauers eat. And Tinkla bakes it all."

"Anna knows the house." Father slashed at a pancake. "And the Bauer girl can—"

"Keep your tongues in your throats, both of you." Anna's lean nose twitched with anger. "Think I was a heifer and for sale, the way you two cluck and clatter over me." She slammed a cupboard door tight. "What's done is done, and I'll not have it said I kicked in the wedding bed. Nor took more'n I brought, either." Malice rubbed in her smile. "You can stay in your own pasture, Vildvogel. And here's more sour jack," she added. "Better stuff than you'll get from now on. New wives—most of 'em don't know enough to spill salt."

Father growled but on Monday Anna packed her things and marched stolidly to the Maises'; wouldn't let us drive her. She stayed a week; scolded Mrs. Mais to tears and left in a huff for her brother's near Mary's Hill. Once more the house rumbled with man-voices. What dishes we had, piled up in the cupboard, and the slop pails filled.

Franz was not sorry that she went, I guess, much as her food suited our taste. He slopped about the house, freer with Anna gone, though he cut a finger hacking the loaf, and his hands reddened from the water poured hot on the separator disks. One night he found a spider stretching webby cords across an upper angle of the new door, and threshed furiously with a broom, as though fifty spiders were spinning there. He paused uncertainly; then took the lamp, careful not to explode it by carelessly shaking the oil, and opened the door.

"Jeppy." His voice rang, as if sounding from an empty water barrel. I braced myself in the doorway. He put the lamp down. A place smaller than the lean-to; hardly room to make your mind up, Alb Hukelpoke said afterward. It was longer than broad, the corners shadowless with two windows, letting in light, and the air strong with the tantalizing odor that goes with new things.

"It will be good, bringing a woman to the house." The room seemed crowded with his words. He pulled at a stray corkscrew of shaving, his voice swallowed up all at once. "A man ought to be on his knees, giving thanks, I guess; only—" He hung his head. "Only, I hadn't figured it would be like this—no, never like this, Jeppy."

5

The churchyard was black and white with people, the folks swinging about shoulder by shoulder, as we drove up. Waiting for the bridal buggy, they were, the men shedding the hot autumn sun with their coats off and their shirts wide; the women, faces eaten by curiosity, filling the lower half of the windows.

Young Sam Bauer, proud in a hat that crowded two inches away from the top of his ears, handled the black lines; kept the team skittish with a sweep of the whip and a loud "Hia there, Napoleon." He was importantly deaf to Tinkla's "Watch out, Sam'l; they'll run away." We could hear her as we rode in the buggy after.

Franz and Tinkla with Matt and Edie Bauer were in the bridal buggy, first to stop at the stone step before the church. Matt was best man—there was no one else Franz wanted, since Fritzie was we didn't know where on the flats, and Walter married—and a pair of crutches was hardly an omen for good at the altar.

Father and I rode with the Bauers, Father less grim, but stiff in his white shirt. Mr. Bauer chewed a willow twig, upset over his bossy, his thoughts work-bound, although this was the day his daughter would leave his house. Mrs. Bauer, smiles on chin and forehead, so jovial she was, bounced on the seat but fretted, "*Ach;* stayed home, that's what I should have. Gina Mais never puts enough salt in the potatoes. I should have told—"

"Keep your petticoat down, Katinka." Mr. Bauer made ready to stop. "Gina Mais cooked potatoes before this day."

Franz was already on the step, straight and starchy in the new suit he got the week previously, the coat and pants matched and of the same cloth for once in his life; steady beside Tinkla, though his hands shook a little as he twitched at his tie. And Tinkla, blooming like a flower, all frills and laces, almost polka-ed at the church door. She flounced away from her mother's fussiness, whispering nervously, "It don't show, now; I *did* pin it up."

Inside, the air was no cooler than outside. Handkerchiefs waved to move the heat from necks and cheeks. Mrs. Mayer was saying: "Sticky, like this; sure going to rain." Mrs. Pilversack bobbed her head: "Hope not, for Tinkla's sake; bad sign, rain at a wedding. But might expect it—wild as that Vildvogel boy is. Don't know what ails Katinka Bauer, letting her girl—" She pushed with the crowd.

Autumn leaves, frost-touched and fiery as on hill after hill of maple and oak, glowed with quiet flame along the carpet edge. Franz's arm was rigid to hold Tinkla's hand. They marched to the altar, Matt's large shoes rustling the leaves that Teena Dorset had brought to border the aisle and tied with ropes of bitter-sweet, beaded with scarlet berries.

The Pastor led the pace, dourly in the lead, his Bible like Aaron's shield over his breast, his beard-ends shaking. He had been mulish when Franz and Father went to the parish house; Franz scared as a chicken, man-grown though he was. The Pastor grumbled about painting with the Devil's brush and needing the church to whitewash our sins. He flung the Ten Commandments about as though they were stone and visible; but growled away into indistinctness when Father offered three cords of oak and a turkey at Thanksgiving. The surliness wasn't forgotten today, however. You could see it in the hitch of coattails and the austerity he bent on Franz and Tinkla as he turned on the altar.

The sun ran a carpet of gold across the faded steps between them and him. He pursued them hotly with the whip of his text, the sermon shoved in their teeth: "Be not unequally yoked with the unbeliever." There was a sort of gloating in his voice, as he pointed to the sorrow and Satan's regret that descended plaguelike upon those who enjoyed the fleshpots of Egypt; until Mr. Prinzing shook his head unbelievingly and Mr. Bauer restlessly snapped and unsnapped his huge egg-shaped watch. Then Franz was saying "Yes," hardly heard, though the congregation held its breath to hear; Tinkla nodding in answer, her throat too quivery for words; and both were kneeling, the sun in yellow slants across them. The shadow of Tinkla's head was dark on Franz's shoulder. But as the Pastor lifted his hands in blessing, the light drained away and a duskiness seemed to hang from his palms. Before they arose, the organ droned the hymn. Mrs. Bauer cried her handkerchief wet. Mr. Bauer nudged her and whispered, "For God's sake, Katinka; this is a wedding, not a funeral." And Mr. Dunkel, glancing out the window, half-called, "Whoa, there, Jenny," when he saw his team had broken halter ropes and was wandering past the church, the wagon bumping behind. With a smothered sound, he plunged over the legs of three men between him and the aisle, and broke for the door.

He was back with the closing of the hymn. "Gonna pour down; any minute," he said so that we all heard. The Pastor was long-winded over the announcements. We sang another hymn. And in the pause between the blessing and the Amen, a shower streaked the windows blind with rain.

They came from the altar. Tinkla almost fluttered, fast to Franz's arm; grown-up and wedded and ready for married women's talk. Franz walked with quick sharp steps, eyes straight ahead; steps that had the beginning of rebellion in them, it occurred to me—a foolish thought. We waited in the gloom at the rear where the church door spilled water through a cracked panel. Waited for the sun, Mr. Dunkel opining it was a middling shower.

"Cover your ring, Tinkla," Mrs. Grosbeck warned aloud. The folks gawked where they remained in the benches. The Pastor, gownless though still in black, frowned from the curtains of his cubicle, but Mrs. Grosbeck continued: "You know the saying:

> 'Rain on the wedding ring,
> Tears to the wedding bring.'

You watch out."

Tinkla giggled and the folks joined her in this proper sort of indiscretion, now that church was over; though the Pastor was still there. A gust of wind jangled rain against the tin that covered a hole in the roof, and under the noise young Dick

Morton, peering through the window at the wet grass in the graveyard, cried brokenly, "My brother, my brother."

A dreadful silence numbed us; the creak of a bench was like a rock striking wood. Mr. Dunkel squeaked the doors open. Franz took a step as if sun-blinded, though the sky was cloudy over us. Tinkla held to his arm—a barrier warding off evil. Then little Maizie Dumke, ten years or so, wriggled among the legs of people, to stand before Franz with a fistful of goldenrod and blue vervain, her face childishly sober. " 'Yellow for the lady, blue for the man,' " she chanted. "Will you pin them, Franz?" As if unthinking Franz lifted her in his arms and put his hand on her hair—hair yellow as the goldenrod.

Mr. Dunkel proclaimed: "Rain's over; just mosquito drizzle now." Sam Bauer was ready with a "Hia over, Napoleon," and the wedding buggy slopped away in the mud. We followed under a watery sun.

It was sprinkling again by the time we arrived at the Bauers'. Franz helped Tinkla from the buggy and together they dashed for the house, rain on their heels. Mrs. Mais met them, aproned and a soup ladle in hand, forgetting both in the excitement of kissing Tinkla and handshaking Franz. But Mrs. Pilversack, dampness glistening on her nose, pinched her lips. "Sloppy housekeeper, that's what she'll be; running over the doorsill on her wedding day, and it rainy outside."

Those from the church began filling the yard, and the house clamored with laughter and shouting. The invited guests, ponderous with gravity and packages of wedding presents, followed a dim hallway to a back bedroom where they added their gifts to those already scattered on the white spread—cups and saucers, pepper-and-salt shakers, soup-strainers, nutmeg-graters, egg-shellers, apple-peelers—all the gewgaws that looked nice in the Montgomery Ward catalog but were useless as a comb without teeth when you came to use them. *"Ach,* what will she do with them all?" cried Mrs. Bauer, raising her hands.

Mrs. Pilversack brought an oak rolling pin (carved by the Deacon and pugnacious-appearing, with a knot like a thumb) and dropped it beside five others. With a cautious look around she rooted for price tags among the presents, trying to find out how much Mrs. Prinzing paid for the dresser set. She rolled her head when Mrs. Dorset came in, lugging a box: "Mathilda Prinzing—she don't fool me, Lena Dorset; that commode scarf, there—she got that from her gra'ma six years ago." But Mrs. Dorset was lamenting: "I told Caspar we oughten to get it; we bought a flowered lamp, and she's got three already."

Downstairs a circle of handshakers kept Franz and Tinkla busy. "It's like a keg of beer, marriage is," Mr. Prinzing was chuckling. "Gotta have a lot of fizz and foam before you get a clear good drink." He slapped Franz heartily and Mr. Mais, laughing, nearly choked on a cheekful of black twist. Heinie Grosbeck hurried to the group, forcing his huge body through the press. *"Na,* Franz." His big hand opened in good wishes. "So you got yourself an old lady, too, huh?" His neck reddened with fellowship. "Me and the old woman—didn't get to town to buy a present. Shucking corn all week. But here's a dollar—wait, now; maybe I got—" He plowed in his pockets. "Yep, here's a quarter, too. You buy yourself a little something."

Everyone became less jovial when the Pastor arrived, the black cloth shedding somberness on gaiety. "I wish you God's blessings," he announced briefly and strode into the next room, in search of Mr. Prinzing and a game of checkers. Tinkla saw the uneasiness in Franz's expression and laughed at him. "That's the way he always acts at weddings." Her tones were low. "So much fun here, he's got to look like that—like he'd walked barefooted through a thistle patch."

Folks eddied into corners, escaping the main stream from door to door. I saw Leff Sperry by the stair railing. The sky was clear by this time and through a window half-shut swept the odor of the wet woodpile and the chatter of men, coats off, in a fight over a town road—whether it ought to strike right through

Hoffmann's sloo-hole, or bend around it. From the kitchen drifted the smell of hot meat and spices. The prittle-prattle of women was noisy: "Just a shake of the can more, don't you think, Mrs. Prinzing?" "Well, I dunno; kinda peppery, the last spoonful I dipped out." Mrs. Bauer wailed: *"Ach,* didn't I say it? Gina Mais forgot to salt the potatoes."

Alb Hukelpoke, six beers (and then some) foaming under his belt, humped from shoulder to shoulder of bystanders and steadied himself against the wall with an arm that shot close to Franz's ear. "Cat's knuckles. So they got you, heh, Franz?" He shook hands. "Got you roped like a bull calf and the knife out to cut—"

"Alb." Tinkla grabbed his fist in a hurry. "Forgetting to shake with me?"

"Aw sheets, Tinkla. Course I ain't forgetting." He rubbed a clear spot in his whiskers. "Can't a man finish what he starts saying, any more?" He insisted on kissing her. "Got to smack the bride, heh, Franz?" He staggered away, finally, just as Mr. Bauer stopped by, distress in the way he pulled at his suspenders: "Gave the bossy salts, Franz. She's real sick, I tell ya."

"Oh, Pa." Tinkla was impatient. "Fussing like that. Get yourself a glass of beer."

"Glass of beer." Mr. Bauer straightened indignantly. "Best bossy I got." He rambled off to find Mrs. Bauer and a bag of "heatened" oats.

Sam Bauer wove along, a box of cigars under each arm. "Pa says you're to dish 'em out," he ordered, still important. "You can use my room, if you want to fix up." Franz nodded and left Tinkla to exclaiming young ladies. He was gayer now, as the folks picked the black lengths of tobacco from the box; invited Leff Sperry to have one.

Leff grinned and spoke—low and with a side twist of his mouth; slipped a small square of paper like an envelope into Franz's hand. Franz listened, startled; made as if to shove the paper back but stuck it into his pocket with a quick thrust and a glance about. He guffawed crazily at nothing; passed cigars, ignoring Leff's malice; blown to gaiety by inner excitement. I knew as surely as though I'd broken the seal whose fingers had folded that paper—and helpless anger stirred in me again.

Before the afternoon pared down to supper, conversation and beer had throttled the shyness in folks. Songs rattled under the eaves, Mr. Mais remembering one from his soldiering days that began:

"I am good Doctor Ironbeard,
Tit-tee, tit-tee, rump-tum-tump . . ."

—a ditty that was shot full of heel slams and shouts. Alb Hukelpoke tried twice to tease fat Mrs. Dunkel into a side room—"for a little waltz," he hiccoughed. Hints about the dance to come and the Pastor were broad as a barn—wasn't he ever leaving? Or was he going to play sour-face all night too, and spoil the wedding waltz? But the Pastor with calmness removed his long coat and drew his chair closer for a third game, his beard limp and his hands groping for the glass which Mr. Prinzing kept rim-high. Glass after glass he tipped excitedly between his narrow lips, so deeply did he play kings and commoners, unaware that Mr. Prinzing drank one to his two, and was pink-cheeked with holding back laughter. Before Mrs. Bauer shrieked, "Tinkle, get Franz and go to supper," the Pastor was froggy-eyed; moved red checkers on black squares and with a chortle of triumph jumped three of his own kings. Then he realized how error had crept like a bug into the clerical gown. Protesting illness, he had his team hitched and with ecclesiastical dignity walked to the buggy and drove home without supper.

It was worse than smashing her best looking glass for Mrs. Bauer—no prayer by the Pastor at table; and that he, of all people, should go hungry—*ach,* this would hang her ears down. But Tinkla hummed *The Flower That Bloomed Too Soon.* She straightened a fold in her dress and pried Franz from the confidences of the Fledermann girls. "Supper, Franz."

[298]

Knives and spoons clattered for an hour, and fingers became as slippery as the forks. Mrs. Muehlbank asked for a fourth helping of boiled cabbage, and a minute later waddled from the chair, sick to the stomach. The men joked and jabbered. Mrs. Dorset not very privately unfastened a hook in her dress. The pickled fish forked out of bowls were soon nibbled to finny bones. Mr. Mais choked over one portion, and Alb Hukelpoke swore he saw a piece of red horse wiggle a tail. Talk and helpings of meat crisscrossed the white cloth. At last Heinie Grosbeck scraped back his chair. "Trough's empty," he shouted. "Let the next batch come," and finished the meal.

With the Pastor gone, steps quickened and the blood ran faster. Folks departed to hurry their milking, and, with chores erased from their minds, were ready to whoop with the bull fiddle until rooster-crow. Darkness blotted out the yard. Lamps flamed in the house and gasoline torches flared in the barn. After a while the house became empty except for a few grandmas.

Boys and girls hustled to the barn, passing the slower groups of older people and tittering over Saturday night affairs and the newfangled dances at Mason's Resort. The flares were red on their faces as they climbed the short stairs and entered the door. Arne Fledermann was tuning the fiddle, the strings twanging. From the stalls below a horse neighed. Mr. Muehlbank stopped me to say: "Kinda let Franz get the jump on you, eh, Jeppy? Marrying before you. In the old country, you'd be dancing in the pig trough for that; Franz fiddling, too." (The crutches suddenly became heavy as rails.) Before the dance really began Father tapped my shoulder. "Got the team hitched." He saw me hesitate and said strangely, "I see. *Bleibe,* Jeppy, if you want to. I can manage. Come home with Franz tomorrow"; a tiredness about him I hadn't noticed before. People crowded him out of sight.

Rows of small boys, perched like chickens at roost on the carriages at the end of the barn, clapped and kicked heels when Arne Fledermann started the wedding waltz. Couples stood in a large circle, waiting, Franz and Tinkla leading . . . boys tickling girls with straws. Mr. Bauer trotted on the floor with Mrs. Bauer, she all giggles, folding him away in her fat arms until only his worried face peeked over her shoulder. Twice around the center posts they waltzed before Mr. Bauer stopped where he had begun, and with a relieved settling of his suspenders pushed his wife toward Franz; hurried off then and five minutes later appeared in overhalls.

Mrs. Bauer gurgled, *"Ach,* Franz; *ich kann nicht mehr,"* but Franz whirled her away, two rounds, bringing her back where Tinkla stood. "There, Mother," he said.

"Ach, but you swing your legs, Franz," she wheezed. Then she put Tinkla's hand in Franz's. "Waltz, now; and take care of her, Franz." The two continued the dance, Franz slow and careful, his head bent over Tinkla, hiding from what he alone knew; Tinkla pressing against him, as if all his slender strength were hers, let sky fall or ridges tumble. "Everybody waltz," shouted Mr. Dorset, and the circle broke into couples weaving a casual pattern under the lanterns.

Whatever it was that made him so, it was good to see Franz happy again; throwing his head high in laughter; moving from group to group, from barn to house and cellar, where the men *prosted* overflowing cups and glasses to the ceiling. He laughed with the rest when Heinie Grosbeck, top-heavy with drink, pawed at him: "Tell ya what, Franz; if you want a boy, you get in bed naked and—" Franz shushed him with "Not so loud, Heinie; women'll hear you. Have another glass," and waved as he pounded upstairs. He danced with the Fledermann girls until Tinkla pouted; waltzed with Tinkla tight in his arms, the scar glowing warmly. Blown like a coal into excitement by that which had come secretly to him.

Square dance and schottische unreeled their lengths, the young bucks restive once and demanding new dances—like those at the Resort. Arne Fledermann snorted above his fiddle, "Dry your noses first and grow up; then talk." Fat Mrs. Dunkel and Mrs.

Bauer joined in a polka. Like two rolled-up feather ticks they spun together; slipped and fell hard, so that a board in the floor cracked and Mr. Prinzing lumbered a cart from among the carriages to cover the broken place. Tinkla rye-waltzed with Matt, leaning from his arm to ask me, "Where's Franz?" I shook my head. Leff Sperry wanted to fight somebody because he missed a round of beer. A little Hukelpoke girl wept, seeing her ma dancing with a strange man. Once there was a loud cry and Mrs. Mais, pushed by a couple of drunks, pitched off the stairs into the darkness outside—her leg broken, they said. Mr. Mais bridled his team quickly.

"Poor Gina Mais." Mrs. Bauer caught my sleeve. "Come to the house, Jeppy; rest a while. This barn—one can't move, so full of people it is." In the house there was quiet after the hubbub of the barn. A few old ladies bye-bye-babied their grandchildren. Even the cellar was vacant. Mrs. Bauer slipped off her shoes. "Poor Mrs. Mais. And I told her yet, 'Watch out for the stairs.' *Ach,* my." She scratched her tired feet. "They burn; like fire. But it is a good wedding." She leaned toward me. "Want a little blackberry schnapps, Jeppy? You get it; all tuckered, I am. Sammy's room; in the closet. He hid it there for me."

Sammy's room was cool and dim with the lamp screwed low, and the air was pungent with the smell of boy's things; the closet a dark cavern into which I groped; boxes and shoes and truck, and finally the bottle. I shifted a crutch. There was a hurry of steps; Franz coming in and shutting the door. I was about to speak but didn't, silenced by the eagerness with which he shook the envelope in his hand and fingered what dropped from it into his palm. He brought it nearer the dim light—a braid of golden hair, shining as if it were still on Liliem's head. His hand trembled as he laid it to his cheek a moment.

"Jeppy, Jeppy," I heard Mrs. Bauer call. Franz turned swiftly, expecting her to enter the room, I guess; blew the lamp and was gone.

"Jeppy, did you get lost with the schnapps?" Mrs. Bauer's voice hallooed from the kitchen. I heard the door squeak shut softly.

By eleven o'clock sleepy quiet drowsed in the kitchen. I'd have dog-winked beside the stove myself, but Sam Bauer said, "Missing the fun, Jeppy," and took me back to the fiddle-and-accordion squawk in the barn. Jollity echoed with the yells between these stout walls—the accordion man tweedling his bellows close to his ear: "Be damn' if she ain't got a leak!" . . . beer never growing flat in the bucket, so often was the ladle dipped . . . Mr. Dorset chanting, "Fiddle in the furrow and the corn rump-high" . . . men's eyes growing small and piglike with drink . . . two whiskered cronies tearfully slobbering into one another's necks: "Hell of a good feller you are, Hank, you old son of a bull-kicker" . . . Tinkla dancing with anyone who asked, even old August Jaahcobs, toothless and lips brown with snuff-spit, who stepped on her wedding veil and sang hoarsely off beat:

> *"Eins, zwei, drei,*
> *Da lag ich im Brei . . ."*

Franz striding into the red light, face glowing, as if he'd tasted more than Mr. Prinzing's wild currant brandy; almost roughly snatching Teena from Matt's arms . . . Alb Hukelpoke trying to light a match but too wobbly to strike the four-by-four oak post, growling, "Got the match, all right, and the post, but damn' if I can get 'em together" . . . Mr. Bauer scurrying from the cow-yard, lantern bobbing yellow on his shoulder . . .

Midnight supper rolled around, cake and cookies piled in dishpans, and sandwiches of rye bread and bolony—"ground steer," Heinie Grosbeck hooted. Mrs. Bauer lamented: *"Ach,* I just know not everybody got enough to eat." A lanky fellow, squinting at his sandwich as he tried to open it, yelled, "Hey, somebody let the bull run out of this bread." The bellow of the caller signaled the after-supper dance . . . squeals of the wall-standers.

But the cookies were tasteless in my mouth. I pushed to the house and Mrs. Bauer's kitchen again, disquiet sagging my heels. It was restful there. Old Lady Katzenmayer and Grossmutter Dunkel rocked together and yawned over gossip about their sons, man-grown and married now: "Jim had nice black hair till he was six."—"*Ja,* it changes. My John—that's the second one; he got a daughter of Prinzing's wife's sister—I thought for sure he'd be bald; over a year and no hair." Upstairs a baby cried in loneliness: "Mama, Mama. I want my mama." Matt led a white-faced boy into the kitchen and hastily out again. A moment later we heard the gugging sound of vomiting and a thin sick voice: "Oh, my belly. I'm going to die. Get me some black coffee. I'm going to die."

The hours of the bridal night slid down the fiddle bow. A rooster crowed and by and by the sheds and the barn loomed into the dawn. A tardy meadow lark attempted two notes and gave it up, out of practice. The old ladies and the grandmas, with many shoulder pats for Mrs. Bauer and exclamations of "*Ja,* the pickled fish—so good," were finally gathered up by the papas and mamas with kids on their arms and driven home. Mrs. Bauer stretched her lips to keep awake but sighed. "*Ach.* Must get on the pillow a minute. Call me, Jeppy, if one looks for me." At her door she said, "Crawl in with Sammy when you like." The kitchen seemed to ache with want of rest. I heard folks rattle off, too sleepy for good-bys, though somebody fare-welled loudly, "S'long, Franz 'n Tinkla. Don't tip the bed over." Freed at last from the scur-and-throb of fiddle and dance, the barn sank into the quiet of rustling hay and the stamp of horses' feet. From the fields streamed the smutty odor of corn shocks.

Franz pushed the kitchen door wide, unsteady in his shoes, Tinkla with him, close in his arms, both pale, but eyes bright as with fever.

"I'm going up to change," she said at the stairs; as if he were a lover still and barred from secrets beyond hooks and eyes. He lifted himself a step toward her. "No; don't come yet. Not yet." Wayward as Liliem.

He looked after her, knuckles white on the post. "I won't wait long," he called, tensely. Her laugh floated from the dark above.

Fire snapped under the water kettle. Mr. Bauer, sad in a draggled cap and like a ghost out of gray light, crawled in, to fetch a bucket of hot water. "No Sammy here yet," he grumbled. "Takes his time, lugging that girl home." He splashed water from the kettle. "Hate to do this. I need you, Franz. You gotta change clothes, anyhow—before you go to bed."

"What?" Franz was only half-listening.

"The bossy. Get into Sammy's overhalls." Mr. Bauer spoke brusquely, as Father would.

Franz straightened and his lips set, as if to shout, "No; this is my wedding night, man." But he heard Father speak in Mr. Bauer's command; the years of obedience spoke. His shoulders slumped. "I'll come," he muttered wearily, and his hand strayed slowly over the front of his coat.

There was only the crackle of fire after he went; the lamp still low in Sammy's room, the wedding suit crumpled on Sammy's bed. Wood fell to ashes. Tinkla called softly, exultantly, "Franz, Franz," her steps soft with the softness of bare feet. I answered. The door clicked on her disappointment. Waiting in the dark.

The coals were nearly white when Franz floundered back, his clothes soiled, and eyes blind with sleep. He slid into a chair. The stove cooled. I stomped off to bed; looked behind me and saw his head falling low. He roused up a moment. The sun crept under the door. But Franz nodded into drowsiness, too tired to wash his dirty hands.

6

It is good to be blind sometimes—eyes shuttered as the tunneling mole to what lies shadow-bound in the crooks and turns beyond today; otherwise each hour's dark glimpses of tomorrow would hagride us into that foggy vacantness which is relief from living. I am certain of that, now that I can see those years of Franz's married life taken as a whole and not looked on in all the number of their separate agonizing days; as certain, at least, as anyone can be, in his blindman's groping after light.

I remember as I do green willow shade those years before I entered this quiet room—those years after Franz carried Tinkla struggling in his arms from the buggy to the step and over the sill. "Such foolishness," she squealed that morning; "my shoe is slipping off."

"But, Tinkla; a man ought to carry his bride over his own door-stone." Franz gasped with trying to hold her. "It brings good luck."

"Fiddle-faddle; you're as bad as Ma is, Franz, with your crazy notions."

He was grinning, but the grin faded as he plumped her down. "Not crazy, Tinkla."

"Well, no." She patted his arm. "But it—it sounds kinda funny, you saying such things; a goose-head like me." She undid her bonnet. "I'll need more wood cobs than that." He let her go, his brow creasing. But Father said: "Good luck. Huh," and waited as for a verdict in his chair.

It was more than soap-and-water cleanness she brought to our kitchen walls, Anna having sudsed them often enough; but a kind of careless cheer that got into her broom and swept the corners clearer of shadows than I ever recalled them. She hung a motto near the ladder: "The Lord is my shepherd; I shall not want," the letters white on a green card. "There," she crowed: "look, Franz; ain't it nice?—the Bible on the walls, like that."

Father missed Anna but, after the first grudges and suspicions, respected Tinkla's housewifery. "By needle and thread a man can tell a good housekeeper," he used to say and nodded assent at her mending. He liked the solid way she put shoulder to a wagon or a tub of washing, I think; soon asked for a second dish of her pudding—a sign of good will from him. And when she stayed at the Bauers' for a week that winter, he was upset and touchy, demanding when Tinkla would be done with doing work in two houses. He accepted her as he would any woman, so long as the routine of three meals never failed (with lunches thrown in for good measure) and clothes were neat with patches; the buttonholes firm.

But Franz would let his knife slip and stare at her; yearning for that which she could never give, and yet recognizing the bolstered strength in her, without which he was empty-fisted. Time and again her laughter would harrow away the furrow between his eyes; though he was restive at her chatter and her chuckle-headness, and shifted under her clinging hands. Like that time at Matt's shivaree.

It took place one dark Saturday night at the Prinzings'—one of the loudest ever given in Pockerbrush, they said. Matt shouted like a fiend in the bedlam, Teena with him in the doorway, happy over the cowbells ringing, pails and dishpans banging, water-tubs booming. The Bauer boys hammered a moldboard into jangles that split the ear. The Klosters clanged a circle-saw with irons, Mr. Mais hoo-wah-ing on his old cow-horn. Dogs howled under the porch, the noise scaring them into frightened woofs. At midnight Leff Sperry fired a stick of dynamite. We heard the tinkle and crash of glass in the barn and Mrs. Mais saying: "Good thing it's fall and no hens setting; chicks'd be dead."

Matt ladled the beer, Teena leaving him to show Tinkla her new stove with "Radiant Home" large on the oven. Young Dick Morton got tipsy and wanted alcohol. Franz hawked on a duck call that Sam Bauer lent him and shouted at me between puffs: "Looking for Tinkla; see her?" Boys and girls knocked into one another, the Dunkel kids stealing cigars and getting puke-sick behind the lilacs . . . shouts and yells . . . Franz meeting Liliem, pushed together by the surge, and letting the noise-maker fall at the redness of her lips, inches away, and clearly seen in the light slanting from a window.

She tugged at his arm. "Don't hate me, Franz," she cried hurriedly, her voice barely heard in the racket. "Don't hate me." As though she must tell him this, if nothing else.

He wanted to put her aside, but couldn't; was speechless before her, his hands reaching for her shoulders possessively before he caught himself, and plunged wildly from her into the rush of people. There was almost a smile on her lips as she vanished from the light.

Franz played for the dance afterward; swung the fiddle and enjoyed the tingling pause before the music sang out and the steps began. It hurt to hear him, somehow—a kind of sadness in the strings, the old boyishness gone, scarred over with heavy-heartedness. The waltzers felt the change and turned heads to watch him, disturbed. Until young Dick Morton, staggering among them, suddenly screeched: "He's hexed. Devil in the fiddle; my grandma says so. Hexed Diah and—" He swayed; somebody grabbed him. "Minica," he cried, breathlessly; "my brother Minica."

Matt helped him to his feet. "Crazy-mad, you are. Drunker'n a two-toed bloodsucker." The dancing floor went queerly silent. Franz put the fiddle down, slowly, ghosts thronging back to mock him, the scar like a red burn. "I—let someone else take it—the bow." He left the platform, head bent.

There was no sleep for him that night, the baffled way he shook his head on the way home. "Guess only the chickens and pigs will listen to me, now. Nobody else."

"Franz." Tinkla squeezed his arm. "You have me. Just play. It goes good, a polka with churning the butter or kneading bread." She made such a cow-face at him, he couldn't help grinning; but he took her hand from his arm firmly. "I have you, Tinkla; yes," he said strangely. Thinking of something worlds apart from us.

Even with Tinkla in the house, salting the meat and shutting windows against rain (and the scattered patches of his happiness gathered for what might have been a second seeding), he couldn't forget a smile unfolding redly. As well command hunger or thirst to cease, with the braid of gold hair nestling like a living thing the thickness of a shirt from his ribs . . . Liliem with the lamplight across her scarlet lips.

A few Sundays after Matt's wedding, Franz had said rebelliously as we stood for a moment in the rear of the church, "Look at Matt and Teena—sitting downstairs like old folks already, and they married hardly a month. No sense in it," and had insisted on marching into the gallery. At once the young folks huzzed— hands slid over mouths and noses were squeezed. Jonas Bluber whispered loudly about a married man up here wanting to tell the unmarried a thing or two. Shame burned the cheeks of both the color of rusty mallow seeds. But Liliem, near the organ, arose quickly and, without a glance at Jonas, sat beside Tinkla— Tinkla, who squirmed in the bench, accepting what she couldn't very well reject; not with Liliem smiling as though honey and cream were mixed smooth on her lips.

At the next service Franz remained properly among the graybeards, not far from Father and Mr. Prinzing. But he ducked low over his hymnal all at once. Liliem rustled along the aisle and took a place three seats ahead of him on the women's side . . . Liliem downstairs among the married and those who were strangers, her eyes vibrant as with words Franz couldn't misunderstand, though her lips scarcely betrayed movement, singing the verses. (Disgusting, she told Lena Dorset after church; the way those kids upstairs behave.)

Franz mumbled half through hymn 350, deaf to sound, before he observed the congregation singing 97. He hinted as we drove away, he might as well read the Bible at home once in a while as be damned Sunday after Sunday at church; which Father called heathenish. But Tinkla, when we were at home, said, touching the gleam of the gold band on her finger, "Liliem— she's regular, going to church this year." Franz looked up quickly, as if her gesture hid a meaning deeper than her words.

There were nights without number that winter when I thought, "A woman in the house—not like Anna, sour as rhubarb going to seed. It will be different now; like Mother here again." I half-prayed that the door would remain locked on us, the windows shut, and what was outside would be shut forever out, leaving us strength for peace within. But I knew, and felt the shadow of things hidden before I knew, that nothing was essentially different—sweat in winter, sweat in summer, a double layer under heat . . . Franz dumping feed into the barrel and bailing out slops as if bucket and barrel were without bottom . . . Tinkla wiping after dinner and setting dishes on the shelves of the worn cupboard; getting them again for supper . . . Father a little more humped each time the mail brought the blue envelope from the Bank—the debt so old, we'd have been lost without its nagging weight.

Franz would say, "Look, Tinkla; the window—frost's growing a whole woodsful of ferns on the pane"; and she'd murmur absently, "Unh-huh," sewing on without heeding him; or he'd point to the sky as the three of us shivered up the path, "Like a big animal, that cloud; eating up the Big Dipper." And she'd be sulky. "You mean it's setting in to snow? Say it straight out, then. You bother me; talk worse than the Pastor." Slivers wedging in the mind, to fester and widen the hurt, and thrust healing away. We'd go for an evening to visit Matt and Teena, snug in the Becker house, Matt in stocking feet and smoking over the Montgomery Ward catalog: "Price of harnesses sky-high again; up fifty cents from the last list"; Teena replying comfortably: "Oh, well; I'll get the hens busy; lay a few eggs more and we can get the harness." Tinkla would say, going home, "So warm and cozy, the Prinzings'; Matt don't gribble over Big Dippers and ferns on the windowpane." And Franz would slap the team, silent while she chattered the whole way home.

What plagued him like a sand-nipper wasn't hidden long. It was on a winter's afternoon, cold, the sun guarded by four dogs, and a wind zooming in the crotches of the oak, that he brought out in a rush the words held as though against breath. "You might as well know. There's a young one—" He stuck the fork deep, a kind of resentment in his voice and the neighbors in his head again; man-fashion, blaming the woman for that which flamed quickest in his veins.

I felt a sudden warmth in my throat, in spite of the hammer pounding in my skull; stammered aloud: "It—Tinkla—"

He flung the forkful. "She's going to have a baby."

"Well, what did you expect—kittens?" I was crusty for no reason, except thinking, "Now there'll be talk, for sure," but admitting to myself, "Matt Prinzing would kick to the ceiling, if this happened to him; wouldn't care if the kid were born the day after the wedding."

Franz dug a tine down savagely. "Laugh, if you can't hold it. But—"

"Franz, man." I dumped oats into the feedbox. "A child is a child. You think he's worse for—"

"The Pastor said it. Again only last Sunday. 'The sins—'" He leaned to pick a strap from the floor. "About sins of the fathers visited on the—the children—" He left forking to go for a sack of oats. There was still feeding to do.

A kind of sickness went over me in that moment, in spite of myself. A shame-child, and coming in our house too soon. (Like Minnie Ochstock, a year ago, married and a mother in five months: and Leff Sperry licking his lips: "Kinda fast work, the way they go after it.")

I can laugh now, almost, older in living and knowing more about this fire added to flame, the uninvited urgings hawklike at muscle and bone; knowing, too, after these years, that the hounds of wrath within us, leashes off and merciless, are snarling a nearer doom than any Bible trumpet. But in that hour I'd have accepted as inevitable the manger boards' exploding into ashes.

I shook the oats from the can into the last box. The door opened. Franz let the oats sack fall. Alb Hukelpoke shivered behind him.

"Cat's knuckles. Cold enough to freeze the soup on your

whiskers, as Old Jens Lindergard used to say." He beat the frost
from his mittens. "Warm, back of your cows here. You oughta
see the ice in my barn."

"Not bad, this year," admitted Franz. Alb slapped him across
the rump.

"Well, I hear you're gonna have a kid—leastways, your old
woman is." He laughed boisterously, but there was kindness in
his eyes. "Might as well cut yourself a birch, right away, and
drag him up right."

Franz had to grin. "Between us, we—"

"Not like my boys." Alb scratched his cheek. "Bull-headed
shavers. I saw Carl—that's the oldest, you know; son of a gun if
he wasn't making eyes at Aggie Prinzing, last Saturday; at Toffmann's store. Yerp, you get 'em out of diapers, and they go
chasing skirts."

Franz was anxious with a question: "Do—do your boys take
after you—" but Alb, chuckling over a new idea, never heard
him. "Say, Franz; your old girl—she's at it again. Broke her
troth to Jonas Bluber."

The sack of oats Franz had hoisted to his shoulder and was
pouring into the feedbox thumped and fell with the grain.
"Yerp. Third time she's yes-and-noed him. Her pa went to the
Pastor and all. She says she's through with a man as slobby as
Jonas is." Franz let the oats slip through his fingers as if flesh
were vacant of nerves. Liliem free and here he was, bound by
oath not his nor any man's to break.

"Jonas is sorer'n a three-day boil," Alb went on gleefully.
"Near chewed up a plug of twist while he was telling me.
'Damn pepper pots, all women,' he says to me. 'They can just
kiss my rump.' Then he spit over his chin—lips all coffee-
colored. 'Yes siree,' he says, 'they can just kiss my rump.' 'Well,'
I says, sorta nodding at his mouth, 'Kinda hard to find which end
is which, ain't it? Both brownish.' It hit him; soaked right
down to his shoes," Alb shouted. "Just about lost my belly-
button, laughing."

Franz laughed with Alb. They shut the door behind them.

Laughter without mirth for Franz; almost like sun without warmth on winter days. And the shapes of dread moved again.

7

Little John was born that spring, on an afternoon loud and blustery for one so scrawny and bony-legged. Tinkla, white and shivering, was deaf to Mrs. Bauer's, "*Ach,* well; born thin, die fat, they say. And he's hungry again, ain't he? You got milk for him, Tinkla?" Franz looked dull-eyed at his son, his hands at his sides, no gladness in him rushing out with his arms; staring at the tiny mark on the baby's cheek. "Tinkla, Tinkla, he's marked; marked to the bone."

The blemish—or whatever it was—vanished in a week. But for Franz it stayed there indelibly red as the scar on his flesh. It haunted him, even when neighbors knocked to shake his hand and joke about the new papa. "*Na,* Franz." Mr. Prinzing was jovial. "Jaw hanging like that; and over just one. Wait till you have ten, like me." Mr. Mais came, sober with news that his Gina was bad with her leg; wouldn't heal, doctor it all they could. Franz greeted them somberly. I'd stomp about the place, easier with the slush gone and the sticky blackness of wet fields shrinking to dust gray, dry for the harrow and the seeder; and see him in the east patch with the team, no whistle on his lips any more than there was on the fiddle dark in the case.

Father jumped from the saw carriage, when he was told, and pounded Kloster's mare homeward; strode in and stopped. "So; it is alive, then." He grunted, neither pleased nor sorry. "Takes after Franz. Pindling legs and a hog-poor farm—they go to-gether." Waiting to blame somebody.

Tinkla hugged the baby close, feeling a kind of danger in his words. "There are things better to have than—than an ox's back or big muscles," she said.

Father waved it aside as woman's truck and of no importance;

tramped outside to give orders. "I want wheat sowed there—in the patch by the creek."

They called him John. Tinkla wanted it so. "After your pa and mine," she said, and gave the Pastor an extra large slice of raisin cake when he finished the baptism at our house. He ate, crumbs and all, but was still dour as ever. Franz said neither yes nor no to the naming, letting Tinkla have the say. "John William Carl," intoned the Pastor, sprinkling the water Franz caught at the pump a while before and Tinkla warmed to remove the chill. "John William—" But Alb Hukelpoke, driving past with a load of feed and dropping in, poked at the swaddled bundle and shouted, "Ain't he a little-john of a feller! Pint-sized. Tight fist, though. Well, kick me through a hornet's collar if he don't look growed-up and sensible already, the little-John." And Little John he stayed. There was about him a wisdom no child should have—as if he knew beforehand what it took years for us to learn; a sadness in the crumpled ends of the lips and the tremble of the mouth—like Mother's, I thought, with a queer pain. He seldom kicked and squirmed, but lay by the hour, eyes steadfast on the glitter the sun made on a pan or the edge of the nickled teakettle. He'd wrinkle his forehead, smaller than a palm, over the buzzing of a bluebottle; quiet. And in a moment, begin to cry as if all the pins ever put into a breechcloth were jabbing his legs. Tears would well up from depths of pain we knew nothing about. And Franz would measure the kitchen with shoe leather, in vain. Until he scraped a tune or so. At the sound of the fiddle the baby unclosed his tight fists and slept. I'd hear him sing *Lullaby, My Little One* after supper, not because he wanted to but because Tinkla would say, "Baby's been howling all afternoon. You take him. My arms are wood sticks, carrying him." And Franz would rock him, hushing the cries gently but with impatience in his hands; moving restless about the room.

The wheat greened and the young corn curled like green twists of yarn across the blanket of new-harrowed fields. As

[313]

summer ripened seed pod and shell, and the binder began to pitch the yellowed grain into bundles, it seemed to me that more and more Franz found a harness broken or a wagon wheel needing splints between iron and rim to hold the tire fast—jobs that kept him from the house. Often I'd come on him idle, the task finished in his hands, lids half-closed and gazing as through earth into nothingness. And the ache in me grew, recalling how he'd almost snatch at her fingers when Tinkla caressed him; how he came to the lean-to, one morning, shoe laces dangling, hastily, as though Tinkla's hands and hard insistence were a drag in his mind, disturbing his dreams; how neither rain nor wet bothered him Sundays nor kept him from church as it did Tinkla—hoping Liliem was there. A bitter mouthful to chew but nearer truth than I cared to admit.

The telephone began to jangle in a few ridge houses the summer Little John was going on three. The poles followed the roads or leaped through fields with giant strides, threading the hollows and ravines with silver wire, in spite of talk and fuss thick enough to fill buckets. Mr. Dunkel grunted he had more trouble with brush and stumps than any man had time to swear at, without having lopped-off trees in his oats to catch eveners and waste grain. He spat angrily and agreed with most—what did some folks think? Did they want all the lightning in a storm to knock walls off the foundations? Oaks by the barns were bad enough and fences a farm long—every farmer had misgivings when the air sang with thunderbolts. And now they wanted to have telephone wires miles over the ridges to catch fire from heaven. "That ain't the worst, either." Old Mr. Ochstock thumbed the bald spot on the side of his head. "The women-folks'll just *hang* on the line; wait and see. You can hardly get them to lift a pot-cover now."

But the Prinzings installed the varnished box with the crank and the silver bells; so did the Bauers and the Maises, Mr. Mais saying he'd just as soon give somebody hell over the wire as to his face—save time and shoe leather. Besides, you couldn't tell when you'd want a doctor quick. But the shining wires passed our place, Father growling that we had all we liked of neighbors' truck without bringing it into the house. At certain hours we could see the gleam of metal among the trees where the sun struck—a ten-day wonder at first.

But there was little we could count as change during those three years. Jonas packed himself off to Canada—to thresh in a real country, he boasted. And Mr. Bauer hauled a new binder to his farm. Mrs. Mais, half in, half out of bed, had misery in her leg, Mr. Mais grumbled. "Guess I'll get me a hired girl." After being grumpy about his rheumatism for we didn't know how long, Mr. Schoen finally went to Fergus to live with his sister and be near a special doctor; but Liliem stayed—working at the Grosbecks'. And it was told in Mary's Hill, a buggy smelling four blocks of oil and kerosene, but without horses, sputtered and smoked and wheeled the whole length of Main Street; trundled up from Fergus, they said. None of us saw it and August Jaahcobs wouldn't believe it, though Leff Sperry, with a hankering for tools, swore he'd get one, first chance he had.

The woods crept over the ridges. Here and there a hill began to show through oak and elm as a man's head through thinning hair. The Maises' barn was open to sight since a storm leveled the basswoods; and the Hukelpokes' windmill, its fan whirling above the trees in the valley, was no longer hidden, now that Alb was selling firewood in Mary's Hill. It seemed odd, if one stopped shovel or hoe long enough to think, that we could peek into a neighbor's yard where five years before dark walls stockaded the buildings into wooded privacy. Each season the logs were sledded farther distances. This year Father went beyond Too Far Lake to help Kloster saw. But these things, being slow as fungus growth, we regarded as no change at all.

Within our house there was even less change. I could have snored years into eternity, knowing that when I waked, I'd be right at home, the milk cans sunning within an inch of the spot where Tinkla always put them. The camomile still hung from the rafters, fragrant over my bed in the lean-to. One summer a peavy belonging to Abel Kloster slanted against a wall, its hook rust-scarred and its point dull with endless gouging into bark. "Going to sharpen it," Father said, but didn't then. I'd see him heft the sweat-dark handle of oak, as if the touch gave him a pleasure he never found in fork or hoe-handle. He sharpened it finally and Kloster came to get it.

There was a new cupboard for Tinkla's dishes and pans; of maple, and ornate with fancy doodads. Franz spent most of one winter, hammering; sandpapered and glued until the house stunk. He'd rub a palm over its smooth and polished sides: "Shines, Jeppy; like my fiddle." But Father with sourness talked about the time spent, when the mangers needed fixing and the bars of the calf pen were splintered and useless. Even Tinkla, much as she praised the cupboard, murmured that the woodpile was small this season; far too small to last the summer's firing. Franz would jerk away, as if feeling that we were leagued against him.

When the mood urged he played; even fiddled for a dance or two, at Matt's or the Prinzings'; with a tremble in the music, afraid of what the strings might reveal. But not often; for the young folks wrinkled their noses. "Old stuff," they said, and trotted to Mason's Resort where strange tunes echoed over the water. Ragtime, they called it; at which Alb Hukelpoke snorted: "Don't know about time; plenty of that, I guess. But with all the twisting and diving they do, 'tain't no wonder their shirttails stick out rags."

At home the fiddle sang so that Tinkla stopped her ironing to listen. It was as if he squeezed a bitter solace for what hurt in him, those days that should have been filled with Tinkla and were half-empty because of Liliem. Until Tinkla, troubled as with a vague uneasiness, said: "It—it means much, so much to you, the fiddle, don't it?" and weariness became shadowed on her mouth; her chatter hushed.

Little John, eyes blinking like a chipmunk's, listened, still where he lay at the first twang; or, as he grew older, crept nearer, caught by the light dancing on the bow. He bawled less as he was switched from diapers to rompers, but was beginning to set a stubborn chin. Once, when Franz put the fiddle on the floor to get resin, his pudgy fingers found the bow and drew it raggedly over the bridge—a strange broken sound that brought Franz in a hurry. He grabbed the bow fiercely, as if this alone remained to bring the wind of melody, the wind of dreams, to him, and he'd give place to nobody—shutting himself behind a thin barrier of four strings and letting the fiddle bring what he never found under our roof—dreams yellowed with the gold of hair.

He'd seen Liliem now and again at parties and the shindandies we took in. He was properly cool, to all eyes, as a married man should be, but uneasy as with urgings inside, the way he had caught her in his arms at Matt's dance the spring before. A house party, it was, and Arne Fledermann had called, "Ladies' choice." She came, then, all smiles.

"I'm left behind, Franz; unless an old married man like you dances with me." Which was hardly true, seeing that Leff Sperry and two others followed her unregarding shoulders halfway across the floor. She was roguish, tapping with a pointed toe.

"I—I guess one can two-step—with a friend." Franz attempted unconcern but a tremor stirred in his voice.

"You don't mind, do you, Tinkla?" Liliem's brows were arched with laughter. Tinkla shook her head, mute.

They whirled past me, and I heard Liliem gasp: "Franz, it's—like iron—your arms; so tight." But Tinkla's eyes followed them, as needle the magnet; as if what she feared were suddenly taking form. She waited the dance out, partnerless, and pulled her handkerchief through fisted and trembling hands.

A long summer, this one, it seemed, but far past prime now and hushing to silence as if waiting for a sign; the robins flown from the roost and the rusty-breasted fledglings on the wing. After dark, when a fan of yellow light spread in the east, I'd see the moon among the corn-rows, the tassels like curved fingers black on the coppery disk. I'd stand stiff as the crutches holding me up, wondering at this beauty disturbing the night; wondering, too, how we'd ever untangle our lives into free and separate strands—if we ever could. The crutches were heavier, somehow, this season, as if insufficient to hold bone to bone and myself upright. I'd wake nights with fire burning down the spine and thirst drying the throat.

Father worried more this year than ever. "Save the leftovers," he'd tell us, crushing the long rectangle of paper he took from the blue envelope and then smoothing it—the Bank again. "Be glad to chew the rind, before long." He never mentioned sums or when interest fell due; his business, not ours. And Franz escaped responsibility in this as he did in deciding a hundred other duties—what acres were to be oats and what barley; when to wait with a field of corn and when to slash the rows into bundles to elude the quick September frosts. These were matters for Father to speak about, and for him alone.

Matt brought the news about Mrs. Mais. He and Teena had a boy now, strapping as the father. Matt would tote him over pick-aback, proud as a peacock and all feathers showing at every coo and gaa the baby made. "Danged if the little duffer didn't grab for my whiskers today," he'd report. "Hey, Franz; how's Little John? You never say much—about him." And Franz would mumble evasively and dig at other news.

Mrs. Mais was in bed again—for good, this time, Matt said, hefting the post maul he'd come for. "Didn't you know? Closest neighbors are the best strangers, I guess. Well, the doctor told Mais aside that she'd never walk again."

A week and Liliem moved in the Maises' house, to keep the cupboard full. And Tinkla would part the curtains of the west window and gaze out, as if more than thunderclouds stalked black-capped across the ridges. Franz tantalized himself again, yearning to jump the seven-acre patch in a leap, but restrained by the thought of Tinkla in the kitchen; raked as by thorns, the way he flung a milk stool with a tight-lipped exclamation.

He finished coffee one supper and offered casually: "Mrs. Mais—she's been fretting the pillows off the bed, almost. Ought to go cheer her up tonight." And with Tinkla's agreeing nod (not wanting to go, not daring to remain away, either), we went, Father staying home. Franz would have carried Little John, except that the boy slipped from him and ran ahead. "That's a big man," Tinkla called; "walking by yourself." But Franz let him go without a word.

Even at this early hour, the moon was huge on the ridge, large with the haze of smoky fires, and promising gold to the wind-torn and rustling mallows. "A yellow night," Franz prophesied, and walked faster.

Mr. Mais, in woollen stockings after eight o'clock, opened to us. With kitchen warmth we thawed to neighborliness, Mrs. Mais wiggling her fingers to say, "A bad night for me, that wedding of yours, Tinkla," and Tinkla grave over her words. Liliem was in a pensive mood, eyes dreamy with a cloudiness in them that was like the mist streamers over the moon; never looking at Franz, although I had a feeling she knew he was conscious of each step she made and turned when she shut the pantry door behind her—her distance plaguing him more than any familiarity, since it gave him no excuse for blame but made him the aggressor.

She was soft-spoken with Little John; brought a bowlful of her best cookies for his sweet tooth. "My, you're big," she cooed, slipping a hand into his hair. "How would you like it—to be my boy?" Little John nodded, his mouth packed to the teeth with crumbles.

Franz, watching with intentness, shuffled and answered Mr. Mais in confusion and without sense, "Well—a— last fall, I guess," when Mr. Mais asked him a second time, "How're your cows milking?" Franz blinked rapidly, so hard had he been listening—and imagining in a swift moment, I think, Liliem in his house and Little John their boy.

At ten-thirty Mrs. Mais said: "Cup of coffee and a cookie—couldn't we have a bite, Liliem?" Tinkla protested, "That's too much trouble, Mrs. Mais; we can't stay; not a minute longer." Franz added: "Cows'll stir us early tomorrow." But nobody arose, our protests being merely gestures to politeness. Liliem went to scratch the fire and put the kettle on, but said, "Water bucket's empty again." Mr. Mais got up, puzzlement on his brow, but Liliem cried, suddenly gay, "You're in stocking feet; I'll go pump it. Such a lovely, lovely night out." And banged the handle. Before she swung the door open, Franz was at her side. "I'll—I'll help." He seized the bucket—almost eagerly, it appeared to me. Then both were gone.

Tinkla made as if to run to the nearest window but settled back to Mrs. Mais's account of what the doctor did and said. Mr. Mais scratched his shoulder. "Empty, so? Funny; I filled them—just when I come in." I saw the yard more yellow than silver in the light, the moon hooded with the smoke of autumn fire. They came back, a breathlessness about them as though they'd run a mile uphill, instead of walking half the length of the yard. Tinkla's gaze was sharp on them—the sharpness of those dubious all at once of their own strength.

It was near midnight when Franz buttoned his coat and Tinkla hushed Little John, who squeezed tears through the sleep prickles and couldn't keep his cap on. He went beside me. We walked through the cornfield, the space between the harvested rows black aisles in the soft radiance, the shocks like autumn teepees stored with leaf and yellow kernel. "Every stalk is plain as day." Franz's voice quivered with inner excitement. "So much light, it—it drips from the corn silk." We unlocked our door to a chilly house. Little John and I thumped in but Franz and Tinkla remained on the step. I could see the moon splash over them, flooding Tinkla and erasing the lines beginning to show in her face; touching strands of her dark hair until they glinted. He caught her roughly to him. "Yellow on your head, even—yellow hair." He spoke huskily, half to himself.

Suddenly she was crying. "Franz, *Liebchen;* how can I say it—what I feel in my heart for you?"

"Like—like the popple leaves—yellow." He scarcely heard her, spun to wild ecstasy. "If all nights were like this—full of gold; instead of—of all the empty ones—" It was winter-still outside, the last cricket folding its wings against the frost. He gathered her in his arms; stood a moment, moon-yellow on his face. Then he carried her through the door. Little John tugged at my hand. I wondered that the hills didn't laugh in thunder at our puppet pretense, knowing with a queer pain that it wasn't Tinkla Franz crushed to himself; not this night, at least; but Liliem, washed in the glow of her hair.

8

It was the next spring that what Mother had always feared came to pass. A mild spring it was, with the peonies rooting their pink snouts through the wet ground and bloodroots whitening by the apronful in the hazel thickets. Little John's fingers were faded orange from grabbing at the bunches I put under his nose. "Smell that; it's got honey in it."

Father spent the winter at Too Far Lake; his last year, he told us. Hereafter we'd have to find a dollar or two extra otherwheres; especially since he had to borrow again and the Bank was snooty about repayment. The old uneasiness began to crawl again—Father getting old and helpless; like Abel Kloster, no more than a shadow of strength; the bins empty and no bread in the house—it was as if foundations of stone turned to unsteady pine and left us in dread of the next thunder-shock. Franz would watch Father, the furrow deep between his eyes. If something should happen to him—

Then on a day tender to new spring grass, they brought him home; silent on his back and shrunken in the hay of the wagon box; eyes open but blank as a lamp reflector without the flame, blind to any recognition. They told us about it—a single log skidded with rubbing noises upon him . . . his legs no longer nimble to avoid the pitching bole, the sinews gristled, and slackening their swiftness an instant . . . the roar of other logs— they peavied him out of the jumble and brought him to us. And on the cot near the loft ladder where Mother had moaned, he lay moaning, a figure of earth, helpless as the pillow against his shoulder.

There was a dreadful interval of voicelessness and Tinkla, as if waking from horror, flew to the corner chest for blankets; washed the spruce-gum from his cheeks—"tears of the pine," they called it—and straightened the battered legs. White-lipped but steady, that day and those to follow. But Franz moved as if he—and not I—needed the crutches stiff at my side; too numb now to do more than lurch from house to barn, dimly aware that he stood on the cliff-edge of things he was to sweat over, even in sleep; and shrank from premonition.

The doctor arrived, our urgency flung over the hills to him along the silver wires. Not Dr. Allbauch, but a young man, and with him, another in white, whose blue eyes crackled over me and whose long fingers seemed to quiver with healing. Remembering the release from agony they brought to my sick bones, I wonder that their skill was as ignorance with Father. Head injury, they said, and loosed a gabble of sounds about paralysis and pressures—I wanted to shout, "Do something; don't let him groan like that—all night and all day." Franz sat, slack-nerved, watching them as an animal its keeper; Tinkla poised to help, Little John allowing no more than a nose and an eye to be seen from behind her apron.

Before they left, the blue-eyed doctor swung close to me. "Pull your shirt." I felt the crackle again for all my befuddlement. "It's Father—" I began, but his hand was at my collar. "Off with your shirt." His fingers were firm but understanding on my skin and over the bones gnarled and knobby in the flesh. "Fine case, Terry," he called. "Papa Bueller would notch his best scalpel to see this." They were gone, medicine in the air but no help. And the sounds, lung-deep, pushing at Father's lips, shaped themselves slowly into words that faltered between pauses. "Franz . . . when is . . . Franz coming?" Tinkla would cry, "He's by you; don't you see him?" And Franz, bending close: "I'm— I'm here, Father." But the trickle of hopelessness continued even at night and in sleep: "When is . . . Franz coming?" All day we heard those words half a room from us. "Franz . . . Franz," taken with our meat and gravy; until Franz shoved plate aside and left more than one meal to cool in the kettle or bowl.

The neighbors came, digging remedies out of their pockets. But when they went home, they took the plasters and liniments with them, grave and almost frightened at what lay beyond the hope of simples to cure. "Lies there like he got the evil mark," Old Lady Ochstock nodded sagely. "Gra'ma Morton said it long ago—he was a queer one."

But Mr. Bauer stopped to tell us, "Your pa—best sawer I ever seen. Shouldn't 'a' been a farmer, seems like. A good man, and down like that."

"I was knocked senseless once," Leff Sperry contributed helpfully, as if aid lay in experience. "Mule kicked me; black in front of me for a week." But Alb Hukelpoke, hearing him, snorted: "A week, heh? Seems to me you've been senseless long as I've known you."

Franz listened and thanked them. Nothing else he could do, longing for a rod of field to hide in where peace and quiet whispered with grass. He was glad when Mr. Mais said, "You got friends—all your neighbors. Just ask. They're friends."

"Are they?" Franz looked his doubt. If they knew about Liliem and the gold braid . . . probably did, at that. . . .

"Liliem, now." Mr. Mais crowded a hunk of black twist between his jaws. "She takes this like your pa was hers." Franz shifted hastily, fearing what his smile might reveal.

"It is good of her," he said slowly. "A man needs them— comforts—at times." As though the message were for him alone.

What the neighbors could do, they did with team and swinging arm. The Bauers tended the corn, and Matt helped with the stacks of sloo grass. Alb Hukelpoke slouched up the valley every other day. " 'Tain't that I want to work," he laughed. "Not me. I got lazy on the bone. But I want to see your Little John, there." And he would grab up milk bucket or shovel to help. Little John hung on his pockets, begging for a shoulder-ride. Once Alb found him crying and chuckled, "Kick me through a hornet's collar. Don't you know you dasn't bawl? You'll get so heavy with salt, you'll—why, your ma'll pinch you up and sift you into the salt shaker." He carried him off to peek at the shiners swarming to break creek water and vanish again in a swirl of fins. Sometimes they'd go fishing. "Acts like the kid was his'n," Tinkla used to say.

"You can't blame Alb." Franz was moody. "All his take after her; and she's crabby as a sick turkey hen." Tinkla didn't answer him, that day, busy with the bread.

But when the neighbors took plow and themselves through the gate and homeward, Franz would walk over our acres, few according to number, though larger than he thought, when seen as a whole—his to manage for the first time. And was uneasy. All his days he had heard commands: "Do this; don't do that." At the haying season, Father set his foot where the stacks were to be; and Franz pitched. At harvest, Father drove the binder; Franz shocked. But now it was Franz who must say when the oats were yellow enough, or the barley golden for the sickle. And Franz was fumble-handed and uncertain. He mounted the binder that summer; sat in the seat as if hornets were raging under him, and reached for the levers awkwardly. Stones like woodchucks poked their gray noses out of the ground and gouged the sections dull as the side of a board. Willow stems flourished in the low places if the wheat didn't; and the stumps of elm were broad in the oats. Franz hung the binder tight on one. I heard the crash and saw him digging at the fragments of a wheel, his hands greasy, and despair in the slump of his shoulders. The bins at threshing time, marked high with the level of last year's store, were piled only three-quarters up.

This is the hour of revelation, I said to myself more than once, watching Franz with pity near to grief in my heart—this the gathering moon of nubbins instead of full ears from seed and stalk planted to hate and cultivated in suspicion. What had been nurtured in the dark places of the mind became plain to see. Franz was as if lost without the rudder-and-guide of Father's hard decisiveness; unskilled at some tasks and waiting, it seemed, for direction that never came. The leathers wore to dry scrapings in the pump, so that Franz had to take the horses to the creek. The cows broke the fences and one died, bellyful of corn; and when Franz drove to Mary's Hill, the machine-shop man refused him the wire we'd needed long before. "Your ole man's sick; I don't know when you'll pay," he said bluntly. Franz patched as well as he could—"with a brush pile and crooked nails," he grumbled. Troubles flew upon his head, one behind the other, like black crows in the evening sky. A horse sickened when Franz, forgetful of an open gate, let the team run, and the gray, heated from tugging the day long at the collar, drank too early of cold water. Franz had to borrow a mare from the Maises. And in the house, Tinkla, "expecting again," Mrs. Bauer whispered loudly to Franz, would meet him with tired exasperation. "Franz, the woodbox is empty; can't you split a big pile once?" Or: "I can't take another step; pump me the water, Franz"; daily demands that one would have counted off with a whistle, ordinarily; but not so easy, with all that had gone before. And eating through closed doors and into ears shut in sleep—those moaning syllables of Father's, "Franz . . . Franz . . . Franz."

We were in the pasture near the seven-acre patch and not far from Mr. Mais's barn, grubbing thistles, and Franz was saying, "Must be something in the ashes that make these stickers grow like this; waist-high where the brush piles were burned," when someone called, "Franz," and Liliem parted the hazels and came, a jug, small and damp with moisture, in her hands. Liliem in a flowered house dress that seemed to cling to every part of her; trembly as to smile and her eyes troubled as pools are, with deep and unsuspected water-whirls; but fresh as a raindrop, in spite of the heat.

"Franz, it's—it's awful. Your Father—so strong, his arms; big to crush one—crush anything." There was a kind of hurt ecstasy in her tones.

"Liliem." Franz could only stare at her. "Liliem, you're—you're—"

Suddenly she began to cry in a helpless sort of way, tears welling over her cheeks; like silver dew on the petal of a rose—a notion crazy as a loon, I told myself in bitterness afterward.

"Crying; for me, Liliem?" Franz spoke unbelievingly. Then as if drawn by invisible powers (as on the day he first met her), he took her in his arms; closely, his eyes shut; with so much yearning in his face, I couldn't speak the warning in my mouth.

"Forgive me, Franz. All the meanness in me—hurting you." She snuggled against him. "It rushes inside. I can't stop it. Forgive—"

"Past, now; all that." He touched her cheek. "It ought to be like this always. You and I—"

"Franz, please." She twisted from him but gently. "Here's lemonade; a drink will settle the sweat. And more for Jeppy." But she offered the jug to me first; with a lift of the chin and a measuring look—daring me to hurl one rock of blame. The lemon bit my tongue. I nearly choked on a swallow. She took the jug. "Here, Franz." He drank, eyes over the rim at her.

He unlocked the fiddle case after supper that evening. Wind stirred over the gray step, loaded with the malty smell of corn. It was pleasanter now, after heat that had crumpled the squash leaves in Tinkla's garden until they drooped like starchless handkerchiefs. The house was duskily still, Little John asleep. Tinkla sat by the table, resting before dishes. From the lean-to door I saw him go to the step, his shoulders cutting into the light of the door, the fiddle in his hands; turning it over and over. He skittered on the strings, halfhearted scraps of tunes, all beginnings and no middles or endings. All at once he began *Liebeslied*, quavery and sick with longing; played it so that I kept my mouth shut though I wanted to speak, and Tinkla left the dishes unwashed and came to him; played as if no vultures hung over our rafters and no death grinned at the cot by the loft ladder. Until Tinkla sat heavily beside him. Then the fiddle snagged and scrippled into silence. She leaned against his shoulder. "Franz." Her voice sank.

"I can't play—your head on the fiddle." His shoes scraped on the stone.

"Don't play; not that piece. It hurts me; you fret over it and—"

He arose quietly; went inside and locked the fiddle away. Tinkla entered slowly. He sank into the hard rocker.

"No yellow moon tonight, Franz. Yellow as—as hair, you said." She stopped at the bedroom door. "Won't be so, always, Franz. It will fade, too. Wheat straw getting gray." She closed the door. I undressed for bed. It was a long while before I heard the rocker squeak sharply as he arose.

9

Leff Sperry bought the automobile in late August; a smoke-shooting contraption if I ever saw one, jerking with every splutter and coughing like a donkey in a conniption fit. The horses on the Sperrys' place waited for one look, kicked and galloped off, to the last colt, far into the pasture, tails streaming hair; and the cows held their milk for a week, old Mr. Sperry grumbled. They hadn't a minute in which to eat, running every time the engine backfired.

Leff snorted into our yard one evening when Alb Hukelpoke was there. Proud as a turkey gobbler to show the big lamps and the gas tank and the line of fender and hood, Alb grunted afterward. Leff tinkered on the dashboard, full of more levers and gadgets to monkey with than two men could handle.

"Good thing Noah didn't have such a damn outfit." Alb was frank. "Or he'd 'a' wrecked the Ark; and then where'd we be?"

Franz touched each shining part as if magic lay in the metal. And when Leff, begoggled and with grim swings at the wheel, gave him a ride, Franz stepped down reluctantly. "It's—it's like flying, Jeppy. You see a hill way off and then—it's past you; like that."

Leff chuckled. "For the money, she ain't a bad jigger."

"Must have cost as much as a farm." Franz tried the wheel.

"New, guess it does." Leff was vague. "I got her from an uncle in Fergus. Dirt cheap, he says. He's getting a new one."

"Dirt cheap, heh?" Alb straightened a suspender. "Took a pretty good wad, at that. Where in Tophet did you get it— money, even for dirt cheap?"

Leff winked at the curtness in his tone. "Where's a mushrat get fur? Hell, a feller can't make money farming." He chugged away. Alb muttered, "Young pup. At something fishy again; and I'll bet it stinks rotten, too." But Franz said, "Wonder if I'll ever handle a wheel like that."

The Bank wrote soon after, about a note due; and would Mr. Vildvogel please talk the matter over with them, when he came to Mary's Hill? Franz hitched the horses, clumsy over the straps with worry. I saw him turn at the mailbox, clear to see since the woods were lopped off.

The horses slowpoked up the road on his return, Franz bowed in the seat. Then we knew; in part, at least—debt like a ridge pressing on us; Father's debt, but ours now, if we wanted the farm. And a note due in half a month—or they'd take the team, maybe; or the cows. Sweat glistened on his forehead. "Not my fault, this; I never asked for it—to be loaded down like an animal." Tinkla, her body shapeless with molding life, sat in the rocker and sobbed, Little John near her, lips quivering and tears large on his cheeks but too scared to cry. Father moaned, "When is . . . Franz . . . coming?" Franz gripped his knuckles. "What do they think I am?" he burst out. "Can't squeeze nickels out of stovewood." He hid his face in his hands.

There were moments in the months that followed when it seemed that life was no more than a fierce crawling through thorns and thistles; when animals at their mangers had the better part, I thought. Not knowing that the worst never comes, no matter how near it is in the mind; nor, for that matter, does the best, both being ends, the one of evil, the other good, and every action bending toward the one or the other. It was hard to see this, then, with autumn mornings so clear the most distant ridge was like a step beyond the closest; with mink in the rushes becoming browner along the back and bolder in the sharpness of their teeth. Nature was closing her doors on another season and we were jumps behind in work, our stores lean as a grasshopper's. We sickled the corn and tied it into shocks, though Franz, listless as one who is infirm after a great illness, let the frost nip the leaves into rustling dryness before we started.

The doctors called again, on an afternoon crisp and sunny. They shook their heads. Nothing in their black bags would arouse a muscle into tugging, or an arm crooking at the elbow. If we had specialists and money—perhaps. But the pennies and dimes we gathered, barely stretched over the groceries we needed. Sometimes they wouldn't have, if butter and eggs hadn't been counted to the score. And with the Bank demanding what we didn't have—there was nothing to do. But the blue-eyed doctor prodded and poked at me again; scowled over words that sizzled in his teeth and went away, remarking, "Papa Bueller's territory, that's what it is. I'm going to see him about this, Terry." And left us without hope. So I saw it. And never dreamed that the blue-eyed doctor would come again and that, far from the hills, I'd find a sort of peace in looking back upon our lives. But on that sunny afternoon, I whispered half-aloud, thinking of Father, "The doctor—it's the last time he'll come."

I'd hear the knife-and-fork clatter of women's talk in the kitchen often, these days, with Mrs. Bauer over to see Tinkla and to exclaim, "*Ach,* you shouldn't be worried; not after your first. And let the washing go." Tinkla would shrill, "What you think we'll wear—grass, like the niggers?"

Deaf Mrs. Sperry, faded as a mullein stock, came to visit and was envious of Tinkla: "Not four years, is it, since you had Little John? Well, wish't I could have a summer once, when I didn't have a kid hanging at my breasts. Pa keeps me busy. Every year, seems like, there's didies to wash—for a new one." Neighbors' torments mixed with ours.

Franz plowed a black furrow across the rain-faded yellow of stubble and, on returning, laid another beside the first; went round and round the widening piece—like Mother, in hooking a rag rug, I used to think. He saw Liliem frequently now; met her by the shelving place in the creek, where the cows drank and where he took the horses to water, since the pump hardly filled the buckets for Tinkla's supply. A place of silver shadow, it was, not far from Mr. Mais's hog pasture; lazy with the water-quarrel of ripples about an old stump; screened by plum and thick mats of willows. I brought the cows there, one evening, and saw them, the horses drinking with a forefoot lifted, Franz with the halter ropes in his fist, and Liliem near, her face eager as she listened—listened to the woe he was pouring out by the bucketful, I thought. It was sweet as honey for him, Liliem there, no farther away than that he could reach and touch her; Tinkla and the moaning on the cot half a pasture away. But it was honey mixed with gall and yarrow on his tongue, knowing that he'd go back. They didn't notice me and I hurried off, letting the cows interrupt them as they would.

I tried to tell him about this madness. "She needs you, Tinkla does; a good woman. And she'll be down before snow flies."

He let the fork thud against the manger. "I know what you

[330]

mean." He was silent, getting a jackknife from his pocket to cut an old halter rope. Thinking of winters before and how Tinkla had added barn duties to house work—milked and slopped when he lay sneezing with the grippe. Another time, when we hauled popple rails, Matt helping us, and tipped the load while darkness settled from branch and limb. We were reloading, when she floundered into the clearing. "Franz, Franz," she gasped, running to him, snowy wet to the waist. She had clung to him, sobbing.

He remembered without pleasure, I think, and was half-angry with me. "Don't speak so, Jeppy. I am married to Tinkla."

"You think that's enough?" I couldn't help reproaching him.

"Enough." He echoed my bitterness. "No; but there are some things that can't—that can't be—be given away; or changed either. Not with gold or silver—or begging on knees." He sagged against the bar. "I'll scratch my finger nails raw— for Tinkla; believe that. But don't—don't ask me to do more."

"Franz, I—"

"There are empty places, Jeppy; inside—deep inside a person. Places that are for—" He wavered uncertainly. "For fiddle tunes and maybe dreams." He turned his shoulder to me. "When a man can't dream any more, he—he might as well die."

The grief in him silenced me. In that moment (and in others soon to come), dubious with doubt, I had a feeling that the direction of our ways had no more purpose than ragged bubbles twisting under shim-ice each spring; and that we were bound for an end awful beyond words, and helpless to avert it as ants under a crushing heel—Father, all of him dead and buried beneath covers, for all the movement that he made; except his hard black eyes and the tongue that moaned over and over again— "Franz . . . Franz . . ." Tinkla wearing herself into peevishness with dishrag and scrub brush, but hushing Father gently, "Here's a fresh pillow; go to sleep now"; crying wearily at times . . . Franz stumbling in a blind manner between hope and desperation, driven to wildness at the urgency in Liliem; fretting himself thin as a shingle-end—Why? Why all this agony in earth, if purpose lay behind action? Until I thought we were walkers in sleep, eyes sealed, and obedient to idiot laughter in the dim and narrow caverns of the mind. Answers there were for the dead, perhaps; there were none for the living. Or so it seemed, the noon Franz trudged in to dinner, hot and with dusty sweat streaking his face.

Tinkla shrilled: "Wash up outside; you dirty too much in here. Besides, I've got the washtubs standing around." Franz set his lips; took dish and water to the chopping block. Inside the door, Little John pushed a square of wood with one of the crutches. I heard the spill of water in the basin, as Franz sloshed off the forenoon's lodging of corn-dust in his ears. Tinkla called: "Dinner." Franz came; half-fell over the crutch. He gripped it and laid the middle over his knee. I saw the heave in his shoulders to break the wood. But he let the crutch slip, breathing quickly; and sat at table. He forked a potato; stopped. Father moaned, "When is . . . Franz . . ." It was like steel scraping on glass. Franz jerked up. "If I hear that again," he shouted, "I'll—I'll—" His shoes were heavy on the floor. The screen sang behind him.

It was on the same afternoon we heard that Carley Sperry, singing his "Jinny, jinny, jinny" to the horses, had lost what sense he possessed and run after his father with a pitchfork. They locked him in a cage in the root cellar, where he could shriek and foam at the mouth, and no one, following the round of chores and field work, hear him or be disturbed.

Franz said, "This is beyond us, now," and saw Mr. Mais about borrowing lumber, sawmill cut, from Mr. Kloster, and spiking up another lean-to—for Father. Mr. Mais shook his head but agreed finally.

The day cooled into evening. I was glad when night began sweeping purple clouds over the ridges. The west stormed in angry crimson where the sun fired a mountain of dark thunderheads. Franz walked into the barn at milking, a wildness about him as if he'd eaten honeydew berries and were wind-mad in April; milked the cows with swift ungentle strokes. "Feed the calves, Jeppy," he yelled, as though I were earless as an owl. With hard jerks he pulled at the halter ropes, taking the horses to water.

"They've drunk," I told·him. "I led them down—"

"Hot day; another drink won't hurt them." He tugged at the mare's halter. "Come on, can't you?"

Going to see Liliem. The thought bounced in my skull like a rubber ball. Liliem weaving a web with her smiles; caressing his tired eyes and aching flesh into calmness—or midnight madness. And this night—soft as spring, now that heat was gone, the wind mellow with wood-smoke and wild grape. I pushed the buckets aside.

After a while I followed him. Shame brought sweat to my collar—sneaking in the bushes like a weasel. But I went (avoiding the black-dirt paths), strong with the notion that I ought to stop Franz—or do something. Half-knowing I wouldn't. The crutches were silenced in grass. I let a hazel bush stand guard between me and the shelving place in the creek.

The sun hurled red arrows of light by the fistful through the interspaces of willow and plum. Shadow and red fire fell on them—the two on the shore. Halter-ropes trailed in the water and the horses were hock-deep in the creek. What wind there was scarcely moved the tips of leaves. Whatever I had to say—if I had words—remained unsaid. Liliem was in his arms, his lips close to her cheek, as if he found rest there; and he was carrying her.

"Franz, dearest," I heard her say. "Kiss me . . . troubles away." Water-ripples hid part of her voice; but Franz's was clear, though soft: "Let me be with you; always. Let tomorrow never come. Never, never."

"Franz, Franz." More like a whisper and belonging to leaf-rustle. A door of willow limbs swept aside a moment and then into place, shutting them away. I stomped the path to the barn—

a long path tonight, and the curve of the crutch-ends was like a chunk of salt thrust against the tenderness of the underarms. I waited by the barn door. With the dusk the horses trotted in for feed, the ropes dangling between their legs.

10

This was not end, much as I thought it was. Tinkla sat with the lamp lit half that night, fearful in spite of my falsehood. "Guess he's gone to see Kloster about lumber for the lean-to." Not end for us, for all our despair, any more than storm ceases because a sparrow falls white-eyed and full of frost. Franz came in at breakfast and, as if he expected bars against further entry, stood in the doorway. Tinkla let the toast slip between her fingers, pleading with him though without sound. He blurted out, "You might as well know. Liliem and I—a man ought to—"

It was an experience met with only in the heat of restless fever, where one is aware that wakefulness and reality are near, but continues in dreams, never certain where shadow stops and substance begins.

Tinkla said dully, "It is so—what kept me awake nights; and all my worry for you—"

"Tinkla." He broke in. "A man grows mad with what is empty in him."

"You—you are ashamed of me." She faltered, and in the pause he was vehement with protest. "No, Tinkla; never that. It is—"

"What shame I have brought—" She disregarded him. "I'll take it away. Yours, too." She began to cry hopelessly, huddled in misery.

Franz said wearily, "It is for you to say. Your father's house— the judgment lies there." But Tinkla held out her hands. "No room there; not for an—an unloved wife." She put the apron rim to her eyes. "This is my home, and what you and I do, be-

longs here. I shall stay until—until my husband forbids me."
She arose quietly. "Franz, Franz—second best under your roof
and with you—it is better, so much better, than—than loneliness
in another's house." She went into the bedroom and left Franz
heavy with the weight of his obligation to her, shamed by faith
not thin and fragile as lichens over rock but durable as the hard
shell of oak.

He lugged the bedclothes from the loft that evening and slept
where he had years before—on the lean-to floor under the window. Tinkla watched him with a tremble of the lips but said
merely, "You'll need an extra pillow. " There he muttered and
tossed until I wanted to yell, "Keep your feet still; waking people
like that . . ."

Mr. Mais began the lean-to and once again the pounding of
hammers echoed in the house. I'd hear it out by the barn—the
beat of iron on wood which Father himself had sliced from the
logs, now made by other hands into a room for him—more like
a box, I couldn't help thinking. For all the saa-zaa, raa-saa of
Mr. Mais's saw ripping pine, and his loud singing:

> "There was a little billy goat;
> Tra la-la la;
> He bumped a lady in the—tra,
> La-la-la, la,"

the house was strange and gloomy, as if strong sickness were
within and lay with the potatoes at mealtime; Tinkla more silent
than ever (I thought of the chatterpiece in the pigtails she had
been). Once I saw her touch the "Lord Is My Shepherd" motto,
where the white letters were frosted with a faint icing of dust.
Her hand slipped down limply.

She took what had happened as oak does lightning stroke;
ready as always with bucket or towel to ease Father. So it appeared to me. I said once, "You tend him like—like—I'd believe
him your father."

"He is." She spoke unemotionally. "Not by blood; but by Franz's blood. And that is part of me." She lifted the dough from the pan at which she was working and reached for the cracked cup, full of flour.

"You hate him—Franz, don't you?" I asked it bluntly.

"Hate, Jeppy? It is cheap, hate; and easy. But Liliem—I could—" Her fingers tightened on the curve of the cup; closed slowly with a hard and terrible fierceness. For that moment, the understreams of her being swirled darkly upward, shattering her calm. Flour shot over her thumb and there was the sound of crockery breaking and rubbing edge against edge. Then she straightened, the breath running from her, and brought more flour. "But Liliem," she went on steadily, her voice sinking, "she is like—for him—I don't know what. Like the fiddle, maybe. Singing to—to him." Her words came in a whisper, barely audible. "What would be left for me, Jeppy, if—if I hated him?" She sprinkled flour into the dough as if it were sand and cutting deeper than her flesh.

The Bank sent another notice—in a polite blue envelope. A note was due next month; would he kindly arrange payment? Franz slipped the notice into the old shoe box where the others along with old letters were piled, and walked to the granary as if he wanted to measure what remained to take. He avoided the watering place by the creek. In a kind of humiliation he tore leather from an old shoe and fixed the pump. The horses drank at the trough again. Franz prepared the farm for winter, and all of us wondered what the Bank would claim.

11

The baby was born the night before snow fell like white blossoms through the bare oak limbs by the granary. The extra lean-to was shingled and by then Father lay behind walls to hush his endless quavering syllables—as if he were in a kind of grave, hidden behind household noises by day but heard like a ghost of agony in the silent dark.

That night mist hung from overhead to underfoot like a gray blanket thrown from the sky. After a while it tumbled in rain. But before darkness hid the ridges within itself, the cold wind hardened the dripping grass, and ice ferns grew and raised their leaves on the rocks. No easy hour for Tinkla, nearly lost in the shadow of birth. Mrs. Bauer wheezed in alarm and finally begged, "Franz, *es ist was*. I can't help her. Get the doctor."

Tinkla moaned, "No, no; the debt—it is bigger now—than we can bear." But Franz hustled into his clothes and ran to the Maises'. And met Liliem face to face again—Liliem with soft fingers to help him. The telephone was out of order. "Always is, when a feller needs it, the golblamed thing," grumbled Mr. Mais. "S'pose a tree fell over the wires, like the last time." Franz drove to Mary's Hill and brought the doctor.

It was a girl, and Franz, touching her hand, almost drew back at the quickness with which she curled fingers about his. He went into dawn gray as sheep's wool; bent over a leaf, its underside ice, its upper frost, rooted from a puddle by the cold snouts of the wind; and raised his head with a strange glow on his face.

Father died that afternoon, when flakes large as apple petals and as white drifted through the oaks. Life beating out of our house to give place to life beating into it. What hour his voice failed over "When is . . . Franz coming?" we never knew; but when Mrs. Bauer opened the door, his lips were still at last. He was buried in our churchyard at the crossroads, the earth black in the snow. And before long his room became the clutter-store for odds and ends we had in the old lean-to and didn't use.

Franz drove to Mary's Hill to see the Bank, and we found once and for all the extent of Father's debt laid now to our account—notes dating to the spring in which he came, when he had bought his first team and plow. There had been payments along the years, yes; but these were little more than mice-nibbles on the whole amount. No manager—Anna's words flew back to mock me. No manager and the debt piling like a strawstack, ours to bear. It was frightening to know that all that ran or walked our farm and that which only stood—all taken together—

wouldn't remove the load. Tinkla buried her face in the shirt on which she had been sewing—one of Father's that she was doing over for Little John. Franz said nothing, too spent to waste himself with speaking. The fear that widened his eyes gripped me like a vise. What now? What now . . .

This, then, is the end, I thought; the threshing-moon of our meager harvest, and the burning of the scattered leaves. The worst here and our bones helpless. Not knowing, that day, that we'd stick here like sheep lice for three years, warding off fore-closure with the promise of a calf or a pig, and then Mr. Bauer would offer his place up north (our farm gone finally); that the blue-eyed doctor would come again, and another one, the old one—people who had places in mind for the crooked and mis-shapen; who didn't look at you as if you were a crippled steer, nor say inside them, the thought plain on their faces: "Take the poor critter out and shoot it, somebody" . . . and that I'd be almost glad to go when the doctor came for me, so great the agony that would not stay chained behind clenched and aching teeth; Franz saying in bitterness, "Don't come back; till I send for you"; bursting out at the question in my face, "I don't know, I don't know when," and hurrying away without handshake or good-by . . . Tinkla red-eyed, and Little John in tears, dripping like a sieve, and crying, "Who will sleep in your bed now, Unca Jeppy?"—Then our farm gone in a blur of trees . . . the Hukel-poke windmill whirling and squeaking harshly . . . Mary's Hill and the high water tower . . . Fergus with its white houses and long avenues of trees . . . clack of wheels under the train (like a loose arm on a fanning mill, I thought dumbly) . . . the city with mist and smoke and racket bulging from its canyons, fright-ening in its crowded loneliness . . . the pain and desolation and the thoughts chased through the head; finally, this interval of peace.

This bright room here, with the acrid smell I disliked at first but have long got used to, and the wheel chair—this is my home. Dr. Bueller and the blue-eyed doctor bustle in frequently, and there are endless consultations, for I am a special case, they tell me as they paw over me. I'm patched up now, as much· as anything half-dead can be. And I'm glad there is something else to think about than bones tearing at the flesh and the heart black with pain. I've mulled over much, these years, and see things more clearly now. I must stay, even if a letter comes from up north of Pockerbrush. There's no place in the hills for a cripple, unless to pasture him on the farm along with old and sore-ribbed horses. And here, doctors come in and starchy nurses and such friends as are less broken than I. Books are here, endless volumes to make me wise if they can. I have found in them what I didn't find years ago.

But right in the middle of a page or somebody's talk, I see the blue gulf beyond the tamaracks and the thorn apples, the blossoms white like pads of snow on their branches, and wonder if the mallards still hatch in the rice lake and the loons laugh crazily over their warnings of rain. So near, those things, and a part of me. But they were too near, then, in that hour back there, when we knew the measure of Father's debt at last, when Tinkla cried into the shirt she was sewing and Franz sat hunched and silent . . .

It was a fierce winter. Snow whipped through the woods and a hissing sound like distant rain on standing wheat whispered through the willows. Often manure lay frosted white under the horses' heels; and steam in clouds billowed from the open doors. Three pigs, dwarfish and runty, of a fall litter, froze in the straw heap into which they had dug. We forked them clear of the pile, their legs sticking out stiff like plugs of wood from huge gray potatoes. Franz banged the gate with bitterness.

He turned his gaze often to the Maises' house, empty as the barn swallows' nests, as far as he was concerned. For Liliem had deserted the Maises after Christmas; ordered Mr. Mais to haul her trunk to Mary's Hill and left to visit her father in Fergus. Mr. Mais told us about it, grumbling, "Didn't get enough spankings when she was a toddler, that one. But gosh"—his tongue-end rimmed his lips—"the cinnamon toast she makes—like nobody else's"; and waited for her return.

The woodpile—a heap that didn't fire us through February—shrank and was lost to the last piece finally in a snowbank, dig as much as we liked. I remember more than one night that we crouched in a drift, letting the crosscut saw (for all its dullness) teeth its width into oak; my crutches buried in snow, Franz slapping his arms. Even in days not far from spring, heavy veils of snow moved before a breath of air and fogged the clarity of sight. Trees dimmed behind slants of gray lines like the chalk marks Little John dotted across the slate. Each tree was dark against a drifted slope, its limbs twisted blackness sharply etched. An early crow, swooping from a ridge, startled the eye with the inky streak it made, flapping across the white of a hill.

In the house warmth gave cheer to the fire crackling under the stove lids and the occasional shouts from Little John, twirling spools on a string. Teddy—for Franz had named her Theodora Louise and this time Tinkla nodded her head—grew and waved her arms from the clothes basket in which she was cradled—except on washdays. There was about her from the first that which caused Mrs. Bauer to cry, *"Ach,* Tinkla; you'll need a strap to keep this one under your apron." A smile that was more than a smile seemed to lift her lips into the beginning of a rogue's grin; but never did. Alb Hukelpoke took one look at her and shouted, "Brown eyes—Cat's knuckles! One's brown, the other gray. Trying to start something new, Franz?" He boo-booed her until she was ready to struggle out of the basket.

Franz played for her by the hour, smiling at her as if she understood his melodies; or rocked her to limp slumber with

> "There were three poodles on a hill—
> Bow-wow, Sic'em and Wolf";

her head pillowed in the crook of his elbow. Little John, quiet as the shoes he scrugged under him, listened where he sat on the floor near the rocker runner. But Franz had his cheek close to her hair, dreamy with singing. Once he stopped in the middle of *Sweet By and By* to pucker his brows at her over a raised bow. He put the fiddle down and touched her hair—a rich growth beginning to be tangly, for one so young. In the lamplight it shimmered like gold. "Look," he cried, excited and off guard. "Teddy's hair—it's yellow, like—like—" and stopped short. Tinkla stuck her knitting needles firmly.

"I know. It was hard not to see," she finished steadily. "I know." A kind of mockery for her; as though Franz's desire blossomed and grew this fruit in spite of her; all this beauty from her plainness.

Spring brought the bluebirds questing in the willows. Phoebes gathered moss under the hanging lip of the gully-rim—the gully where the wood's road crouched away from the edge. The cows followed the road and the horses. I'd see hoofprints above and white phoebe eggs three feet below.

The crutches were somehow lighter, with snow thinning to layers, to water soaking into earth spongy after release from frost; to vapor hanging over the meadow levels where soon violets smoked the grass a faint blue. I was glad that the short days were past and the storms that huddled us closer, we who were valleys apart. I'd remember almost with a shudder the winter-long nights, the hours when I thought somebody must scream soon, if only to break the dull pauses between the tick and tick of the clock on the shelf; unable to speak sometimes, any of us, the length of a meal, all that had gone before lying crooked as a pin in our consciousness; when each glance was looked at twice and a word was inwardly fashioned anew by an interpreter's tongue of suspicion. Hard to keep ire from leaping then.

I'd remember too one evening when we were sawing wood and Franz, as if he sensed what roiled in me, said slowly, "No use keeping it to yourself—what you think." The wind rubbed dry branches into mews of protest, and a long pointer of frosty flame stabbed upward where the sun had plunged into clouds dusty-colored with storm. "But all that you can pitchfork at me—I've said it to myself, in the night and no eye shut." Dusk hid his face.

"A man ought to have reasons—" I began solemnly but he thrust me aside. "Reasons. What are words or reasons when there's—when there's—" The saw rah-zah-ed to scrapings. "Jeppy, Jeppy." There was pleading in his voice. "So far we've come, you and I; and now blame lies on your lips." He grabbed the ax and split a chunk of wood, anger in the swing of the blade. I lifted a crutch and longed to drive the end against stone—anything to vent what was gathering in me. But the crutch was like an iron bar, sagging my arm. I pointed a hole in the snow. We sawed again . . .

But that belonged to winter, I said, breathing deep of new air; and was glad most of all that Liliem no longer moved across the Maises' yard, invitation in the toss of her shoulders. Let her stay in Fergus, I thought, and hoped with a blind hope that spring would not fail this year to heal with balm and scarred growth the frost wrenches of hate that had split and broken us.

Jonas Bluber returned from Canada in May; a hard-muscled man with a vestful of northern cusswords and tales of Canuck wenching, they said. He drove an automobile shinier than Leff's and with newer doodads; roared over the hills like a demon—"Made forty an hour," he bragged. Though we agreed with Mr. Prinzing: "Goes almost as fast as his tongue, his auto does." But he was the peacock's eye of Mason's Resort before June had run its length. We talked about it, getting to work.

We harnessed the team for the fields, knowing that, let hate spill over like a kettle boiling, or grief wring the heart crookedly, the earth waits for no man. Disk and harrow dug their steel across the curving furrows, and now it was Franz who had to decide what patch ought to head in oats and what in barley. "Guess wheat will do for the creek patch again," he'd say, though wheat had sucked fiber and kernel from the soil twice in a row before. Rain fell, and the seed he dragged into the ground poked pale reddish needles among the dirt chunks; greened and parted into arching leaves, the hope of harvest and the year's supply against hunger in the young blades.

I wondered about it, times enough, that summer, when sweat was mixed with the coffee and bread Tinkla sent to the fields, and the shocks pointed shadows in the stubbles—this hen-scrabble to keep belly-button from rubbing against backbone. There was the grain stunted by heat and drought and the shallow plowing Franz had done to save the edge of plowshares; the corn wind-shrunk before it had a season to mature, and the puffballs breaking the solid bed of roads, whitish, the color of a snake's belly—countless upthrusts like the endless vomiting of earth sick with bearing-pangs and the ripping out of life. What did it bring in the end, for all our sweat and swearing, but chaff rushing with straw before wind in the blower, and the Bank like a bloodsucker at our veins? At least as far as I could see. But we clicked tugs to the evener and pulled our belts tighter.

Leff Sperry tooted the horn regularly in our yard, though Tinkla scolded, "Poor salt he'll ever earn." He talked mysteriously about trips and the money cold in his shirt. "You ought to drive," he told Franz. In a burst of good feeling he added, "Damn' if I don't learn you"; and waved a wrench over clutch and shift and the complicated business of advancing and retarding the spark. Franz, after a while, would come driving, his face alive as it was when he fiddled sometimes; as if he'd climbed mountains, and saw earth like a plain below, the sense of flying and taking hills at a leap stirring his blood strongly. He'd catch up Teddy where she crawled on the floor: "See; we can go sailing—sailing through the air." With her on the seat beside him, he'd wheel over the road to turn at the mailbox and dust back.

Leff grinned a broken-toothed smile, jingling his keys like silver coins in his pocket. Once, when we were at the blacksmith shop and Old Wibart was grumbling, "Franz—*es tut mir leid,* but the bill you owe—I have to pay for coal in my fire—" Leff slipped the money into Franz's hand. Franz would have refused, enjoying Leff's automobile better than his company, I think; but Old Wibart was grim with coal-dirt black on his cheeks and eyes white. Franz paid with Leff's money. This will bear sorry interest, I thought; never guessing how sorry it was to be.

Matt came over on a Saturday, bubbling with ideas. "Let's have a picnic Sunday. Two-toed—why, neighbors ought to get together. Teena's in a lather to go, and Alb's bunch, too." Franz was dubious but Tinkla glad to escape four walls for an hour. In the end we didn't go to Long Lake, but decided on the hill in our pasture, where a level space overlooked the creek and the lake, beside a valley of oaks.

Matt and Teena with Junior hiked over, but Alb hustled through the gate alone—his wife had got a quick mad on, and made up her mind to stay home. "But I got the grub along," he chuckled, mopping sweat.

Little John was excited—his first picnic. He was a long-armed, long-legged boy, solemn as a barn owl but lively; wearing his pants thin at the knees. Only that morning he'd punched holes in the door screen and smeared sirup around, to coax flies in; and in they had buzzed by the hordes, until Tinkla discovered the trick and walloped him with Franz's razor strap. On hot afternoons he'd chase bullfrogs in the path, herding them out of the protecting grass, till, weary of hopping, they lay with blowing sides and put their forepaws like little hands over their eyes. The melodies that Franz played were never long enough for him. Once when Franz was away, Tinkla let him scrape the bow on the strings—and a laugh bubbled from his lips.

We trudged from the gate, that Sunday, Little John and Alb's lunch in the wagon that Mrs. Bauer had sent the last Christmas, Little John rustling the packages and teasing Alb, who hauled at the pole: "Wanna fis, Unca Alb; get a pole." Alb pulled a face as long as the Pastor's. "Fish? Today? Cat's knuckles, Little John. Why, I can just hear the Lord up there. He says to Gabriel, 'Gab,' he says, 'Lookit, once. That Little John feller—

fishing on Sunday again. And I just hooked the church-day on the calendar. Better give 'em a little toot, Gab.' " Alb shook his head. Little John, so interested he forgot the packages, asked, "Will he toot, Unca Alb?"

"Will he?" Alb investigated the clear place among his whiskers. "Kick me through a hornet's collar, young un; I hope not. If he does the whole sky'll bust right slam on your head." Matt laughed and Tinkla smiled, but Franz said, "You listen to Uncle Alb, and you'll be a smart man, John."

We came to the first hill, short and steep on its further side, where the gully lay like a wide gash. Trees grew at the bottom, taller than the gully was deep, so that a robin's nest in a crotch halfway up was on the level with our shoe tops. The road crowded between the edge and a tumble of mossy slabs. Someone years before had hatcheted a trail this way to avoid the rocks cragging the broken hills three-quarters to the wind. And with the contrariness of people clinging to old paths (and old ideas), everybody followed, as we did, without gumption to make change.

Franz with Teddy on his shoulder—her usual perch—and the rest of us stopped for a moment's breath. Matt kicked a stone at the ruts. "Have to watch, next winter, Franz; or you'll slip in." Franz nodded. "Get the horses shod sharp."

Alb began a story to quiet Little John, who wiggled with curiosity about Gabriel's toot. "Well," Alb told, "I heard about a boy long time ago. His name was Peter Prackbrush and his old man used to lick him and lock him in the cellar with the rats." Alb sat on a stone and pushed the wagon handle backward. Little John caught it. "Well, Pete ran away and killed a whole pack of wolves; got a rich farm and made—oh, bushels of dollars." Little John humped in the wagon. "And Pete came home and licked his old man good." The wagon began to move. "Hey, where—" The wheels rattled.

"See, Unca Alb," shouted Little John. "I'm running away, too." Down the slant rolled the wagon, Little John screaming with laughter. Tinkla dropped her bundles; Franz swung Teddy to the ground, and Alb set off at a run. The wagon hit a rut; John and the packages spilled into the dust.

"You little two-by-four." Alb was ready to shake him but set him gently into the wagon, grinning at the boyish mirth. We all thought of the rocks and the thorn bushes below.

Alb grabbed the handle and we followed the road to the cleared place. There was a lightness even to my dragging heels that day. This once I forgot the ache that left me sometimes helpless; forgot it in watching Matt gobble sandwiches and shout at his son, head down in a plate of potato salad, "Hey, Junior; come up for air, now and then, can't you?" Tinkla, some of the old chatter brought back to her with talk and fellowship, admitted that the wild currants were wormy this year; hurt by frost, too; and clucked her tongue sympathetically over Teena, who bemoaned the seven chicks a weasel sucked of blood the night before. Matt tamped his pipe and smoked. Tinkla nodded in answer to whatever Teena asked, and said: "Two farms, up north. Pa got them for a song. It would be nice, living up there, away from—" She stopped with a quick lift of her head in Franz's direction. But Franz played "Bear" with Teddy, who waved her arms as if flying. An afternoon as far from the days past as the hill was from the valley.

We went home before dusk, Matt sure that one of his heifers had calved and not wanting to scratch in the brush after dark for it. The moon, almost round, tagged us on the homeward trail. Franz pointed to the dark figures on the white disk. "See; there's the old lady raking hay, and the old man pitching manure." As we unlatched the gate, Little John asked sleepily, "Can they toot?" The horses whinnied, nosing beyond the fence for oats, welcoming us. But the house was chilly—autumn-chilly, I thought. And the overhalls, slung on a nail in the wall, were pungent with barn smell.

Three days later Liliem was back; rode from Mary's Hill with Charlie Abendsmeyer. (Charlie bragged afterward, "Sure was a warm lapful.") She bounced in with the Maises again. No one else, it seemed, was pleased to have her. It was autumn then, the maples red on the ridges. A strange excitement ran in Franz, when he heard. His tunes, unquiet with longing, became wilder. Often he'd pitch Teddy to his shoulder, evenings, and, with sun red in her curling hair, walk to the creek. Tinkla would watch them, her fingers tightening.

Teddy more than crawled now and was beginning to reach for the rungs of chairs and peer wistfully at the tallness of the table top. "I can't make her out," Alb Hukelpoke used to say. "Looks at you like she's laughing—one eye granite and the other brown—and warm as rain water."

Franz liked to take her where he worked, though once she fell into a nettle-bed and he spent the night hushing her and running his fingers through her locks. She was with us, teething a willow twig while we stretched a wire between two posts, the late afternoon Liliem came. She was beside Teddy before we knew, and holding her close.

"So sweet—like sugar she is, Franz."

"Liliem." His voice frogged with huskiness. Nothing changed, it came to me; nothing; nothing. Only unaltered yearning that brought, now passion, now reproof, like fire and slow ice in them. The wire zummed under his hammer. "It is as I thought—the same yellow, both of them." He became bold. "She should be yours, Liliem."

"Mine," Liliem murmured, a far-awayness in her eyes. "She should be mine," and hugged her; then shivered and suddenly cried, "No; never. Not me. For others, but never me."

"For you, Liliem." He dropped the hammer, denial flung to the winds, and came for her. "You. It is plain. What is in my house—it can't go on."

She stared at him. "No." Her tone was violent. She tore the hazels aside and fled, as if his demand had shamed her into flight. Nothing changed.

Teddy daa-daa-ed and pointed the willow at the bushes. Franz squeezed her in a quick burst. "She will come again," he said with steadiness. We finished the fencing. Easy enough to say "Forget," I thought, as we followed the path. "Forget; tomorrow will unsnarl what today left behind." But harder to accomplish—all the bitterness crowded between sunup and sundown not lightly put by or washed like a stain easily from what we remember. His resolve echoed in my head: "This can't go on . . . this can't go on" . . . Tinkla like a ridge-hen in her quiet patience. I wished in a wild moment that Liliem were a man and my crutch at her throat . . .

Teddy, shouldered high, twitched at Franz's hat, screaming, "Cah, cah" (which Franz insisted meant "car," though, to me, it might have been any sound from "bah" to "wah"). We opened the cow-pen gate just as Leff Sperry headed a cloud of dust into the yard; in haste and nervous, it struck me, the way his fingers twiddled at the gas levers. "Can I put her behind your machine shed?" he shouted, slapping the wheel. "Forgot to get gas," he explained hurriedly; "won't make it home."

"Sure thing," Franz nodded, trying to calm Teddy's excited "Cah, cah," and keep her from wriggling down. Before he could ask a question, the motor barked and Leff drove behind the shed. He waved at the corner but didn't wait, except to promise, "Get her—in a day or two," and struck into the woods.

"Road's easier than brush—and no farther." Franz pulled his lip. "Wonder what—" He glanced at me. "Getting along chore time," he said.

"Cows ain't far," I agreed, turning on the crutches. Leff's in for something, I thought; trouble again, and we're going to be mixed in it. It was there under word and action—an uneasiness, as if things we couldn't fathom were trooping in the shadows.

It grew when Mr. Mais puddled over after milking and told us, "Town board's sure kicking a fuss; leastways some are." He spat a cheekful of black twist. "Gonna clean house on Mason's Resort and them fellers peddling booze."

"Mason's too, huh?" Franz asked quickly, thinking of Leff and the car behind the shed.

"Yup. Whore-hole, that's what it is. Rooms wide open, and a lot of half-naked women. Needs a brushing."

"Town board—that bunch." I threw a handful of oats into the milk for calves. Franz got the old broom handle he used and began to stir rapidly. "You'll wait yourself tired before they do any cleaning."

"Not so sure." Mr. Mais stretched his legs. "They're gonna get the sher'ff to help, too." The broom handle slowed and the thick whorls Franz made in the slops flattened to the evenness of milk and oats. He scraped the bucket without looking up— the lean man with the gun, crossing the meadow, large in his mind.

"Liliem—she says the board better keep their noses to home. Can't figure that one *atall*." Mr. Mais chewed a moment. Franz stirred again. "She went on a tantrum tonight." Mr. Mais inspected the black plug for a fresh cut but shook his head regretfully and put it away. "Tantrum, all right. Broke Ma's best yellow water pitcher. Said we're nothing but old brush-hooks anyway, and she's sick and tired of the whole kit and boodle."

"She—she said that?" Franz waited with pails uplifted. Mr. Mais nodded, rising, and went home. I held an extra bucket to a crossbar. We carried the feed to the calf pen near the shed, where the automobile returned a curve of the afterglow. "Smelly old devil," I muttered, sniffing the foul air. Franz guessed so, and clattered the pails to the barn, shuffle-footed with thought.

I poked at the levers, wondering what madness people would take notions to next; and saw gasoline dripping. I unscrewed the cover of the tank without knowing exactly why, except for the skulking look I'd seen in Leff's eyes; measured with a splinter of wood—an inch of wetness at the bottom. More than enough to carry him and his old fire-eater the three miles to the Sperry farm.

A week passed before he came to get it; mumbling about shocking corn and having his hands full, with fall work. He laughed when I told him Franz and Teddy had circled the yard in the auto, and gone for the mail once or twice. "Hell, yes; good thing he did. The buggy needs limbering up." But he acted as if he didn't know about empty tanks or lack of gasoline.

I had an awful feeling that people could see in my face what was happening to us; the mask no longer rigid to cover our real selves—all those months, when crimson and scarlet burned themselves pale on the ridges. Franz was curt and goaded himself for the moment when he'd blurt out what he meant to do . . . the beginning of every speech one to hold the breath . . . Tinkla washing dishes and boiling coffee, waiting . . . each moment put by for another.

Then, before rains froze the roads to rutty tracks, Jonas Bluber roared over to see Liliem, his car shined to a hen's feather, Mr. Mais informed us. Franz was banking the house against deep frost and digging the pebbled earth. "He jollied her along and sorta made up to her." Mr. Mais poked a bit of pine between his teeth. "Hefted her in those big arms of his. And goldarn if she didn't skin off with him. After all the sassy names she used to call him, too." Mr. Mais growled to himself.

Franz gripped the handle of the spade; the knuckles shone white. "She—she and Jonas—it can't be—" He mustn't let on or say more; not in front of neighbors; not so they'd know.

"Sure is. Pert she was, too, crowding in beside him."

Franz leaned the spade against the house, his hands unsteady. "Guess—guess I'll get a drink." He hurried, as if his twisting lips betrayed him; turned in the path and went by the pump, forgetting what he'd come for, smarting under the fire-weed of jealousy, that day. He waited for an excuse to see her and finally crossed the field to the Maises', asking to borrow a five-tined straw fork. He was pricked as with needles then. She had left—left without a word, riding kit and suitcase with Jonas Bluber.

She shouldered herself into the Grosbeck family, distant cousins of hers; threw scorn at the Pastor when he rebuked her for absence from church, we heard; and danced at the Resort with any man sober and straight in his legs enough to hold the floor. Until I was ready to believe Alb Hukelpoke: "Keep her where she belongs? Huh! Takes more'n six feet of man-muscle and a hard belly to do that."

Franz had the scabby bone of frustration to chew, that winter, when the white dust of snow fled over the plowing like the shadow of jack rabbits, wan and ghostly, pursued by the wind-hounds. Tinkla would shove back a chair from the table sometimes, lips trembling, as if she wanted to cry, "Franz, it is lonely and cold—without you"; but wouldn't, slipping into the bedroom . . . Little John grave except when Franz was gone and Tinkla opened the fiddle case . . . Teddy uncertain on her legs and toddling but steadier by the time snow ran northward on roofs slanting from the sun.

Franz met Liliem in an unforeseen moment at Toffmann's store one April day. He had just laid out the money for shoes, a pair for me, and was crooking his brows over the list Tinkla sent. "I'll have a pound of coffee—cheapest, and don't grind it," he was saying, and looked up to see her near him. His lids flickered. She whispered, "Franz, please—" But there were people there, eyes alert, however guarded. He swung back to the counter. "Five pounds of sugar—wasn't it, Jeppy? And some pepper." He hunched sidewise, though, in order to watch her hastening to the rear of the store.

For once I didn't care whether spring thawed the creek into ripples again or not. A sort of numbness that was worse than red-hot coals crept along my spine, and the path to the barn seemed miles long. We muddled through work, Franz, early in the morning, shoving collars on the horses as if he wanted to get into the harness himself.

But I wondered how we'd ever manage another winter with thistle seeds and cockles instead of oats and barley for feed. The dreadful ache in one at seeing cows nuzzle moldy hay or straw—and eat it finally, despair in their ball-eyes at the hunger drying up rib and udder; the awfulness of throwing down the last forkful of sloo grass, the barn empty to the boards, and knowing there'd be only wet straw and little of that from now on. Each morning the awful certainty of slop pails sour and clotted with yesterday's milk . . . the stumbling in a death of sleep, mornings, and touching a pan or bucket without knowing how or why . . . manure fetlock-deep . . . the stink of horse stalls so heavy we ate it with oatmeal and flapjacks . . . on hot summer days the thick scum of flies on the feed buckets . . . God, if there were one morning to wake and find the barn clean and the hills without furrows.

We picked up the fork where we stuck it the night before. Franz seeded and harrowed, the sweat draining away restlessness and dulling memory, though he flung the milk stool the length of the manger, crying, "Why? Why? I've *got* to know why!" Looking as if uncertain whether this were his voice or an echo of his silent shouting. Wanting to find out and, like children and wise men, sorry when he did.

12

We were in the blacksmith shop when the "Why?" began to unravel, for all we didn't know it, our thoughts then being on a broken casting Franz brought. John Bluber was there with a feeder apron that needed new slats; Charlie Abendsmeyer and a couple of men from near Jenny's Peak. John was complaining, "Never seen the beat; kids nowadays tearing like crazy. Jonas gone half the week." He hammered on a slat. Old Wibart dusted cinders from his leather apron. "Hanging around the Resort all night, and so weak next day, he can't pick his own teeth."

Old Wibart took the casting from Franz. "How you want I should do it?"

Adam Kloots limped in and clanged two plowshares on the floor. "Dull as a sled runner," he said, and began packing his lower lip with a thumb of snuff. A father at last, he was, though the men still ragged him.

"Kinda late hopping, for you, ain't it, Adam?" John Bluber slapped a fat thigh. "Must have been the hired man."

"Well—I kinda diddled long enough." Adam grinned good-naturedly. "Kid takes after me, all right. Gave him the snuffbox and damn if he didn't put a thumb in."

Adam was still laughing when the car with the red wheels slowed at the door and a man leaped from the running board—a lean man with hard eyes and the curve of the hawk in his cheek. The men in the shop became grim-lipped—remembering how he'd taken a neighbor boy from them. Adam spat loudly. Franz drew into the shadow of a post, as if guilt—he didn't know for what—showed on his face.

"Just getting acquainted." The sheriff was complacent. He had them spotted, the men he was after, he said; and he'd pick them—like plums from a tree. He got into the car and drove off.

"Red wheels." John Bluber peered down the road where the sheriff had gone—the road leading past our mailbox. "Rolling trouble for somebody."

Franz had more than one glance backward on the way home. "Hunting a man." He walloped the team. "Like he'd hunt rabbits with a shotgun." Remembering the meadow and how Diah Kloster broke from the tamaracks.

We trotted opposite the parsonage, and the Pastor called from his porch, "Herr Vildvogel," and hurried over the plank walk.

"Your place is empty often, Herr Vildvogel." He announced it as he would a text on fornication. "What would your father say?" He hadn't changed much, the Pastor; still worried himself into a sweat running from tar-paper shack to story-and-a-loft house, shouting Law and Gospel where accident or design brought two or three, or the whole congregation, together—doses of religion bitter as snakeroot. I wondered about him—and those like him—offering peace and quiet to others and never finding it themselves; chasing sinners out of the Devil's under-brush—as well roll the white stones on a ridge to find a one-legged ant; about as easy and about as profitable.

"What did I teach you in school?" he demanded, waggling a finger, anger swelling his jowls. No different from German school. The years had brought gray to his hair but little heaven to the hell of his preaching; stooped a little, sloping at the shoulders, as if the Law he upheld with his two arms had been heavier than he thought. "The word is clear, Herr Vildvogel," he concluded; "come to the Lord's house."

Franz mumbled about cold weather and bad roads. The Pastor grumphed and whipped on his heel. We continued homeward, Franz disturbed as Mr. Mais was whenever he went to the Pastor to announce himself for communion.

There was a letter waiting for him—blue and polite, a jog to Mr. Vildvogel's memory—about the note at the Bank. Franz lifted a tormented face. "A feller ought to go with Leff. He has money." Desperation rang in his tone.

"Franz." I couldn't keep still. "Enough trouble on this place—"

"Trouble?" He swung on me furiously.

"No, no." Tinkla dropped the overhall she was patching, terror in her voice. "Franz, such madness—"

"Madness," he threw at her. "Is it madness, then, to want meat for the cupboard? or buy hay for the cows?"

"The land, Franz; it will bring hay and feed; jelly for the cup-board. Only plow well and seed the land." Her fingers curled at his shoulder. "Otherwise it is wrong to—"

"Wrong." He shrugged away. "Tired of it—hearing I'm wrong. All my life—wrong, wrong, whatever I do; that's all I've heard. If crying would help, I'd—I'd—" He blundered into a chair. Tinkla let her hand drop. Teddy caught at his knee, struggling with sound. "Papa, Papa—" the only word her tongue commanded. Little John banged the screen door.

"Unca Jeppy, Unca Jeppy." He gasped for breath. "The

cows—all in the wheat, and the bull's bellering over the fence."

Franz stumbled up from the chair. Milking to be done and feeding. We corralled the cattle, did the chores. . . .

Leff Sperry came by after dark, the first time since he'd put the car behind the shed. He was pointed with slyness and hints. "Hold an extra dollar, your pockets, won't they?"

"Empty as mine are?" Franz was sour. "They'd hold a lakeful."

"Guess there's ways to get a couple of shekels." Leff guffawed smearily. "If a feller ain't caring about smells."

Franz hesitated, knowing what he meant. I wanted to shout, "Watch out what you do." Then Franz shook his head, the sheriff in his eye. "Got trouble enough."

I felt Leff's smile crumpling into crookedness. "Sure. I know. But you owe me—"

"God's sakes, Leff." Franz whirled on him fiercely. "If it's that—"

"A couple of quarts at a dance—you could pay me. And have some yourself." Leff slipped the offer in. "No risk for you and it'd help me, you're such a churchy sort of feller. Besides you'd see her again—Liliem."

"Liliem." Franz stiffened. "What's she got to do—"

"A high stepper, she is, at Mason's. Comes regular." Leff struck a match for his cigar. His smile was sticky. "She and Jonas got a room—"

"Don't believe it." Franz balled his fist hotly; clinging to his dream, as if it were hope slipping like mist from his grasp. "Not till I see it myself." The match died.

"That's easy. Come along with me—any time." He slapped the wheel, as though hit by a new idea. "Why not tonight?"

"Tonight!" Franz eased aside, taken aback.

"Sure. Why not? Scared?" There was a taunt in his voice. Franz jerked up. "Good night, too." Leff spoke eagerly. (I thought bitterly, "He was just waiting for such a chance.") "Everybody there. Fact, Jonas asked me to bring him a bottle or two—in case his hip goes dry." Leff heehawed nastily. "Get in."

I sensed the shadow of evil. "Franz, don't—don't go." He jumped in beside Leff. Chill swept through me. "Franz, this belongs to me, too." I hardly knew what I said. "If you go, I go." His silence was worse than a measuring look. Finally, "Get in, then," he said roughly. I knew without being told that Leff was ready to protest. I didn't care. Leff swallowed what he had to say but the gas lever squeaked as he ripped it down angrily.

I noticed how yellow the lamp in the window was, how dark the night, the moon, low in the east, struggling with clouds. Tinkla was a bent and anxious figure outlined a moment against the glass before we turned the corner and lost her. We clattered over the nine miles of twisty cow trails that passed for roads beyond Long Lake; rumbled over tamarack bridges, hollow-sounding and unsafe. "Spooky as hell, these swamp places. Gets ya." Leff's face seemed pale in the dimness behind the glare of the headlights. "Gets ya, all right. Feller feels safer, somebody along, like this." We tunneled from gloom into the light reflected from the waters of Pike Lake. Leff wheeled around a bend and we were in Mason's Resort.

The cottages were dark, until one saw the faint white threads in the windows and knew that a length of cracked shade hid whatever was inside. But the dance hall was garish with carbide lamps, we could see without stepping down. Franz leaned toward every passer-by; sat back, relieved. Not here, for this blowout.

The band tootled a ragtime piece from the platform and the dancers, with arms spread like bony wings, curved around, bobbing like calves on a hobble; belly-squeezing in the shadows. There were women with more paint on their faces than on many of the barns in the hills. Etta Rippey was among them, squealing and shaking her breasts, bringing the men nearer, desire in their eyes. She jiggled with a black-mustached man, half-drunk. They halted in the whirl to hug tightly. Like Liliem, she was. The thought bored into my head. Like Liliem.

A girl shrilled, "I ain't got my corset on," and the boys with her yawped at the joke. Once I thought I saw the lean mouth of the sheriff among the crowd, and uneasiness filled me. If we should get caught with Leff and what he had hidden— A man loomed out of the night; beckoned to Leff. Suddenly Franz joined them, before I could crack a thumb or stop him. There was low talk. Leff brought a jug from under the hind seat; a jingle of money and Franz's refusal, "No; not this time." He hopped into the car, a shrug of the shoulder for my scowl. "All there is to it," Leff snickered. "Open your pockets and the silver rolls in."

The dancers were getting heated. Here and there, boys with girls pulled to them went behind the building—"to cool off," Leff smirked, rolling in his seat. A pimply fellow, lurching by, held upright by a flowsy girl, was saying, "Didja see 'em? Old Mason'll have a fit; swimming without any clothes on—that yellow-haired tootsie and—"

Franz was out of the car in a leap; caught the youngster's arm. "Where'd they go?"

"Jeez, you're hurting—"

"Where'd they go?" Franz shook him into pointing unsteadily. "In that house—there." He pulled free. "Christ, you don't have to sprain a feller's elbow."

Franz didn't bother to knock. He banged the door open, Leff and I at his heels. Not even a bar prevented us. He pushed in and stood as if hammered into immobility.

It is smudged over and over again by what came between— that night and the small sleazy room, indistinct with gloom, the lamp-flame almost smothered by the chimney smoked black . . . Liliem in the bed, the startledness in her eyes hardening to anger; radiance in her tumbling hair . . . Jonas breathing thickly with drunkenness and grabbing for the shirt that hung at the bed-end, his eyes piglike and unfriendly, peering at Franz.

Franz clenched a fist into tightness. "Liliem," he cried, and the word was as if torn root and branch from deep inside him. No need of protest from her—he saw the shame which the anger on her face could not hide. And knew. Husks, now, all that belonged to his yearning (valor in the sun, a prayer under the moon)—husks like those blowing from the shock after the corn is harvested, ear and kernel gone. "Liliem, that you could do this—anybody who—"

"What th'ell's goin' on here?" Jonas lumbered up, the ugliness in him growing. "Talkin' t'her like that, ya bull-wiper, ya—" He lurched toward Franz.

Franz whirled and shoved him, hard. Jonas fell back, wobbling grotesquely as he hit the curved iron at the foot of the bed, and landed on the floor; tried to get to his knees, blood on his mouth, slipped back and lay still. Liliem screamed.

Leff grabbed Franz, who went suddenly limp. "God's sake! Let's get out of here—quick. Want to get me into trouble?" He hustled Franz through the door. I followed, into the dance-noisy night.

Iron scraped iron as Leff pulled the throttle along the guard. Lightning flickered, throwing the western ridges out of the dark for one instant, catching them into obscurity again the next; flooding us with pale fire, Franz indistinctly seen, huddled and bent to hide himself. The moon, not yet swallowed by storm, had a scud of cloud across it, like matter smeared over an eye. Leff swerved around a sloo-hole—had the decent sense to keep his mouth shut. He braked the wheels in our yard. "See you later, maybe," he said gruffly. "Gotta get along; couple more jugs to deliver."

Franz walked stiffly across the stone step. Tinkla, as if she knew, was up and had the lamp lit; trembling, though this was summer and the fire not yet dead in the stove. "Franz, you are back. Now let it be what it is." She touched him, half-timidly. He slouched from her.

"Don't. I'm—I'm dirty." He spoke as if he couldn't escape

the room at Mason's any more than he could the lightning's flare beating against his closed lids. As though he had to speak, he burst out, "Liliem—and Jonas—they—" He waited for her bitterest scorn.

But she said, as I think Mother would have, "Franz, up north— Father has land. It is clean there. We'll make home, you and I—" Tears choked her. For a moment he turned and I thought he wanted to bury his head like a child in her lap. Then he straightened and went to the lean-to; closed the door and was alone in the dark, knowing with certainty all that he had avoided since Liliem departed from the Maises'—the false face removed and the grim visage of reality thrust before him; stung to fury and yet uneasy with guilt, too.

Beyond the walls storm rattled the loose shingles and rain spattered on the step. I entered the lean-to; put match to wick and found him sagged on the quilts. Lightning tore the sky to shreds. The artillery of thunder blasted earth until the house shook. No sleep this night, I thought, listening to the racket. Franz sat bowed. Once Tinkla leaned in the door—to bring him to her, I thought. But she asked instead, "Want another blanket? A wet night."

He roused up. "Tinkla, you're— I—" He twisted toward the window, humbled in that moment by her patient acceptance of hate or love, or the slow strangling of corn by creeping vines.

I ached for morning, sleep like salt on my lids, no rest in my bones. But when dawn pushed the darkness up and overhead like a great curved sash, blankly purple with night, the sun on the step was no harbinger of courage but a gusty omen among the rack. Crimson splashed the sky above the trees and the creek wallowed in redness. Franz was grim at breakfast, crumbing the toast, a glower for me; Tinkla silent, her stockinged feet padding on the floor and the kettle-cover noisy in her fumbling hands; Teddy and Little John grave, but inquisitive as fawns, spooning curiosity unsatisfied with their bread-and-milk. I wanted to yell, "Say it, why don't somebody? Say it."

All morning the sun was hot, a mugginess in the air hard to breathe and like gravel under the shirt—too wet to cut the last of the grain, overripe and shelling on the stem.

Franz jerked past me, as if this humiliation were a hurt deeper than he could bear to have me witness, and it galled him that I had stumbled behind, last night—a wedge widening between us. He paused at the gate and stared into the northwest—with a half-fearful expectancy, as if he saw Jonas Bluber falling again. . . .

Once he grasped my shoulder. "Are you laughing?" he demanded savagely. "If you and Leff Sperry—"

"Franz. What are you thinking?" That he should accuse me with Leff! There was a mistiness I couldn't clear from sight, for all my head-shakings. "Franz—"

He flung off to pump water. The tar-paper on the chicken coop seemed to crawl, a dancing floor alive with heat-quivers. I saw Teddy and Little John playing "Toad" by the lilac bushes and the peony beds, Little John cracking his shrill soprano:

"Toady, toady, how is thee?
Just as well as I can be.
And how is toady next to thee?
You stay here and I'll go see,"

both scampering around the clumps. A yard full of ordinary things—the old wagon, the binder near the shed, one wheel of a buggy visible around the corner of the granary . . . chickens scratching; but because of what was inside us, a Devil's nest of hate and fear . . . growing . . . growing.

I creaked to the barn and slanted a crutch over the sill to prop myself across; not seeing Franz striding quickly out of the dimness of the stalls, ahead of the mares. He stumbled over the crutches and wobbled to his knees; was on his feet again and at me. "Damn you, you cripple"; pushed me hard. I plunged against the wall and slid to the wet ground; gritted teeth to hold from yelling—pain like a veil over my eyes; the crutches thudding on the edge of rocks; Franz staring at his knuckles and lurching by to slip halters from the horses.

As one tired and lacking sleep, I pulled myself up; gathered the crutches under my arms and began crossing the yard. I saw the length of the road from where I stood, empty now; the popples growing on one side and Teddy dodging in the bushes near the gravel; saw Franz throw the halters over a post and come toward me, as if to speak.

It is clear now what was roily with rinsings then—the sun hot and a rooster crowing . . . the roar of a motor and Leff Sperry's auto splashing mud almost to the barn where I waited for Franz . . . the car half-swinging around to avoid the wagon, so that it was at angles with its own tracks . . . Leff shaking and so frightened the spit dribbled unwiped on his chin; falling from the seat, one arm limp in the rolled-up sleeves, blood wiggling like a red swollen worm over his hand; shouting, "Franz, he's after me—the sher'ff; a gun" . . . Franz going white, his hands grabbing at his hips . . . the engine droning under the hood . . . Tinkla in the doorway . . . Little John and Teddy pointing up the road . . . Leff groaning and sinking to the ground . . . seconds of slow moving . . . Franz shock-still. Then red wheels in the yard and the sheriff leaping from the running board; Franz wagging his head in a mad way . . . the sheriff clawing at Leff . . . a gleam of steel . . . Leff moaning, "Don't; don't; don't."

It is hard to remember the jumble of those moments and what happened. Franz shouted all at once, "No; not me," wildness in his face, the vulture of fear ripping in his skull; all the hours of terror smashing in him—Father with whip or fist upraised and he cringing to save his ribs . . . Pete Prinzing shrieking into the night . . . Sornas Tetzlauf's knobby thumbs groping for the eyes . . . Diah with fear stretching his lids, being jerked forward and crying, "Don't; don't; don't" . . . the blood on Jonas' mouth . . . fear . . . the sheriff. . . .

He jumped into Leff's auto, paralysis broken. "You won't get me; you won't get me." Clash of iron gear on iron . . . the car rolling . . . the sheriff's hard query, "What's he beating it for? Got my man" . . . wheels gaining speed . . . Teddy running into the road, waving her arms excitedly *(Papa! Cah, cah)* . . . Little John trying to catch her . . . his figure blurred . . . the rattle and crash of tires on gravel . . . Little John falling back . . . Tinkla running . . . the car skewing off and braking to a stop among the popples . . . Franz leaping out.

She was in his arms before Tinkla or I were there, the sheriff hesitating beside Leff, in dead faint . . . red stains on Franz's naked arm, where the shirt was torn away, but none in his cheeks. He called, "Teddy, wake up; can't you hear me?" stumbling to his knees in front of Tinkla, as if he offered her a gift—or a sacrifice.

Even now I wake sometimes, Tinkla's cry loud in my ears, and see them stricken and helpless in the road beside the peony bushes—her fingers curled in Teddy's rumpled hair, lying so still . . . Little John stiff and tearless close by, the sheriff coming soon.

Franz shivered. "Tell him—the sher'ff; I'm here."

My voice was ragged trying to tell him. "Not for you, the sher'ff; not you."

"Not—not for me." His head swayed, knowing in a strange way that this too was error added to the sum of errors. "Even the baby. They might have left the baby."

"Franz." I shook him.

"Empty." His gaze cleared. "Empty, my hands. I killed her."

"Franz, *nicht so,*" Tinkla pleaded.

"So empty—"

"*Stille,* Franz. I am here."

His hands swept the golden curls. "She—she had fiddle-music in her hair," he whispered softly. "Gone now."

"We'll make it right." Tinkla's voice, in spite of tears, was strong with an urgency that could rise above death even. "Up there—there's place for us. We—"

"If—if I could—" he faltered.

"I am here, Franz. Together we can—"

"Tinkla here." A sad wonder filled his mumbling. "Mütter-chen—Liliem—Teddy; gone. But Tinkla here."

The curls slipped free and his hand went limp; slid down where Tinkla cupped the small head in her palms. His hand stayed there. His head was bent, but she heard the words—words he'd said once, years before, at the Prinzing baptism, when he staggered and fell into her arms out of storm. "Your hands, Tinkla; so warm . . . so warm."

13

It was evening with a sunset the like of which we saw no more than once a year. Fire tinged the blue haze over the swamp to cherry-brightness. The sun was a red-hot ball flung against a rock pile of clouds, its curve flattened. The Maises' yard dimmed with shadows and over north Mr. Prinzing's voice drifted with the dusk from the pastures: "Ca' boss, ca' boss, ca' boss."

Tinkla walked slowly from the barn, milk foaming from the rim of the pail, Little John beside her, shoulders sloped with the weight of another bucket. Franz was in the house, ahead of us, the team unharnessed and bedded down. "Let them run to water," he'd said, worn as a rag and his legs wobbly from tread-ing behind the walking-plow.

Tinkla lowered the buckets and straightened to unkink the muscles. Milk splashed over the edge of Little John's pail; he scraped it up on a finger and scattered the whiteness with a swing of his hand. A car roared past the mailbox, its shininess catching the red of the sky—Jonas', likely . . . on a spree again. Over the seven-acre patch we heard Mr. Mais shout, "Sic 'em, Rover; sic 'em into the yard." I watched from the pump.

All at once, so that I shivered, hearing it, the fiddle cried in the house—the quavering lullaby of *Liebeslied*. It was a part, somehow, of that evening quiet, as much as the throbbing notes of the night sparrow threading his song from the creek. Sad beyond words to tell, choking the breath; the strings vibrant with grief. Tinkla put her arm about Little John with a quick gesture. A kingbird climbed to see the last of the sun and slanted earthward again.

The fiddle sang with a loneliness even beyond tears. But under the grief, like crumbly ledge-rock under hills, lay strength, I thought; crumbly but holding together. And hope, however moldy and moth-eaten. Or so it seemed.

Our yard was hollow with sound. Little John moved impatiently under Tinkla's hand. "Never lets me play; never." He looked up at her. "Why?"

"*Stille, Junge.*"

"Scolds so, too."

"*Stille.* It's—it's something in him; hurting—I can't say it—"

Little John stamped a foot. "But why? He hurts me, too." Young anger brought the tears. "You wait. I'll run away; like Peter Prackbrush. Unca Alb says—"

"Hush, Little John. You mustn't talk so. Ever." Tinkla was crying now. "He—he needs us, your pa; both you and me. More than ever, if—if God's peace is to come to our house."

Little John touched her hand, awed by sorrow. Tinkla lifted the buckets. The music thinned to whisperings. The creek and the willows faded into indistinctness except for a clear patch of water; and dark swirled up and over the hills. I saw a lantern flame like a red coal jerk among the trees over at the Maises'. Tinkla and Little John carried the milk to the house. I saw them at the step.

The fiddle was still now, still as the early night, the day a closed chapter and the heart too tired to wonder about tomorrow. The house door slammed. I lurched back to water the horses.